BEYOND DIAMONDS

Veronica Mahara

BEYOND DIAMONDS

ISBN 978-1-7323712-4-8

Dedicated with love to my dear sister and friend, **Beth Anne**

Part One

.

CHAPTER ONE

Cincinnati, Ohio—1879

HER INDISCRETION HAD BEEN MINOR, BUT THE TINGLE OF feelings lingered in her body. Jane's brief flirtation yesterday with Martin would have stayed between them if not for the women in her mother's society witnessing their closeness and then gossiping about it. The heady moment now felt shameful as she sat in her father's study waiting for his reprimand.

At nearly twenty-five years old, Jane felt she had a right to do as she pleased. However, being unmarried and living under her father's roof took that privilege away. The upper class of Cincinnati had become a burden to her instead of it being the status symbol she had enjoyed growing up. Considered an old maid, she needed to be even more discreet. A pillar of society. The woman who never found love, a sweet thing who worked tirelessly to help with the family business, for what else did she have? She felt the opposite. Part of her wanted the freedom to explore her passions for botany and horticulture, and part of her wanted and needed the protection and advantages of her family and society. Today she felt caught in a web she no longer desired.

Looking at the occupied leather chair by the window, she wondered why her brother, Chadwick, had to be present. He teased at a hangnail as he lounged nonchalantly, his legs out in front of him, crossed at the ankles. Jane wished this didn't have to involve him, but being the oldest and heir to the jewelry empire, her father had become more dependent on him in business as well as in family matters.

Jane sat before their judgment in the fine wood-paneled study of their Franklin Avenue manor. It stood among the other estates and away from the dirt and acrid smoke coming from the many towering stacks along the Ohio River.

John P. Wallingford came into the room and sat behind his large desk, ignoring his offspring as he looked at his well-worn daily journal. It was still early morning, and Jane and her problem were first on his busy schedule.

Casting her brown eyes to the floor, she fingered the light green ribbon on the lace of her day dress, her nerves on edge. She bit her lip and took in a slight breath while she waited in agony. Her hands became clammy, and sweat pooled under her stays. She wished the large double-hung windows were open wider on this August morning. The north side of the house was always a bit cooler in the summer. Looking out onto the private back lawn, she yearned to be a child again walking barefoot on the green carpet.

Catching her brother's smug grin made her more uncomfortable. She wanted to slap the silly expression off his face. She was his junior by six years, and he never let her forget the fact that his station in life was vastly more important than hers, which gave him great satisfaction. It sickened her.

Jane's father grunted as he set aside his journal. She caught his gesture and became attentive. He was known for his generous nature toward those who did his bidding, but his quick volatile anger if they did not meet his expectations made the tension in the room palpable. To her advantage, she rarely experienced the latter—their relationship was different.

She hoped today would not be one of those rarities, yet something inside her fought with that hope. Would he remember the daughter with whom he shared travels to New York City and Paris? Their shared love of history and poetry? His willingness to not only see her for the bright and ambitious person she was, but to acknowledge it in public? Would today cross the line of no return? It seemed in recent years his affections had grown thin as he continued to work endless hours on his growing business, Wallingford Jewelers.

"We are here to discuss what you were doing at my downtown store with my apprentice, Mr. Cabot. What do you have to say for yourself, young lady? If you still consider yourself a lady worthy of society."

Jane bristled at her father's words. Although she was guilty, she wasn't prepared to be considered unladylike. It erased all her efforts as a good daughter. All her hard work to prove herself to him. Helping with the accounts, inspecting inventory at the store, putting her touch on displays, and mostly using her social standing to delicately lure the wealthy clients to buy exclusively from Wallingford's. Every inch of her spoke decorum and grace. None of that seemed to matter today.

"Father, of course I still consider myself a lady. How could you—"

He held up his hand, and she quit her defense.

"A lady such as yourself is not seen with a man's hands around her shoulders, especially not in one of my stores in front of our most cherished patrons, the Mallery sisters! I dare mention your poor mother was told he even whispered in your ear. How could a daughter of mine be so thoughtless? Have I taught you nothing?"

A whistle from Chadwick had Jane twist in her seat to glare at him. He merely grinned. She turned back to meet her father's eyes.

"Well?" her father asked. His baritone voice bounced off the walls, making her jerk. She straightened her back and cleared her throat. She knew he would take no nonsense, so she was direct.

"Father, it was quite innocent. The necklace was for Mrs. Harper's niece, and I happened to be in the shop to make sure that day's delivery was on time. Martin, I mean Mr. Cabot, was adjusting the clasp." She silently cursed her misstep. "He forgot the exact measurements and asked me for my assistance since I have a similar stature as Mrs. Harper's niece."

A cluck of the tongue from Chadwick sent a wave of anger through her. She exhaled, calming herself, and tried to ignore him. She focused on what her punishment might be. In the past if she dared to step out of line, her father would send her to her room for a whole day or refuse to let her attend a dance, the theater, the ballet, and other functions he knew she had her heart set on. Too old for that now, his coldness toward her for several days would be disheartening. She thought for a moment. The worst would be his disappointment in her. Was she still her father's good and worthy daughter?

Her father sat back in his large leather chair, his eyes never leaving hers. She knew it was his way of breaking down her defenses. Today she held steady, but a moment longer would have her confessing sins she had not committed.

Her brother let out an irritated huff. The pound of her father's fist on the broad desk had her taking in a quivering breath.

"You must be careful! He's a man well below you in every way. The gossip traveled down the street and into my office in no time and to who knows where else. Your mother and I will have to explain our daughter's behavior for several days to come. Do you think I have time for this?"

The smell of her father's pipe and old leather furniture refused to offer the usual comfort; in the past, she had been invited into the sacred room to be praised for her accomplishments in school, riding, and dance lessons, but mostly her ability to help raise the family into society. One wrong move from any of them and her father's hard work in establishing the most prized jewelry stores in Cincinnati might slowly come to ruin. Their reliance on their wealthy patrons was clear to Jane. Her guilt from adding to his worries compounded her misery.

"I'm sorry, Father."

All her life she had tried her best to win his love. Lately, it felt as if she had to fight for his attention and approval at every turn, and today was no different. As her unmarried status raised questions, her interest in botany and horticulture grew. Instead of raising children, she wanted to grow plants from seeds and nurture them into their full potential. Jane's mother, Elisha, lamented nearly daily that all the invitations to teas, committees, the theater, and parties might be her last—and the last for her daughter as well—if Jane didn't show more interest.

"You will first apologize to your poor mother, whose nerves are frayed from this. Then you will go to church this morning and pray for your soul. If Father Goodman is there, you will ask him to hear your confession."

"Father, I did nothing wrong." Her voice was low, her eyes not meeting his.

"And another thing . . ."

Jane held her breath. What else could there be? Then she remembered. Her shoulders slumped.

"Take those botany and horticulture books back to the library. You graduated in literature, not in farming. I've allowed you to write your social column, as silly as it is. Nevertheless, this is taking your desires too far. What's next, Jane? A visit to the farmer's guild?"

Jane thought of her weekly column filled with the superficial social goings-on of the city. It did not fulfill her. She hoped it would possibly lead to being assigned to write about what she was truly interested in.

Her father stood. She followed him to the door. Before he let her leave, he dictated his harshest blow.

"You are banned from any association with the backroom help, especially Mr. Cabot. I will not have this incident happen again."

It made her angry. Why was she being treated like a child?

"But the storeroom is—"

"Have one of the clerk girls handle the storeroom."

"Father, you know that's a job only I can handle. I have been keeping the inventory up-to-date for several years."

He cocked one eyebrow. "Are you saying you enjoyed Mr. Cabot's advances and want more?"

A sharp laugh from her brother had her swinging around to face him.

"I'll have you keep your rudeness to yourself, Chad," she said. "This has nothing to do with you. Father, why have you brought him in?" Her face warmed, and her upper lip became moist. "I have nothing to defend." She knew this wasn't true. Her secret desires were indefensible. Her guilt was clear, yet today she felt none of that. Martin was a good man. "Please, Father, don't take such drastic measures."

Her father eased his stance, something she rarely saw in him. His chest was no longer puffed out, and his shoulders lowered. "You will continue your work at the downtown store, but you will have nothing to do with Mr. Cabot. Is that clear?"

"Yes, Father."

"I have business to discuss with Chadwick. Go to church."

He ushered her out and closed the door.

A stab of grief pricked her heart. This was a turning point in her relationship with her father. She could no longer be his darling girl. She had experienced a man's touch, and there was no going back.

She turned to look at the carved wood inlays and brass knob of the door. She had stood in front of this entry so many times while waiting for an audience with him, the ruler of their household. The staircase was only paces from his study, and she climbed the steps that led to her bedroom. She would have to be careful with Martin, but a smile came to her face when she thought of him.

The morning sunlight streamed through the first-landing window, sending pink hues onto the floral wallpaper and down to the red-and-black woolen hall runner atop the walnut wood floors. She was outgrowing this house. The walls were closing in on her. She ached to have her own home, her own gardens and more. A conservatory? Looking at the dark colors and heavy fabric that reflected her mood, she wondered when she would be able to find her way to her own house and present to society her own tastes and style. She would dress her home with flowers and plants, not the dull dusty paper roses her mother insisted on having along with the forced arrangement from the strictly planted and pruned garden borders outside. Her gardens would be rich with all kinds of plants, some she was still learning the names of. The kitchen garden would be filled with medicinal plants as well as edible ones. She had already mapped out her plans on paper, but where would they become reality, and when? Would she do this alone or with a husband? The path to her dreams always began with her finding a husband first. She knew no other way.

Entering her bedroom, she went to the window seat and fingered the books scattered in front of her from her late-night studies. She let her mind wander. Her feelings for Martin had become apparent last winter when she had forgotten her muff on one of the counters. Martin had rushed it out to her before she had entered the carriage. The cold wind had picked at his shirt and rustled his straight brown hair.

"Miss Wallingford, your muff," he had said, handing it up to her.

She had caught his sweet smile, and their eyes had connected for a moment longer than necessary.

It had sparked something she couldn't let go of. It confused and delighted her. Thoughts of the jeweler became forward in her mind.

Her work in the store had her asking the floor manager, Mr. McMann, if he would tell Mr. Cabot she needed his advice on designs and stones and the best way to display his work. When he appeared from the back room, her nerves ignited, and she could barely speak. His attentiveness gave her reason to believe he felt the same toward her. It was delicious in a way she had never experienced before.

These hints of attraction happened more often now. Then yesterday he had asked her to model the necklace for him as she was on her way to the back room to inquire about a shipment of pearls from the stock boy.

He brought her to the light of one of the display cases. His breath on her neck as he fiddled with the clasp filled her with a welling of anticipation and excitement. He talked into her ear. "Almost got it. There. Now let's see how it looks." He took her by the shoulders and turned her around. She was the daughter of his employer, yet he seemed calm and confident. He smiled as his eyes met hers. "It's just right," he said before taking a look at the necklace.

Her face became warm as she nodded shyly. The moment seemed timeless.

Finally, he gently turned her around so he could remove the piece from her neck.

He should not be touching me, she thought, but she didn't move away.

Again, he whispered in her ear. "I think this will not look as beautiful on any other neck as it does on yours, Miss Wallingford."

Jane had felt a blush on her cheeks. She looked around, and staring at her were two of her mother's friends and the store's most reliable customers: the Mallery sisters. Feeling the necklace slide from her flesh, she had rushed to help the pair.

"May I show you something from the case?" she asked.

Lynda Mallery's pert reply was, "No, thank you. I think we've seen enough."

Jane knew she was in trouble, yet she had floated through the rest of her day feeling a strange sense of euphoria mixed with danger. It was exhilarating.

Today she'd been told to ignore her feelings and stay away from him, but it was no use. A flutter trickled up from her belly, like a little bird trying to escape. For all her confessing to their innocence, Martin had lingered much too long with his hands on her neck, and she hadn't pulled away as she should have.

She stacked up the library books with determination. If her father knew she not only read about plants but had also visited several farms on the outskirts of town, he would be furious, and she'd have to face his wrath: a scolding and warning followed by a cold shoulder.

Her emotions welled in sadness at the thought of her father being angry with her. How would she continue to visit the farms and learn from the farmers if he was against it? The library provided her with more than plant knowledge. One day as she'd perused the new arrivals, she'd heard a farmer's wife talking about their growing land. They had just acquired another ten acres. Jane was curious. Where was this vast farm?

She struck up a conversation with the woman and soon found herself asking if she might come to visit. The shocked farmer's wife reluctantly gave her directions. Soon, Jane hired a hackney to take her there. At first, she had just looked at the land and animals and house and barn at a distance. Part of the land was covered in a crop she didn't know. The hackney took her back to the city. It had piqued her interest. She would have to go back.

Her following visits had become as covert as her feelings for Martin. Wallace, their carriage driver, was in on her secret. He was fond of his charge, and she was fond of him, though he warned her he could get fired for taking her to these farms.

"It's just an innocent ride in the country to soothe my nerves," she told him with a mischievous giggle.

"Yes, ma'am," he had replied in his stoic way.

On her second visit, she went to the door of the farmhouse. The woman, Prissy, let her in, and they got along quite well. Jane told her of her desires to learn about horticulture, and Prissy laughed.

"My, you are a strange one! Never heard of a society lady such as yourself wanting to come to a farm. The smell alone would discourage anyone! But if you'd like, I'll show you around. I have a patch of flowers growing near the medicinal garden and the kitchen garden. I have to get back to work, but you can watch if you like. Just weedin'."

Jane was excited to learn in a practical way and not just from books. Prissy introduced Jane to the farmer's wife on the other farm, and before she knew it, she was invited to help with planting some of the medicinal crops, including lavender, calendula, St. John's wort, and feverfew. This was proving to be such a valuable experience!

The farmers' wives welcomed her with more than a little curiosity. She didn't mind. Helping them and learning from them felt as if she was making progress on her path. Getting her hands in the dirt felt freeing. Tying an apron around her plainer day dress and donning a wide-brim hat and scratchy gloves gave her a new perspective. Each time she made sure she left with clean hands and that her dress and shoes were intact.

Mostly, she rode back with a big smile on her face and in her heart while she thought of all the possibilities. She'd always be a society lady, she decided, but one with a very interesting hobby. Perhaps she could start a lady's horticultural guild. She'd heard of other guilds in nearby counties, but so far, the society she associated with had nothing of the kind. Her head spun each day with the possibilities, and now Martin had been added to the list.

She lamented over her desires. Why couldn't she have the simple pursuits of all her other friends? She knew the answer: she loathed the thought of doing nothing but being a support to her husband, raising children, and staying in the good graces of the establishment.

Reminding herself she would have to dress for church soon—a humble attire would be required—she leaned back on the green velvet pillow in her window seat and gazed at the morning sky.

The light gray blue was heavy, already hazy with humidity. A slight breeze snuck into the open window, and she breathed in some of the late-summer aromas of carnations and bee balm.

She looked out onto the strict garden borders her mother had dictated and noticed the joe-pye weed still trying to make a claim at one end of the long garden border along the back fence. Though her mother didn't mind it when Jane had made her a tea from the plant to help soothe a very troublesome stomach, she still thought of it as an invasive thing needing constant pulling. Leroy, their gardener, was at her mother's command.

When Jane claimed they could grow a number of such medicinal plants in the kitchen garden, her mother told her to discuss it with the cook but warned not to take it too far and not to let anyone know lest they be seen as women associated with brewing up concoctions. Jane could only chuckle to herself. Elisha Wallingford could never be cast as the kind of bohemian who dug in the dirt to make medicine she could easily acquire at the apothecary.

Jane felt stifled by her mother's rigid way of life and her father's overbearing presence. She knew she had to break free from their world. It both frightened and excited her.

Chapter Two

The next day, Jane and her friend Sadie Longworth stepped out of Jane's home and onto the sidewalk.

Sadie's family owned a chain of retail stores. Longworth's catered mostly to women who had the time and means to browse its array of expensive wares, and Sadie, now Mrs. Leonard Manford, was its biggest advertisement. Her dress and adornments were always impeccable.

Meeting her friend's appearance, Jane wore her summer attire with equal adornments. A tight flourish of ruffle cascaded down the length of her striped yellow dress, and her small light blue version of a man's top hat studded with tiny silk blossoms sat slightly tilted on her upswept hair. Her ankle boots with yellow fabric-covered buttons matched perfectly, and her cream-colored day gloves, which were light enough to suit the weather, fit snugly on her delicately long fingers. With her parasol in hand and a small daytime reticule swinging from her wrist, she felt ready for the day.

The sun's searing rays filtered through the lingering dust of the freshly swept street. Jane shaded her face with her parasol and brought a gloved finger up to her nose. The scolding from her father had left her less cheerful than usual.

Attending church yesterday for no good reason had seemed a waste of time. The only other person who had been in attendance was the priest instructing a novice on the ways of the Mass. Father Goodman had not the time to hear her confession. Her mother was put out. Jane had knelt and said a few prayers. While waiting for her mother to say her own prayers, she sat back and daydreamed about her future. At her age, she reasoned, she should be on her own. Would Martin marry her? Was that the answer? Society deemed him below her, in the same way she was discouraged from pursuing her own career path. Two strikes against her. Yet she envisioned herself wrapped in Martin's loving arms and living in the horticultural world. It gave her such joy to picture a grand garden estate all her own with society begging to know her secrets.

"A picnic in the upper park with the river view," Sadie said as the straw basket swung from her elbow. "I can't think of a better way to spend some time to ourselves. It will be so very refreshing. Besides, I have some news."

They crossed the street, avoiding the oncoming carriages.

"I was wondering why you invited me out today. How were you able to manage it, Mrs. Manford?" Jane said without her usual good humor.

"My father and Leonard are visiting the next county on business. I told the house staff I'd be back later, and Leonard's mother is visiting her daughter today. All is in hand."

Jane didn't reply. Sadie was younger than she was by two years and was well established as wife and helpmate to her husband and both of their families. A stab of jealousy hit her, and she reminded herself that she had her own plans—as out of reach as they may be.

"You're a bit of a Gloomy Gus today," Sadie commented. "Whatever could be wrong in your perfect world?" Holding tight to the basket and her parasol, she stepped around a clump of fresh horse dung. "Oh!" she exclaimed with a wrinkled nose.

Jane hurried alongside her friend to the sidewalk across the street as they walked on. "Father scolded me for being seen with Martin the other day."

"Oh, dear." Sadie adjusted the basket and brought her parasol down across her face and whispered, "What happened? What did you say? Have you told your father about your feelings toward Mr. Cabot?"

"Of course not. He would have me in a convent for sure."

Sadie clucked her tongue. "I doubt that. Your beauty would be wasted in a convent. Your father is ready to have you married to one of the many wealthy prospects in this city, and you know it."

"I think he still sees me as his little girl," Jane said as they made their way up the nearest hill. "On one hand, I'm free to write my column in the *Daily Star* and work tirelessly at the store. On the other hand—"

"How is your next entry coming along? I can't wait to hear your take on Bessy Morgan's hat at the theater on Friday." Sadie leaned forward with a laugh. "It was simply hideous!"

Jane cleared her throat. "*On the other hand*, I can't love whom I please or pursue my interest in horticulture and medicinal plants. Did you know that white willow bark is what our mothers give us for fever? The little tablets are all wrapped nicely in brown paper, but it actually comes from bark. And I've learned that the plant called feverfew can help with headaches. I know chamomile tea is a soothing remedy. Also, the beauty in a landscape is not accidental."

She waved her hand toward the fronts of houses along the sidewalk. Their small entry gardens were filled with shorn shrubs, fluffy flowered hydrangeas, topiaries, and blossoming summer flowers, some with tiny green lawns giving her fine examples.

"These are too stiff and limited though. This was all once a great wilderness. Taking a stroll in that wilderness is to take a walk in Mother Nature's landscaped gardens. I wish to combine the two."

"Jane, you do go on. Stick to social events and fashion. It will keep you in touch with what's important."

Struck by her friend's reproach, Jane drew back her enthusiasm. As they made their way up the wooden steps to the landing on one of the many hills along the great industrial Ohio River, her friend huffed and puffed with the effort. Bunching the layers of her skirts in her hands, Jane took the last few steps with the energy of a child. Finally at the top, she leaned against a large shading tree and decided it would be their picnic area. The sudden exhilaration felt delicious, if not a little dizzying.

"Jane, wait, I can't run!"

Jane laughed, slumped against the tree, and waited for her friend. She looked out from the hill. Over on one of the highest tops stood the luxurious Bellevue House, which was more of a mansion. She'd heard the grounds were spectacular. The new incline railcar was exciting, and she was looking forward to taking it up to the mansion. Her mother had said it was strictly for tourists and only an invitation to the Bellevue House would see her or her family boarding the steep climbing rail. But they knew none of the family who lived there. Jane would have to find a way to ride it to the top. Another clandestine act to add to her growing list.

Sadie came up the last step and looked as if she were about to faint.

"Oh, Sadie, are you all right? We used to run up this hill like it was nothing. Do you remember? Especially when Winston and Benton chased us?"

Sadie nodded and smiled as she tried to gain an even breath.

They spread out the thin blanket from Sadie's basket and sat down.

"Don't you ever want to run as fast as you can until the wind lifts you up and takes you away?" Jane asked.

Still catching her breath, Sadie answered, "What? You're talking nonsense. Sit completely on the blanket, dear. You're going to stain your dress. What's gotten into you, Jane?"

"Nothing. Just restless I suppose." She dared not expose her truth to Sadie for fear of further reproach; she had enough of that whenever she hinted to her parents of her ideas on gardening and her study of plants.

Jane smiled and helped Sadie unpack the basket and lay out its contents. They settled into their small sandwiches, pastries, and fruit.

Looking out onto the docks, called the Public Landing, with various sizes and colors of passenger boats, Jane thought it was a lovely sight away from the smokestacks of the industry downriver. A soft breeze blew their direction, and the aroma of summer caught her nose. She inhaled the rich scent of the citrusy bee balm and the heady smell of goldenrod. The combination of colors—yellows, deep reds, and a variety of greens—touched her senses. A swath of black-eyed Susans swayed in the open area, intertwined with false indigo and blades of field grasses and meadow flowers. She sighed as the air returned back to its thick stillness.

Arranging her skirts, Jane removed the pins of her hat and laid the pretty little thing beside her on the blanket. Her rich dark hair remained in its arranged order except for a few wisps, which she didn't try to put into place. The sound of the water, today a steady stream of babbling coolness, blocked out the noise of the bustling city. Her corset felt too close, the bustle too lumpy underneath her. Pulling her gloves off, she let her hands feel the air. If only she could wear a plain dress like the farmers' daughters wore, then stretch her body on the cool grass. She positioned herself to the side and held her usual pose of a straight back with her legs neatly tucked under her many layers of dress. The idea of a fresh apple with its tart juice made her mouth water, and she reached over and grabbed one. Crunching into it, she noticed Sadie surveying her.

"You *are* restless. What's going on, Janey?"

"I'm getting old and have no prospects. My parents are becoming impatient with me. And the other day, Mrs. Perkin's precocious daughter asked me why I wasn't married and if there was something wrong with me."

"Oh, pay no mind to her brats. I swear, they will find themselves in trouble one of these days." Sadie bit into one of the peach tarts and gracefully wiped the crumbs from her chin.

"Still, she had to have heard it from her mother, and her mother heard it from, well, you know how these things get passed around." Pausing to swallow her bite, Jane continued her lament. "I want something more than writing a society column. Why can't they put me on the county pages? I have more interest there."

"That page is for common folk and farmers. We might only be merchants' daughters, but we're quite above that class, especially you, Miss Wallingford." Sadie gave a mocking look of indignation and shook her head. "Your parents did you some great favors by letting you attend college. Mine only hoped to marry me to an intelligent man from a wealthy family who would take over the stores once my father became incapable of working . . . or deceased. Thank God I love my Leonard, and he is doing a fine job."

"Yes, Leonard fits the bill all right."

Sadie furrowed her brow. "That didn't sound very generous."

"I'm sorry, Sadie. He's a fine man, but would he have been your first choice if you'd had a choice at the time?"

"You talk such folly! Please stop. It's quite unpleasant. I'm not restless, if that's what you're getting at."

"No, you're settled and happy, and I'm just jealous."

Sadie leaned over and patted Jane's hand. "You'll find love someday. Mr. Cabot may just be a fling for now, but your parents will find the right one for you. Give their choices a chance. You never know."

Jane bit into her apple and turned her thoughts to Martin, and her heart skated. A fling indeed. Their mild flirtation whenever she was at the store had turned into something she considered more than a fling. His keen eye for jewelry making; his fine hands, which hadn't seen a day's hard work; his lovely open expression; the way his soft brown strands of hair touched the collar at his neck. Although some wouldn't think him especially handsome, she loved his larger nose and wide-set brown eyes. His look was warm and welcoming, much different from the squeaky-clean, pale-looking young and not-so-young men who swarmed around the girlish socialites like bees in a jar.

She wasn't fooled by their rigid manners. Too many of her friends and acquaintances had referred to their lewd behavior, such as a whistle toward a woman walking down the street or talking about the size of a woman's chest in low tones or what they might find under a woman's bustle, always when the young men were in a group. Jane and her friends caught the comments and behavior as they walked the mall around the fountain in town or at a party where spirits were served. It had the ladies discreetly turning away sometimes, hiding their heated cheeks behind fans or gloved hands. The most socially respected young men could be indecently forward. Her own experience added to the others.

One such fellow had her fending him off once he had danced her into the outside balcony at a ball last spring and tried to kiss her on the lips while his hand traveled to her bodice. He became angry at her rebuff and shuffled her back onto the dance floor, bowing curtly and leaving her to walk back to the sidelines alone. It was most embarrassing, and as far as she knew, he got no flak for his rude behavior. She had fortified her shield against all of them. Martin, on the other hand, had dissolved her armament, and she trusted him. He always treated her with the utmost respect. He was older than her peers by several years, and his demeanor was very much in accord with that of a gentleman.

A woman of her age was settled into a proposal of marriage or wed with several children, their life path clearly defined. Unsatisfied to simply report the news of the influencers of society, she desired to become one herself. If Cincinnati was considered the Queen City, she would be part of its royalty. She dreamed of Martin having his own jewelry empire and she the lady of their fine home where a conservatory and still room gave her plenty of space for plants and potions. She dreamed of the opportunity to write a more important column of the events and people in the city while entertaining the grand society of Cincinnati, hosting exquisite garden shows for charity, bringing in the rich and revered. She'd be known for being more than just her father's daughter.

It all seemed quite reasonable to her, yet whenever she approached her parents with expanding her life into the realm of horticulture, they quickly diverted her attention to the importance of being a good wife and supporting a husband in his endeavors. Mostly, she was told to continue working for the company of Wallingford Jewelers until she was married.

"You're not a child, Jane," her mother would say. "It's time to give your life over to a husband and children and, of course, first and foremost, to God." Those words always had the opposite effect on Jane. She didn't share her mother's faith in the church and God. Although she believed in a higher power, she found too many disparities in her mother's religion to believe without question.

She looked at her friend. Sadie reflected what was held up as the cornerstone of society.

"Do you ever dream of a life other than the one you have?" Jane asked.

Sadie thought for a moment. "I want children. We've been married long enough to start. And, well, I believe we may have succeeded on that account." She smiled widely and blushed as she looked down at her gathered skirt.

Jane clapped her hands. "Oh, Sadie, that's wonderful!" She came forward, and they both stared at Sadie's stomach before dissolving into laughter.

"It's too early for that, but Mama says I will be taking out some of my dresses soon."

"Congratulations. Give my regards to Leonard. What good news."

Jane meant it. Her childhood friend was going to be a mother. Would she be wed and pregnant soon also? Would she and Sadie be like their mothers and tend to their husbands, homes, and children, playing the part expected of them?

Smiling at her friend, Jane leaned back on the great oak tree and let her mind wander. The sun-filled day made her lazy. She felt herself dozing with the warm breeze on her cheeks and the thought of Martin's arms wrapped around her waist, his lips so close she could smell his clean yet musky scent. If only she could convince her father of Martin's worth to the business and to her happiness.

The day was too glorious to spend on worry. She and Sadie sat in easy companionship for the rest of their visit.

On her way home, Jane's predicament returned to her heart. What would become of her? Would she be working for her father until she was too old for any man to want her?

CHAPTER THREE

𝒥T HAD BEEN A MONTH SINCE JANE WAS FORBIDDEN TO associate in any way with Martin. It was easy in theory, for she had no business with him unless she made something up. Emotionally, however, neither one of them could help a side glance when they crossed paths. A bowed head and a small smile from her. A part nod and grin or a silent wink from him. She found this to be quite sensual and looked forward to the possibility of a chance meeting each day. It fueled their relationship in a way she knew her father hadn't anticipated.

Today as the summer was in its last weeks, she strolled to the store. Wallace let her off several shops away. She wanted to take in the center of town this morning. Wallingford Jewelers sat on the right side of the large oblong walkway. Its mall was the perfect place to see and be seen. It was named Fountain Square and held court to men discussing the politics of the day and women entertaining their own discussions, some with great zeal for woman's rights, such as the right to vote, and others simply passing the latest gossip. The women's rights movement was a curiosity to Jane, but she couldn't be seen finding interest in it—not with her father's office windows overlooking the square. Although he was busy with his own affairs of acquiring gems and other precious jewels for his stores and doing business with diamond mines in far-off places, she couldn't take any chances.

Surrounded by commerce of every kind, Fountain Square attracted wealthy and common people alike. The magnificent fountain with its statue of a graceful woman standing unabashedly atop the pool of dancing water below filled Jane with pride in her city. She loved its clean, cultured look. Browsing the shops, she strolled up the sidewalk closer to the store.

Knowing Martin was seated in the concrete back room with a loupe in one eye and a steady hand upon a jewel made her thighs pulsate. His quiet strength fueled her imagination of his hidden passion. Picking up her pace, she noticed today the square was speckled with men talking business and a few nannies with their charges probably exchanging lamentations about their employers. The bright sun had her pinching her small sunglasses onto her nose.

September was one of her favorite times of the year. The late summer turning to autumn had a rich smell all its own.

Finally, she got to the store and went inside. Her own small office was toward the back, but she casually took the longer way to get to it, past the door that led to the jewelers' workspaces. No sign of Martin today.

She placed her sunshades in her purse and went into her office. Her small desk had a pile of orders on it. It was a tidy desk set with matching pen and holder, a green glass lamp, and a vase of flowers. Behind her was a shelf of boxes filled with older files. She would have the floor girl take them to the cellar. She liked to keep this part of her life uncomplicated, for just outside this windowless room her life was complicated enough.

At lunchtime, she stood and stretched her body. Mr. McMann, whom she considered to be one of her father's spies, went to lunch, and he never returned until half past one. The store clerks paid little attention to her as they helped their customers.

Leaving her office, she gracefully walked around the wide aisles along the display cases, inspecting them indiscreetly. Wallingford Jewelers was geared mostly toward women. New York City was far away, and other jewelry stores in the area served men's needs, such as cases for cigars or watches. The large store surrounded a lady patron with displays of hats decorated with plumes of peacock feathers nestling a gemmed pin or brooch, glass cases with white satin gloves and cream-colored scarves as backdrops to diamond and ruby jewelry, and the mannequin heads adorned with the latest fashion in necklaces. It was like a candy store for the rich as well as a reliable place to have work done on any piece of broken or damaged jewelry. A sitting area was arranged for waiting for a piece of jewelry to be tried on or adjusted. Serving champagne and small cakes to the clients had been Jane's idea. Tea and coffee were available for those who didn't want to indulge in the sparkling wine.

The store was buzzing as she finally reached the back rooms. The two other jewelers, who shared a separate workroom, paid no mind to her entering Martin's larger workroom, which had the vault in it for the pricier inventory. She had to inspect that inventory, didn't she? The other workers' doors were closed most of the time for privacy and to minimize the dust.

The pleasant coolness of the workroom refreshed her, and she sighed his name. "Martin."

Martin looked up from his bench, and his loupe popped from his eye as his hand jerked. Jane saw a bloodred ruby fly from its stand.

"Gads!" Martin sprang from his seat and went down on his hands and knees to retrieve the pricey gem.

After finding it in one of the cracks of the floor, he gingerly brought it back to its setting.

"One moment, Jane." He replaced his loupe and concentrated.

She waited and watched until he came up and took out the eyepiece and set down his tools.

"You shouldn't be in here," he said.

"Don't be silly. I can come and go as I please," she said, casting her eyes downward.

Martin got off his stool. "Now, we both know that's not true—not here anyway. I'm glad to see you though." He rubbed his neck and looked sheepish. "I've missed you, Jane. We have to be careful. Your brother put me on alert that I was not to associate with you. It was unpleasant. He seemed to think I was some low-life, gold-digging hick. I need my job until I get—"

"Oh! I'll have a talk with him. I wish he'd stay out of my affairs. You and I have different ranks in life, but that makes no difference to me. You must know that."

"Yes, of course. But like I said, I need my job until other plans come to fruition."

Jane wanted to learn more about his plans. He mentioned them so vaguely to her, but there never seemed time for him to go into detail, and now she had only these brief moments when Mr. McMann left the store. The last thing on her mind was his plans. She wanted to know what *their* plans would be. She became curious.

"Will you tell me about these plans?"

Martin returned to his stool. "Oh, never mind. We just need to be careful."

"What if I don't want to be careful anymore?" She stood next to him, and he took her hand.

"Now, Jane."

She tilted her head, feeling the weight of his gentle grip.

"My father says he wants to promote one of his jewelers, and that could be you. Once you establish yourself as the head jewelry designer, you and I could . . . I mean, it would go well for both of us, if that is what you want."

Looking deep into her eyes, he nodded. "Yes, it's what I want. To be with you, I mean."

It gave Jane a thrill of excitement. No man had spoken to her like this before.

Martin took on a more pensive expression. "But . . . what if I don't want to work in this particular business forever?"

Was he teasing her? She furrowed her brow. "Don't be like that. I have plans for my life. For our lives. We are the next generation in a city that welcomes change."

Martin guffawed as if he were choking on food. "Welcomes change? For whom?"

Losing her patience with his lack of foresight, she withdrew her hand. "We could make them see how it is. New designs in jewelry, in décor, in the way gardens could be used and not just seen."

Martin's face lit up. "Yes, land and plenty of it."

"Well, enough land anyway. We're not farmers. A few acres perhaps? That should be fine. A good house. Something grand but not too fancy. I've found a few plans in a magazine."

"But I want to be a farmer. A sheep farmer. A land owner. My own boss."

"A sheep farmer?" Jane was taken aback.

"Yes, Jane. A sheep farmer. My cousin, Harry, has sent me a plan to buy the farm next to his."

"Where?" She felt confused. Her mild-mannered Martin was excited, and it was contagious, but she felt cautious.

"California, across the bay from San Francisco."

Jane stepped back and placed a hand to her chest. "Oh. That's quite a distance from here. Isn't San Francisco wild and filled with derelicts?"

"No. What have you been reading, Jane?"

"I thought it to be common knowledge."

Again, he took her hand in his. "Land where a couple could join their interests. Gardens of all sorts. Mild and sunny weather most of the year. Fruit trees and livestock. Mostly, freedom. Think about it, Jane. No one to tell us what to do. No society to pamper or please."

Her head was spinning. What was he offering? How could she ever think of leaving her bright and modern city for a farm in the wilderness of the West? She didn't see herself as a pioneer. The thought frightened her.

"Martin, that sounds very adventurous, but quite out of step with what I have in mind for what *a couple* might achieve in Cincinnati."

Slumping his shoulders in surrender, Martin placed his arms around her waist. She tingled, forgetting what they were discussing. Their eyes met, and for the hundredth time, Jane thought the moment had finally arrived: he was going to kiss her on the lips. The cool, dank back room of her father's jewelry store wasn't the most romantic place to have a first kiss, but she wasn't going to back down if he decided it was time to take their relationship a step further.

She waited in anticipation as he reached out and touched her cheek while his hand touched the side of her bodice. Her heart beat rapidly. He stood as if anchored to the floor. The clock ticked loudly on the wall. Precious seconds were speeding by. Jane couldn't wait any longer. She leaned forward and planted a kiss on his lips.

The intrusive clang of the front door had Martin rushing her out of the back room and into the store. He receded to his workroom and closed the door. Mr. McMann's loud voice rang out.

"Good afternoon, Mrs. Jenkins. How are our girls treating you? Finding everything you need?" His voice came closer to the workroom. "Was there much activity while I was out?" he asked one of the clerk ladies.

Jane's heart thudded as she hurried back to her office. Catching herself, she slowed her pace and looked around the store as if she were interested in each station and its clerks. Instead, her head was spinning with the reality of her actions.

Had she actually kissed him? She giggled to herself as if half-mad. What could he possibly be thinking of her? This assertive action had ripped the fabric of her neat, confined world, and she felt exhilarated.

Coming back to earth, she thought, *A sheep farm?* She shook her head and entered her office. There was more to this man than she'd imagined. Could she join him? What about all her lovely plans? A knock came to her door, and she let in the floor girl.

"Yes, what do you want?" she asked her.

"You told me you wished to see me after lunch."

Jane stared at the young girl. "Oh! Yes, take these down to the cellar please."

After the boxes had been cleared away, Jane closed her door and sat at her desk. She would get little work done today—she had too much to contemplate.

CHAPTER FOUR

*T*HAT SAME DAY, WHEN THE FOUR-THIRTY FACTORY WHISTLE blew in the distance, marking the end of another work day along the banks of the Ohio River, Martin began to collect his tools and straighten his work area. Mr. McMann left at four o'clock sharp each day, leaving Martin to clean up and close. He sometimes felt as if he were comanager with all the added responsibilities Mr. McMann had given him.

"You're the only one I trust in this place," was the reason the tall gray-haired manager had given.

Martin went over his inventory for his work tomorrow, when he would set a sapphire for a necklace and restring a strand of pearls before adding an embossed silver clasp. After placing the small boxes of expensive pearls and rubies into the heavy black vault along with the items he had finished today, he went back to his bench to tally his hours and prepare the report of his day's work.

He checked off the list of precious jewelry he had made ready for the customer servants to pick up, and he set those items aside.

His thoughts were not far from Jane along with the kiss he still felt on his lips. He didn't know what to make of it, and he tried his best not to think about it. A futile exercise.

Continuing his job, he gathered the more modest jewelry, such as silver-plated bracelets and pewter rings set with cheaper stones, which would be retrieved by the customers themselves. Martin preferred that class of people. They often gave praise to Mr. McMann for the jewelers' fine work. Sometimes the prideful Mr. McMann would pass on the compliment to Martin or the other jewelers and sometimes not, but Martin's keen hearing always caught the words meant for him.

He knew one of the servants from the Rochester estate would be coming in before closing to pick up an emerald-and-diamond pin. He swept the floor and continued tidying up as the chatter from the clerk ladies drifted out the door. Not long after, the Rochesters' servant was entering the store.

"I'll be right with you." He went to the back and brought out the precious pin in its black velvet box. "Here we are, then," he said to the astute older man, who always behaved as if he were on a mission for a king or queen. Martin wanted to tell him this country was no longer under such rule, but he had to admit, the high society in Cincinnati seemed to think they were royalty or at least equal to the Asters of New York. After the servant left, Martin continued his end-of-day tasks while his mind wandered.

Cousin Harry has the right idea. Buy a farm and work it for yourself and to hell with society. California called to Martin each time Harry wrote of its vast land and extraordinary beauty. Martin had saved every penny he could manage outside of rent and food, and at twenty-eight years of age, he felt time was quickly slipping by him. First, he would follow his heart and find a way to make Jane his wife. With her interest in plants and what could be rendered from them, he was sure she would want to live on fertile land. He needed to get around her parents while showing her the possibilities outside of Cincinnati, Ohio. It wasn't a small undertaking.

The door chimed again, and Martin hurried to the front and welcomed Mr. Holcomb. "Sir, I have your wife's watch all repaired."

Behind the bulky Mr. Holcomb was a flair of a peacock feather and the smell of orange blossoms. His chest tightened. He'd know her scent anywhere.

He rushed to the back to retrieve the watch and steady his nerves. What did she expect from him? Would she be as forward as she was this afternoon? He wanted to be in control of their relationship. He was the man, after all, yet he had spent several hours thinking about her lips pressed against his, and he desired her more than ever. How could she bring him to such a weakened state?

JANE HAD COMPLETELY FORGOTTEN SHE was to pick out a piece of jewelry for her upcoming outing tonight. She immediately asked the housekeeper, Charlotte, to have Wallace bring the carriage around and take her to the store. Leaving work early to rest up for the dinner and dance, she rushed to make it back before Martin closed for the day. It was nearly four thirty.

After changing into her best day dress, she dabbed her favorite perfume behind her ears and on her wrists, adding a bit on her collar too. She planned to linger at several jewelry cases for a pin or necklace to accompany her outfit. Her father had made it clear she must always wear the latest trend in jewelry from one of their stores.

Her excitement at being alone with Martin was tempered by the fact she would be going to the affair tonight with another of her mother's choices of potential suitors: Tommy Ruch, a nice young man she'd grown up with but considered a complete bore. Her mother reminded her he was rich and in line to inherit a great fortune. Complying with her parents' wishes kept them from hounding her about her lack of a husband. Besides, she had pent-up energy from today that needed to be let loose on the dance floor. She would imagine she was dancing with Martin.

The sidewalk surrounding the square would soon be crowded with shoppers retreating back to their homes, followed by the shopkeepers and their workers. She stepped inside behind a customer and waited for Martin to finish his business. It gave her time to gather her composure.

The thought of kissing him today flared her nerves. It had been wrong of her to be so forward. Now she was about to face him and find out where she stood.

For all his goodness, she sometimes wished he were more commanding of their relationship. It dampened her spirits that he hadn't been the first to kiss her. It wasn't enough for him to touch her glove or brush his shoulder on hers. Her very reputation depended on him knowing her true feelings. They would present themselves as a united force in front of her parents. From what she knew about old unmarried women, she believed the world would soon be calling her Spinster Wallingford as simply a matter of fact. She cringed at the title. It spoke of lost opportunities and disadvantages. Even a rich spinster was looked upon as less than whole.

The portly gentleman left, and Martin came around to greet her.

"Hello, Jane. What a nice surprise. What brings you back?"

He seems unaffected. Maybe the kiss didn't mean much to him. He thought it was a joke perhaps?

"I was looking at the new pins. I'd like one for an event tonight." She ran her finger over the glass case that held the bejeweled items. For a brief moment, she noticed how clean the glass was, how the pins were arranged, and how she might arrange them differently. Matter of habit.

"You caught me in time. I was just about to lock these in the safe. Let me bring them out for you to take a closer look," he said. He went behind the case, and reaching into his vest pocket, he retrieved three keys on a silver ring. He chose the one he needed and slid the glass open. With care, he brought out the blue velvet-covered board.

The pins caught the light and glimmered. She waited as he placed them on the counter. She went for the peacock-shaped pin and met his hand on the edge of the board. She felt the sweat under her glove and ached to remove the cotton choking her hand. She also ached to feel his flesh on hers.

He pulled away. "I'll let you choose, but I like the ruby one with the diamonds around it."

"Yes, I was looking at that one too!" She folded her lips inward as if to think. "But it might be hidden on my maroon-colored bodice. What do you think?"

He came around from behind the counter and bent down to examine the board more closely. "I think the sapphire may be more suited."

Jane didn't care if any of them were right. The smell of his sweat and the nearness of his body made her want to fan the heated blush rising into her cheeks. Her fan stayed at her wrist, however, and she asked him for a glass of cool water.

"Yes, of course. I'll get that for you." He hurried to the back room.

Jane scolded her girlish nerves. Her determination came back to her, and she felt bolder when he returned. After taking a sip of water, she asked, "Do you have any others in the back?"

He shook his head. "I don't think so, but I could go check."

Her patience waned. "Never mind. I'll take this sapphire one. Thank you, Mr. Cabot."

"Jane." He let out an exasperated sigh. "I suppose we could take a peek in back." He went to the door and looked up and down the street, then turned the sign to *Closed*.

A chill of excitement ran up her spine.

They stood alone in his workroom. It was tidy and dim with light. He faced her and reached to touch her cheek, but then withdrew his hand. He cleared his throat. "You're the highlight of my day, of my life."

"You are for me as well."

He took her gloved hand in both of his and stared into her eyes. Looking up at him, her heart skipped a beat. She came up to his chin and he lowered his head and kissed her.

She closed her eyes as his warm lips touched her lips. She felt her world tilt. A tingle of heat engulfed her, and then his passion lessened, and he pulled away. The heaviness between her legs and the expansion of her heart were left unsatisfied.

What was happening? This was supposed to be the monumental moment she had read about in so many novels. She thought she might have been transported to another world, but she stayed as earthbound as ever. Where was the romance? Where was the solidification of their relationship?

Stepping back, she saw his face was flush and his breathing was audible.

"I'm sorry, I shouldn't have done that," he said.

Bringing her hand to her lips, she replied, "I don't mind."

"You should. If your father and brother knew what we did today . . . you kissed me . . . I just kissed you . . . they'd have my job and my neck!"

"We can do what we want, Martin. We're not children."

She kissed him again. He took her by the shoulders and brought her away from him.

"We will wait," he said.

Jane felt extremely agitated. Why was she still to be treated like a little girl? "Don't you desire me?"

"For goodness' sake, Jane. Don't speak like that!"

"I want to know, Martin."

Running his hands through his hair, Martin stared at her as if he had no words in his head. She waited.

He whispered, "Of course I do."

She smiled. "I do too. I mean I desire you."

"Jane, please. You're talking like a hussy!"

She brought her hand to her mouth, confused.

He lowered her hand down and held it tight. "I'm sorry, I didn't mean it. I'm just not used to a lady of your station talking like that. Please forgive me."

She suddenly felt like an oddity. Was she the only woman on Earth with these feelings toward a man? Some of her readings had her thinking she may not be. The new women's movement meant equality, but where? In politics only? What was she supposed to do with all these wanton feelings she was having? Her mother would say, "Go to confession." Her father, well, it would be unspeakable.

"I do very much desire you," he whispered. "But your forward-ness is . . . a bit off-putting. I think you're wonderfully outspoken and different from anyone I've ever met."

She raised her chin. "I am different. I admit it. I will try to be more ladylike if that's what you mean."

He huffed. "I will try to be more accepting of you just the way you are."

Smiling at each other, they came closer. The sound of a key entering the front door lock and the ringing of the chimes had the couple pulling away. Martin poked his head out from the back room. He stepped back in, his eyes wide with horror.

"Jesus, your father!"

He rushed Jane out the back door, and she heard her father call for Martin.

She was practically shoved into the back alley, the door closing in a rush behind her. She took a breath of the air, which was filled with the commerce of industry. The thick, acrid smell seized her lungs, and she coughed into her gloved hand.

Her heart raced as she hurried along the backs of the many stores, dodging the debris of boxes and other trash. Finally, she was on the sidewalk. The clip-clop of horse hooves had her turning and waiting for Wallace to come alongside her. He helped her in and closed the door.

She sat heavily on the leather seat, tore her gloves off her hands, and removed her hat, then fanned herself vigorously. The carriage lurched, taking her away from near disaster.

Soon after she returned home, so did her father, who questioned her about her day and other business before inquiring about why Wallace had been parked at the store.

She looked right at him and said, "I was looking for a piece of jewelry for tonight."

"I didn't see you."

Jane's mind quickly produced an alibi.

"I was tempted by the hat store down the street. Then it got late and Wallace caught up with me." Using her innocent large brown eyes to her advantage, she satisfied any of her father's misgivings.

"And what will you be wearing? I want you looking your best for tonight."

"I have something among my jewelry that will look lovely with my gown."

"Very well," he replied and left her for his study.

Jane wasn't worried about what to wear; she had already decided she was going to have a "tremendous headache." Better yet, woman's ailments. Her father wouldn't dare pursue that subject. A night of reading in bed with a hot water bottle and a cup of tea would suit her just fine. This new suitor would have to find someone else to escort to the ball.

A tinge of regret poked at her. She did love such affairs, with all the dancing, mingling, secret dramas, and gossip. The pain of losing out on all of it would be well worth the sacrifice. Perhaps Tommy would find a nice girl to court and she'd be free of his impending advances.

Her assumptions were short-lived. The morning after, a box of red roses was delivered to the house for Jane. The card read, *Get Well Soon. Your ardent admirer, T.R.*

"How awful!" Jane exclaimed.

"That is a fine thing to say about a possible future husband. I think it shows great concern about your health and well-being!" her mother answered.

"Get well soon? Red roses? Did he think I was dying? How is that an indication of concern? It's rather dry and unfeeling."

"Charlotte!" her mother called to the housekeeper. "Put these in a vase and take them up to Miss Wallingford's room."

"No, Charlotte," Jane said. "Please keep them down here. My mother will find greater pleasure in them than I will."

"Oh!" Her mother stamped her foot. "You are impossible!"

CHAPTER FIVE

October 1879

THE COOL OCTOBER WEATHER MADE JANE HUNGER FOR THE warm meals Miss Ellen, the cook, would serve. Gathering for supper, Jane and her mother waited patiently for her brother and her father to come to the table. They both knew Miss Ellen would be agitated and the server would fret about the temperature of the food. Her father and brother could talk nonstop about the jewelry business: where to obtain the best gems and diamonds, what company was giving the best deals, what costs could be cut if they went with smaller gems for their less expensive designs, and so on.

Usually, Jane's curious nature was intrigued, yet she was not privy to their conversations. As long as she kept the store looking beautiful and the inventory well accounted for, she was little else use to her brother and father. Now she had a greater reason to be involved in the business. Martin would benefit from its ongoing success. He could become an integral part of the designs.

Finally, they came to the table. Jane looked at Chad seating himself across from her. Medium height and handsome, he had a confidence she envied. Chad had only to be himself and he would be given the world. Beyond her looks, she had to use her femininity, her charms, and her wit to get any attention, especially from her father.

She took heart as she continued to plan her future with Martin. Yes, she was different, and they would be a different kind of society couple. It thrilled her to no end to think of creating a life with him. A part of her was curious about the land Martin spoke of, where one could grow an array of plants all year long. She was so curious she had taken books from the library on California gardens. It sparked her interest, but she was determined to stick to her plans.

It helped that Martin believed in her and felt the same as she did about the new wave in women's rights. The ability to cast a political vote was a near-impossible thought to her, though the freedom to weigh in on the politics of the day enlivened her spirit. Martin had said to her one day as a group of suffragettes gathered in the square with signs and pamphlets, "I think a woman should have the right to vote. Why shouldn't a woman's opinion matter? And if a married couple work together on a project, more the better." She had ignored the last part. The jewelry business in itself didn't interest her, only what it brought to her life. Now she knew he was talking about farming. She had to cope with this new complication.

Then it had come to her last night—they would purchase a piece of land in the countryside where he could hire a man to tend some livestock. It could be a gentleman's hobby of sorts. She would use the land as well. It was a perfect solution. Tonight, her thoughts focused on making her father and brother accept Martin as more than an employee. She would have to approach the subject carefully.

After the dessert of raspberries and cream had been served, Jane seized her opportunity. The cool vanilla pudding was a refreshing end to the warm veal tureen with braised potatoes and carrots along with the baked bread. Jane's stomach felt more fluttery than full.

"Father, I think the store is looking very well-kept. By the way, Mr. Cabot was very polite and helpful to me and the other ladies yesterday. And he's quite talented, don't you agree? Have you thought about advancing him? Perhaps to one of your designers? He also seems to manage the store well when Mr. McMann is out."

Her father raised his head from his dessert, wiping his lips. "Is that so?" He went back to enjoying his pudding.

"Mr. Cabot does a fine job, don't you think? I've heard from the women in my circle what a talented jeweler he is. Very confident. It's how you began. Why not be as generous as Mr. Fromm was with you?" Placing her spoon to the side, she became aware of the three of them staring at her.

Her mother stopped midbite. "My dear, what are you saying?"

"I'm saying that I think he's a fine gentleman and an asset to our family." She bit her bottom lip. She was getting in over her head now.

"So, you do take a fancy to him after all," Chad said. "I thought so, little liar."

With her anger flaring, she spit out, "At least he's single. Unlike some of your—"

"Enough," her father demanded. "Not at the supper table and not in front of your mother. My own daughter talking in such a way. You may excuse yourself and go to your room, Jane."

Placing her napkin on the table, she rose. "I'm not a child, Father." She looked at her brother with a smirk. "I think I'd rather take a walk if that is acceptable. I need the air."

With a grunt, her father conceded.

"Have Charlotte walk with you, and only up to the Brightons' house and back. My daughter doesn't need to parade herself in public for no good reason and at this time of day. Why, it's nearly dark."

"Father, I think I can take some air without your consent. I won't be long."

"Jane!" her mother cried. "What has gotten into you?"

Her father slapped his napkin onto the table. "I'd like to know that myself."

"She's all turned around over that Martin fellow, I bet," Chad said.

Her father stood and rang the sideboard bell.

Charlotte came into the dining room. "Yes, sir?"

"Take my daughter for a short stroll. She's having a bit of a tantrum and needs some air."

Jane turned and briskly walked to the foyer before she made more of a scene. His dismissal was like a slap across her face.

Retrieving her wrap from the brass knob, she swung it around her shoulders and rushed outside. Charlotte followed close but never caught up completely. The lowering sun cast long shadows from the maple trees lining the street, a vivid array of color on their leaves. The cold damp evening had her crossing her arms tightly around her bodice. Walking with purpose around the block, she tried to clear her mind of anger. She had to think of how she could get from under her father's rule and her brother's antagonism. It would take so little to bring Chad to his knees; women talked, and she knew all too well of his affairs. His money affairs were more convoluted, and she kept clear of that part of his life.

She knew she had to find a better way for herself, and as the wind pricked at her uncovered head and the sky turned a moody blue, she vowed to set herself free.

"Thank you, Charlotte." Jane accepted the cup of tea from the housekeeper's hand. The morning was sunny, and a new day was before her. She would go into the store and perform her duties as usual. She let out a breath. Her mother came into the dining room.

"Your father is in his study and would like a word with you," she said. Her eye cocked in that expression that alerted Jane she was in for a lecture.

She walked down the red-carpeted hall past the staircase, wanting nothing more than to rush out of the house and start her day at the store or retreat to her room and work on her weekly column. She knocked lightly on his door.

"Come." His voice boomed from the other side.

She entered and stood waiting to be invited to sit. He gave her the gesture to take a seat. Sweeping a hand over her fringed forehead, she stared at his books neatly lining the back wall. So much knowledge in every bound edition. She had read several of them and wished to read more. Business, history, and even philosophy. Fascinating! Yet of what use was having knowledge if she wasn't allowed to apply it in her life?

"What is this all about?" her father asked.

She came away from her thoughts. This was her moment, and she would not run scared. "Mr. Cabot and I have formed an attachment to each other."

Her father's eyebrow arched. He rubbed his chin. "Oh, have you now?"

She scooted forward. "It began last fall. First it was friendly talk, then—"

"Then what?" His temper rose.

"We just talked some more."

"Of course, of course. Yes, talking is fine, but I have a feeling it might have gone further. God help you."

"I like him very much, but I have been nothing but a lady in his presence," she lied.

"He's not for you, Jane. I'm sorry. Now, let's have no more of this. I think your mother has planned a little something with a Mr. Hale. A fine young man, with several prospects and from an excellent family. Hopefully this one will be the man you let court you. Your mother has all but exhausted the pool of eligible young men within the city limits. We must keep to our own, Jane. I've worked too hard for you to marry a simple employee of mine."

Slowly coming up from her seat, she felt something inside her stir, a rebellious feeling. She faced her father. "He isn't simple, and he doesn't have to be just an employee. Mr. Fromm was a wealthy merchant who gave you, his jewelry maker, a chance. How can you look down on Martin, I mean, Mr. Cabot? He could be as successful as you are."

"Fromm was a stroke of luck, and I worked hard to benefit from that opportunity. Men like that don't come along every day. He gave you a chance as well and introduced us both to a rung of society our family had not known before. I have no intention of squandering what good fortune we've attained on some young man with poor relations. At least we come from some good stock. Mr. Cabot's family was poor, God rest their souls. His father worked on the docks. Is that the kind of story you want to tell your children about their lineage? I should say not."

Jane pursed her lips. "I will marry whom I please, Father. You can't stop me."

Her father leaned back in his leather chair. She trembled, yet she didn't lower her eyes or slump her shoulders.

"I would never think of disinheriting you, my dear, but you will break my heart into pieces if you go against me and your mother and end up living a penurious lifestyle."

He dangled her future wealth in front of her like the bait he knew it was.

"If my happiness breaks your heart, I am truly sorry. We will not be penniless, I'm sure."

His fist came down onto the desk, and she jumped. "Go tell your mother of your foolish desire to marry Mr. Cabot. I have no more to say to you."

Jane put one foot in front of the other, and finally, she was in the hallway. Leaning against the thick stair post, she closed her eyes and took a deep breath.

Finding her mother in the kitchen going over tomorrow's menus, she reluctantly got her attention. "Mother?"

"Yes, yes, dear?" her mother answered, not looking up from her papers.

"I am determined to marry Mr. Cabot."

"Oh!" Her mother's eyes widened on her slim face. "I should say not! Have you told your father?"

"He said to tell you."

"Oh, this is awful." She wrung her hands. "We have a guest coming tomorrow to dine with us. Mr. Robert Hale Jr. I want you to meet him. It may change your heart. Please give him a chance."

Jane gave little weight to her mother's distress. She was always in a tizzy about the least important things. How the roast was cooked, how evening visitors would have to come only after all the cooking smells left the parlor. Sometimes the windows had to be opened in the depths of winter. The winter snow was particularly vexing. She couldn't miss church or a social event! Keeping a clean home was her greatest pastime, even with a housekeeper. Jane's room had to be kept immaculate, or she'd get a lecture from her mother on God and heaven. Apparently, He also appreciated cleanliness.

Jane huffed. *I suppose these things are important to her.*

"Mother, I wish you would stop inviting these men to dinner. It's not fair to me, and it's not fair to them. They only accept because of Father's money."

"What a thing to say!"

Her mother's shrill voice was like looking into the sharp light of the sun. Jane rubbed her temples.

"You are one of the most beautiful, talented, and intelligent young ladies in the whole of Cincinnati—or at least one of the last ones left. I see Miss Harper has secured a date at the church with Mr. Murphy. And I had him in mind for you. He comes from old money I'll have you know."

Jane could not wait to be free of her mother's hysteria. The love between them had always been lukewarm at best. They never saw eye to eye on anything, and Elisha Wallingford had worked diligently throughout Jane's childhood at being in all the right social circles to the neglect of her children.

"I'm doing this for you" was the routine excuse each time Jane complained of her absence. Elisha noted with great pride each time one of her parties was considered noteworthy in the paper the next day. The charitable committees she headed or cochaired took up much of her time—not to mention her devotion to the church.

Jane had been raised by the housekeeper, and she felt Charlotte was more of a mother to her than her own. It wasn't uncommon in her mother's circle to have a nanny or housekeeper take care of the children, so Jane had given it little attention throughout her growing up. When Jane had been introduced by Mr. Fromm into his social circle at age eight, Elisha took it upon herself to take every advantage of that opportunity.

Sometimes Jane felt more like an instrument to her mother's climb up the social ladder than a daughter to be loved and cherished for herself.

Today, as she witnessed her mother's small stature become physically agitated, her heart felt sorry for the woman. At the same time, she vowed to not be like her in any way. Her God would not be so judgmental and harsh. The church would have no hold on her soul. She would not be overwhelmed with the guilt and fear Elisha tried to cultivate in her children. Chad certainly hadn't let it sway him.

No, she would not follow in her mother's footsteps. Her father's strength and determination were Jane's template. How he tolerated his wife's brittle humor, she did not know.

The wildness of California came to her in a wave of desire. She ignored it. She had to show them all that she could be an accomplished woman in Cincinnati.

Leaving the kitchen, Elisha reminded her of the guest coming for dinner the next evening. She would have to dress in her finest gown and play the part of a charming available prospect. She moaned.

"I don't like that sound coming from my daughter!" her mother said from the kitchen.

"Yes, Mother."

In her room, Jane was locked out of the world. She gazed at the back lawn. The main house was on the street front, and the bedrooms and her father's study faced the rear of the estate. It was quieter, and Jane could think or daydream. Tonight, she did both.

How had it come to this? When she was young, she felt she had it all. Mr. Fromm, the jewelry mogul who with one invitation to his estate could advance a man to the higher ranks of society, had taken her father under his wing. The business of acquiring the finest diamonds, rubies, and other valuable stones, along with the silver and gold to surround and hold the beautiful gems, was now her father's business. Long past dead, Mr. Fromm had left a thriving trade that her father had taken advantage of and made his own.

At a young age, Jane had been invited to take riding lessons with his two older daughters. The Fromm stables were renowned for their fine horses and expensive tack, along with the clean large stables. With that introduction, others followed, and Jane was invited to join the ranks of the wealthy. Then there was the Alister couple, who had no children and gave her a full scholarship to Wesleyan Female College. Her two-year liberal arts degree gave her some advantages over most other girls her age, but it wasn't what she really wanted to study. She wanted to take classes in botany, but Mrs. Alister thought literature would be best, with classes in household economics. Jane took it upon herself to secretly study plant life, fueling her love of horticulture.

Her thoughts went to Mr. Hale. *What if he's handsome? Will my heart be taken by him? Is Martin the only man in the world right for me?* Leaning against the fluffy pillow on her headboard, she contemplated marriage. *Perhaps it's only a practical arrangement after all.* Then a flash of his face gave her a thrill. *Mrs. Martin Cabot.* She frowned. *Mrs. Jane Cabot.* A smile swept across her face and lit her heart with joy. She removed herself from her daydreaming and got ready for her day at the store. Perhaps Martin would have an excuse to come out of his workroom today.

CHAPTER SIX

A FINE MAN INDEED. MR. ROBERT HALE JR. WAS AN average-height, fair-haired fellow. At nearly thirty, he had already developed a bit of a paunch under his well-tailored vest and waistcoat, indicating his fondness of rich food and lack of exertion. He carried himself as one suited to a certain lifestyle, all pomp and regal.

The rose-flowered wallpaper reflected the autumn light, creating a pinkish glow in the room. Jane couldn't help but notice how it lit Mr. Hale's scant crop of blond hair, revealing his scalp. She thought his chubby face looked quite infantile, like the Stewarts' new baby boy. She pinched her lips together to keep from laughing at the image of a baby's face on a man's body. His round face and cigar-shaped fingers gave her no pleasure. Intelligent and kind, perhaps, but he caused no stirrings. She was greatly relieved.

"I've read your column, Miss Wallingford. It's not my usual read, but I thought it was well written and probably quite engaging for your readers," Mr. Hale said during the main course. Other than their introduction, he had simply glanced at Jane with a smile. Mostly he talked with her father and brother.

"Yes, I enjoy writing it."

"My daughter has many talents. We've allowed her to indulge in this particular hobby," her mother said.

"It keeps our name in the papers," her father added. "Free advertisement if you like."

"Indeed," the gentleman replied. "Yet . . ." He looked up in contemplation.

The family turned to their guest.

"I prefer wives with a less public showing in a man's arena," Mr. Hale said. "I mean to say, hobbies are all well and good, but ladies must keep to the drawing rooms and attend to the needs of the household. A well-run home is a blessing to a husband. Don't you agree, Mrs. Wallingford?"

Elisha swiftly brought her napkin to wipe her mouth. She had managed a bite as she listened to Mr. Hale speak. "Yes, indeed. I've raised my daughter to know how to run a home, and well, she has many other talents, such as in dance and riding, and she knows how to . . ." Her mother searched for the word. "Garden."

Mr. Hale was correct in his assertions about a wife's duty. It was no surprise to Jane a man of his station would think so, yet she thought very differently. She hoped her role in a marriage would be one of partnership.

"What of equality in a marriage, Mr. Hale?" she asked. "I feel it would be a greater benefit if the wife had a role in running more than a home. The study of horticulture has always fascinated me, and my interest in it goes beyond helping in the kitchen garden, as much as I enjoy getting my hands in the ground. I assist the cook in deciding what the gardener will plant. Why, the carrots on our plates are from that kitchen garden. Are they not a delight?"

Mr. Hale examined his plate. "Yes, quite." He cleared his throat and bent his head to his meal.

Jane ignored her mother's piercing glare. The room went silent. She knew her opinions would go unrewarded. She didn't care. It was time for her life to reflect her likes and dislikes, her desires and needs. A husband was all well and good, but not to the extent of giving herself up entirely to him.

Mr. Hale spoke, breaking the heavy silence. Turning to her father, he stated, "A woman may dream up many hobbies." He turned to Jane and raised one eyebrow. "I would grant you the opportunity to dabble in your own kitchen garden." Leaning forward ever so slightly as if to insinuate something more intimate, he added, "A contented wife is also a great benefit to her husband."

Jane lifted her chin. The thought made her ill. She had to put a stop to this.

"However," she said, "I feel a husband should honor his wife with respect to her own career. As you say, a happy wife can benefit—"

"Jane." Her father's strong voice caught her attention. "That will be enough. Mr. Hale doesn't need to know your every thought."

There was nothing more to be done. She smiled generously at their guest.

"Of course," she said demurely.

Knowing her parents barely accepted her need for independence, it was now on display in front of a potential suitor. There was a hush that even Chadwick didn't break. He wiped his mouth with his napkin, placed it back on his lap, and continued to eat. Jane caught his gesture.

Why did she hope he would defend her now? His manner toward her hadn't always been disrespectful. When they were young, he was her champion, and bullies never dared trouble her. As he grew older, he became more distant from her, and recently, the estate and the business were all he cared about. As Jane became aware of her own stake in the company and estate, Chad treated her more as a rival than a beloved sister. She attributed his behavior to drinking and greed. It troubled her heart, but she wasn't going to let him get the better of her. She would ignore him for the rest of the dinner.

At the end of the supper, her father invited Mr. Hale into his study. After a moment, Jane crept down the hall and put an ear to the door. She could pretend to be on her way upstairs if caught.

"Your daughter has turned my head, Mr. Wallingford. Although I prefer a woman with less of a mind toward her own life and more of a mind toward supporting her husband's pursuits, I think I can manage her well enough. She's quite a beauty. I'm surprised she hasn't been married by now. I'm sorry to be so blunt."

"I'm afraid my daughter takes after her father, Mr. Hale, head-strong and independent. I don't think you will have an easy time at managing her, as you say."

Jane heard only muffled conversation after that and went to the parlor, where her mother sipped a cup of tea and Chad stood beside the long lace-curtained windows, parting one with a finger. He liked spying on passersby on the sidewalk below.

Ponderously, Jane sat on the chair and huffed. *Manage me?*

"What is it, Jane? You look disturbed. What were they saying? Did you catch a word?" her mother asked.

"No, I shouldn't have been at the door."

"No, you should not have been." Her mother looked up at the ceiling. "Yet these are important matters that concern us all. I don't blame you and won't tell your father."

"Thank you, Mother."

Jane placed her hands in her lap. The wait was excruciating. How would she bear it if her father let him propose? Refusing would cause an uproar.

Once the gentlemen returned to the parlor, the evening was over, and Mr. Hale took his leave with great praise to her parents and a promise to call on Miss Wallingford again soon. Jane couldn't tolerate any talk of future plans with this man.

"I will have to look at my diary, Mr. Hale," she said. "I think the next several weeks are quite taken."

"Never mind my daughter's reserve; we will be happy to welcome you anytime," her mother interjected.

Defeated, Jane gave a slight nod of her head and wanted to turn on her heel and run to the stables. A good gallop through the northern woods on this moonlit night would calm her agitation. She held steady and watched her father and Mr. Hale leave the room.

"That went well, I thought. Did you think it went well enough, Chadwick?" her mother asked.

Jane looked at her brother, whose body language was as much engaged with the whole affair as the chair he stood next to.

He turned and kissed their mother on the cheek. "Yes, I suppose. He's a bit of a bore, but I'm not marrying him. I'm expected in town, Mother. Good evening." The siblings looked at each other. As her brother brushed by her, he whispered, "Good luck with that bit of puff pastry."

She choked back a laugh. He could be disarmingly glib, and his remark broke the tension in her.

"I'm quite tired," her mother said. "Good evening, Chadwick. Do come in at a decent time. Jane, I'm going to bed. We will talk about you and Mr. Hale in the morning."

"I didn't find him very appealing. I don't want him to pursue me."

Bringing her hand to her mouth to cover a yawn, her mother said, "In the morning, my dear." She left the room, and Jane felt abandoned. Her father walked in.

"He's a fine man. I'll bring him into the business. I believe his degree in finance will be a great asset. I will meet with his father next week. He's a bit older than I would like, but I think still pliable enough to learn new things. I want no resistance from you. That show of arrogance tonight will not do. I don't want to hear any more of it, do you understand? I've made my decision. Good night, darling daughter."

She accepted his kiss to her cheek. "Good night, Father." She lowered herself onto the chesterfield with her hand clutching its arm.

How was she going to get out of this? Martin Cabot was her man. Her future was clearer to her than ever before. They would settle into a grand estate, and she would pursue her love of all things growing wild and cultured. She would collect information on botany and the workings of plants as remedies. Committees would be formed, elevating a hobby to a real contribution to society. Then one day she would take her journal entries to a publishing company. Her children would know about such things and spread the word also. More natural gardens would flourish on every estate. Martin would contribute in his own way as he worked to become head designer and partner in the company. How lavish their wealth would be and how generous she would be in showing Cincinnati her own exquisite gardens as teacher and donator. The heady thoughts had her dizzy with anticipation.

Two days later, Jane spied her father in the parlor, a neutral ground. The afternoon was dark and drizzly, and she had not been needed at the store. To her relief, Chad was in town on this particular afternoon—he couldn't insert his opinions.

Her father sat in his high-backed chair, his legs crossed, reading the newspaper. It was a rare sight at this time of day. He must've been waiting for her brother to return. On the round polished table near him sat his cup of coffee and a plate of apple Danish. She strained her neck and noticed they were half-consumed. He would still be in here for a little while at least. His burgeoning waistline revealed a lifetime love for the pastries.

She entered the long high-ceilinged room. In one corner sat a baby grand piano with an intimate seating area for listeners.

Biting her lip, she knew she'd eventually be asked to play for Mr. Hale if she didn't make her feelings clear. Her layered skirts dusted the carpeted floor as she passed the chesterfield, her hand skipping over its carved wooden frame. She seated herself in the flowered-upholstered chair at its end. Today the light flowing into the dark greens and bluish hues of this formally decorated room invited her to be adult and forthright.

"Father?"

"Yes, Jane?" he said, still buried in his paper.

"I'm glad to have found you here. I hope you're enjoying a bit of rest. You work so hard."

"What is it, Jane?" he asked without looking up.

"I want to say that . . . well . . . I believe Mr. Cabot could be a fine asset to our family and to Wallingford Jewelers. He has talent and drive and, most of all, integrity, and I love him." The last part had slipped out of her. She marveled at it. This truly must be love for the words to come out so naturally.

He closed his paper and placed it down on the table. Then he sipped his coffee and took a bite of the flaky Danish. She waited, watching his every move.

Finally, he wiped his mustached mouth on the white napkin and put his cup down. He'd been a handsome man at one time. Now the rigors of his business had brought gray to his slicked-back dark hair and wrinkles under his hooded brown eyes. At only forty-five, he looked older. Jane put aside her longing to hug him and have him hug her back.

"My dear. You have been quite sheltered from many sides of life, as you should have been. A beautiful rose flowers with great care. Let me and your mother decide what is best for you." Her father paused to take another sip of his coffee. Wiping his lips, he continued. "And I must say you have become an astute learner of the business. I need your continued work at the store. I daresay some of those clerk girls don't know a stitch about design and placement."

"Thank you. I do enjoy it but—"

"You are correct in assuming Mr. Cabot will be of great benefit to us. I will have a talk with him, and we'll go from there."

"Father, what changed your mind?"

"Never underestimate me, Jane. One has to see both sides of the coin. We must discern how we can benefit from others as well as how they can benefit from us. Remember that, my daughter. In your dealings with others, you must stay alert and take everything into account. Have I not taught you as if you were a son? It's my own damn fault for raising you this way. You have too much of your own mind. The fact hasn't escaped me that you are very clever, more than you are allowed to be. If you were a man, I would have you run the main store without hesitation."

Flabbergasted, Jane sat back in her chair. He had been paying attention to her all this time. He knew her. She felt silly for all her frivolity in the past. She could only stare at him now as he continued.

"Martin Cabot, as I said, is a worthy man, but not as a husband to you. We must promote him to a higher level, that is true, but as my employee, not my son-in-law. That is my final say on the matter."

Deflated, Jane stood and walked to the window and looked out from the haze of lace curtain onto the wet pavement below.

"We will promote him as the manager of production. I will have him visit the other three stores as well. It may be helpful for him to see what my other jewelers are doing lately. You may need to tour them as well with one of the clerk girls. Of course, separate from Mr. Cabot.

"I haven't been able to keep an eye on those stores as I want to. Also, I will put Mr. Cabot in charge of designing a limited release, and we'll see how it goes."

As her father rattled off his plan, her throat tightened with anger. Turning, she came to stand in front of him. She coughed into the back of her hand, then blurted out, "We are in love!"

"Now, listen to me, Jane. I have confidence in you. I know this is difficult, but you must see to your own future. You know nothing about a life without money."

Would the room stop spinning? Her plan was collapsing before her.

His expression softened. Her heart skipped a beat.

"Love is a fine thing. I understand it, I do."

"Yes, Father, but—"

"Let me finish. One word of you being seen in that store in the company of Martin Cabot and I will have him put out of my employ no matter how talented he is. I'll put George Miller in his place."

Jane furrowed her brow. "Oh no, not that dolt! He's not nearly as talented as Mr. Cabot. You know that as well as I do."

"I would remind you to contain your opinions. And yes, I know this. So, it will be up to you to keep Mr. Cabot in our employ by staying away from him. We need good people in our company for it to continue to succeed. I am training your brother as best I can, but I fear . . ."

Jane looked down at her shoes. She had to save Martin *and* her brother? By what means? Keeping away from the man she loved and keeping her brother's reputation clear of gossip?

"I can't help you with Chad, Father. I'm sorry to say, he has made his own decisions."

"Don't say a wrong word about my son. I was about to say I fear he may be taking on a great deal once I am no longer in charge."

"But that won't be for ages, and Martin and I could be a great benefit to him as a couple, as a married couple."

She held her breath. Her father rose and looked as if he was about to speak. Had she said words that had given him a change of heart?

"I hear your brother coming in. Go to the store and mind yourself concerning Mr. Cabot." He left the room.

She stood alone, shaken by his dismissal. A clap of thunder

startled her, and she brought her arms around her waist. It was only thunder, nothing to fear as she had during thunderstorms when she was a child. A thought crossed her mind. Her father was the thunderstorm that threatened her peace now. She would have to find a way to brave this storm.

CHAPTER SEVEN

*J*ANE AND MARTIN STOOD OUTSIDE THE BACK OF THE STORE. It was damp and cluttered with the discarded remnants of commerce. She winced from a mouse scurrying under a collapsed wooden container. It was the only place where they might have some privacy, but it certainly wasn't ideal for their rendezvous.

"I was able to catch the postman before Charlotte got to him," she said. "I threw his invitation directly into the fire."

"Is this Mr. Hale so bent on courting you? Or is he bent on adding to his wealth by marrying into your family?" Martin asked.

Jane shook her head. "Both. I think my father has his mind made up. What are we going to do, Martin?"

"I spoke with your father."

"Oh, Martin!" She hitched a breath and waited as patiently as possible. Mr. McMann was on his lunch break, and they had precious little time. One of the senior shopgirls was temporarily in charge, and she might need Jane at any moment.

"It was a good meeting. He—"

"When did you meet with him? What did you say exactly? What was his response *exactly*?" She knew what her father's plans were for Martin, but a slight glimmer of hope rose in her. Maybe meeting with Martin might have changed her father's mind.

His hand moved to her waist. A slight squeeze sent her into a daze and her loins into heaviness. What was this? How could he be romantic at a time like this? Her mind cleared, and she stepped away.

"I'm sorry," he said. "What were you saying?"

She adjusted her waistcoat. "Your conversation with my father."

"He said he would promote me and give me a position as manager of production and design."

"Yes, I know. What else?"

"He told you?"

She cocked her head. "In the two years you've been at this store, the profits have been steadily increasing. He sees your value."

Martin rubbed the back of his neck. "I'm glad for that, but—"

"This is a good step in the right direction, is it not? I think you should ask my father to provide you with more diamonds. They've been very popular in all the ballrooms and in the best of houses. The gaslights make them sparkle even more brightly."

He nodded his head.

She eagerly waited for more. Had he asked her father for her hand in marriage? When he offered no further information, she felt let down and betrayed. Wasn't he going to fight for her?

"Did he also tell you he's letting me have my own design this winter for a springtime release?" Martin asked.

She clapped her hands. "Martin, that's wonderful! Just think, your own designer's release! It could be the talk of the town. I'll get busy telling everyone to get some trinket or bauble to help boost sales. By Christmas you will be our number one jeweler, and my father will hear your name in every ballroom and parlor. I'm sure he will see you as a worthy husband for me as well as an asset to our family and business."

Martin stepped away, his face crestfallen. "I'm afraid as much as I tried, he did not want to talk about me courting you, least of all marriage."

Jane put a gloved hand to her mouth as tears welled in her eyes. Her optimism couldn't withstand the force of her father once he had made up his mind.

"Oh, sweetheart. Don't be sad. There will be a way. I'm sure of it. As for managing the production, well, truthfully, I think it's his way of keeping me too busy for a social life, if you get my meaning."

Jane did get his meaning. They would have less time to spend together. Martin would be locked away making the jewelry and trinkets for the stores or consulting with the other jewelers. She curled her lip and tugged on her waistcoat, and then drying her eyes with her handkerchief, she rallied.

"Do your best, Martin." She thought for a moment. "I will make sure your name is on invitation lists that aren't so formal so that a man of your station would be invited. The library's annual fundraiser for one. I'm determined to raise you up in society! I have faith in you. I have faith in us."

"Thank you, Jane." He swept her up in his arms and planted a kiss on her lips. "I will do whatever it takes! I've been saving my money, and with your dowry, well, we can make a real go of it in California!"

She made a sighing sound, coming away with heated cheeks. His sudden kiss had her lost in a swirl of emotion and hope and . . . California?

"We don't need any of this." He swept a hand toward the dark wooden door that led back to his workroom, the store, and her small office. "We can have land and sheep and sunshine all year long! Breathe in fresh air and freedom!"

She laughed and stepped away. "I need you to be strong and grow in the Wallingford business."

"But, Jane, I'm serious. I have plans."

"As do I."

She held out her hand, and he took it without hesitation and pulled her into him. His show of strength just about undid her. He lifted her chin and brought his head down, pressing his lips on hers. She felt the warmth of his mouth igniting her sexual desires. His passion was so different now. Perhaps the promotion had given him the courage to pursue her more ardently. Whatever it was, she liked it. If she stayed a moment longer, she would welcome him to take liberties with her. Not here.

Keeping to her word, Jane talked to everyone she knew about the value of diamonds on a woman's neck and ears. She wrote about it in her weekly column without sounding as if she were an advertisement for the store. She wrote: *With the expertise of the jeweler, diamonds will put a spotlight on you at any gathering. The glow of your skin will light any man's ardor.*

Only a few days later, Martin overheard her talking to a clutch of women in front of the store.

"In certain light, say at a ball at the Davenports' or Rothchilds', the glow created on one's face is quite flattering."

He had to laugh to himself. He had come to know her as a force of nature once she set her mind to something. Like her father, she didn't give up easily.

It wasn't long before Mr. McMann found himself surrounded by the ladies of society. They all had a bauble with some diamonds in the settings, but the excitement of new designs brought out women looking for something different.

For his new endeavor, Martin worked with Mr. Wallingford's designers and was given an additional inventory of clasps and settings for rings, necklaces, and brooches, all in 18-karat gold and the finest silver. Along with the small pouches of diamonds and other gems, Martin was so busy he had no time to think.

He had come out of his backroom shell to serve the ladies of high society. After a few of the bejeweled pieces made their way into the best of homes, he was the one the women swarmed to in their eagerness to place their order. Necklaces, rings, hat pins, hair adornments, and more were commissioned in an array of settings—some a whisper of elegance, others a shocking display of wealth. One woman asked if a diamond necklace could be made to fit her Pomeranian.

Even with all this, the invitations to attend certain social events were not forthcoming—Jane had been overconfident with the acceptance of his standing in the ranks of society. He was a servant to society, not one of them. He wasn't disappointed but rather relieved. His own nature was quiet and reserved, and he valued his time in the country away from the world Jane seemed to thrive in. It concerned him greatly, but then his mind would settle on her love of plants, and the fog of doubt would clear and his heart gladden.

When Mr. McMann would slip out for his morning break or again at lunch, Martin waited for the timid knock on his workroom door. Jane would slip in and settle herself in a chair while Martin worked around her. Cautious, Jane kept the door ajar and talked more loudly at times. "What was the gold chain count last time, Mr. Cabot?"

It gave Martin a twinge of excitement coupled with a feeling of dread. As much as he was falling in love with her, he didn't want to lose his job—it would ruin his plan. At times he felt as if he might be better off if his heart weren't so engaged. Greedily, he thought of the hefty dowry she would come with, which would secure the land he was bent on purchasing. Ashamed, he would think of how he could obtain the money through his work at Wallingford's. It would certainly take longer, and he knew Harry couldn't wait. His cousin had purchased the neighboring farm at a good price but needed to sell it soon and at a profit to support his own farm.

That afternoon as Martin secured the clasp on the string of cultured pearls, his mind drifted. He envisioned a country home with loads of children playing among gardens and animals. It gave him a deep sense of joy. His wife and offspring by his side, a good horse and wagon to drive into town, and a loyal dog would set him up for life. Although his experience in sheep raising and farming in general was nil, Harry had assured him he would show him the ropes, and that was good enough for Martin.

First, he would prove his worth to Mr. Wallingford. The diamond-and-ruby brooch design he worked on in his spare time had been more difficult than he had anticipated. There were so many talented designers who had already made their mark on the jewelry world. What could he contribute, and did he care? The pile of crumpled paper next to his desk in his small apartment was proof of his lack of talent and will. Had he taken on more than he was capable of?

A new, more adventurous life could be had, and if he was honest with himself, his focus on the jewelry business had decreased greatly as his love for Jane and his yearning for the West increased tenfold, especially after his latest letter from Harry.

Dear Cousin Martin,

The land is ready for purchase. All conveyances have been cleared but for your final payment. I have placed the order of fifty sheep to be delivered in January. Be prepared for some good hard work. I hope sitting at your stool all day hasn't made you too soft. A new life awaits you, my friend.

I look forward to working together to make our farms more prosperous.

Best Regards,
Harry

CHAPTER EIGHT

November 1879

$\mathcal{E}$LISHA WALLINGFORD'S PINCHED EXPRESSION RELATED HER dismay at having Martin Cabot dine with them tonight. It had been a heated topic ever since John Wallingford had announced it three days ago. Jane was ecstatic.

"It's a business dinner," he said to the family. "I have to know who this man is outside of the store if he is to represent me on this new level."

"But, John, at our house? Why couldn't you arrange something at your club or one of the restaurants in town? Surely his manners are up to that level."

"Yes, Father," Chad inserted. "You seem to be dangling the bait before your daughter here. I mean, look at her face!" He laughed.

Jane gave him a serious look, trying to hide her pleasure at the idea of having Martin right there at the dinner table with her. Inside, her heart was beating faster, and her face felt flush. She had to speak and expel the energy building in her.

"Brother, if you had taken a moment of interest in my life, you would know that Father has forbidden me to marry Mr. Cabot. It would be to your advantage to know him and his capabilities. He might serve you well in the future. Lord knows you may need all the help you can get."

"Father, are you going to let her talk to me that way?"

"Sit down, Chadwick!" Her father loosened his collar and unbuttoned the top button. He seemed out of breath, and his cheeks were flushed. "I have no patience for sibling rivalry."

"I'm sorry, Father. I spoke out of turn," Jane said.

The look Chad gave her made her cautious. He had no temperance, no forgiveness, and his ability to seek levity was gone. For the first time in her life, she felt afraid of him.

Her father nodded his acceptance of her apology as Chad left the room.

That night, she wondered why her father would have one of his employees for dinner. What game was he playing? The state of his health concerned her. Though John Wallingford was above seeking help for any ailment, she knew he had recently sought advice from their family physician for shortness of breath. She knew nothing more than that and speculated he'd been told to rest more—a state in which he would become quite agitated.

Perhaps Martin was more important to her father than he realized. She hadn't slept well since her father's announcement. What would she wear? What would be served for dinner? The appearance of the house, her brother's caustic attitude, her mother's disapproval—all of it worried her beyond measure.

JANE WAS BEYOND ANXIOUS ON this cold and drizzly November evening. Her hair was drawn up into a neat bun with a braid tucked underneath at the nape of her neck. Her attire hung on the large hook near the floor-length mirror. The long modern fitted bodice-style dress with a lower laced neckline was accented by a mass of ruffled material trailing down from the hip along one side. She loved how the different hues of blue would highlight her dark features. A soft fringe over her forehead and she would be the ideal figure of fashion. It would surely provoke the inner stirrings of their guest without the others any wiser. Tonight, she hoped, would be the first step toward softening her father to the idea of Martin being more than an employee.

Jane let out a sharp puff of air and leaned forward as Mrs. Simms, the Wallingford ladies' dresser and hairstylist, laced her corset. Mrs. Simms was called over for all their special dinners and occasions. For her mother to call her tonight gave Jane another indication of this being more than just business.

"Is this tight enough, miss?"

Jane winced. She took another breath. "Just a bit more."

"Yes, miss." With her strong arms, Mrs. Simms pulled on the laces and then brought them against Jane's lower back, securing them with a double-knotted bow.

The rest of the layers were draped over Jane's head, followed by the dress itself. Mrs. Simms helped assemble the fluff of ruffles, then retouched her hair. Jane then went to one of her large jewelry boxes. Appraising the sparkling diamonds, emeralds, and other opulent gems, she opted for a multistrand of pearls with pearl drop earrings to match.

Satisfied with her choice, she stood in front of the mirror with an approving nod from Mrs. Simms. Lifting the heavy dress slightly above her feet, Jane slipped into her evening shoes. The higher heel and heaviness of the lopsided fabric had her swaying before finding her balance.

"Thank you, Mrs. Simms. Would you help me downstairs please?"

Gingerly, Jane took each step, and finally, after the last one, she was able to relax on the solid floor. This new fashion had her at a slight disadvantage. She would try to act as if she wore these types of clothes all the time. However, her other gowns were not severely ruffled. The dresser hurried back up to tend to her mother, and Jane stepped as gracefully as she could toward the parlor.

Before Martin was about to arrive, her father spoke to Jane and her brother. "Chadwick, you and I will try to refrain from business talk at the table. Jane, I see you are quite decked out tonight, which I approve of since I've also invited Mr. Hale. Apparently, his recent invitations to you were declined, or worse, have gone unanswered."

"Mr. Hale is coming to dine also?" Jane couldn't believe it. Now she knew why Mrs. Simms had been called for. Her mother wanted her to look her best for Mr. Hale! "He has sent me a few invitations to the theater. I didn't have the time or inclination to accept."

Her mother was now at her elbow.

"After all I have done to secure a good match for you?" she said. "You will make it up to him tonight by accepting whatever invitation he gives you—if he does at all." Elisha turned away in disgust.

"I'm sorry, but I don't care for him." Jane addressed her father now.

"My dear, no worries. I have it all in hand. Settle your nerves, both of you." He turned to Charlotte. "Pour Mrs. Wallingford and my daughter each a glass of sherry."

Jane let out a huff. A glass of sherry was hardly the answer. She hated being managed like a half-wit. Didn't her father have more respect for her than this?

With her dress keeping her upright and prim, she stood in simmering silence and waved away the offer of sherry.

"I want Mr. Cabot to feel comfortable in meeting Mr. Hale," her father said. "The two may cross paths in their new positions as financer and jewelry manager. We will discuss the finer points later in my study."

THE DINING TABLE WAS FORMALLY dressed, as if their guests were of greater importance than they actually were. Charlotte had brought out their finest china, and the cook was to dress up the three-course meal with extra flare, a flourish of parsley, sliced apples in pretty rosette shapes, and the more expensive wine from the cellar.

At the stroke of seven, the doorbell chimed. Jane's nerves flared. Charlotte brought the men, who arrived together, into the parlor to be greeted by the family.

"Welcome to our home, Mr. Cabot," Elisha said obligingly.

"Thank you for your invitation, madam," Martin replied.

To Jane, Martin looked fine for an informal dinner, but he was not as appropriately dressed as the rest of them were. Had no one informed him of tonight's dress? Or had he not the correct attire for a formal dinner? Before she could fixate on it, Martin gave her a sweet smile, and she relaxed.

"And Mr. Hale, it is a great pleasure to welcome you back," her mother continued.

Mr. Hale gave a bow of his head. "I am very pleased to be in the company of the Wallingford family again." He then shook hands with Chad and her father.

Jane acknowledged Mr. Hale with a thin smile, then turned to Martin while her mother chatted, bringing in her brother and father.

"Oh, the weather has been dreadful, has it not?" Elisha said. "Mr. Wallingford, tell him about the temperature in your office the other day. It took all day to get warm!"

"Have you met Mr. Hale?" Jane asked Martin.

"Only just now." His reply was marked with a confused look on his face.

Turning sideways, she whispered, "My father's idea, not mine."

Her father's loud voice cut through the chatter. "Mr. Robert Hale, this is my jeweler, Mr. Martin Cabot. I am making him a manager of design. I wanted to have you two meet each other."

"A pleasure," Mr. Hale said. "It's good to know the staff, as I have many plans going forward."

Jane closed her eyes and turned away. This night wasn't starting out as the triumph she had hoped it would become for Martin. How could her father put her in such a position? She took a breath and tried to act as if nothing were wrong with having these two men meet. Her father's choice for her husband and her own choice standing in the same room!

As the courses of soup, fish, and meat were served, Jane found herself becoming more uncomfortable. Mr. Hale was trying to meet her eyes as much as Martin was trying to avoid them. Not only was her outfit clutching her body in a vise grip, but Martin was not selling himself as readily as she had hoped. But what could he do? Robert Hale had the family in the palm of his hand.

"I look forward to immersing myself in the jewelry business. And with your talented and charming daughter by my side, I feel we'll be able to reach new heights."

Mortified beyond belief, Jane ate with steady purpose. She didn't look up to agree or disagree with what Mr. Hale was saying. *Poor Martin!*

When Martin met her eyes, she saw in him a polite resignation. He was enduring the situation, and she loved him for it. Another part of her wished he would speak up! *Sell yourself! Sell our relationship!*

"Time enough to talk business, Robert," her father said.

"Yes, indeed, Mr. Wallingford." Robert wiped his mouth with his napkin.

"I'd much rather we talk of your talented daughter," Martin inserted.

Jane looked up with surprise and great pleasure. Her heart expanded while her family looked at him with curious stares.

"Jane's interest in the study of horticulture is remarkable. My parents had a small plot of land they tended, and it certainly is in my blood. She will contribute a great deal to any man willing to be open-minded to a woman's need to express her talents."

She wanted to laugh out loud at the raised eyebrows and tab-leau his remarks had caused. It was as if the world had stopped revolving. She wanted to applaud his courage and confidence and hug him for championing her interests. However, the family and Robert did not find his views worthy of continuing a conversation over.

"Our cook has prepared the most wonderful apple tarte tatin with fresh cream. We must save room for dessert," Elisha said.

After dessert, the men rose, and her father led them to his study.

"I've yet to see your design, young man," her father said as he escorted Martin down the hallway followed by Chad and Mr. Hale.

Oh dear, Jane thought. She knew Martin was having trouble coming up with an original design. She waited in the parlor with her mother, who took up her knitting. An hour passed, then two. What could they be talking about? She thought most men loved to talk just to hear themselves speak. Her brother was one such man, but what would Martin contribute? She got up and paced the parlor.

"Sit, dear," Elisha said. "There's nothing to be anxious about. It's all settled. I think your father was good to invite Mr. Cabot after all. He seems like a fine young man, and Mr. Hale can use his input on business matters, I'm sure." Elisha knitted several stitches and looked at her daughter. "And Mr. Cabot saw how it is between you and Mr. Hale."

Knowing her mother knew nothing of "business matters," Jane didn't bother to argue. The other matter of Martin seeing any rela-tionship between her and Robert was a different matter. Was her mother so oblivious to her wishes? She tried again to enlighten her.

"I have no feelings for Mr. Hale."

Elisha continued knitting. "I will not engage you in such talk."

It was no use. Jane did not reply and continued to pace the floor. Finally, her gown became too heavy, and she sat down and took up her embroidery hoop. Elisha nodded her approval.

Only Chad and Martin returned to the parlor. Jane rose from her seat, her cumbersome dress making it difficult to stand quickly. She forgot her embroidery, and the hoop fell to the floor, where it would have to lie. Her heart pulsed in her throat.

"Thank you for a wonderful evening, Mrs. Wallingford, Miss Wallingford," Martin said.

Jane searched Martin's face. His expression was placid. What had been said? She'd mine his thoughts tomorrow. Tonight, she was to perform her duty of a gracious hostess along with her mother. Oh, how she wished to be free!

Elisha was on her feet as soon as she heard the men's voices. "Mr. Cabot, it was a pleasure. Now you can see how we all have our place in the business. We hope to have you join us in the future when we give our annual reception for all of our hardworking employees."

Martin smiled and tipped his head.

"And," her mother continued, "you should consider yourself very fortunate tonight. Mr. Wallingford has never had one of his employees for dinner like this. So intimate. He must think very highly of you. Meeting my daughter's future husband, who will be our future financier, was quite an honor for you."

"Mother." Jane had to stop her. Martin remained polite, however.

"I am most grateful, Mrs. Wallingford," Martin said.

"May I see you out, Mr. Cabot?" Jane asked. She was desperate to talk with him.

Chad stepped in. "I'll see him out, Jane. Mr. Hale expects you to be waiting for him."

She and Martin exchanged a knowing glance. It soothed her nerves. They would meet and talk tomorrow. She went back to her seat in the parlor and waited. Grabbing her embroidery hoop from the floor, she nearly toppled over. She wanted to go upstairs and tear off this horrible dress!

Recovering, she plunked down onto the chair and began poking wildly at her taut fabric, making horrible stitches while praying to Mother Mary, Saint Anne, and Saint Teresa. Maybe one of these sainted women would help her cause. Then the wait was over.

Robert Hale stood confidently in the parlor entrance. "May I have your daughter join me on the veranda? The evening air might be good for us both."

She looked at his reddened face gleaming in the light of the gas lamps. Was it pudgier than just a few hours ago?

"You may go," her father said to her as he came up beside Robert.

"Take your shawl, my dear," her mother said with glassy eyes.

Jane walked out with her mother's emotional voice behind her. "Oh, John! How wonderful!"

It wasn't wonderful at all. It felt dreadful. The cold night offered little comfort, let alone a romantic setting for a proposal. She tried as hard as she might to think of a gentle refusal.

He reached for her ungloved hand. She felt his doughy, sweaty fingers. A slight nudge of compassion rose in her, and she didn't withdraw. His upper lip was moist. He reached with his other hand into his pocket and took out his handkerchief and wiped his mouth. He placed it back and cleared his throat.

"I would be honored if you'll be my wife. Your father has blessed our union."

His words came out in a rush. She waited a beat before answering.

"I am sorry, but my heart belongs to someone else." It felt good to finally tell him where she stood.

Robert's eyes went wide with disbelief. "Who?"

"Martin Cabot."

"Martin Cabot? Why, he's a simple worker. His station is well under my own. It was pleasant to meet him—I need to know the employees—but surely, I will have a greater importance in the business. I have wealth and standing. What does he have?" He rubbed the top of his head and then smoothed out the thinning hair. "Your father assured me of your answer."

"My father is not me. *My* answer is no." She breathed in and let it out, the cold air making her breath appear. It felt as if she was letting out all the worry and anxiety of hiding her true feelings. Then she felt her hand drop from his as if it were on fire. The moment of relief was replaced by the reality of her life. This was not going to be easy.

"Then why was I led to believe—I mean, your father has hired me onto the business."

"That is not my doing. I'm sorry, Mr. Hale. I'm sorry my parents led you to believe I was in on their plan to have us wed." She felt awful for not forewarning him. "I thought my lack of response to your invitations would alert you to my lack of interest in you."

"Why, I must say, you are the bold one! I may have dodged a bullet! If you think I needed the job from your father, you are both mistaken. It was to be a hobby of sorts. Something new. I don't need any of this!" He left in a huff.

Though disturbed by his change in temper, she was happy to have the awkward moment over with. She followed him in but took a different direction up to her room. She heard voices rising from the foyer. Struggling to take each step while she managed her dress, she couldn't escape fast enough.

"Jane!" Her father's baritone stopped her in her steps.

"Father, I did what I felt was best for me."

"He's quite put off. I've asked him to give you time."

"Oh, Father, please!"

He approached her as if weariness had overcome him.

"Come down here," he said.

She gathered the ruffles and began a slow descent. He looked at her, and his tiredness turned into a sharp look of determination.

"If you do not marry Robert Hale, I will put you out of this house and you will have to fend for yourself. Your mother and I have lost patience with you. And if you think this opens the door for you to go off and marry Mr. Cabot, think again. He will no longer work for me. I will destroy whatever reputation he has built in this city, which I gave to him! Make up your mind to this. It's the best for everyone involved."

His words were like a punch to her gut. Would he actually turn her out?

"Why are you so bent on Mr. Hale?" she asked, but it soon came clear as day. *His fortune.* "Of course, I now see. You are using me—and him—for gain."

Her father didn't waver. "How dare you! I see the future, and this is what is right for our family, the business, and you. Have you become so against me and my care for my family?"

Jane felt neither shame nor victory, just sadness that it had come to this with her father. "No. I'm sorry."

He turned from her, and she struggled back up the stairs. Once in her room, she sat on the edge of the bed. The feeling of defeat engulfed her. Martin hadn't yet proposed. Why was she planning a future with him? Her dreams were crushed. She felt abandoned by her father. The thought of Robert Hale as her husband turned her stomach sour.

After Mrs. Simms came up to help her undress, Jane went to bed and wept until sleep took her.

CHAPTER NINE

$\mathcal{G}$OOD DAY, MISS WALLINGFORD," said JOEL, JANE'S COWORKER at the paper, as she left the offices to head into the heart of downtown.

"See you tomorrow, Joel."

Her column was done, and she could leave early—one of the perks of being on the paper as a part-time worker. She placed her hat and gloves on and walked the four blocks to Wallingford Jewelers. The autumn sky was a brilliant blue, and the air was crisp and clear, if not completely fresh from industry. A steam engine's horn blared in the background as she hurried to the store, passing the usual commotion of people.

It had taken her two weeks from his first proposal to accept Robert's second proposal. It was not with happiness in her heart, but dread. Knowing Martin would not be ruined made it easier but no less grievous. Her heart was broken; it was as if a death had occurred. Today she had to talk to Martin. She had to see him before the announcement came out in the paper.

She entered the front door and looked for Mr. McMann. He was helping a customer at the far corner of the store. She was about to go to the back when he came upon her.

"Miss Wallingford, what a pleasant surprise. I thought you'd be at the paper today."

"Hello, Mr. McMann. I finished early. I'm here to see Mr. Cabot about a few business matters."

The look on his face told her she wasn't treading on solid ground. Did he not suspect in the least her and Martin's secret visits? He looked to his left and then to his right. She waited.

"I'm afraid your father has given me strict orders for you not to be let into the back rooms. I can relay your message to him."

"I don't care what my father told you. I will see him if I like. Now excuse me."

She brushed by the manager, her heart beating loudly in her chest.

"Miss, please," he said as she hurried to the back room. She opened the door to Martin's workspace.

"Jane!" He stood up from his stool, nearly knocking over a box of pearls.

She stepped forward in the hope he would embrace her. He looked concerned, and she stilled herself. "Martin, I had to see you."

"Jane, your father had some harsh words for me the night I came for dinner. He forbade me to have anything to do with you. I thought you were aware since you've been distant from me these last weeks. You've not come to this part of the store. I just assumed . . ."

"I'm sorry."

"Your father threatened me with ruin if I had anything to do with you. How can I work here in the same building with you and not . . . I mean, it's quite impossible, but I need my job for at least another six months. Then I'm going out West."

Jane stepped back. "The sheep farm? Martin, you're not a sheep farmer. You belong here. We belong here."

His expression was one of amusement. She became cross with him and folded her arms over her chest. He smiled and took them down and held her hands.

"I don't belong here. I choose not to anymore. I—that is, *we*— could make a new and completely different life away from all this society business."

She was speechless. He went on.

"I want you to be my wife and share my life with me. You could plant any kind of garden you want! Several even!"

"Did you just propose?"

He got down on one knee and looked up at her, sincerity lighting his face.

"Jane Wallingford, will you marry me?" Looking up at her, he quickly added, "I'm surrounded by diamonds, and I have not one to place on your finger!"

"Yes!" she said, caught up in the moment.

He stood up, and she felt his warm embrace. Realizing what she had done, she withdrew sharply, her hand flying to her mouth.

"I've accepted Mr. Hale's proposal. I had no choice. I thought you might forget the farming idea and stay here and become well-known and wealthy. At least I could see you and—"

"And what?" His voice was no longer syrupy. He became angry. "I see you have it all figured out! Well, so do I. Your father is not the ruler over my fate. I'm sorry he is over yours. We could leave. We could make our own decisions. I no longer wish to be under your father's harsh rules."

"You make him sound like an ogre!"

"We all freeze back here in the winter because he says it's too expensive to heat and sweat in the summer for lack of windows and air. I don't want to live this way. I want to be my own boss. I don't want to ask another man for the comforts of life. I want to live on my own terms. This jewelry making is for someone else to benefit by. I get nothing but a paycheck from it."

Jane was struck by his passion. He wanted more from life, as did she. But a farm? In the wilds of the West?

"Martin, I didn't know that my father has treated you so poorly. I suppose I didn't notice. I'm sorry."

"It's no longer your concern. You're probably better off with Robert. You'll continue to get anything you want. I'm sure you'll charm the pants off of him for every inch of freedom you can get."

"I'll ignore your assumption of me," she said. Before he could apologize, she continued. "I want to be as free as you do, but not in the same way, I suppose. Oh dear!" Tears flowed from her eyes. First her father's abandonment, now Martin's. "You have no more feelings for me, Martin?"

Martin raked his fingers through his hair. "I love you. Don't ever forget that."

She stepped into his arms, and they embraced for what she knew would be the last time.

With a hiccup in her voice, she said, "I love you too."

"I won't say goodbye, Jane. I won't stop hoping."

"Oh, Martin. I wish I could be so confident."

Holding back her emotions, she left the store.

ELISHA PRESENTED JANE WITH A book of illustrated wedding gowns including all the accoutrements a bride would need. Jane stared at each page. Was she actually going through with this? Elisha fawned over every last detail on offer and gave her opinion freely.

"This is very beautiful, but it might make you look thick in the waist. Now, this one is just right, but oh my! The price! Your father would have a fit over it. What do you think of this one, Jane?"

Jane looked at her mother's choice. "I suppose so."

With a huff, Elisha stopped her page turning. "I've looked forward to this time with you since you were a little girl, and this is your response?"

"I don't want to marry him. How can I be excited about the dress when it means marrying a man I don't love?"

"May I remind you your father has said there is to be no more talk of that? You will come to love him. He will come to love you if he hasn't already. The look on his face when he told us you had accepted his second proposal was, well, it brought mist to my eyes."

"The only reason I am marrying this man is to keep the man I love from ruin. How can my father be so cruel?"

Elisha shook her head with a satisfied smile. "My dear, you are maturing. You have come to know the sacrifice we women make. Children will bring great joy and even greater sacrifice. God will keep you on the right track, as He has for me. It's good you know all this now." She patted Jane's hand and continued the search for the perfect wedding gown, then added, "And what may seem cruel at the moment may turn out to be just what you need."

Jane couldn't think how this arranged marriage could be beneficial to her. With a heavy heart, she let herself bend to the moment and joined her mother in the search for the perfect dress. What did it matter anyway? Martin would be gone soon to California. A place where land could be used all year round. A seed of "what if?" began to crack open. Would she dare let it grow?

CHAPTER TEN

November 1880

$\mathcal{E}$LISHA WALLINGFORD BEAMED FROM ALL THE ATTENTION she received after the announcement of her daughter's betrothal last year. No one could've been prouder.

She thought of Robert Hale as an upstanding citizen in society and the perfect husband for Jane, rich and full of promise for the business and the family's future. Some in her circle looked down their noses at the family's choice of husband for the Wallingford daughter. He was not the handsome young man she was expected to marry, not to mention how he would be put to work for Wallingford Jewelers.

For once, Elisha didn't let the pettiness of society squelch her joy. Her true friends had assured her that it was better than no husband at all and agreed he would be a great asset. She was also reminded of the grandchildren coming her way. This was as much her grand accomplishment as it was her daughter's.

Being the quintessential society mother, Elisha had sent her daughter to finishing school and accepted all worthy invitations to tea, lunches, and parties, not to mention the annual season of balls. She had planned Jane's coming-out with great care and had recently planned the engagement party and now the climax of all her efforts: the wedding.

Jane let her mother arrange most of the wedding. Martin became a lovely dream while the days of winter passed by and spring turned into summer. She forced herself not to think about him.

He had stayed on at the store longer than she had expected. He probably needed the money. They saw each other when she went to the store, which had become increasingly rare. When they did meet, he was pleasant, yet distant, and she couldn't be more than that herself. Her duties were being curtailed, as her duty as a wife would soon take over her life. Not only did she miss Martin, but she missed working and the worth she felt in her job there, along with the conversations she and her father would have about how things went that day. It had all been taken away to be replaced with a life she cared nothing for.

Spring was her favorite time of year, and yet it was with a heavy heart she walked through it and into the summer light, the flowers full of scent, and the many hues of green. She thought she might be able to follow her dream and Robert might not rule over her.

As fall arrived, a feeling of something new filled her with an odd joy. What could she anticipate that gave her hope? Perhaps it was only the nostalgia of the start of a new school year and the excitement of learning. With a heart steeled by fate, she decided she would be her own woman no matter what.

She dived into her column and continued her study of botany and horticulture. Visiting the farms and asking the librarian for more books on the subject kept her from falling into a melancholic state.

Now that she was in her good graces with her father, he paid little attention to her daily life, and she had the freedom to come and go as she pleased. Oddly, it was what she'd craved, but it had come at a heavy price.

Robert Hale was robust in his attentions to her. It gave her no pleasure to stroll with him around Fountain Square or attend the theater or balls with her arm on his. She had little choice, for her father had fixed her future as if he were signing a deal for the store—an acquisition for his daughter and jewelry empire.

Although her friend Sadie was sympathetic to Jane's plight, she didn't hesitate to include Robert in her own social circles. Dinners at the Longworths', where Sadie's parents and Leonard welcomed the new couple into their fold, were polite agony for Jane. How could Sadie not see her discomfort? Sadie and her handsome husband and Jane and Robert formed a neat and stylish quartet and were seen about town together as often as Jane could stand. Sadie mooned over her new son while Leonard talked with Robert about business.

At least once a week, Jane would come down with a "headache" or some other ailment. Her excuses ran thin, and she would have to go out with Robert. His presence in their home was most awkward for her. He had nearly moved in. There was nowhere to hide accept in her room or at the paper.

She wrote of plants, not wedding plans. Her readers were quite upset, and a few even commented in the editorial section about her lack of interest in her own wedding arrangements. An inside look into the wedding of a socialite would add to the paper's sales, and Jane was given the order to indulge her readers. So, after observing her mother and becoming involved with the planning, she wrote of the rigors of all the important details, including the dresses, flowers, and food; the venues which were best suited for an autumn reception; and on and on. It was a distraction of sorts, as if it were someone else's affair. Her readers ate it up, and her editor loved her for bringing more subscribers in.

Jane's father was more affectionate with her than in recent years. It added to the surreal feel her life was taking on. Each night when he kissed her on the cheek, he said, "Good night, my daughter. You've made me a very happy man. I'm truly at rest in my heart."

She felt wrapped in his love again, although it wasn't the same. Her love for Martin outshined her father's affection. Her father had gotten his way, but she had sacrificed hers.

Only weeks away now from the big day, she, her mother, and the household were steeped in all the last-minute arrangements. The house was filling with gifts, and a room off the parlor had been dedicated to them alone. Her mother gave thanks each night at dinner for God's good grace in choosing her daughter a husband. Jane knew her mother had prayed for this and had overheard her say to her friends that God had answered her prayers.

Jane often wondered if her mother and her mother's friends thought God was a genie in a bottle granting all their wishes as *He* saw best—especially through prayer and church attendance.

All of her mother's efforts to find her a husband and her father's insistence in her marrying Robert faded into the background as her wedding day grew nearer and the excitement built. In less than two weeks she'd be a married woman. Martin would be gone, and her life would be one of social engagements and supporting her husband, father, and even her brother in every way she could. Her garden would be grand but subdued as to fit into the nature of their estate. The Capital Hill manor had already been purchased and was being renovated in preparation for the newlyweds.

In a small way, Jane was looking forward to her new home and possibly a life she could be content in. Her creative nature couldn't help but plan the arrangement of furniture, the color of walls, and the placement of plants inside her home and out in her gardens. With a slight glimmer of hope, she moved forward.

However, it came to be that her mother's god had other plans.

As JANE SAT IN THE front pew of the church and listened to another person eulogize her father, she felt the power of God in no uncertain terms. His decision to change her life in the blink of an eye astounded her.

With only days before the biggest event of her life, her father had passed away in his sleep. Instead of walking her down the aisle, he lay in a coffin before her.

Her heart was broken into pieces. She remembered the trips she'd taken across the Atlantic with him. Paris had been one of those trips and was the one she cherished the most.

Chadwick had come down with the measles, and he had been left behind with the doctors and their mother to care for him. Clear of the virus, her father had taken her and Charlotte instead.

She'd been fourteen and full of excitement. She and her father roamed the streets of Paris, eating pastry and chocolate while pointing at all the sights like the tourists they were. Dining at the finest restaurants and staying at a luxurious old hotel right on the banks of the Siene. They met each morning for strong coffee and French rolls. Jane had him all to herself, and she made him laugh, and he made her feel special. Uninhibited by the smell of the city—a mixture of baked goods, riverbank, and urine—she had been given plenty of time to roam the shops with Charlotte while her father conducted his business with the jewelry merchants.

Her father, her strong-minded hero, the only man she thought she would ever love as a child, had been taken from her without warning, without a chance to say goodbye. Paris, London, New York City—those places would never be the same for her without him, most of all Cincinnati.

Looking at her mother clinging to Chad, a black veil over her face, Jane couldn't help but feel twice as grieved. What would they all do without the devoted, intelligent, often unyielding influence of John Wallingford? How would her mother cope as a widow?

Robert's hand was on Jane's as she sobbed quietly into a handkerchief. She didn't withdraw, but she offered little of herself to him. In her grief, one constant thought ran through her mind.

I do not have to marry this man.

Chapter Eleven

Only a day after her father's funeral, Chad informed his mother and Jane he would be the head of the household now. He'd taken it upon himself to take care of the funeral arrangements and the obituary. Jane was glad for that, yet his authority felt bullish to her.

"I will hire a secretary to help you with a proper response to this event. Most of the wedding gifts should be returned with thank-you notes. From now on, you and Charlotte will care for Mother's daily needs while I take care of her financial needs."

This was his speech to Jane as he walked back and forth in the parlor after their mother had retired with a headache. He stopped in front of one of the long windows, looking out as he always did with one finger drawing back a piece of the lace curtain.

The colors of fall were fading as the bare trees braced for the harsh winter ahead. With a blaze of reds and oranges, the sunset lit the room with a soft glow. Jane thought of how her father had remarked on the beauty of the season. Even with its threat of winter, he found it a time of solace. She failed to find such solace today.

Jane looked beyond her tall, lean brother and felt her experience was none her friends or acquaintances could relate to. Her life was an anomaly now, something no one she knew had experienced. All she craved was normalcy, but she had no idea how to bring it about.

Turning to face her, Chad continued. "I'll inform you when I've made my decision about the date of your wedding. Until then, you may continue to work for the paper. Father let you write your dribble without his approval, but that will change. I will need to see the final drafts before you send them to your editor. This reflects on all of us. I daresay Robert will have you quit the paper as soon as you're wed. I'll be keeping a tighter rein on how this family is viewed. Now, if you will excuse me."

He strode across the room past her and took a turn down the hall to their father's hallowed study. She heard the door close with purpose.

Clenching her teeth, she sat down very slowly. Her life could not—would not—be dictated by him. She had to be married, and soon, but not to Robert.

After making up her mind, she stood to retire to bed, if sleep was even possible. As she was about to climb the stairs, she heard from the other side of her father's study a strange sound. She went to the door and pressed an ear to the engraved wood.

The sound of a man in grief had her anchored in place. Her heart swelled. She touched her forehead to the door, and her tears silently flowed. His sobs unnerved her, and yet she felt this would be the closest she and Chad would come to sharing their grief.

After a short while, she went to her room and let her own emotions flow as she gripped her pillow and shed the unstoppable tears that would not fill the vacancy in her heart.

STUCK IN THE HOUSE WITH Mrs. Crowley, one of the secretaries her brother had brought in from his office, Jane did her best to write to each and every one of the 150 gift givers. Her back hurt, her hand cramped, and her heart felt as heavy as a lead ball in her chest as she wrote a brief note of thanks. She excluded the line Chad wanted her to write: *Miss Wallingford's wedding announcement will be forthcoming after a respectful period of mourning.* She felt it was too much for her. It was just like her brother to be a bit crass. This was not the time to talk about her wedding—at least she didn't think so since she was not going to marry Mr. Robert Hale.

She attributed her brother's ways to the time he spent with boorish men and easy prostitutes in the lower part of town. It was something she wasn't supposed to know about, but people loved to gossip, and the stores in town where women met were where Jane had heard the unsavory talk. She soon realized it was no secret the city had its dark places, and Chad seemed to know every seedy crack and crevice.

His lifestyle gave her anxiety. How would he run the company as well as her father had?

Her temples throbbed, and finally, she declared she could do no more of this writing. She left the rest to Mrs. Crowley. Her mind had shifted with anxious anticipation to the end of the week when the reading of her father's will might change everything. She tried not to worry, but it had kept her up at night.

CHAD SAT AT THE HEAD of the table, and the family lawyer, Mr. Shipman, and his clerk sat opposite of Jane and her mother.

The atmosphere in the room was tense. Elisha held tight to her handkerchief, dabbing her eyes now and then. To Jane, Chad reminded her of a racehorse ready to run. She, however, was stoic and braced to receive the news that she would be obligated to follow Chad's rules if she was to receive a penny of her father's estate. It was unfair, yet it was not up to women to be in charge of money.

"To my loyal and loving wife, Elisha—"

A sharp intake of breath came from Elisha, and Jane placed a hand on her mother's shoulder.

The lawyer continued. "I bequeath our home and all its belongings. I hand over her inheritance from her father, including all the interest it has earned in my care, to our son, Chadwick Wallingford. This amount will pay for her personal expenses and the running of the household until her death. To my son, Chadwick, I leave the business of Wallingford Jewelers and all its assets, to be listed in detail within these pages. I also bequeath a sum of $60,000 to him, half of which is to be invested into Wallingford Jewelers in its own account."

Jane saw the acceptance on her brother's face as he gave a knowing nod. Chad had obviously known what was going to be left to him before the lawyer spoke of it.

"To my daughter, Jane, I bequeath a sum of $50,000 to be deposited monthly into an account under her brother's name until she is wed, at which time it will be signed over to her husband. An added dowry of $20,000 will go to her husband."

Jane held her breath and waited for Robert's name to be announced as her husband. It wasn't, and Mr. Shipman continued to read the details of the will, mostly about the business and diamond mines, which Jane had no interest in. Relieved, she thought of Martin. Her money would be in good hands. He would be her husband, and they would enjoy her wealth together.

Mr. Shipman paused in the reading to let the family take in what had just been stated. He then continued.

"All of these financial matters will be under the control of my son, Chadwick Wallingford, as the head of the household from this day forward."

Chad raised his chin and huffed. "My father was wise to think ahead," he said.

Jane made up her mind there and then. She and Martin would marry as soon as possible. Taking her money out of her brother's hands couldn't come soon enough.

When the proceedings were done, Chad saw the lawyer and his clerk out while Jane and her mother retreated to the parlor. Elisha sent Charlotte for tea. Jane sat in thought.

She had the means to marry Martin and pursue her dreams. Her father had taken care of her financially, and now she would take care of herself and marry the man she loved. She couldn't keep still.

"Mother, would it be all right if I ride into town? I need some fresh air."

"Very well. This whole matter is too much for me. I daresay we must marry you to Robert as soon as all this business is over. You mustn't expect your brother to manage everything."

"Yes, Mother."

Jane left her and summoned Wallace to take her into town. She hoped Martin still wanted her. Chad was another matter. She and Martin would have to present a strong front.

Walking straight to the back room of Wallingford Jewelers, Jane didn't even look for Mr. McMann. She opened the door and stood in its frame. Martin was eating his lunch and quickly put down his sandwich and wiped his mouth. He stood from his workbench.

"Jane, what a nice surprise. How are you? I'm so sorry about your father. It's such a shock." Martin nervously rolled out his words. "Come in, come in. I was at the funeral but far from the crowd. A few of us thought we'd pay our respects."

She let down her tense shoulders. "That was sweet of you. I didn't mean to interrupt your lunch."

"No, not at all. Are you hungry?" He raised the second half of his sandwich.

She shook her head. Her anxiousness was mounting. She needed more than a lunch break to tell Martin what was on her mind. She mustered her courage.

"Martin, I feel with all my heart that we must be married." Her heart leapt in her chest. She had said it, and there was no taking it back.

Martin put down his sandwich and wiped his mouth on the cotton napkin. He stepped closer and grasped her hands. "My dear Jane, I didn't know if you still felt the same. And what about Robert Hale? You're committed to him."

"I will write to Robert and break off our engagement. I've never felt committed to him."

Martin embraced her and then held her apart. She stiffened. *What now?*

"Jane, I'm still leaving for California."

She lifted her chin. "I've inherited a great deal of money from my father's estate. We could live very well off it. Perhaps buy land here? Please say you'll reconsider."

His brow furrowed in disbelief. "But I don't want to reconsider, Jane. Won't you come with me?"

"California is so far away."

"It's beautiful! Across the bay from San Francisco."

She threw up her hands. "Why would you want to live there?"

He took her gently by the shoulders. "I love you, and we would not be living in the city. Besides, San Francisco is not what you think. We would live in a small town with good people. Harry says it's a well-established place but welcomes new residents all the time. You and I could make our mark there."

Jane thought for a moment. Creating a whole new life away from her brother and the side of society that kept a rigid hold on her was tempting. She'd never have to encounter Robert Hale again or the gossip that would surely follow her for some time.

"I have to think about it," she said.

"Yes, think about it, my love. You and I together!" He picked her up and spun her around. "What an adventure!" he shouted. "And to think we'll have the money to do it with!"

"Martin! Shh! Everyone will hear you," she said through her laughter.

He put her down, and their eyes met. Jane felt a giddiness that sprouted from his gaiety. It faintly veiled her fear of the unknown.

Mr. McMann's voice came close as he spoke to a customer just outside the door to the back rooms.

"I have to get back to work. I'll walk you out."

Martin planted a kiss on her lips, and they entered the showroom. Holding her head high, she addressed the store manager, whose gaze was one of confusion mixed with sorrow.

"Hello, Mr. McMann."

"Miss Wallingford, please accept my sincerest condolences on the passing of your dear father. We are at sea without a captain."

"Thank you. Rest assured my brother will know what to do. I think your position is safe."

Mr. McMann blushed and looked at his shoes. "I didn't mean it like that, miss, but thank you for that information."

"Of course."

Looking at Martin, Mr. McMann asked if they might help her with anything today.

"I was just visiting with Mr. Cabot. Thank you. I must go now."

"Good day, miss, and give my condolences to the rest of your family."

"Good day, Jane," Martin said.

Jane felt her cheeks get hot at Martin's familiarity. McMann cleared his throat and looked at Martin with a furrowed brow. Jane felt her future husband was already done with Wallingford Jewelers and heading out West.

As she stepped onto the sidewalk, a shiver went through her body. The cold air held the scent of the coming winter. Her head felt dizzy, and she hurried to place her gloves on.

Entering the carriage, she leaned back and let the wrapped brass container of warm coals beneath her feet do its job. Wallace always knew to take care of things. She contemplated a place where hot coals under one's feet might not be needed in late November. How strange that would be.

Back home, she sat by the parlor's fire and studied the flames, her mind filling with thoughts of her and Martin's future. With her brother absent from the house today, she could relax before going upstairs.

Having noticed the smokestack above her room as she entered the house, she knew her small bedroom fireplace was also going. Charlotte must have snuck in and lit it after Chad left. He was setting the rules of the house, including how much coal could be used and how much wood for cooking. Gas lamps were turned down lower, and there were to be no lit fireplaces in unoccupied rooms and not until the temperature gauges on the walls dipped below sixty degrees in occupied rooms. She had been coming home to a very chilly house.

As she climbed the stairs, it hit her—this would no longer be her home. Where would she live next?

"Is that you, Jane?"

Her mother's thin voice took her out of her thoughts, and she quickened her step. "Yes, Mother."

Her mother's bedroom was dark, and Jane wanted to leave as soon as she entered. It smelled dank and heavy with grief. To her relief, though, it was warm. Her mother placed her book to the side. Jane was glad to see her sitting in a chair and not in bed.

"Good, you're back. Remember, your brother likes his supper early. Get dressed soon, and don't be late again."

"How are you feeling?" Jane inquired.

"Oh, don't ask me that. I can't say really. It's all been too much. Chad is my anchor now. He must be yours as well. We must let him be the head of things. He should set a date soon for your wedding."

Jane did not share her mother's sentiments. Her brother would not control her. "Chad will take good care of you, but you don't have to worry about me, Mother." Jane started to leave the room and then turned. "Mother, I . . . I will not be marrying Mr. Hale."

"Oh, Jane. My nerves!"

"I think your nerves will be fine. I wish to marry Mr. Cabot."

"Well, then go! Marry your Mr. Cabot and leave me in my grief! God help you both!"

"I will take that as your blessing."

"I'm too weak to argue. Oh, but what will people say?" Elisha lay back in the chair.

"I'm sure it will all blow over," Jane said. "Society has many other things to occupy its time than the Wallingford family." Jane wasn't too sure of her words. The society she knew loved to witness such drama.

Her mother squinted her eyes and turned her head sharply away.

"I'm sorry, Mother, but I have to follow my own destiny."

Her mother's head snapped back. "Destiny? Wherever did you get a notion like that? My dear, you are not a man. Please don't talk as if you are one. It's very unladylike!"

Jane restrained from rolling her eyes. She knew her mother was never going to understand her independent nature. She almost felt sorry for the woman.

"Go and tell your brother what you intend to do. God knows what havoc this will cause!"

Jane's heart felt as if it had dropped into her stomach. A wave of nerves flew up into her chest. Another confrontation with Chad. She was hoping to marry Martin in private and face the consequences with her new husband together. She wanted to flee. Perhaps as far as California?

CHAPTER TWELVE

*T*HAT EVENING, JANE BRACED HERSELF FOR HER BROTHER'S anger. He did not disappoint.

"Of all the disrespectful and selfish things!" he shouted. "Our father is buried less than a month, and you decide to go against his wishes? I won't have it!"

She tried to skirt around him and leave the parlor, but he grabbed her arm. His squinted eyes frightened her, and her arm burned with pain.

He brought his face closer to hers. "You always did have to have your own way. I blame our father, God rest his soul, for not seeing how he spoiled you."

"Let me go!" She yanked her arm from his grip, causing more pain.

He backed off, but she could hear his heavy breathing.

"Well?" he barked. "What have you got to say for yourself?" He stood by their father's chair, his agitation abating. "I insist you marry Mr. Hale. You will stay in this house and care for our mother. I will run things as Father did. We must all chip in and do our part to keep the business going and the estate running well. Our standards cannot collapse because he's no longer with us. Mind my words, Jane. I could have Martin Cabot run out of town. Then where would you be? A wealthy woman without a husband? I won't have it!"

Jane stared at her father's chair and at her brother, who'd seated himself into its worn upholstery and wooden armrests.

"We should take Father's chair to the attic. I can't bear to look at it."

Chad rubbed the cushioned part of the arm. It was already threadbare from her father doing the same when he was thinking. No one had been able to convince her father it was time to take it to charity.

"I don't see what that has to do with our conversation. We shall keep the chair where it is. Now answer me."

Jane looked away, her mind clearing from the discomposure of her brother's anger. "I really don't care what you can do to us. We have plans."

The room went silent as Charlotte brought in the tea tray and set it down on the table beside Jane.

"Thank you, Charlotte."

Charlotte gave a smile and bob of her head. "Chamomile, miss. Thought it might soothe you."

They exchanged a look that let both of them know how they felt about the overbearing Chadwick. She sat on the couch and took a sip, letting the warm aromatic liquid flow down her throat and into her being. The housekeeper left, and Chad was about to speak again when Jane began.

"I accepted Martin's proposal without your approval. I'm a grown woman and have the right to marry whom I please."

"And our mother? What about her? We all have to face this shame."

"My dear brother, do not talk of facing shame. I know about your escapades—at least some of them. The women, the gambling. Is this why you keep the reins so tight on the money? Who do you owe, Brother?"

"Enough!" He sprang from his seat. "You know nothing!"

Jane brought the cup of tea to her lips as a shield. Her hand was trembling. She took a gulp, but the tea would not dampen the fire she had lit between them.

"You are a shameful disappointment to this family, and I will make sure you and Martin Cabot do not succeed in any plan you might create."

He stormed out of the room, and Jane felt the breeze from his exit. She was frightened.

That night as she lay in bed, sleep was impossible. A new reality emerged. An acute awareness was palpable. She would not be anyone's property to rule over as they saw fit. Martin would never do that to her. Freedom was calling her, and she couldn't ignore it.

THE RECTORY OF THE CHURCH surrounded Jane with the heavy aroma of burning frankincense. The cold light pierced through the windows, making long shadows in the room. Its dark paneling made her feel as though she were standing in a wooden box filled with religious relics. The candles flickered from the air flowing in waves through the old windows. A whistle of wind added to her feeling of doing something behind the backs of society.

Why hadn't she had the judge at the courthouse wed them? Her mother's influence was greater than she'd thought. A priest had to marry a couple for it to be a true union. This was not in the church proper, but close enough. She dismissed her concerns; after all, this was what she wanted.

Martin cleared his throat and adjusted his tie. Jane thought he looked handsome in his gray suit even though she sensed his feeling of dismay at this not being the wedding he might have liked—a wedding surrounded by onlookers in support of their union. It certainly wasn't the affair she had planned for her nuptials with Robert. Her brief note to him had said it all.

My circumstances have changed dramatically with the death of my dear father. In consideration of these circumstances, I wish to break off our engagement.

She had signed it respectfully and prayed he would be reasonable. He had been and wrote that he accepted her wishes. It was a sign to her he had never loved her to begin with, and she could move on without the guilt of having broken his heart.

Before the priest entered, Jane had to speak.

"We're not committing a crime, for goodness' sake," she whispered. The tension eased, but not completely. Martin smiled and squeezed her hand.

The priest and two witnesses came into the room. Jane smoothed her wedding dress. It was voluminous in its many layers of silk with lace overlay. It was the dress for a much bigger affair, but it was the only wedding gown she had with no time to shop for another more modest dress. It took up a fair amount of space in the small room. The priest stood in front of them holding his book of vows.

The ceremony was short, and with the priest's blessing, Jane was a married woman with none of her family to witness their union. The witnesses smiled at her, and then she turned to Martin, who kissed her gently on the mouth. It felt odd for her to show such intimacy without the walls of the store's back room or the alley behind it as protection. A gush of joy filled her heart. She was free! Then she signed the wedding certificate and felt a twinge of regret. Was she going from being ruled by her father and brother to being ruled by a husband? She quieted her feelings, replacing them with the thought that Martin was different. The wedding night was ahead, and she was nervous and excited. What would it be like to finally unleash her passion for him?

THE SWANSON HOTEL STOOD ON nine acres outside of the city with views of the many hills and valleys of the surrounding area. Jane marveled at the beauty of its glorious arboretum. So many mature trees and lush lawns. Martin wrapped his arms around her from behind. He kissed her cheek.

"Does it please my new wife?" he asked as they gazed out from the balcony of their room.

She turned to him. "Yes, very much so."

"This is nothing compared to what we will find out West."

Suddenly, her mood changed. How could she leave this city, this state? Even with her brother's threats, her heart clung to the place she loved. "Can we talk about that later? I want to enjoy what we have right here."

Martin nodded and turned her in his arms. "I want to enjoy what I have right here."

It was an invitation, and Jane's passions were ignited.

He led her back into the room and helped her get undressed. The cumbersome gown fell to the floor, leaving several layers yet to free her from the bonds of clothing. They giggled as Martin made an exaggerated effort to unlace, unbutton, and finally pull off the last remaining piece.

She stood naked in front of him, her husband. Immediately, she wrapped her arms around herself and hurried under the bed covers. He quickly disrobed and joined her. They shivered under the fresh crisp sheets even though the lavish room's roaring fire heated the room.

Holding each other close, they warmed to each other's bodies.

He whispered, "I'll try to go slow, but I . . ."

She groaned as he touched parts of her no one but she had ever touched. It felt exciting and a little dangerous. Reminding herself she was a married woman and this was natural, she relaxed and began to explore his strong body.

He was lean, and his muscles flexed under her touch. The world slipped away, and it was only the two of them under the trance of love and lust. She met his hungry kisses with her own passion. He was on top of her, and she looked at his chest pulsating with the beat of his heart as he slipped his manhood into her wetness. She arched and cried out as he continued slowly. The pain was followed by a feeling of pleasure. Mostly it was the pleasure of being so close to him. She felt all-powerful at that moment, as he seemed completely entranced with her and her alone. He whimpered as his body stiffened and then dissolved like water on a rock onto her body, his breathing labored from the effort. After a moment, he slid off her.

Between breaths, he said, "I love you."

"I love you too," she replied. Her mind couldn't comprehend why she was not as breathless. Had she missed something? Was there more to this for her? Perhaps as she learned about this ritual she would find out.

He kissed her lips gently now and closed his eyes. She turned onto her side and formed her body into his. She was awake and energized, but her husband was snoring. His breath touched the top of her head like a warm breeze.

Closing her eyes, she soon found she was tired too, but her mind wouldn't rest. The day had been long, and she had gone against the wishes of her brother. Her mother was another story. Elisha would be disappointed in her and robbed of a good match for her daughter. Society may not be kind, and Jane felt wretched for that. She didn't want to think about what her father would say. The grief of his passing left her troubled. Nothing would take away her sadness at losing him, yet fate had intervened, and here she was with Martin, not Robert.

She cringed at the thought of doing with Robert what she and Martin had just done. A laugh escaped her, and Martin groaned and held her closer. She let his warm smooth body take her into a restful sleep. Tomorrow would have to wait.

Rolling over to face her new husband, Jane ran her hand along his cheek. He opened his eyes and smiled.

"Good morning, wife," he said.

"Good morning, husband," she replied.

Martin stirred and sat up. "I want to talk to you. Let's order tea and coffee."

"Is it about our future?"

"Yes, but I need coffee first."

He kissed her mouth and rose to ring for service. Jane felt comfortable beyond measure and looked forward to the same comforts in her new home with her new husband.

Martin relished his coffee, and Jane waited as she enjoyed her tea.

"I want us to move to Clermont City. It's the small town my cousin lives in. I want you to know that my decision has been made. This is my choice for us, but I want you to be happy with it." He looked into her eyes. "What do you say, Jane?"

His sincerity touched her, along with the gleam in his eye he always got when he talked of going out West.

"I will go with you. We will make our own life there."

He grabbed her hand, nearly knocking the teacup out of the other. "Jane."

"Martin, careful." She laughed. "But I wish to live in the style I am accustomed to."

"Of course. Of course. Oh, my love, you've made me a happy man!"

CHAPTER THIRTEEN

December 1880

MARTIN MET HIS LANDLADY IN THE COLD AND DAMP entryway of the brick-clad apartment building. The low glow of a single gas lamp above their heads. She had her hand out and a package under her arm, reminding him that the last week of his rent was due, plus the extra to get the lease broken.

"I'm a married man, Mrs. Whitley," Martin said proudly.

"Yes, so you stated in your letter." She was not a woman easily impressed. "Still need to sort out the rent," she said.

Martin was feeling quite prosperous, and he reached into his coat pocket and handed her the exact amount.

She shook off her surprise with a raised chin and puff of air. "Married into the right family, did we now?"

He ignored the barb. "You can fill that apartment any time. I'll be out by tomorrow."

"Then I certainly will." She held the heavily strung package out to him. "This came for you."

He took it from her, anxious to get into its contents, and waited while she counted each bill.

"Very well," she said and shoved the wad into the pocket of her stained apron. "Important business, looks like to me. I had to sign for it. Stamping says California." She raised her brows.

"Very important indeed. It will change my life, Mrs. Whitley. Thank you."

"Bah." She wrapped her shawl around her chest and went back into her apartment.

After taking the stairs two at a time to his rented rooms on the third floor, Martin hurried to unlock his door. He removed his gloves and warmed his hands above the small brazier. It barely emanated heat on this frigid December evening. He didn't mind, for soon the cold days would be behind him.

He and Jane were staying at the hotel, where he would join her before they set out on the train out West. He had packed up his belongings, and now the last piece of the puzzle lay before him.

Without removing his overcoat, he sat down at his kitchen table. Taking his penknife from his pocket, he broke the string and unwrapped the brown parcel. The contents included a letter from Harry and a stack of papers. He read the brief note.

Congratulations, Cousin. I will look forward to seeing you soon. Best Regards, Harry.

Putting that aside, he went over every piece of paper as carefully and mindfully as he would any fine piece of jewelry. There was the surveyor's document and a map of the land's boundary lines. He read the title document with his name on it. His heart swelled with joy. He looked over more of the papers. Some issued by the city, the county, and the state. His signature on many of them. An official seal on some. So many documents for the twenty acres of land.

Once the price and survey had been settled and the city had allowed the sale, Harry had had a lawyer draw everything up. The endless weeks of back-and-forth to make it all happen had been tedious for Martin. He'd been sure he would have to spend several more years working under Chad to make the final payment. Marrying Jane and he and Chad's recent agreement, signed and sealed, had brought the long agonizing wait to an end. This was his chance. Along with his life's savings and the final sum coming from his wife's dowry, he had purchased his dream.

Chad had made it clear: it was to be an investment, and after three years, Martin would have to pay back the dowry money to Wallingford Estates, plus 5 percent of the profits. Mr. Shipman would take care of the legalities. The papers had been drawn up, and Martin had looked them over. Most of it he couldn't decipher, but with time being a factor, he signed where he was told, and the money was his. Although he felt confident in his decision, the look on Chad's face had given Martin a brief moment of pause. His brother-in-law's expression had been one of satisfaction. Was he counting on getting this money back sooner rather than later? Martin was young and healthy. The farm would be successful.

After shaking hands, Chad handed Martin a banknote. He was anxious to deposit it and then wire the money to the bank account Harry had set up for the land deal. Chad had added a sum for expenses, which Martin thought was quite generous of him, considering his opposition to him marrying Jane.

"Thank God you and I are in charge of my sister's inheritance. Who knows what she would have spent it on? Mr. Shipman has transferred her inheritance into my account. Don't worry, I will transfer a good amount monthly into your account out West.

"But, Chadwick, your father stated it was hers," Martin said.

Chad became irritated. "My father was ill. I know he wanted me to run all things, and this is part of it. You should be glad you even get her dowry from me. Just make sure this investment makes me money." He added in a lowered voice, "And this deal of ours is to remain between us and no one else. I daresay my sister would have you in this city for the rest of your life while she spent every last penny." He looked over at the lawyer as if no words needed to be spoken, and Mr. Shipman gave a stern nod.

Martin had agreed half-heartedly. Giving up his control of his wife's inheritance was a small concession for what he was getting in return. Her monthly allowance would be plenty to get the farm running and produce a profit. Martin was sure of it.

Now he held the precious receipt for his payment in full. It was well worth his brother-in-law's bullish ways.

He placed the receipt with the other papers and cupped his hands and blew his warm breath on them. Soon the bright sun of California would bathe him and Jane in its warmth. Martin felt confident in keeping the details of the deal with her brother from her. He was the man, after all, and perhaps Chad had been right and she might have spent all of it on foolish adornments and lavish parties. Though he knew Jane to be reasonable about these things, he also knew she had been brought up without a care for what things cost. Her inheritance would be enough to satisfy her wants and needs, while he proved himself to her and her family.

THE MORNING LIGHT PIERCED JANE'S head like a sharp knife. Why were the curtains open? The reflection of the sun off the snow could cause her terrible headaches.

She sheltered her eyes with her arm. Peeking through the crook in her elbow, she saw Martin was not in the room. Her throat was tight, and she reached for the glass of water on the nightstand.

It had been three weeks since their wedding night. For now, this would have to be their temporary home. Her brother refused to have them stay at the house. Jane visited her mother, but it was always strained. She avoided Chad. Charlotte was her company and the kitchen a place to have tea and a chat with the beloved housekeeper.

Charlotte had helped her pack up her dresses and sort through what she might take to California. Martin suggested leaving the heavy furs and cold-weather clothing behind.

"We can store those in the attic," Charlotte told her. "Who knows if you might be back someday."

Another day, Jane had strolled the square and dropped by the jewelry store. It all looked the same even though her perspective on life had changed dramatically. It was strange knowing how far she would be from the city in such a short time.

In the evenings, she and Martin would dine, then retreat to their room, where Martin would talk nonstop about Harry and land and sheep. It bored her to tears, and her mind wandered to the house they would purchase and the gardens she would have installed. Jane looked forward to the nighttime when they made love and fell asleep in each other's arms.

Today she decided to visit Sadie. She presented her card to the butler and waited. Unsure of her friend's opinion on her marriage to Martin, Jane was relieved Sadie came to the drawing room with outstretched arms and a wide smile.

As usual, the tea service was a delight, and the two friends conversed easily.

"I can't believe you are married to Martin Cabot!" Sadie said. "You got your wish. How lovely for you. Though Martin Cabot is, well . . . What are his goals? Will he stay at Wallingford and help your brother run things?"

Jane took a breath and let the air out. "Oh, Sadie. I'm so happy. Martin is wonderful. He's taking care of business so we can leave as soon as possible for California." Jane watched Sadie nearly choke on her cake. "Yes, I came to tell you. We are moving to a town across from San Francisco. It's called Clear . . . Cleary City." She put a finger to her chin. "No, it's Clermont City. Yes, that's what it is."

"I'm in shock! To be honest, I thought you would never leave Cincinnati."

"Well . . ." Jane leaned in. "I doubt I'll be gone long, Sadie. I think once Martin sees what we've left behind, he will gladly bring us back. I'm looking at it as an adventurous extended honeymoon."

Sadie laughed in relief. "And some of us choose to go abroad for our honeymoons! Oh, what we do for our husbands!"

Jane laughed, shaking her head. When she had left Sadie's home that day, she was in good spirits even though she'd had to say goodbye to her friend.

Today she was heading to her family home to pack up the rest of her things. Martin had told her they would be on the train in a few days. This would be a different goodbye, and she dreaded it.

As she waited for Martin to return from his business with his landlady, she penned a few letters to the friends she had not had time to see. They would be as shocked as Sadie, yet she knew Sadie would soon comfort them with the same words Jane had comforted Sadie with: they would return before too long. She wasn't sure what her other friends thought of her marrying below her station. She added in her letters that she hoped they would welcome her new husband into their fold, and she promised great parties and social events when they did finally root themselves in one of the grand estates in this fair city. As she secured the last letter, she felt false.

Would they be coming back here, or had she concocted a nice story to make everyone feel at ease? Nevertheless, it was how she would make her graceful exit.

Martin returned with a bright red face and a smile from ear to ear.

"We own a twenty-acre sheep farm. Land! All ours!" Taking her in his arms, he swung her around, then planted a kiss on her lips.

Jane laughed and couldn't help being swept up in his joy. But now they had to face her mother and brother.

"Are you ready, Martin?"

"I am, my wife. Let's face the dragon head-on!" He stepped into a pose with his imaginary sword piercing the beast.

Seeing him so animated helped to remove some of her trepidation.

Chapter Fourteen

Chad was in a foul mood. Jane could tell by the squint of his eyes and the tightness around his mouth. She took another sip of tea and a small bite of the scone Charlotte had brought in for them.

"As the executive of this house and estate, I must warn you against this move. I am Father's replacement."

Jane scoffed. "You are hardly a replacement for him. My husband and I will do just fine without your interference. I have my inheritance and don't need you."

Chad smirked. "You're a child. One who knows nothing about the world." He whirled around to Martin. "And you, wanting to take her away from the only home and life she has ever known."

Chad was being his usual self with a bit of artificial flair, but Jane was concerned with Martin's silence. A shadow came over his face as if he was hiding something.

"Look at your mother, Sister," Chad continued. "She's heart-broken."

Jane turned to her mother and found the same expression on her face as any other day. Had she forgotten her prompt from Chad?

"Mother?"

"I am heartbroken, but you must follow your husband as I followed your father. I will miss you both." A tear rolled down her cheek, and she caught it with her handkerchief.

Jane swallowed. She had not given her mother credit for her love. A swell of emotion bubbled up. "I'm sorry, Mother. Will you come to visit us?"

Her mother sat up straight. "Oh, goodness no!"

Jane was immediately snatched out of her remorse. "Of course not."

"Indeed," her brother said. "Martin, when you find you have had enough of this farming deal, you will come back to work. I still need a jeweler for the downtown store. So far, I've had a damn hard time trying to replace you. We will work together as a family." He turned to his sister, his hands spread out in front of her. "You see, Jane, I am here to set all things correct again. Never let it be said I don't protect my family. With our resources, we could build a greater business than Father could have imagined. I will guide us."

Chad's words sent an electric current through her that sparked her rebellion. Her father was by her side now. His courage and strength seemed to buoy her in the tumbling sea of new ideas and old ways.

Facing Chad, she stated, "I am a married woman. You can take care of the business. I want no more of it."

Chad stood his ground. "You're too young to know what's good for you. This marriage was a mistake."

Turning to Martin, she asked, "Will you not defend me? Us?"

He rubbed his chin. "Chad, don't be unreasonable."

Her brother ignored Martin. "I promised Father I would watch over you and see that your foolish mind didn't get you into trouble. He knew you better than you know yourself."

Jane's anger was rising like flames on dry timber. Martin stood aside as if he weren't the cause of this disagreement.

"Martin?"

He shrugged. "Your brother cannot stop us. I have nothing to add to your family feud."

Her mother looked away in disgust. "Spineless," she hissed.

It was all too much for Jane. "When did you say our train leaves, Martin?"

He snapped to attention, his eyes wide with eagerness. "In two days."

"You see?" Chad said. "This is the foolishness Father was afraid of. Taking the rail in the middle of winter?" He shook his head and turned away with a cluck of his tongue.

Martin spoke up. "It's quite safe. There have only been a few delays this time of year and only one tragic delay that I know of."

Chad placed a hand on his hip and scratched his head. "This is not to be tolerated. And there is one other thing."

She had a feeling there was more to his objection than merely his concern for her.

"Father wanted us to continue the business together, Jane. He didn't command it, but for all intents and purposes, your inheritance was to go toward that end. I made plans expecting you to contribute your share."

Jane saw Martin shoot Chad a tense look. What was that about?

"So, that's it? You want me to stay for my money?"

"And to hold our family together." He waved his hand dismissively. "That's fine. I have other plans and insurances for Wallingford's future. Be the impulsive young thing you are. Mother and I will be here in the comfort of our lives."

Her mother stood. "I have had enough of all this. Let me know what you've decided, Chadwick."

"Mother, he decides nothing. We are leaving in a few days. Have you not heard me say so?"

She turned and faced Jane. "My dear, California is a very long way from what you know. Please listen to your brother. And Mr. Cabot, Martin, this cousin of yours, is it Henry?"

"His name is Harry," Martin said.

"Yes, Harry. We hardly know anything about him. You've been quite secretive, and it has us at a disadvantage." She arched her brows and sighed. "Your father would take care of all of these matters. I'm overwhelmed, to be honest. He's not been gone for more than a few months, and now all this upheaval. Why can't you two just settle down with a nice country estate here? Live in one of the apartments on Broadway or a house on Pike? It's become quite fashionable there, though I wouldn't care for it in the least. Then visit your country place whenever you please."

"Mother, I agree, and perhaps we may consider it if this adventure of ours doesn't pan out."

"There now, I've solved the problem. Just let us know before you return, and I will secure a place for you. It would be no problem. I think my dear friend Mabel and I would find the perfect apartment."

Martin looked aghast, but Jane felt a bit reassured by her mother's plans.

"Mrs. Wallingford," he said, "I have no intention of failing at this and returning here."

"Well, I will leave you to it. I've given my suggestion." Her mother turned and left the room. Charlotte went to her side as she entered the hallway. She seemed frailer than when Jane had seen her only days ago.

Jane looked at her brother. "She doesn't need your overblown theatrics!"

"As she doesn't need your uprooting yourself from her."

"Mother has never been as fond of me as she is of you," Jane said. "We both know that. Be her rock as Father was for her, and she will do fine."

"Now you are dictating *my* life?" His sharp laugh was filled with indignation.

"We've made our plans, and there's nothing you can do about it." She left the room, leaving both men to stew on her statement. Feeling empowered, she climbed the stairs, gliding her hand along the dark wood banister that had led her to her sanctuary for years, through lighthearted times, heavyhearted times, and every non-eventful day of her life.

The drapes were still drawn, letting only a soft light filter through. She sank into her bed, and for a moment, she let her mind rest. The smell of her quilt and the softness of her pillow brought comfort, if only for a moment.

She got up and sat on her window seat and looked out onto the garden beds, which were void of their color and dusted in icy white with the bare-limbed trees outlined in snow. They were no longer hers, for she could never call this place home again, even if they returned. She was a married woman now with a life that would lead her far from this room. It was empty of her.

While her gowns, furs, and adornments had found a new home in the attic, Martin had recommended she not take her jewels, a small fortune in themselves, and they had been placed in the family's safe box at the bank in Cincinnati.

His overabundance of caution gave her trepidation. Did they not have a safe on the train? Was it safe to travel at this time of year?

When she questioned Martin about it that night, his irritation was sharp and immediate.

"Do you not trust me? So soon in our marriage, my actions are in doubt?"

The thought of arguing with the man she loved so shortly after their wedding was more disturbing to her than leaving behind her gems and clothes.

Sadness was soon replaced with excitement for the adventure ahead.

CHAPTER FIFTEEN

January 1881

$\mathcal{J}$ANE LEANED BACK ON THE PLUSH VELVET SEAT IN THE luxury compartment of the Pacific Railroad's Pullman car. The warmth of it embraced her, and she closed her eyes and let out a breath. Saying goodbye to Charlotte and the staff had been harder than she had expected. Charlotte had hugged her with the love of a mother, and Jane had dissolved into tears. Her heaving chest had taken her back to her childhood. Charlotte had brought her away with a hand on each of Jane's shoulders.

"I will miss you, my dear. Take care, and remember to write. Wipe your face now, and be brave." Then she whispered, "You still have a home here."

Jane nodded. "I hope it's not too awful for you. Chad and Mother can be unbearable."

"Don't worry about me. I have my own family, and thank God I can go home to them each night now. Your brother has let me know I will no longer be living here."

"Oh, Charlotte," Jane said.

"It's fine with me. I've wanted that for some time now, but your mother would hear none of it."

"Take care, then." Jane gave her another hug, then turned to say her goodbyes to the rest of the household as they stood on the porch to send her on her way. The cook, the driver, the gardener. One day she would have her own staff, and she hoped they would be as wonderful as these people.

Composing herself, she walked down the stairs to where Martin and her mother stood.

Her mother kissed her on each cheek. "Write to us now and then. Let us know you're alive," Elisha said, dabbing her eyes.

"Yes, of course."

"I don't know what you're thinking," Elisha said. "I would have no desire to see any more of this country. I have it all right here. You do too. I've no idea on earth what you can find out there that you can't find here." She waved her hand in dismissal and looked up and down the street. "Be on your way, then. I can't be seen standing on the sidewalk like this. Charlotte and I have the luncheon to arrange for the ladies in the card club. God bless you and guide you, and I pray you will heed His guidance." Her mother lifted her skirt, and Charlotte came down the stairs to help her to the door.

"Goodbye, Mother. I . . . I love you."

Her mother took the housekeeper's arm. "Well, yes, yes, of course. I love my children as God loves His." She turned and took the stairs.

Her brother had insisted they say goodbye in the study, and he wouldn't come out to the carriage to see them off. "It's unseemly," he said. "Mother may, but not I." He had shaken Martin's hand and given her a curt nod.

As the train chugged along, she felt her eyes mist at the whole scene. She was leaving so much behind and had nothing to fill it but Martin's promise of a better life. Taking one comfort, she saw herself able to garden in the mild weather all year long. A scrap of hope for happiness.

Coming back to the present, she arranged her skirt, feeling the soft emerald-colored fabric beneath her. Their roomy train compartment offered her a rest from the hustle and bustle of traveling. So far, they had traveled by coach to the Cumberland train station in Chicago before taking the rail to Omaha, Nebraska. Those compartments had been outfitted in a more practical sense compared to where she sat now. She thanked her lucky stars for the fine room, which would be her home for nearly a week as they journeyed to Oakland, California.

It was filled with polished wood and shiny brass fixtures and had a chandelier in the sitting area, where one could relax and enjoy a view among sumptuous fabrics. She felt she was in a tiny replica of the salons of her wealthy friends. What a marvelous way to travel! The bedroom was just as lovely, and Jane looked forward to sleeping with Martin in the cozy bed, though it was only mid-morning.

Thinking again to her goodbye with her mother, she felt a strange longing. She had never said "I love you" to anyone but Martin, and even that felt awkward. It would be the first of many firsts, she figured. It wasn't as if she and her mother were very affectionate with each other, but she'd always thought that deep down her mother loved her very much and simply couldn't express it and perhaps one day they would be more comfortable with each other. It felt as if she was leaving behind unfinished business. Her thoughts went to Chad, and she hoped he would look after her and take care of Wallingford Jewelers.

Voices all around the train took her attention. The bustling of passengers and well-wishers outside her window sparked her sense of adventure. She pulled down the window and poked her head out to view the long snaking locomotive. Her breath was visible in the air. The steam rose, and it was cold, acrid, and damp. She'd been on several long trips, but this one gave her stomach trembles of anxious anticipation. She pulled herself in. Martin sat across from her, contentedly reading the menu for tonight's meal.

As THE DAYS PASSED, THE snow blanketed the vast landscape of the country with barely a soul in sight. It captured her imagination of tall imposing cowboys and rough riders, Indians and buffalo. She saw no signs of any and wondered if it was all a bunch of tall tales. Then one day in the middle of nowhere, in the distance was a splattering of teepees, yellowish cones against a stark-white background and strikingly clear blue sky, smoke streaming up and clouding above their peaks. It was like a picture she once saw as a child in a book about the Native people of the West. She wasn't alone in her fascination, as she heard other passengers' oohs and aahs.

Coming away from the window, she sensed a great dichotomy of cultures. It suddenly felt odd to look upon the teepee village as if it were a tourist attraction. She saw figures of people moving around the homes. These were people going about their business. She had heard of Indians raiding the trains, killing passengers, and setting fires. Was it possible such savagery could impose itself on such a beautiful way of traveling? The train was slowing, and an overwhelming fear gripped her. She felt trapped and couldn't breathe. She pulled at her high collar. Martin reached out his hand to her.

"My dear, you're as white as a ghost."

Fanning herself, she took a sip of cool water offered to them throughout the day. "What if the Indians raid the train?"

"Oh, they have no reason to. I hear the Indian agents have it well in hand. I haven't heard of any since . . . Well, it won't happen to us."

"So, it has happened on this train?" Her anxiety rose. She took out her fan and waved it vigorously over her face. "This was an awful idea! There are no dangers like this in Cincinnati!"

Martin rose and came to sit beside her. "We are in no danger. They only attack in the spring and summer. It's the dead of winter. We'll be fine."

She looked at her husband. If he was telling her a lie, she didn't care. It made sense, and it eased her mind. She could breathe again.

After several hours, she noticed the landscape held no real danger, and she felt silly for her childish behavior. She was a married woman now, and it behooved her to act like one.

The stations they passed were surrounded by wooden shacks and some houses farther along the track. Nothing remarkable. As they continued on, the distant mountains stood like sentries to a hidden world. They traveled closer, and she was both in awe of and disturbed by their grandeur. How were the train tracks built through these mighty fortresses? The thought of being swallowed up in snow among the high jagged rocks renewed her fear. Martin was reassuring, however, and again she took his word for it.

Still, when they reached Wyoming with snow as deep as she had ever seen it, she couldn't help but ask a porter if he had been through this part of the country in the winter.

"Oh, yes, ma'am. They clear the rails. No need to worry."

Who were these men who had to clear the snow for the train? She was disturbed by them doing the work in such awful conditions. She was told the train's scheduled time to arrive in Oakland would be set back by two days at least.

It began to snow, and a shiver ran through her as she tightened her woolen shawl. Although the compartments were warm enough, the cold air circulating between cars gave her pause each time she walked from her compartment to the dining car, reminding her of the fact she was in a desolate wilderness in the middle of winter in a very long tin can.

After the delay, the train was speeding down the tracks to make up for lost time. The scenery had been steadily changing. Along with the many tunnels cutting through the mountains, green fields and hills appeared. This evening as the sun dipped below the horizon, creating a beautiful orange-red silhouette, Jane felt a lump in her throat. It was magnificent to behold. It softened her, and she wanted to cry. She breathed in and let out a small puff of air.

It had been six days since their departure, and they would be in Oakland in a day. Harry's description of their new home was lacking detail. It sounded no more than a sparse stick-built structure alongside a large barn. She hoped it would be decent enough to put her mark on. She also hoped her and Martin's lovemaking would improve in regularity. He thought it was vulgar to have such intimacy with so many people on board. Knowing he was a conservative man, she let it be, but not without giving her side of it.

"Our compartment is quite private," she argued.

"Nevertheless, there's a time and a place for such things," he had stated sternly.

Her heart ached. He sounded like her father, her brother. Were men just practical by nature? She would try to follow his wisdom, though it felt as if she was still under someone else's control.

At breakfast the next day, they were served the usual tea and coffee with a tray of pastries followed by a menu of more substantial foods. Eggs Benedict was Martin's favorite while Jane preferred the French toast.

She ate, feeling a bit out of sorts. She reminded herself that this part of the journey was nearly over. The woman at the next table struck up a conversation with the couple, which reassured Jane. The man and wife were moving to Oakland.

The woman, a large imposing figure, declared between bites of pastry, "Because of the railroad, we will have no problem bringing in goods from the East. I plan on making my parlor quite grand indeed. I have relatives who will expect no less. And I hear there are some very interesting imports in San Francisco."

Jane decided she would spend what it took to make her own home as worthy as any home in Cincinnati. She was determined to show her brother he was wrong about her not knowing her own mind. She would prove she was an adult in charge of her own destiny, or at least her own home.

Chad's words repeated themselves in her head. "You'll be a farmer's wife with drab hair and an ashen complexion before next Christmas."

There would be no "I told you so" from her brother if she had anything to say about it.

Part Two

Chapter Sixteen

January 1881

$\mathcal{J}$ANE STEPPED DOWN WITH HELP FROM A PORTER AND SAW the third-class passengers embarking from the far back of the iron snake. Their bodies looked tired. Turning away from the scene, she planted her feet on the ground of the West.

She felt a strange sense of unity with all the passengers who had traveled across the vastness of the country. We made it together!

Martin took her elbow and led her to the stagecoach by the side of the station. Her shawl fell around her arms. She wasn't cold. The winter was no longer a threat. It was warmer than she had ever felt in January. She had barely noticed the change until she was away from the steel of the train. It was lovely, and she wanted to stop and take it in.

Pausing for a moment, she let Martin's arm slide from hers as she stood facing the sun by the side of the train station. What a strange thing. She didn't see her breath billowing out into the frigid air. Her face was not accosted with the bite of winter. Her spirits were lifted. Another first, and this one was most welcome.

"Jane! Hurry along. The coach is waiting," Martin called to her.

She looked among the crowd and spied him with a suitcase in one hand and his arm stretched above his head, waving frantically to her. His hat was slightly askew. He reminded her of a child with a nickel for the sweetshop. Where was his dignity?

She weaved her way through the crowd. The stagecoach was being loaded with her belongings, among many other pieces of luggage. A man strapped them down with little concern for their contents. The carriage bobbed and rocked as one by one the passengers entered its cab. She raised her skirts as Martin helped her inside. She lost her balance and sat with a plop on the well-worn wooden bench. Opposite her was a gentleman of sizable proportions. A woman and child sat next to him, and lastly, Martin and another gentleman squeezed in alongside her. It became very warm in the cab, and she felt overwhelmed by the closeness. It was a rude awakening after the luxury and openness of the train.

"Martin," she whispered into his ear, "how long will this take?"

In his regular voice, he answered, "We're two, maybe three hours or so from Clermont City, my dear."

The thought gripped her. That long in these conditions? She had too many layers on, and there was no room to remove her outer jacket. She desperately wanted to ask the other passengers if they, too, were headed to Clermont City, but she dared not reveal her discomfort to them, these strangers.

To her relief, the man was let out at a station only twenty minutes after he had boarded. The woman and child rode longer but were soon gone as well. Finally, the man was able to take the seat opposite her and Martin, and she felt some relief. She swiped at the wrinkles on her dress, and as daintily as she could, she removed her jacket and folded it carefully on the seat. When she looked at Martin, he had a concerned look on his face.

"What is it?" she asked.

"I'm sure Harry knows a woman who can help you get acquainted with the proper dress for this area. A more proper dress for this climate, I mean."

She glanced at the man across from them, who seemed thoroughly taken with his newspaper.

"Proper dress?" she whispered. "I daresay I would be able to teach her the proper dress, whoever this woman is."

Martin nodded. "Yes, dear, I know, but you might want to save your good dresses for special occasions."

Jane leaned back in her seat, her heart racing. The reality was sinking in. Remembering her visits to the farms back home and how she wanted to dress more casually to suit the environment, she now questioned her sanity. It was an occasional outing, not her daily routine. What strange world was she entering into, and how long would this last?

THEY CAME TO CLERMONT CITY. The stagecoach station was neat and clean with a whitewashed building and a few carriages to the side. Martin helped her down, and her fixed smile soon turned to a grimace. Her legs were stiff, and her back felt as if it had grown elderly. Enduring the pain, she pulled herself up straight.

They were just outside the town itself, but Jane could see down the main street. Some of the storefronts were still decked out from the Christmas season. She found it odd to see the decorations past their time with no snow to give them credence.

On either side of the dirt street were buildings, some two stories high, and a wooden platform for a sidewalk skirted them. A hotel, a saloon, and a general store. Across the street from the station was a bank and land company. Farther down the road, she spotted a sign that read *Carley's Restaurant*. Her stomach growled at the sight of it.

A few men stood outside of the saloon talking, or were they arguing? Two women walked with purpose past them, and a few children played in the road. Horses whinnied and shook their manes into clouds of dust, and a flatbed carriage loaded with shabby furniture stood to one side, letting other riders pass by.

This was a Western town in America, but it was strange and new to her. She felt as if she had gone back in time. In her studies at school, she had learned that Cincinnati was considered a Western town at one time. Oh, dear! How long before this town became a shining city?

Then her attention was drawn to a man approaching her husband with a broad smile. Was this the cousin so much talked about by Martin?

Harry Cabot stood taller than his cousin, with broad shoulders and an obvious hard-worked body. His sun-kissed brown hair was to his shoulders, and he carried himself with an air of confidence her husband lacked.

Jane watched him embrace Martin, and then they patted each other on the back. She smoothed her hair and adjusted her hat, then slightly shook her skirt on either side to let the wrinkles out. Why she suddenly felt self-conscious, she didn't know, but butterflies danced in her belly, and she felt sweaty.

"My dear, this is Harry," Martin said as if producing a miracle man on the spot.

Harry doffed his hat and stuck out his hand. Catching his sultry brown eyes and ready pearly-toothed smile, she offered him her hand. The strength of his shake rode up her shoulder. He must have sensed her discomfort and apologized for his eagerness. She didn't mind.

"I'm so glad to see you both here. Safe and sound. That rail can get mighty dangerous in the winter. But here you are."

Harry's statement sobered her from feeling a bit giddy in the presence of this strong handsome man. Jane looked at Martin with hooded eyes. He had known it was dangerous ahead of time!

Before she could find justice with her husband, Harry was striding toward an open clapboard carriage. Another first. This was a farmer's wagon. It was the kind she'd seen in the farmers' fields when she would go to help them, but she'd never ridden in one.

Martin took her bag and his and loaded them onto the flatbed of the carriage along with their luggage from the stagecoach. Their belongings were sparse, and Jane now wished she had brought more. Her thoughts rushed to finding a woman's dresser and the proper outlet to purchase what she would need in fabric and lace. She was helped up to sit on the leather covered board seat of the carriage. It was dusty and well-worn.

Harry again apologized. "I thought with your belongings and all, this would be more suited than my smaller rig."

"This is a grand experience, Harry," Martin said with a laugh.

The carriage lurched forward, and Jane grabbed tight to her hat with one hand and to Martin's arm with the other.

To her dismay, the carriage loaded with furniture followed behind them with Harry pointing out that he had found many good pieces for them to furnish their new home with. Jane turned back and looked at the stacked carriage of mismatched plain wood chairs and tables of various sizes. Pots and pans hung from the sides, clanging as the loaded wagon rocked from side to side, pulled by an old spotted horse moving with steady purpose. Their carriage hit a pothole as she turned forward and nearly toppled her backward. Martin laughed at her and held on to her waist.

"Isn't this fun?" he said.

She didn't think so. The bright sun added to her dismay. She'd have to unpack her parasol and veiled hat as soon as possible. Her delicate skin would not take such an assault, and she was wary of the headaches it might cause.

A sharp stab of homesickness struck her, and it took a great effort to not break into tears.

She held tight to Martin as they swayed and jerked while Harry drew the horse down a long winding road. Jane took in the many tall trees skirted with tall grasses and bushes. Along the road, she spotted wild strawberries and vines with dots of flowers. The lush green of the land and pungent smell of plants and vegetation was unrecognizable, and it took her attention away from her lack of repose on this bumpy ride. She'd have to learn all about this new landscape.

A sudden gust of wind took her small stylish hat, and she would have lost the precious thing if not for Harry's quick rescue. She felt him secure it back on her head with a strong hand. How odd to have him touch her like that. She looked over and thanked him, and he gave her a wink and grin, and then his attentions were back with the horse.

A flutter of nerves flew into her chest, and her cheeks warmed. She told herself she was tired and his attentions meant nothing. Her hand went to the crimped material on her head, and she felt ill at the thought it may be unsalvageable. She took it off and held it with her free hand.

The ride seemed to last forever. Still clinging to Martin, she noticed a white house peeking out from the trees. As the carriage veered onto the dirt road, it became apparent they had reached their destination. This sorry-looking structure was to be their home, and the stretch of field around and beyond it was the land Martin had bought. She put her hand to her mouth to smother a gasp.

Groupings of trees here and there gave a break to the hilly green landscape. The air smelled of grass, hay, and animals. A faded red barn stood off to the side. A low enclosure with strewn hay inside was next to the barn. Chickens roamed freely, pecking at the ground. The glimmer of water caught her eye; they had a small pond complete with ducks. There was nothing beyond that but more hills and a dotting of trees. But for the fowl, the house and outbuildings looked abandoned. Whatever was Martin thinking?

With his help, Jane stepped down from the wagon and looked around with unbelieving eyes. This was where he thought she would make her mark on society? It was almost laughable.

After a thorough tour of the barn and animal pens, they finally came to the house. She was exhausted and disheartened. She cared little about the animals' living space. Her focus was on her new home.

Stepping inside, her head caught on cobwebs, and Martin rushed to help her brush them off. Everything was in dire need of repair and remodeling. The scuffed wood floors would need redoing. The rugs left by the previous owner were threadbare and dirty. Who would think of painting the inside of a home such a gaudy brownish color?

When she peeked into the kitchen, she was given some hope. It seemed large enough for a cook and assistant, yet the whole thing would need updating. Harry assured her the well was in good working order. The pump attached to the sink basin was rusted. The paint was peeling, and a window in the parlor was broken.

Jane turned to her cousin-in-law. "What on earth led you to believe we could live here?"

Harry looked directly into her eyes. "I was led to believe you have a way with interior design and the money to make something of the place."

"Martin?" Jane implored her husband to speak.

"Jane, it's true. This is your blank canvas, as it were."

She looked around and shook her head.

"Harry wants to show me the pump house. Can you manage in here?"

"Go, I'll be fine."

Carefully, she roamed inside the rest of the house. The sitting area off the kitchen might serve as a parlor or dining room. The stillroom off the kitchen smelled of soured milk and bad meat. She choked back a gag and turned away.

The staircase at the entry looked solid enough. She held on to the banister and made her way up to the bedrooms. A wobbly board had her nearly falling onto the next step. Fisting her skirts, she continued up.

The top of the hallway had a window crisscrossed with dusty webs. The view—or what she could see through the layers of dirt on the panes—was breathtaking. So much open land, and the blue sky went on forever. Continuing her investigating, she concluded the six bedrooms were too small. One could serve as the water closet. The house would need indoor plumbing. The dilapidated outhouse would not do. A few walls would need to come down to expand the main bedrooms.

Going back downstairs, she noted the ceiling was chipping and the wallpaper in another sitting room was stained and had bubbled. The list in her head was as long as her arm.

When she stepped outside, she found Harry and Martin unloading the awful-looking furniture. She walked to the flatbed and looked inside. She saw material she thought might be suitable for curtains, small tables, a box of kerosene lamps, and a number of other boxes she didn't dare look into.

"Stop!" she said, louder than she'd wanted to.

The men, including the driver of the housewares, froze in their tracks.

"I will not have these—" She chose her words carefully as to not insult Martin's cousin. "We need to do a bit of cleanup before the furnishings go in. Can you please place these items in the barn perhaps?"

The men raised their shoulders and loaded the chairs back into the carriage. Harry hopped up onto the flatbed and brought it around to the barn. He called to the driver.

"Gil, run ahead and make room for all of this."

Martin ran along with Gil, and Jane felt the awkwardness of her decision, but she wasn't about to have that junk in her home.

Rolling her eyes, she went back inside to take another look and continue the list of things that needed doing. Deciding this would take all her courage and determination, she took heart in small measure. The woodwork looked sound as far as she could see, and the windows were a decent size. She returned to Harry's rig and waited.

The men came back from the barn with an empty flatbed driven by Gil while Martin and Harry walked close. Jane heard the sound of their voices, men talking business. It wasn't any different than her father talking about the store with her brother, except this was not about the acquisition of precious gems and diamonds, but about sheep, and as she heard, cows and pigs too. She stood there feeling rather dumbstruck at the lowly turn her life had taken. It came to her that this was no temporary venture. Martin wouldn't get this place up and running and then leave it. This was a commitment her husband had made.

Gil doffed his cap at her as he drove by. "Good luck, missus," he said with cheer.

She tried to smile, but she couldn't find any reason to be glad. Taking in a deep breath, she let it out, and her mind went to the quaint homes they had passed down the road. They stood close to town and looked sturdy and well cared for. The gardens seemed well tended. One of them might have to do. It was impossible to imagine herself living in this ramshackle house with the most grotesque furnishings she had ever seen.

Harry stood to the side. "I'll let you folks take it all in. Let me know if you decide to spend the night here. My place is pretty small, or I'd invite you to stay with me. There's a decent hotel in town too."

"We'll stay here, Harry. I want to start early tomorrow," Martin said.

"I'll leave you my rig," Harry replied. "I can walk back to my place from here. Have a good night, folks, and I'll see you bright and early, Martin. Sure glad you're here. And you too, Jane."

Jane nodded and watched as Harry walked back to the road. She held steady. "Martin, I think we should stay in town."

"Jane, I need to be here to start work on the farm," he said.

She had no idea what that might entail and knew for sure Martin didn't either.

"But this isn't a home. It's an abandoned building that was once a home." Jane looked around.

"I can't be staying in a hotel! What would Harry think of me?" He went inside and climbed the staircase. She followed, tired and hungry. He sat down on the soiled mattress placed atop an iron spring frame in one of the smaller rooms and nearly fell into the middle. Jane helped him out. He laughed, but she found no amusement in it.

"One of these bedrooms must be fit to sleep in," he said, then went off to inspect each room.

She waited for his return. Looking at the banister and pickets along the hallway, she saw another job to be done. They moved under her touch like loose teeth.

When he returned, he didn't look in any way dissuaded. "Isn't it all just marvelous, Jane?"

Slowly, her hand went to her mouth, and tears welled in her eyes. She turned away.

"It will be beautiful once you put your own touch on it. Don't be sad."

Martin's hand came to her shaking shoulder. He whispered in her ear, "Wait until you see the sheep and other livestock."

Her quiet sobs turned audible.

Jane was finally able to bring her husband to the realization that the house was uninhabitable for now.

As MARTIN SNORED SOUNDLY BESIDE her in the small hotel room, she took up pencil and paper and began her list. The task of hiring the right people to bring the farmhouse and land to a proper estate would be daunting. The one bright light was she had the money to do so. A trip to the bank would be one of her first tasks. As her eyes grew heavier, her mind worked over every detail. The shock was wearing off, and she felt a tiny spark of excitement. *It will be the grandest estate this little town has ever seen!* Once her lids closed, she let sleep take her.

Chapter Seventeen

Martin woke early the next morning, as he'd said he would. He was as chirpy as a baby robin, whistling away. Jane rolled over. When had she ever heard him whistle? She watched as he got dressed. He pulled on a pair of brown cotton pants and got into a plain cream-colored shirt, which he tucked in and belted. His footwear was a pair of leather boots. She sat up and suppressed a yawn with the back of her hand.

"My dear, what are you wearing? Where did you get those clothes?"

"I can't very well show up with my suit on. Before we left Cincinnati, I went to Granger's and had the salesman pick out some of the clothes the farmers wear."

She was speechless. He looked rustic and rather handsome, but she wouldn't concede that fact. She was still upset by what she'd seen yesterday. "I hope you'll change before we are seen in public together. What about breakfast?"

"Harry will have something for me, and there's a restaurant across the street."

"Can't I ring for a tray?"

Martin looked at her with raised brows. "We're not at that kind of hotel, dear."

"Of course." She got out of bed and wrapped her robe around herself. "Will you be back for lunch?"

"No, Harry said he'd bring lunch too. Why not join us? Perhaps Harry's farmhand, Gil, could come get you."

"I'll see. I have to look for help today. I need a secretary, and we need to find several good tradesmen."

Martin spread his arms to each side. "How do I look?"

His happiness was charming, and she didn't have the heart to tell him he looked as if he were going as a cowboy to one of the costume parties frequently held in Cincinnati. She waved him out.

"Fine. Now, go do your farming."

"Thank you, Jane. You know I love you."

He kissed her mouth, and she wanted more, but then he was off in a mad dash.

AFTER TEA AND A MUFFIN at the quaint restaurant in town, Jane headed down the boardwalk skirting the shops in Clermont City. She stepped over another nail sticking up from the wooden planks as she made her way to the general store. Her shoes were not fit for such a rustic walkway.

Martin had told her the general store was usually the hub of any town. She wondered how he would know such a thing, and then she remembered his family's station in society. He had grown up in a place that had a general store.

She came to it without tripping. Before entering, she stood aside for a man twice her height, or so it seemed. A cowboy, by the looks of him. She stared up at the burly man, and he tipped his hat to her and passed by, leaving in his wake an aroma of hay, sweat, and cow dung. Holding her breath, she brought a gloved finger to her nose and stepped inside the darkish store.

Taking a minute to breathe normally, she let her eyes fall on the barrels of produce, the shelves of canned goods, and the case of breads and pastries. The store had a pleasant smell, a mixture of textiles, bakery goods, and licorice. A kind-looking clerk with sandy hair and a white apron tied around his slim middle approached her.

"Good day, madam. You look new to my store. Would you like me to show you around?"

"Thank you. I am new here. My husband and I just arrived yesterday from Cincinnati by train."

"Welcome, then!" the clerk said as he extended his arms. "I hope you will find our little town pleasing. Are you setting up a homestead, or will you live in Clermont City proper?"

Jane smiled and wished she could say they'd bought a home in town. "A home on land."

The clerk smiled back. "A homestead, then?"

"Actually, a sheep farm."

"Oh, now that must be the old Duncan farm just outside of town and around the bend. Am I right? Harry Cabot bought it and sold it to his cousin . . ." He scratched his head. "I forget the name."

"Martin Cabot, my husband. I'm Jane Cabot," she said as she extended her hand to him.

He shook it as he looked her up and down. His inspection made her self-conscious.

"You might want to look at some of the cotton dress material we carry. Maisy, the seamstress, makes most of the dresses around here for the women who can't sew themselves. There are a few, believe it or not."

"What makes you think I can't sew, sir?" she asked with a smile.

"I . . . Well, to be honest, you look more city-like than country.

But I have a fine array of pretty fabric toward the back of the store, and my wife will be better suited to show you what would work for you as a farmer's wife."

Jane took no offense but didn't care for the title "farmer's wife." Of course, she would put together the appropriate wardrobe, but she'd have to see what the city of Oakland or San Francisco had to offer. Noting the clothes on the women she had passed on the way to his store had told her that the general store's fabric and Maisy were not to her taste.

"Thank you. I'm here to inquire about finding a secretary. Do you know of any I could employ? I will need someone who's honest, skilled in math, and knowledgeable of finding trained labor. The house needs a total revamping, as you probably know."

He scratched his head. "Why don't I get my wife to help you." Another customer came into the store as he was about to go find his wife.

"Clarence, did you get my hammer handle in yet?" said the customer. "Don't know how much more pounding the old one is going to do."

Jane turned to see a farmer of sorts looking at her as if she was an oddity. He couldn't take his eyes off of her.

"Danny, this is Mrs. Jane Cabot. Her husband purchased the Duncan homestead."

The man's eyes went wide. "Oh. Nice to meet you. Good luck with the place."

"Clarence?" A woman approached from the back. Now, Jane thought, she would get somewhere.

"Gladys, this is Mrs. Jane Cabot. Her husband bought the Duncan place. Harry's cousin Martin. Mrs. Cabot, my wife, Gladys Cornby. By the way, I'm Clarence."

"Nice to meet you all. Mrs. Cornby, Clarence, Danny," Jane said, anxious to get the pleasantries over with so she could get on with her business.

"Oh, call me Gladys, please. And nice to meet you too, Mrs. Cabot. You'll certainly have your hands full with the old place. Harry's been talking of getting his cousin out here for over a year now."

"Oh, has he?"

Gladys smiled and nodded. "That's right."

"I was just telling your husband that I'll be needing a secretary or assistant to help me find the right laborers and designers. We may even need an architect."

The stocky woman scratched her loose blond bun. Jane wondered what all the head scratching was about. She wasn't asking for the moon, after all.

"Hmm, you might want to check the newspaper here. They can put an ad in next week's edition. It's a small publication, but it's circulated throughout the county. Lacey at the front desk will help you. It also serves as our telegraph office in case you need to send a message for your folks back in . . ."

"Cincinnati," Jane said.

"My, that's a long way from home." She looked up at her husband. He gave a lined smile to Jane. All the while, Danny was still staring.

"Sorry we can't be more help than that. But we can sure start you a tab with us. You'll be needing plenty until you get yourself up and running."

"Thank you, I will take you up on that. We're good for it."

"Oh, we know you are. Harry says—"

"Clarence!" Gladys elbowed her husband.

Jane said her goodbyes and left feeling downhearted. This wasn't going to be as easy as she had thought. And what had Harry told these people? How very vulgar!

She continued down the boardwalk and spied the very man she'd just been reprimanding in her head. Harry was coming out of what she'd seen the other day as the town saloon. He walked over to her.

"Jane," he said. His surprise was equal to hers. He tipped his hat in greeting.

"Harry! I thought you'd be at the farm helping Martin."

"I was, but needed to take care of some business. Gil is showing him the ropes."

Jane nodded. "I don't suppose you would know where I could find help? I'll be needing several people to get that place into shape. After all, it was you who convinced my husband he could be a farmer . . . and of sheep." She pressed her lips together.

Removing his well-worn brown hat from his head, Harry gave no notice to her grievance. "Well, that depends on the kind of help you're talking about."

His brown eyes, easy smile, and openness unnerved her. He stood too close. His height had her looking up at him. This familiarity was unheard of back home. He stared down at her, and she shifted her weight.

"I think you know what the place needs, Harry. Carpenters, roofers, plumbers, an architect, and so on."

The impish grin growing on his mouth sparked her anger. Was he making fun of her?

"Martin said you were a bit . . . commanding. I think that's good in this case. He'll be mighty busy with the rest."

Drawing her eyebrows together, she placed her hands on her hips and couldn't help but let out some steam.

"You have no remorse for leading Martin on about his prospects here? We left a perfectly civilized and prosperous society in one of the most cultured and modern cities in this country to come to . . . this!" She waved a hand as she turned to show him the small town.

He laughed and placed his hat back on his head. "I'm sorry, Jane. It was my impression you came here of your own free will."

She folded her arms and was about to speak when he leaned down.

"You'll have to sort this out with your husband, ma'am."

His smooth delivery made her heart beat faster, while his lack of engagement agitated her. Before she could respond, he continued.

"I only gave my cousin the opportunity to change the life he told me he was desperate to change."

"Desperate?" She was confused.

"Yup."

"He never said he was desperate!"

"Not my words, his."

"You may have painted a rather different picture for him than what's actually here." Her patience with him was running thin.

"Nope."

"Oh!"

He looked at her with raised brows.

She took in a ragged breath. She realized her disappointment and frustration had made her angry and defensive, and she wanted to release it onto this man.

"I'm sorry. I thought you and he were of one mind," he said.

"I really don't see how that part of my life is any of your business." She let out a breath. "I will make the best of this situation. Now, as I was asking before we got into this rather fervid conversation, do you know where I can hire a secretary to help me get organized?"

"I do not." His broad smile indicated his humor at her question. "And I don't mind an ardent conversation with a beautiful woman."

"I didn't mean that. I meant . . ." She felt flustered at his forwardness. This exchange needed to come to a close. "Well, Harry Cabot, I will let you be on your way."

His brief nod gave her a need to continue.

"I know Martin is a ready pupil, and maybe I will come around to all this once the house is done to my satisfaction. I have to admit, I'm a little overwhelmed. I'm sorry I was short with you just now."

He laughed at her, and she wanted to stamp her foot and tell him exactly what she thought about a man like him. Had she met a man like him?

"Where do you intend on staying as you fix up the place?" he asked.

"The hotel is fine for now, but I think we could rent one of the cottage-like houses I saw, perhaps down the road there."

His response was as if he were watching a comical character perform.

"What is so amusing, Mr. Cabot?"

"Oh, now it's *Mr.* Cabot?" Harry mused, his grin never leaving his face. "I'm sorry, Mrs. Martin Cabot, but you are so far out of your element you don't even know how to fake it."

At this she wanted to burst into tears. He'd hit a sensitive nerve. She felt like a fish out of water, and the heat rising in her was beginning to scorch her scales.

"Good day, Harry. I have to find my way to the newspaper. Excuse me." She walked by him and felt a tap on her sleeve.

"It's just there, across the street, Mrs. Martin Cabot. Good day."

She stood for a moment and watched him walk away and untie his horse from the railing alongside the boardwalk near the restaurant. Suddenly filled with regret, she wondered how she could have let them get off on such a bad foot. He lit a strange emotion in her—one of anxious anticipation, like the night before a big event. She didn't like it. Refocusing, she headed across the street, but not before stopping to let Harry ride by. He lifted his hand in a wave, and she returned the gesture without a smile.

With her chin up, she continued across the street.

Why isn't he married, for goodness' sake? The answer, in her opinion, was due to his lifestyle, but surely his looks and manner attracted many a wide-eyed young lady in such a small town. She, however, was a married woman and glad of it.

Bringing her mind back to her purpose, she opened the door to the newspaper's front room.

CHAPTER EIGHTEEN

ENTERING THE TALL WHITE CLAPBOARD BUILDING, JANE took out her fan and swiped it across her hot face. How could January be so warm?

The newspaper's reception area had one desk with a young woman seated behind it. The top of her head, a loose bun of curly red hair, could barely be seen above the high front of the desk. Beyond the room was a hall with the sound of muffled men's voices. Familiar clicking and beating sounds and the smell of ink and paper brought Jane back to the *Cincinnati Daily Star*. A feeling of loss pricked her heart. She had fond memories from her time there. She had to remind herself to go forward and not look back.

The smell was not pleasant today, and she rubbed her nose and fanned herself. *Don't they have a separate building for printing?* She was used to the hustle and bustle of a newspaper. In such a small town, she wondered what could be all that important here.

"Yes?" The young woman's voice came from behind the desk, though she didn't look up.

"Excuse me." Jane leaned forward to get the woman's attention.

When the woman did look up from her work, her expression told Jane what Harry had revealed to her: she was sorely out of place. The woman's wide eyes held great curiosity.

"May I help you?"

"Yes. I'm Mrs. Jane Cabot. My husband, Martin, and I have just moved into town. We purchased the old Duncan homestead." She waited for the woman's acknowledgment, but nothing registered on her face. "I would like to place an ad."

"What sort of ad?" The woman took up a pencil and grabbed a piece of paper.

"Help wanted. I need a secretarial assistant to help me organize the refurbishing of the place."

"Is it full- or part-time work?"

"I suppose two to three hours a day."

"Very well. What does it pay?"

"Two dollars a week."

The woman popped up from her seat. "I'll take it!"

Jane stepped back. "Oh! Wait. Do you have experience? What's your name?"

The young woman was full of life as she whipped around her oversize wooden desk, nearly knocking over a jar of pencils. An energetic redhead not much taller than Jane, she stuck out her hand and announced with enthusiasm, "I'm Lacey Bennett. Pleased to meet you, Mrs. Cabot. I can start right away."

Jane reluctantly shook her hand. "Nice to meet you, Miss Bennett."

"It's Lacey."

"Lacey. What will your boss say? I need to interview several candidates before I make up my mind."

"I work here in the mornings from six to ten. I could help you the rest of the day. I'm not just a front desk girl. I can do figures, and, well, I know just about everyone in town too. Mitch, the plumber; Eli, the roofer. Eli and his team just roofed the Hoopers' home. I'm educated up to eleventh grade and graduated three years ago top of my class. I'm willing to learn anything you throw at me!"

Jane had to smile. She was certainly eager, and she would need someone who matched her own energy in turning the old house around.

"You won't find another girl more up to the job than me! Most of-age people leave this town as soon as they can. Not me and Hilary. Hill is my friend and works here too. She's the boss's daughter."

With little hope of finding anyone else, Jane agreed to hire Lacey. It was a rash thing to do. Maybe this was how she could fit in. Maybe this was how things were done here.

"We're staying at the hotel in town. I forgot its name."

"There's only one," Lacey said. "The Clermont Hotel."

"Of course. Can you meet me in the lobby today after your shift?"

Lacey nodded and stuck out her hand again. Jane shook it with misgivings.

"Thank you, Mrs. Cabot. You are a beacon of light that just shined on my life today!"

Jane raised her brows with an apologetic grin. "It's just an assistant's job. Nothing fancy. Perhaps quite grueling."

"No matter, ma'am. I am truly grateful. My job here is as boring as watching grass grow!"

Jane smiled at the reference. This woman was charming. She hoped Lacey would live up to her self-recommendation.

An unsettling feeling came over Jane as she walked to the bank. First Harry and that unwelcomed conversation with him, and now this haphazard way of going about employing someone. What else would she face in getting herself a real home? Would living in Cincinnati under her brother's rules be all that bad? She could be in a safe and well-known place decorating a stately home surrounded by friends. Instead, she was feeling out of sorts and very much at sea without a paddle. Then she recalled her last encounters with Chad and her mother. Their words would not leave her, but they couldn't harm her here. She soldiered on.

The clerk behind the barred window in the small bank told her the account was in her husband's name and they would need his signature to release the funds.

"Yes, I know," Jane replied. "I'm Mrs. Cabot. I think my husband signed a paper stating I could take the funds out without his further signature." Jane was vexed. Though they hadn't talked it over extensively, she thought for sure Martin would have done this. It was her money, after all.

The clerk left to consult a gentleman who looked like he might have more authority. He returned shortly.

"There seems to be a misunderstanding," he said. "I see that a sum of $1,680 will be deposited into your husband's account the first of each month. The full amount of $5,072 was already deposited with $1,075 payable to Mr. Harry Cabot for land and buildings. You're asking for a good amount of money, ma'am. I will need your husband's approval, and he must receive the money himself. I'm sorry, that's all I have to tell you, and it's more information than I should give you." He rubbed his cheek. "Harry says you folks are good people though."

"Thank you, Mister . . . ?"

"Call me Simon. Most folks here do."

Again, Jane felt the informality of this place unnerving. A bank worker being addressed with such casualness? How was she to trust this institution? And was Harry the town crier?

"Very well . . . Simon. I will inform my husband. I need to fix up that old house. You probably know my husband and I recently purchased the Duncan homestead."

Simon nodded in agreement. "You'll need to get those funds at will. I understand. If you'll have Mr. Cabot come in and sign for his part, you can start fixin' up that place mighty quick. Believe me, Mrs. Cabot, the town would be grateful to see that farm up and running again. The Hendersons left quick like when Joe couldn't pay his gambling debts. Left the place in mighty bad shape."

Oh dear. A gambler's house as well?

Jane left the bank feeling she was taking on too much. The history of a house was part of its charm, but no one back home would find out the history of this one.

Walking back to the hotel, she knew she would have to make sure Martin took out large sums of money so she wouldn't have to rely on him each time she needed to pay for something. Trying to get around the norms of society made her weary, and it was just the beginning.

What would this town think about a wealthy woman taking on such a project? She was betting on the fact that no one would mind. It gave her an independence she savored like a delicious meal at a fine restaurant. The satisfaction was palpable. Her thoughts went to the restaurant in town, and her spirits were dampened. When would she taste another meal as she had in Cincinnati's finer eateries?

MARTIN SLUMPED IN HIS CHAIR, his eyes half-open as he ate his dinner. Carley's Restaurant was filled with locals, and Jane ate quickly to avoid their stares.

"Martin, sit up," she whispered.

The aroma around her was heavy with pot roast, cigarette smoke, and something with too much cinnamon, not to mention hay and earthy musk. Dust motes danced in the remaining daylight that streamed in from the windows. The yellow paisley-print curtains glowed from the setting sun.

"Huh?" he said with a jerk. "Oh, I guess I was dozing off." He adjusted his seat and finished the last of his steak and potatoes.

"You need a good night's sleep. You still haven't told me what you did all day."

"Sheep. Lots of sheep. Herding them. Corralling them," Martin mumbled.

"Sheep already? I thought Harry would teach you a few things before you had to deal with the sheep. Can't we hire men to do that?"

Martin seemed beyond the conversation. "They were out in Harry's field, and we had to move them to our field. I need a sheepdog. We borrowed Gil's. It bit me on the leg."

"Oh my!" Jane brought her napkin to her mouth. "Are you in need of a doctor?"

"What?" Martin was about to doze off again.

"Martin," she whispered impatiently.

"Oh, no. I'm fine. I need to get someone like Gil. He's Harry's man, and I need a man like that."

Jane nodded her understanding. Meeting Martin at the restaurant before he'd had a chance to wash and change hadn't been the best idea. He was now a laborer and looked the part. His farmer's outfit was dusty and grass stained. His boots already looked worn in, and he smelled of acrid sweat.

She glanced around and noticed the other male patrons weren't much better. The women looked clean and tidy enough, but the men looked as if they had come straight from work, as did her husband.

Why aren't these people at home eating?

One woman must have read her mind, for she heard her say to the waitress, "Give Carley our thanks for another Tuesday steak and potatoes." Her husband concurred as he wiped his bearded mouth on the daisy-print napkin.

I guess Tuesdays are meant for eating out around here. Jane dreamed of the day she'd have her house in order and a fine cook, a dining area and sitting room for tea or brandy. Her dreams sat beside her reality, which was sharp and imposing.

"Let's go back to our room, Martin."

He stood with a wince and paid the bill.

"Here's a little something for afterward," the waitress said as she handed Jane a wrapped package. "I make them special for this time of year." Jane smelled the cinnamon coming from the paper bundle. "And would you like me to send over a pot of coffee or tea?"

"Tea would be nice, thank you," Jane said. "With sugar and cream please."

Suddenly more awake, Martin said to the waitress, "Why, that's very generous of you."

Jane gave him a furrowed brow. Again, she had to remind herself of his previous station. His landlady had probably never offered to bring him tea or coffee.

They walked across the street and were greeted by another couple who said hello and smiled. An old man grunted his greeting when they reached the boardwalk. Before entering the hotel, a woman and her young son also gave their hellos as they walked by. Everyone greeted her as if they had known her for years. She made haste to their hotel. Politeness was one thing, but this familiarity was something she wasn't used to.

Once in their room, Martin got out of his grubby clothes, and Jane made note to have them taken to the laundress on the corner of Main Street. Perhaps tomorrow they would survey the land and take notes on its purpose outside of keeping sheep and livestock. She wanted a proper flower garden, kitchen and medicinal gardens, and plenty of formal landscaping, along with a future conservatory and gazing pond. Martin would wear his brown suit. It would be casual enough for their review of the homestead. Tonight, however, he would be all hers. She missed him and his touch. Their sweet kisses and intimate moments seemed so long ago.

"How was your day?" Martin asked with a yawn. He sat down heavily on the large upholstered chair in the corner.

Jane placed the wrapped dessert on a sideboard, then removed her shawl and unpinned her hat.

"I hired a young woman to help me. Lacey Beckett is her name, and I daresay she might be a helper or just a handful." She would wait until after they were settled with tea to tell him about the general store, then her meeting with Harry, and finally the bank. Her hesitation to bring up the last two subjects disturbed her. Martin must've known she needed the money, and as far as Harry was concerned, she wanted to know if he'd exaggerated Martin's discontent back home.

"Good luck with the new girl," Martin said with half-closed eyes.

Before the tea arrived, his head had fallen to his chest and he was snoring soundly. Jane shook him gently and led him to bed. There was a knock on the door, and Jane opened it to a young girl balancing a tray with a teapot, cups and saucers, a small pot of cream, and a bowl of sugar, spoons and napkins included. Taking the tray to the sideboard, the girl paused to look at Martin. She smiled at Jane.

"Our menfolk work mighty hard around here," she said.

Looking at her husband and back to the young girl, Jane could only nod her head in agreement.

"Would you leave the tray outside so I can pick it up on my way to work tomorrow morning?"

"Yes, I will. Thank you. Good night."

Jane closed the door, and her shoulders slumped. Feeling disappointed with the lack of attention from Martin, she poured herself a cup of tea and brought it to bed with her. They hadn't made love but a few times since their marriage. Did Martin not find her desirable anymore? She wanted to be irresistible. It had bothered her throughout the day, but she dispelled the worry and hoped in time it would be different once things settled down.

She'd hoped to tell him about running into Harry. She knew so little about his cousin, only that Harry and his parents had visited Martin's family in Ohio several times throughout his childhood.

Harry was two years older, and being single children, both boys had enjoyed their time together getting into boyish mischief. The kind of man he had become was a mystery, except for the fact that Martin looked up to Harry and trusted him with his future.

She sipped her tea and listened to the steady breathing of her husband. It gladdened her heart to see the way Harry and Martin had greeted each other and how easily they fell into their relationship. She hoped it would last and she, too, could have the same manner with Harry. Why not? He was now her family too.

If only the thought of him didn't rattle her in a way she wouldn't confess to a priest. His handsome face and charm gave her an odd desire to flirt with him, to spar with him. He seemed so different from her husband. She wanted Harry to hurt for her.

She shook the indecent thoughts from her head, but the feelings remained. Perhaps it was just as well she didn't tell Martin about running into Harry today.

Turning her thoughts to her new home, she went over her many lists.

CHAPTER NINETEEN

To Jane's dismay, Martin was up early and climbing into his dirty clothes. She gathered the blankets around her and sat up.

"Martin, they need to be cleaned."

"Jane, don't bother to get up. It's early yet."

"But I thought we could explore the town together, then talk about our plans for the house and the land."

He looked at her with worried brows. "No, Jane. This is important. I must get to the sheep and make sure none of them got out of the pens. They're in need of repair. Harry's meeting me there, and we have to take stock of the buildings. Fresh hay needs to come to feed the horses. And . . . And . . . Oh, yes, I've decided on two milking cows. Pigs too."

"Horses? When did we get horses?"

He brought his suspenders up and onto his shoulders. To Jane they looked as if they weighed him down.

"I had Harry pick out a few riding horses and one for the carriage. I'll have Gil come get you today around noon, and your new gal, what's her name? You two can start taking stock of what the house needs. You know I have no talent for that thing, my sweet." He kissed her hard on the mouth and touched the top of her head. His curly brown hair was long on his forehead under his brown cap. He swept it away, then slung the heavy cotton coat over his shoulder and said goodbye. The door shut neatly behind him.

Jane leaned back on the pillows. Her heart stung. Soon a *tick, tick* on the window announced the rain. Perhaps the day would be short and he would be back in the room with her. She had a feeling the rain was not a concern for Harry, and so it wouldn't be one for her husband. His clothes would be a muddy mess.

The early-morning chill had her pulling on her shawl and wrapping it tightly around herself. Burned-out embers in the fireplace gave no warmth. The hotel owner had promised to have someone come up each morning and light a fire for them, but she had a feeling she would be doing that herself.

How do you light a fire?

She let out a breath. Another thing she would put on her list.

Her father's voice came to her. "Be less concerned with the trivial things in life and look at the bigger picture."

She sighed. *I will try, Father.*

JANE STOOD IN THE FUTURE front parlor of her home. Lacey sat on one of the old kitchen chairs brought in from the barn.

"Take notes. Don't let me wander off track," Jane said. "I'll need to concentrate on one step at a time. I tend to go straight to the décor. It's what I know. But we need to focus on structure, roof, and . . ." Jane stopped short, shaking her head, her hands on her hips. "Oh, why don't they just tear down the whole thing and I can start from scratch!"

Lacey scribbled in a notebook, whispering as she wrote. "Structure, roof, décor, tear down . . ."

Jane puffed out an impatient breath. "You don't have to dictate my every word."

Lacey looked up with a mischievous grin.

"All right, let's continue."

"Sorry, Mrs. Cabot."

"Call on the men you said you knew. The roofer, carpenter, plumber. Is there someone who can install gaslighting?"

"Yes, I mean, no. I mean yes to everything but gaslights. We don't have that in these parts yet." Lacey's eyes lit up. "They say a line will be forthcoming though."

"All right, then. Kerosene will have to do. I'll have to buy new ones. Those in the barn are unacceptable, along with all that furniture and other . . . relics." She spun around. "We'll go to the city when the time comes for the finishing touches."

"Oh, I'd love a trip to Oakland!" Lacey squealed.

"No, San Francisco."

"Oh my gosh! I've never been."

Jane moaned to herself. Of course Lacey had never been to the city. Secretly, Jane still feared San Francisco. Martin wouldn't have agreed to her going if it were dangerous, she told herself. From what she could ascertain from Gladys at the general store, all the good furniture and "fixin's" could be found in the big city. Though, she'd added, Oakland was nice too and so much easier to get to. Jane made note of it, but she wanted to experience San Francisco and find out for herself what it was like.

"Yes, I think San Francisco will have what I need. Do you know where I can get a few catalogs?"

"My aunt. She collects every one of them. All that fine stuff you can order now that the train comes through to Oakland."

"Very well."

Gil came by the house to offer her and Lacey lunch. She heard Martin and Harry coming up the porch steps behind him. The rain had stopped, and the sun was piercing through cracks in the clouds. Jane's heart raced at the thought of seeing Harry again, and she brushed it aside as she swept a strand of hair back into her bun.

Martin came over to her and gave her a kiss on the cheek. She immediately wanted to wipe away the salty grime his lips had deposited on her face but waited until he turned around. He grabbed a sandwich from the sack Gil held out and devoured it.

Jane declined. She had an unsettled stomach. Lacey reached in with gratitude. Harry ate his along with the rest of them.

"Lacey, I'll need to have you send a telegram for me later," said Harry. He looked at Jane and smiled. "We all need a good secretary, don't we?"

Jane felt he might be teasing her. She smiled but didn't answer.

"Sure thing, Harry," Lacey said. "But I'm working all afternoon with Mrs. Cabot. We're going to go to the city sometime soon. I'm talking about San Francisco," she said with satisfaction.

"Sounds like an adventure, Lacey," Harry said. "Good for you."

Martin finished his last bite. "Jane, come on out and see the sheep."

"Oh, Martin. I'm sure I'm not properly dressed for it."

"Please, Jane."

Jane glanced at Harry. She didn't know why, but she needed to prove to him she wasn't afraid to get a bit dirty. "Well, all right."

She and Lacey stepped outside with the men. Looking up the hill, Jane saw a swath of light brown fur moving like a gentle wave. The bleating was loud. Where had they all come from?

There must have been over a hundred of them, by her quick figuring. Martin led her up the nearest hill to take a closer look. They were furry and round with small faces that Jane thought were quite adorable, and she wanted to pet them. A tree was being felled in the distance, and a loud crack had the flock moving as one. They ran closer to Jane and Martin. Martin's grip on her arm made her alert of sudden danger as he practically pulled her off her feet. She lost her balance in the wet grass and fell to the ground. He forced her up and over to a nearby tree.

"Martin! Wait!" She stopped to catch her breath.

"Get out of their way, Jane, or you'll get trampled!"

She lifted her damp and grass-stained skirt as he led them to safety. They watched the sheep pass in a riot of hooves beating the ground with the sound of so many off-key baas.

After the rumbling of the herd, the sight was that of Harry, Gil, and Lacey at the bottom of the hill. Jane felt embarrassed. What she must have looked like!

"Why did they do that?" she asked as she swiped at her skirt. Gil and Harry ran up the slope to join her and Martin.

"They spook easily today. New ground and all," Gil said, puffing with breath.

"They'll settle over there, and later we can bring them back here, where the grass is sweeter," Harry added.

Gil and Martin were discussing their next move as Jane continued to brush her skirt, and then she wiped her neck with her handkerchief. Glancing up, she caught Harry's stare. He looked tentative.

"Are you alright?" he asked.

"Yes. That was unexpected, but I'm fine, thank you." It was getting warm, and she regretted her layers of clothes and snug-fitting bodice. She looked down to see part of her hem was torn. "I suppose I should purchase the proper clothing if I'm to set foot on this land," she said mostly to herself.

"That's smart of you, Mrs. Cabot," Harry said.

It brought Martin's attention to them. He gave a chuckle. "Harry, you don't need to be formal with Jane."

Harry looked at her and winked. She didn't respond, but her heart quickened.

Jane walked down to Lacey, who was writing in her notebook.

"Can you drive a carriage?" she asked.

"Well, of course."

"Good. I need clothes. May we borrow your carriage, Gil?"

"Um, I guess. Watch the potholes, Lace. You know how Babe gets," Gil said.

"Will do," Lacey answered, then lifted her skirt to hitch herself up and take charge of the rig.

Martin helped his wife up. Jane settled in. Lacey commanded the horse, and with a jerk and wobble, they were on their way back to town. Jane held on tight, but still, she nearly fell backward onto the flatbed. It added to her awkwardness and embarrassment.

I'll have to learn how to ride atop one of these things. Better yet, I will buy a small buggy for myself or ride my own horse—astride!

CHAPTER TWENTY

May 1881

*A*s THE CARPENTERS, ROOFERS, AND PLUMBERS RESTORED and renewed the old farmhouse, Jane grew impatient to begin the decoration of her home. Spending long hours going over every detail of the design with them was necessary but tiring. It was time for her to do what she loved most. Today, her energy was recharged; she and Lacey would take the coach up to Oakland, then the ferry into San Francisco to search out fabrics, furniture, and décor.

Having taken the ferry on the Ohio River many times, Jane was used to the water boats; however, this one seemed far more seaworthy. It was crowded with passengers, and Jane and Lacey had found a wood bench on the upper deck of the *Central Pacific*. The choppy waters and cool winds had Jane bundling her shawl around her snug woolen jacket and holding on to the brim of her hat. She'd been told to dress warm and was glad she'd heeded the advice.

The ferry looked as if it could meet the challenge of the furious bay, but she was still nervous. The rolling and rocking of the steamer had her gripping a rail and swallowing her breakfast. It was truly frightening at times. She and Lacey talked only a few words during the whole crossing.

Relieved to finally see the shore, Jane stood to get her legs under her as she watched the steamer navigate a narrow docking area. Once off the boat, she was not prepared for the stench of fish. So many round barrels with sharp acrid smells that permeated the air. She took Lacey's arm as they made their way onto the solid boardwalk. A handkerchief to her nose, Jane asked a passerby how they might get to the center of town.

"Take the cable trolley, ma'am, or hail a hackney. One is quite more expensive than the other though."

He left her to decide.

"Oh, Mrs. Cabot, let's take the cable trolley! I've heard they are quite the thing!"

Jane had the funds for a decent hackney, but the adventure of the trolley called to her too.

They waited for the trolley on a designated corner. As it clamored toward them, Jane felt it looked a bit dangerous. Lacey hopped from foot to foot in excitement. Lifting her skirt to enter the steps up to the sitting area, she was like a child on a new toy ride. Jane was presented with the hand of a young gentleman, who helped her aboard. She paid for their tickets, and they took their seats in the enclosed cab while in the open area in front of them stood men and young boys holding on to the sides of the trolley's canopy. Lacey giggled, and Jane held on. She had not experienced the rail up to the hills in Cincinnati before leaving that city. She reminded herself to be brave, for if she had stayed, she would have had to endure the steep incline. The ups and downs of the ride made her lightheaded. Focusing on the many rows of buildings and houses crowded atop hills helped to divert her mind. The city was more populated with homes and people than she had expected. Her thoughts of having to skirt around murderous thieves and filth-ridden derelicts faded. Everyone looked normal and was going about their business. It was a great relief.

The conductor called out names of streets, stopping to let passengers off and then slowly picking up speed as they made their way along the trolley tracks.

"What street, madam?" he called to Jane.

"I'm looking for shops selling fabrics, housewares, and furniture."

Shouting out his next stop, Market Street, he told her this was where she would get off. They were in the middle of a place clamoring with people, horses, buggies, and carriages. Jane and Lacey were helped down and stood aside while the trolley went on to its next destination.

"I feel dizzy," Lacey murmured, putting her hand to her head.

"That certainly was an interesting ride. I thought Cincinnati was hilly!"

She ignored Lacey's curious expression.

The day was dry and windy with the sun playing peekaboo in the sky. Jane held on to her brimmed hat as a gust of wind threatened to turn the silk and lace inside out. She re-pinned it into her upswept bun, hoping it would stay.

The air coming off the water gave her a chill, and she couldn't help noticing how much cooler San Francisco was than Clermont City.

As she and Lacey walked along the crowded boardwalk, weaving in and out of people, she began to form an opinion about the city. It definitely lacked the well-established charm of Cincinnati, yet it had a vibrancy that lured her in. On the trolly, they passed a row of small colorful houses along either side of the street, looking crowded as if strung tightly together. Now as she stood at the beginning of Market Street, the many large brick-and-stone buildings spoke of commerce, and she was anxious to start exploring what they had to offer.

After shopping in a few stores with great success, she came to Mr. Witmore's fabric shop. He was, by his own admission, a merchant with knowledge of everything textile. His store proved that in the rich fabric samples he showed her. Before establishing an account, she paid cash for the first several yards of fabric. Then bought yards of material to be made into pillows and curtains and later upholstery for the new chairs and settee—her other purchases that day. Armed with a list of measurements, she kept the fabric salesman hopping to her requests. Mr. Witmore knew of a decorator who may have been willing to take the trip over the bay to her house—if the price was right. She got the notion the merchant knew who he was dealing with.

After a few hours, she felt famished.

"Can you suggest a fine place to dine, Mr. Witmore?"

Without hesitation, the man replied, "The Palace Hotel, madam. One of our city's finest."

Soon a carriage waited for her and Lacey, who had been busy scribbling down what fabric would end up where. To Jane's relief, she didn't have to use the trolley again. The merchant offered his carriage and driver for their use for the rest of the day.

Jane felt that the ambiance of the luxurious Palace Hotel rivaled any in Cincinnati, and she was well pleased. The courtyard was grand, and the carriage circled it before stopping in front of the impressive entrance. Gilded to the nines, the hotel gave Jane a feeling of belonging. Large palms in giant gold pots flanked the entry to the dining area. The tables were set with white tablecloths and gold utensils. Flowers were everywhere, arranged in enormous bouquets, and smaller ones decorated the middle of each table. Ferns and feathers draping from pots were affixed to the sides of the mirrored walls. Jane was duly impressed. She looked over at Lacey, who was simply awestruck. It made her smile.

A large woman sat at the next table eyeing Jane. Her dress was brass-colored silk accentuated with an oblong ruffle of patterned material around the neck and chest. The rest of the dress was of a satin in dark burgundy. It looked tailor-made for the woman's voluminous figure. Finally, she leaned over and Jane had to acknowledge her.

"I love your attire, my dear. So fresh! Heavens, that fashion is not from around here, is it?"

Jane knew her afternoon dress with its deep blue silk and gold satin trim fit her as perfectly as any worn by the elite in New York City. She had purchased the ensemble on one of her trips there with her father and mother. The matching jacket and shawl now draped on the unoccupied chair at their table showed the inner workings of satin and finely woven wool. She felt well-appointed in this grand atmosphere.

"Thank you. It's haute couture. New York City," Jane replied.

Lacey looked anew at Jane's attire and gave a low whistle.

"Are you from there?" the woman asked.

"I'm from Cincinnati, Ohio."

"Oh my, a long way from home. I'm Berta Hathaway. My late husband was from the New Orleans Hathaways."

Jane lifted her eyebrows. Was she supposed to know of this family?

"We must get acquainted," Berta said. She reached into her small bejeweled purse and brought out a card. "Here is my address. Call on me anytime between eleven and two."

Jane took the card. "I don't live in the city. I live . . . well . . . across the bay. My husband and I have renovated a most charming little farmhouse, and I'm in town to collect fabric and find a decorator. Mr. Witmore was being very helpful today. He may know a decorator."

"Witmore does know his stuff," Berta said. "But I have the perfect man for you." She brought a finger to her mouth. "He's coming to one of my soirees this week. I'll let him know. Ned Graves is his name. My dear Ned. He's helped me countless times, and not just in decorating." She gave a hearty laugh. "Where is this charming fixer-upper?"

"Clermont City," Lacey said.

Jane fingered her napkin, worried this might put off any chance of her making acquaintances with someone from society.

"It's a sheep farm, and a very good one," Lacey claimed. "The land is quite expansive. The house is a complete mess, but Mrs. Cabot and I will bring it back." She gave Jane a wide smile.

The flush of Jane's cheeks could not be contained. She felt ashamed of her new house and circumstances in front of this lady of culture and obvious wealth.

"A project for sure," Jane said.

"I love a project!" said Berta. "My own estate was not to my liking, and Mr. Hathaway had given me a free hand with it. Bless his heart." She bowed her head in reverence, then declared, "The grounds alone are beyond romantic! Think of the English manors, my dear."

Jane was intrigued. She loved a formal garden and was anxious to set one up on the farm.

Berta and she talked nonstop for the next hour about everything from chintz to the rules of society in San Francisco, which weren't much different from the ones back home, yet she had a feeling there were nuances to be learned. By the time the waiter came with the bill, Jane felt she had found a new friend. Berta was forthright and effervescent in her love of fine things. She seemed to almost flaunt her wealth. Jane couldn't help but notice her necklace of pearls and rubies surrounded by stiff gold lacework. Where had this woman gotten such a gaudy piece? It made her think of Martin and her father and the fine jewelry in Wallingford's. Mostly, Jane found Berta to be quite amusing, and she was having a good time. Lacey yawned and scraped at the remaining cream on her flowered dessert plate.

Berta looked at her in amusement. "The flowers stay on the dishes, my dear."

Jane felt abashed at Lacey's table manners. It was always lady-like to leave a bit of dessert on one's plate.

"I will leave you ladies now," Berta said as she stood and walked out of the restaurant.

Jane noticed she left without paying her bill, a sign she had an account at the restaurant. Jane was determined to acquire the same. She and Martin would make this city their second home.

"The meal and service were exquisite," Jane said to the waiter who took the leather book from her.

"Of course, madam," he said as if she were insulting him instead of offering a compliment.

Jane's humiliation sent a wave of heat from her toes to the tip of her head. She had never thanked the service people for the meal back home. It caused her great concern. Had living on the farm outside of a small town dulled her sense of decorum?

Minding her own reputation, she was sure to leave the waiter a sizable gratuity. She had to prove her worth. It would be the beginning of establishing her place at the exquisite Palace Hotel. She was determined to stay here with Martin. They must be part of this world.

Her marriage was not what she had expected—a balance of working on the land and being together in society, in cultured environments. If only she could persuade him to find time for them, for *her*. As the weeks and months had gone by, Martin seemed to have become obsessed with the farm. Was there anything she could tempt him with outside of it? On the other hand, she had come to know Harry better. His sharp wit showed his intellect, and she looked forward to seeing him at their dinner table or out on the property. She wasn't sure if their competitive banter was innocent or a bit flirtatious, but each time she left his company, an emptiness engulfed her only to be replaced by a disturbing feeling of guilt. Brushing her thoughts aside, she took heart in today's progress.

Although four hours away from Clermont City, Jane felt through Berta she had found a niche in San Francisco. The carriage ride back to the ferry was less bumpy, and the water in the bay looked less choppy. Jane felt a calm she hadn't felt since before her father died. The clouds broke, and beams of sun shined down on the water. What had felt like the end of one lifestyle was now the beginning of a new lifestyle rich with possibilities.

CHAPTER TWENTY-ONE

August 1881

AFTER MANY MONTHS OF RENOVATIONS ON THE EXTERIOR and interior, the Duncan homestead, now Cabot Farm, was looking more like an estate, or as close to one as Jane could make it.

The stables and barn were painted a deep red, and old timbers had been replaced. It was all she could do for those buildings, and after all, they were made to house and feed livestock.

From the new white veranda at the front of the home, one could view the winding paths meandering to the potager garden full of greens and delicate white flowers. In the distance, the eye was drawn to the beginnings of a small arboretum. Its trees cast lovely shadows onto the green field.

The wide borders that skirted the house were filled with flowers of various colors, and the kitchen and medicinal gardens flanked the side of the house where the sun shined most of the day.

In the back of the house was a gazing pond surrounded by special tall grasses Jane had brought in from a nursery south of them.

The tile around the pond was another specialty from Italy, and it had taken many weeks to arrive. Only one worker had been able to treat the stone with the care it needed, and the results were magnificent. Jane was entranced with the eucalyptus trees and bright flowered bougainvillea, a kind of shrub she'd never seen before. Thanks to her new gardener, Mr. Hill, she was learning all about the flora in this new land. Jane thought it an appropriate name for the strong, stocky man who helped to tame the wilderness around her home.

The young poplars lining the long driveway that turned into a graveled entry would grow tall and straight, welcoming guests to the oasis that awaited them.

The front of the house had a convenient turnabout for horse and carriage. The conservatory would be close to a giant fir tree. Its shade would help with the searing sun in the summer.

Inside the house, two guest bedrooms were stately and comfortable with a shared washroom down the hallway. Her and Martin's was the largest bedroom and was outfitted with its own washroom at one end and three large ornately carved armoires along the other end on the opposite wall. A four-poster bed with sumptuous linens was Jane's way of bringing herself and her husband comfort, and she hoped it might liven up their lovemaking.

His work left him either too tired to be aroused or less than romantic when they did come together. Their hopes of starting a family seemed to take a back seat to Martin's desires to see the farm make a profit.

She had never felt such loneliness in all her life, and she let the house and land projects fill the void. His anxiousness to be successful nudged at her. Why did he feel as if it were a race? Why did he worry about money when they had plenty? She had learned to keep such thoughts to herself, as it would cause them to argue. Martin would defend his actions concerning the farm with vigor.

Today she stood looking at the back garden from their bedroom. The windows on each side of the bed looked out onto a stretch of manicured lawn, topiaries, and the pond, which would be given the finishing touch of a fountain placed in the middle.

With an extension onto the side of the house, the white-trimmed light-yellow home looked more like a dwelling to sit and relax about in than the working farmhouse it had once been. Adding to her dream of a complete estate, she had hired a cook named Bell and a housekeeper named Margie, and along with Mr. Hill and Lacey, she had only a personal dresser to find.

Jane took in a deep breath and let it out. She found joy in all of what she had created, and not the least, her medicinal garden. She grew chamomile, feverfew, peppermint, marsh mallow, and mugwort, and she added to it each time she went into town to the general store when a new shipment of seeds and plants came in. By now, Clarence was privy to her lists. The garden was surrounded by a mixture of lavender and marigolds to ward off the deer. It was somewhat successful, but each morning she noticed something had been nibbled on from the night before. The wild rabbits favored her kitchen garden mostly. She would have Mr. Hill put up fences. The plans for the large conservatory were coming along and would be finished soon—that was if Martin would let her take out another sum from the bank for the architect. He was being tightfisted with their funds, and again, Jane wondered why.

She left the ruminating for later; there was much to do, and Harry was coming for dinner. He had become a regular at suppertime, and she was beginning to feel more at ease with him. His manner with her was light, and she'd grown to love his sense of humor. Although most of the time he seemed to mock her way of doing things, she didn't find it offensive; indeed, it gave her a certain thrill that someone noticed her efforts. Martin would comment only on how much money she was spending, and she would find herself prodding him for validation.

Harry brought levity to her life even if it was teasing. The other night he had commented on how sinful it was to waste a good piece of farmland just to gaze into a pool of water. In her defense,

Jane had replied, "The peace and harmony of a beautiful landscape can bring many benefits to one's well-being. There's more to life than herding animals from one end of the land to the other. There's plenty of land for practical use, some of which I intend to cultivate further."

Again, Harry listened to her, and despite his grin, she felt he was interested in what she was doing. His opinions had come to mean something to her. She wondered if it was healthy to rely on them and chided herself for even caring.

"Just be careful the wild animals don't go swimming in your pool," he said.

"Who said you were invited?" she retorted.

It brought the three of them to laughter, and Martin shook his head.

"I'm glad you two are getting on. Don't be too harsh on my wife, Harry. She's brought this place out of ruins. I'm quite proud of her. Now if she can only control her spending habits."

Martin's backhanded compliment had disturbed Jane. Would he ever see her and her efforts without a reprimand?

Harry had looked at Jane. "I think she can take it. And yes, she's done remarkably well. My hat's off to you, Jane." He'd pretended to take off an imaginary hat and dip it toward her.

Today as she stepped into her parlor, her mind thought of the exchange. Harry's comments had brought a warm feeling to her heart.

Oh! Why does he light something in me? Something new and exciting, yet so fragile and unreal? Was it just the reality of marriage that hadn't settled well with her? She knew what her duties were. She would do the woman's work, and Martin would do the rest, including the bookkeeping. Though it was a job she had done for her father, Martin forbade her from looking at the books as a matter of his male pride. "As my wife, you must trust me."

Letting her have an allowance below the amount her father had given her put her off, yet it was still enough for her own needs and wants. As far as she knew, he kept the bill collectors at bay. So why was she so suspicious of his actions concerning their money, her inheritance?

With the sun at its peak and the heat rising to a dry, nearly insufferable temperature, Jane looked about her parlor with satisfaction. She had done it. Lacey had told her Cabot Farm was the talk of the curious townspeople. She wondered if she might host an open house to let them view the modern décor of handcrafted furniture and lively floral upholstery.

The light blue striped wallpaper in the parlor was the perfect backdrop for the art she'd acquired in San Francisco. The artist was so delighted to have her as a patron—apparently, her wealth and good taste were no secret among the vendors in the city, and he had come to their home to suggest the perfect placement of his works. Berta's decorator, Ned, had become Jane's personal decorator and had been a great help and comfort when things became too much for her. A tall thin middle-aged man, he had worked over two decades in the business. He was full of sympathy for the trials of not getting the correct floral fabric or the right pillows, and he also knew how to negotiate with the merchants. He was charming, and Jane had liked him immediately.

"As they say, money talks, and you surely have enough to talk with, my dear!" he had said to her one particularly difficult day. "Now, let's get that chintz ordered for your bedroom."

The whole process enlivened her. She had acquired the appropriate clothing for working outside and felt quite at home in the cotton day dresses and aprons, high leather shoes, and large straw hat. She was ready for her work this morning.

With her journal in hand, she went out to the medicinal garden and marked the progress of each plant. Within the dirt-stained pages were recipes and practical uses for each species. As the season had progressed, she had noted how well her small plants had thrived in the rich soil. Some had perished under the sweltering heat, so she'd made note to put them in a shadier spot. It was a miracle to her how tiny seeds developed into plants for food, medicine, decoration, and scent.

Rubbing the top of a sprig of lavender, she released the soothing earthy aroma. Bringing her fingertips to her nose, she inhaled, then let out a breath with a soft sigh. Soon she would bundle the lavender for drying and set them in the stillroom. The thought of using herbs right from her own garden in creams, ointments, and tinctures for healing and aiding in minor cuts and bruises, or for making into soothing poultices for chest colds, filled her with joy. The horticultural books and a book on medicinal recipes she had ordered from Clarence at the general store had her staying up late into the night to devour their knowledge. Clarence's wife, Gladys, and Bell were a wealth of information on canning and preserving fruits and vegetables. Jane was keen to learn what to do with all the citrus, apple, and pear trees in the orchard.

Lacey had become an astute learner and great help with organizing the plants and planning for the winter ahead. Martin felt they needed neither her or the household help but she had convinced her husband that it took all of them to keep the estate running. Had he forgotten the lifestyle she was used to? In many ways, it helped him also. Bell cooked delicious suppers and baked mouthwatering desserts. Margie kept the house spotless and the laundry clean and folded neatly. Jane knew little about cooking or baking, and cleaning a house was out of the question.

Her desire to be among the socialites of San Francisco had translated into a good part of her life. Berta and Ned had introduced her to the city's wealthy and influential. Her newfound friends had her venturing across the bay once or twice a month. The wives of wealthy men provided her with the outlet she needed as a lady of means. Martin had balked at her absence at first, but she'd convinced him if she was to stay in Clermont City, she would have to have more than its meager society. She had yet to make friends with the local women outside of Lacey and Gladys.

Each time she went to the city, he advised her not to spend her money on trifles. Ignoring him, Jane played the card games, paid for drinks at the tables, and shopped for dresses and adornments she could wear while attending parties and luncheons there. It was always at least a three-day stay, and Berta was more than happy to accommodate her. It was a different life from the one she led on Cabot Farm, which would remain her little secret among her city friends. No one needed to know she was considered a farmer's wife in Clermont City.

CHAPTER TWENTY-TWO

October 1882

*T*HE DINING ROOM LIGHT WAS A MIXTURE OF RED AND ORANGE hues as the sun began its descent. The shorter days of autumn meant shorter workdays in the fields and gardens. It had been a little over a year since the last of the renovations were completed, yet it was just the beginning of all the work required on a farm. Bell helped in the kitchen department, and Margie kept the home as neat as a pin. Jane indulged her love of planning her gardens and working in them to create their beauty and practicality. The longer evenings meant a bit more rest, and she had to admit she welcomed the change. If only Martin saw it that way too.

Margie came in with two lit kerosene lamps and placed them on the side tables along the wall. She was a tall robust woman in her forties and not afraid to speak her mind. She didn't come and go softly, and she balked at wearing a uniform.

"My clean day dress is my uniform," she'd stated without any sign of compromise.

Jane had let it slide.

Due to the fact Jane hadn't found a dresser for her more formal attire, Margie had taken on that task—to both their dismay. A few extra dollars tacked on to her wage helped soften Margie's attitude, and Jane had to admit, the woman had an eye for detail. Having few reasons to dress up but for a dance in town or an outing in Oakland, the two women could tolerate each other on these rare occasions.

In general, they did their best to get along. Margie had come from an elderly man's estate and took no guff from anyone. Apparently, the man had had a difficult personality. She didn't seem to mind his passing, as she'd shown little emotion when she spoke of him in her interview with Jane.

"Thank you, Margie," Jane said. "Would you please bring us coffee?"

"So late in the evening, ma'am?"

"Yes, please," Jane said between tight lips.

Martin continued going over his notes about the farm. He carried the tablet around with him and was always scribbling in it. She'd noticed him stopping midstride to reach into his shirt pocket and pencil in another thought.

It was a common practice now, even on the beautiful polished wood table.

When did he become so crass?

"Jane, you know I need to get a good night's sleep. No coffee for me."

Reaching over, she placed a hand on the dirt-stained papers. "Martin, can we talk?"

For a brief moment, he stiffened as if she had violated his right to work.

"Yes, my dear. What is it?" He looked up at her. "I'm aware I've been busy, but it's for the both of us, my sweet."

"That's what I want to talk about."

"Again?" he asked curtly.

She took in a breath and continued. "Couldn't we hire more men to help you? You could run things in an office, manage the workmen. We might convert a room or build on to the house. Why must you be so hands-on? Just because Harry is doesn't mean you have to be."

"This is my life. This is our future. Yes, I must be hands-on!"

"Don't be upset. Why are you so concerned about money? We have enough, do we not?"

Leaning back in his chair, Martin took a deep breath and let it out. "I have acquired two cows. They'll provide milk enough for our household, and we can sell the rest. The eggs are selling well, and Clarence said he'd be glad to take the milk and cream. I've rented out some of the property, which will bring in more income. The sheep need shearing, and the horses need shoeing. We've sold to market the two pigs, and Harry and I will purchase a few more at the auction next week. He said those will have to have the piglets we need to grow our business. This farm is worth more if it's kept up in a proper manner. I want to be independent, Jane. I need to assure our future is solid. We might have plenty of money now, but . . ."

A side glance to Margie coming in with the tray had Martin holding his tongue.

"Will that be all tonight?" the housekeeper asked.

"Yes, you may go," Jane said. "I'll see you tomorrow, laundry day."

With a quick nod, Margie left. Soon after, Jane heard the front door close. They were alone. All the staff had their own residence, and Bell had left after cleaning up for the night.

Jane's stomach was in a knot. "But?"

"If we don't succeed, it could all be taken from us. And Chad seemed very convinced we—I—would fail. I don't intend to give him that satisfaction."

"My brother is far away, and we are living our lives independently of him. I don't see why you're so concerned about his opinions." She reminded herself to write to her mother. It had been nearly eight months since her last correspondence.

Jane looked at Martin's concerned expression. The tightknit brows and turned-down mouth showed through his lengthened hair. She continued her inquiry about the state of their finances.

He brushed the sun-kissed strands out of his face. "Just let me handle things. And for God's sake, stop spending so much money!"

She stated as calmly as she could, "You forget, it's my money."

"*Our* money," he said.

Steaming with pent-up resentment and feeling utterly unloved, she lashed out. "It's my money. You had nothing before you married me!"

He stood and left the room.

Jane closed her eyes, admonishing herself for her harsh words. She went after him. "Martin."

As he was about to open the heavy carved front door, the low-hanging sun shined its light, touching the long, stained-glass windows on either side of the entrance. It streamed the colors of amber and red between them. The beauty was in sharp contrast to the battle in its wake. Martin turned, and she looked at the expression on her husband's face. His eyes were misty, his mouth downturned. What was this about?

"I thought we could have a good life here. A life we could share," he said.

"We share nothing. You don't pay attention to me. Don't you want children?"

Martin came to her and embraced her. "Why, of course I do."

"I'm sorry, Martin. Please forgive me. I'm just feeling . . . lonely."

He held her close and kissed her lips sweetly. His voice became hoarse as he whispered in her ear, "I'm sorry. Perhaps we could begin tonight in making our family?"

She was filled with relief. He still loved her.

Martin drew the silk damask curtains over the large windows in the luxuriously decorated bedroom. Jane turned around for him to unbutton her day dress. He untied her padded bustle and un-buttoned her under slip, letting it fall to the floor. She stood in her chemise, the coolness of its thinness giving her body pleasure.

He undressed himself, showing his well-defined muscles. It was done with efficiency as he placed his clothes and hers on the chair. She smiled but longed for him to let their clothes fall where they may in lusty abandonment. Then he turned to her and cradled her head in his hands, kissing her with a passion she remembered from their courting days. A bubbling of joy fountained up in her as the heaviness of her loins had her returning his passion with her own. She had learned to temper her lust and let him take the lead, but tonight she was hungry for his body.

They were entwined and tossing in the soft cotton sheets, and their mouths found pleasure in each other's flesh. She wanted it to go on forever. Martin's need turned urgent, and she finally lay on her back as he brought himself to enter her. She moaned and welcomed him inside. The sheer abandonment and heady pleasure made her dizzy. As she rocked her hips, his heavy breathing was soon punctuated with a sharp cry, and then he came down on her in a breathless heap.

"Oh, Jane," he moaned as he rolled over. Before she could cuddle into him and let him know how much this meant to her and how perhaps they could find more time to be together, he was snoring.

She sat up and was very still, the sound of her own breathing audible in her head. After her emotions calmed, she wiped her tears, redressed, and went downstairs. She couldn't listen to him sleep.

Tonight, she would stop hoping he would want what she wanted in their intimacy. Her dreams of him were only that: dreams. He was her steady, hardworking Martin, her practical thinker, honest and humble. She would keep her desires to herself and learn to live in contentment and gratitude. Wasn't that what she'd been taught? With all her might, she would strive to be a good wife and take what he had to offer, nothing more. Beyond that, perhaps tonight they may have started a family.

She had not become pregnant yet, and the reasons were obvious. When she felt the time was right, Martin was away visiting other farms or too tired. When she had asked him to take note of the timing from her so they could make love and produce a child, he had turned red and replied, "Jane, that's not my department, dear. It will happen as God wills it."

Although each time he said he would try harder, it hadn't been enough. Jane felt her time was running out. What if she became too old to carry a healthy child? Her want for children had turned into an unquenchable desire which she'd turned on the animals around her, despite Martin's continual reminders that the animals weren't pets. The sheepdog, the chickens, and the lambs had become her outlet for her maternal affection.

Then there was Harry. He was a complication in her life. Her efforts to not think of him were useless. His handsome face would appear in her mind with little effort. His humor and attentiveness didn't help either. She often wondered what it would be like to—

No, she wouldn't let herself go in that dangerous, tempting direction. It was all in her own mind, she told herself. Harry had no feelings for her in that way. He was Martin's cousin, a member of the family.

The next day she wired Ned to meet her at the ferry dock in the city. She would get satisfaction by buying a trinket for the house and gardens, perhaps a new platter for the kitchen or new clothes for herself. It didn't hurt that everyone, including the men, in their group told her how beautiful and charming she was. A dinner with them and their wives would give her an outlet for her pent-up sensuality as she flirted back in playful abandonment.

CHAPTER TWENTY-THREE

November 1882

BERTA WELCOMED JANE WITH OPEN ARMS. THE TWO friends embraced, and Berta had tea waiting for Jane in the airy sitting room. The fall day was warm and sunny, and Jane let all her worries melt away.

Later that day she strolled by herself, taking in the mansion's beautiful gardens. The soft but cooling breeze and the fragrance of flowers and plants mingling with the ocean's salty smell were lovely to her senses. She took note of the pleasingly arranged garden in formal circles and squares. It was more formal than she could ever achieve on her own land. Even with all her efforts at Cabot Farm, she could not make it into the mini-Versailles that Berta had done with her estate. Here there were no pigs to escape their stinky pens and trample the new sprouts of corn or squirrels to dig up the potatoes before they were ready. Everything seemed expertly manicured down to the last blade of grass. It gave Jane a sense of peace and order.

Ned arrived that night, and instead of joining the rest of the group—they had become quite a clique of eight to ten wealthy city dwellers—the three of them dined alone. This night they enjoyed fine food and aromatic wines and champagne. All were served on the richest silver and gold dishware. To Jane's eye, the crystal glassware was among some of the finest she had ever seen.

Ned was aware of her true life, yet he never gave one hint of it to anyone, including Berta. As far as any of them knew, she was a wealthy woman from back East dabbling in an adventure with her equally wealthy husband.

"How brave!"

"So interesting!"

"I'd never!"

"You are something, my dear!"

Such were the comments from her city friends. Tonight, she felt relaxed with just Berta and Ned. The rest of her four-day visit floated by without a finger to lift or a problem to solve.

When she arrived home, feeling much restored from her getaway, she was expecting Martin to be waiting for her at the coach station as usual. Instead, she spied Harry, and her heart lurched. His tall lean body rested against one of the posts lining the boardwalk in front of the station, his arms folded on his chest. He was clearly waiting for someone. *She* was the someone. For some reason, it made her feel special.

Gathering her satchel, purse, and nerves, she waited for the passenger before her to be helped down. Minutes before seeing Harry, she'd been ready to go home, get comfortable, and take a short nap before getting ready for supper. Now her adrenaline gave her a strange energy. Where was her husband? She would find out soon enough.

Harry approached the carriage and helped her down.

"Harry! I didn't expect you to be here. Where's Martin?"

"He and Jason had their hands full with a few strays. I had some errands to run in town, so you're stuck with me."

His familiar teasing and boyish grin sent her blood rushing through her body.

"Oh, I see." She felt tongue-tied.

The afternoon sun beat down on the dusty road as she looked away from him. Swirls of dirt danced along its corridor.

Her luggage came from the coach, and the driver doffed his hat. A fellow passenger said good day to her, and then Harry took her bags and they walked to his flatbed rig. Martin had bought a decent horse and buggy, so why was Harry using this to pick her up? Her answer lay in the back, which was filled with lumber, tools, and two boxes of groceries.

He helped her up, and she seated herself beside him on the bench, acutely aware of their closeness. With the warmth of the day, most men had a repugnant odor, but his smell was not offensive; in fact, it lit her desire. His arm touched hers as he took up the reins, and she moved over. After settling her skirts, she glanced over to him.

"Don't worry, Mrs. Cabot. You're safe with me," he said with a chuckle.

Dismayed at his assumption, she replied, "I have no doubt, of course." She adjusted her skirt again and straightened her back. The carriage lurched, and she grabbed his arm.

"You did that on purpose!" she said.

He laughed. "Sorry, I thought you had braced yourself." He looked down at her arm still wrapped around his.

She went to take it away, and he clamped it to his body. His strength was gentle but firm.

"Why not hold on to me? It could get bumpy," he said.

For a moment longer than natural, their eyes met, and she let herself look at him. He was tan and rugged. His deep brown eyes and generous smile invited her to smile back, and she did. Then she felt something exchange between them, a connection not like before as they teased each other. There was a deeper look in his eyes, and she returned it with a longing that made her want to kiss him. She physically ached for his lips on hers.

When he swallowed, his open collar revealed his Adam's apple moving up and down. His sweat glistened in the spot where his clavicle bones met. It nearly undid her. Harry cleared his throat, then carefully took her arm from around his and placed it on her lap.

"On second thought, I'll let you hold on to the seat. Might be safer for us both," he said.

She nodded, feeling he was just as aware as she was of something more between them.

Gripping the seat on either side of her, she felt a tickle of excitement. This was the first time he had looked at her in that way—the way that spoke of interest beyond friendship. It was wrong to have such feelings for Harry, her husband's cousin. If her mother's god did exist, she was surely on the wrong side of his laws.

They rode in silence. Perhaps she would visit church this Sunday. She hadn't attended for two weeks.

The ride home was quiet but for the singing of the birds and the flatbed's wheels crunching over the dirt road.

Martin came out of the house as Harry was getting Jane's satchel. He rushed around the flatbed to retrieve the rest of her luggage.

"Thank you, Harry, for fetching Jane for me," he said, pulling the two cases from the back. "We finally managed to get those strays into the pen. Coming for supper tonight? I think Jane can have the cook make your favorite stew." Turning to Jane, he kissed his wife's cheek. "Welcome home, my sweet. Did Harry tell you we have several pregnant sheep? The ram did his job!"

"No, that's wonderful, Martin," she said. She noted to herself how easily his sheep became pregnant and not his wife. "You can show me them in the morning. I'm quite worn out. I think I'll go inside and rest before supper." Harry handed Jane her satchel.

Was she imagining it, or had he held on just a moment too long before letting go? "Thank you, Harry," she said. "Please do come for supper tonight."

"I will, Jane. Thank you."

Before Harry's eyes could make contact with hers, she stepped away and walked inside the house, where Margie took her luggage and followed her mistress upstairs.

"How was your visit, ma'am?" the housekeeper asked.

"Very nice. It's good to get away and good to come home." Jane took off her hat and gloves, releasing the oppressiveness of them. "Will you draw me a bath, Margie? I'll be glad to take the travel dust off before we dine."

"Yes, ma'am. Do you want lavender this afternoon or the citrus?"

"Lavender, please."

After she was completely undressed, Jane put on a light robe and entered the bathing room.

She let the pink silk whisper off her slender body. Slipping into the warm water with its heady aroma sent a tingle through her. The world melted away, and there was only her and Harry. Closing her eyes, she let her fantasy develop.

A rough handsome man, a dainty woman. His lips on her bare neck. She brought her wet hand to her chin and let the warm liquid glide down onto her chest as his tongue would, silky and sensual. Cupping her firm breast, she imagined his hand replacing hers. She breathed in and out as she ran the soap along her smooth thigh, longing for Harry to see every satiny curve. She hitched a breath and came back to reality. It had only been a moment of pleasure, but she knew she couldn't let herself indulge in those thoughts again.

God help her. She still felt young at twenty-eight and sought the attention of her husband and received very little. The emptiness was a pang of hunger so deep and wanting she could feel the void of it in her stomach. Yes, Martin was good to her. Indeed, he cared for her well-being.

Can I not want more from my marriage?

Wanting, her mother scolded her, was a sin. Jane dearly wanted it to be untrue.

How can we move forward in life and make plans if we do not want?

As always, her mother's beliefs confused and dismayed Jane, and as always, she dismissed it and decided to find a more suitable belief system. She would still attend the service on Sunday, however, just in case. She rose from the bath and rinsed off the soap and guilt of her wanton heart.

THE ROASTED POTATO AND BEEF stew Bell had cooked smelled wonderful, and Jane found her appetite. Bell was a sweet natured older sister-type to Jane. She was also a no-nonsense person as was Margie, but Jane and Bell got along quite well. Bell tried teaching her many things about the kitchen and larder, and Jane felt it was good knowledge, but she let Bell do most of the work. She didn't need to know about kitchen work as she didn't need to know how to do laundry or clean a house. She could devote herself to other more pleasurable pursuits and some not so pleasurable tasks when Martin and Jason needed an extra hand with the livestock.

Martin and Harry talked about farming, as she had expected. Then Harry turned to her and asked how she was. She swallowed a mouthful of food and took a sip of water.

"I'm well, thank you."

"Good. You seemed rather tired this afternoon. But that would be expected after your trip."

Martin looked up from his stew. "My dear, are you recovered? I think you should forgo any further visits across the bay if it makes you weak. I need you well to help run things."

"Why, Martin, I'm quite refreshed. I don't know what Harry is talking about." She looked at Harry with squinted eyes.

"Oh, I'm sorry," Harry began. "I . . . I didn't mean to say you looked bad. Just, well, you look quite refreshed indeed. Martin, I think the city does your wife wonders. We all need a break from the farm now and then. Why, I may take a small holiday myself."

Jane hid a smile. She was amused with this composed, self-assured man now stumbling over himself. It endeared him to her even more. Yet she thought by right he should be tongue-tied. He had made a terrible misstep on her behalf. She needed those trips into the city.

Martin looked at his cousin in surprise. "How would you take a break away from your farm?"

"I . . . I don't know actually," Harry replied, rubbing the neat beard on his chin.

Martin gave a grunt and went back to eating.

Jane glanced at Harry, and he shrugged his shoulders and mouthed, "I'm sorry."

She shook her head. What was she getting into with him, and why was it so damn enjoyable?

Having gotten through supper in her current state of infatuation with her cousin-in-law, Jane was ready for a long night's sleep. As Harry was about to say good night, a sheep cried out, loud and strong. It wasn't coming from the pen. The trio rushed outside to inspect the situation. They looked in three different directions. There was another loud cry in one field, followed by one in another field.

Harry turned to Martin. "I'll take the upper."

Martin answered in a run. "I'll take the east. Jane, stand by the barn in case they come back."

Jane watched the pair sprint off in their chosen directions, her gaze darting across the landscape. She prayed it was only two lost sheep and not a coyote attack.

After a while, Harry came back with one smaller sheep. He had the animal around his neck like a scarf, holding firm to a pair of legs in each hand. It was a comical sight, and Jane had to laugh as she approached him.

She helped the poor thing down, and they both corralled it into the pen. The other sheep made noises as if welcoming it back into the fold. Harry immediately inspected the pen enclosure and found a chewed hole in the fencing. The opening was big enough for a smaller animal to wiggle through.

"Damn, that needs fixin' right now."

Jane looked on, then followed him to the barn. He lit a kerosene lamp and found what he needed. The cows made sounds, and the horses rustled at their intrusion.

"I fear the other one is further afield or Martin would've been back by now," he said as they walked back to the pen.

Jane looked at him. "Hope he finds it before something else does."

"Me too."

They looked at each other with mutual concern that turned into a lingering stare. His presence tantalized her as the last of the evening sunset cast its light on his well-defined features. The land turned into a magical place of shadows and light. The song of the birds settling in for the night and the crickets and frogs joining the chorus made for a symphony of nature. They were a part of it, and it added to the natural attraction she felt toward him.

His smile made her heart sing. It was a wanting smile. She returned with her own. Before she could check herself, their bodies were touching. His muscled arm pressed against her arm. She lowered her head, and they walked together with less urgency. Then Harry stopped in mid-stride.

"I'm sorry for putting my foot in my mouth at supper," he said.

"It's all right. I doubt Martin has given it another thought."

"Jane, how unhappy are you? This certainly doesn't seem like the life for you."

"Why, Harry, I'm absolutely delighted to be on this farm!"

They both laughed, and he brought her closer. "I wish I could take your unhappiness away."

"I'm not unhappy. There's many things about this place, this land, that I've fallen in love with."

"Good. I like having you here."

He brushed her cheek with his finger and leaned in to kiss her as Martin came down the east side of the field with an armful of bleating wool. They jerked apart. Jane's heart was beating hard in her chest and her body trembled.

Harry brought the back of his hand to his mouth and coughed. "Where did you find it?" he asked as Martin came closer.

To Jane's eye, the sheep looked fine as it tried to struggle to be free, yet she felt its struggle.

"The stand of trees, of course. It was crying like no tomorrow under the biggest one. Couldn't move an inch."

"Oh, poor baby," Jane said, and once she got it safely into the pen, she petted it and offered comfort. She was happy for the distraction.

"They're dumber than you think," Martin said. "Don't baby it, Jane."

Ignoring her husband, she waited for the others to crowd around it, then left it to the flock.

Harry showed Martin the hole in the fence, and the two of them worked on a temporary solution, both agreeing it would need more reinforcements tomorrow in the light of day.

"Well, time to get going," Harry said. "Think I'll go settle in with a brandy. Have a good evening, you two."

"Sounds like a good thought to me," Martin said. "Thanks for the repair."

"Good night, Harry," Jane said. "Thank you."

"Anytime," he said as he walked down the path that led to his road. It was a long walk, but Jane knew it would be quite pleasant on a warm evening. She and Martin had made the walk many times, and she loved emerging from the woods onto his land.

Mostly, a horse ride was the more practical way of getting from one farm to the other. Tonight, she longed to join him. Just her and him. Harry had struck the match that now lit the fire in Jane. It felt warm and disturbing. How was she going to resist this new awakening in their relationship?

CHAPTER TWENTY-FOUR

November 1883

*J*ANE'S ABILITY TO ENDURE HER MARRIAGE WITH MARTIN as a "farmer's wife" depended on Harry's presence in her life and her trips into the city.

A look from Harry could right her world for the day until the next time when he came for supper or she ran into him on the land or in town. Their relationship was not set in stone as her marriage was; instead, it was as unpredictable as the dappled light through the trees on a breezy day. He knew how to show her affection in a way that spoke to her—a hand on her back as he let her go first through an entry, or his extended arm as he led her over a rough patch of land on the farm, not letting go right away—and she returned it with an accepting nod or smile.

When he stared at her as Martin read aloud by the fireside after the meal, it fueled her passion for him. He was out of reach, yet he sat right there, so close. She didn't have to please Harry. He was his own man. Nothing she said was right or wrong. He wasn't concerned about what she spent or how she looked, yet he would tease her about her fashion and grin his grin, the one she felt was just for her, when she got too hoity-toity in her manner. He also praised her when he came into the house after surveying her gardens and the stillroom, where she stored the products she developed like salves and creams. In short, he let her know he saw her. Those moments, however brief, were building something between them.

Martin and Harry and several other men erected the conservatory, which brought a new direction to Jane's own farming of the land. She would have more space for plants and seedlings. In winter it would produce food such as peppers and tender greens. It sparked a new venture in her, one that may take her mind off of Harry. Her desire for him was taking up too much time in her heart and mind.

Her trips to Berta's estate helped in another way. It gave her evidence she was still good enough to be in high society. The notion was still important to her, yet she sometimes found herself being less than her authentic self in the city.

Still without a child, she wondered if something was physically wrong with her. Or maybe it was Martin. He was not as strong as Harry. He was not as agile as Harry either. She couldn't keep count of the many times Martin had hurt himself. His soft jeweler's hands took a beating from the start and had been slow to callous. She kept a large jar of calendula cream in the stillroom to soothe his blisters and lavender oil to remedy his sore muscles. Feverfew for his temples when the headaches of bookkeeping became too much. Ginger and peppermint teas for his digestion. Bell made him hearty breakfasts and lunches, and the dinners she served would squelch any farmer's hunger, yet he remained himself, a jeweler trying to be a farmer.

Jane couldn't help comparing the two men. It was quite obvious Harry had done this type of work from the time he could walk. His father had farmed and his grandfather before him. Her heart softened toward her husband when she thought about him working so diligently to become the man Harry was, to make this a successful venture. Why couldn't he be as diligent at making their marriage as successful? It occurred to her this was his way. She wondered what kind of marriage they would've had if they'd stayed in Cincinnati. Would he be more attentive? Or would jewelry making take him away from her? What if he were a gentleman farmer? Would he be so obsessed? Perhaps not.

She remembered what Harry had said about Martin being miserable in his life there, and she sighed. There was no place in her new life for what-ifs—there was too much work to do.

Today the kitchen garden was in its autumnal change with seed heads forming and leafless stems turning brown and brittle on some plants while others were ripe for harvesting and still others ready to be planted to mature in the mild California winter. Oranges and lemons weighed their branches down, and Mr. Hill was busy carefully gathering the fruit to be sold in town and around the county. It was one of the ways Martin chose to help pay the expenses.

Taking what she needed from the harvested citrus, Jane squeezed the fresh fruit into a tall glass and looked out the kitchen window, going over in her head what she needed to do. Helping Bell in the kitchen garden was top priority. As she sipped the sweet juice, her eyes landed on the swirl of dust down the drive. Someone was coming, and at a hurried pace.

John, the messenger boy from the newspaper's wire service, came riding in on his horse, Lester, kicking up dirt and gravel as he brought the bay to an abrupt stop.

Jane went out to meet him, lifting her hand to her forehead to shield her eyes from the bright sun. "John, what's so important that you have to make a mess of my courtyard?"

He swung down from his horse. A sprig of youth, his appearance was in a constant state of dishevelment. "I have an urgent telegram for you, Mrs. Cabot. Lacey got it in just now. She says it's come from Cin-cin-aty and told me to take it to you right away."

Jane paused with concern. This was not her family's way of communicating. "Very well, hand it over." She reached into her apron pocket and brought out a nickel and gave it to John.

He took the money and gave a slight bow of his head. "Thank you, ma'am."

"I may need you to take back a reply. Go into the kitchen and tell Bell I sent you for some refreshment."

He doffed his hat. "Thanks, ma'am. Always happy to see what Bell's been baking."

Jane didn't look at the telegram. If it was bad news, she'd receive it sitting down in the parlor. She went inside and found her favorite chair. Unfolding the brown paper, she saw her hand tremble. The message was brief.

Mother is dying. She has asked for you. Chadwick.

She turned the paper in her hand. Was he too cheap to send more words than this? Warning bells rang in her head.

What did the Wallingford Jewelry Company look like now? She had been so occupied with her life, she had lost touch with her friends and family in Cincinnati. Now her mother lay dying, and she was to go to her and . . . and say what? Do what? Hold her hand? Listen to her confessions? Her regrets? Was this what would happen at the end of her mother's life?

A stab of love hit her, and tears swelled in her eyes. She was the one with regrets. She hadn't written often enough, and when she did, it was to let Chad and her mother know she was doing well. She wrote that Martin was a great success at farming and that they had a fine home and lived in great comfort—she knew her refurbished and outfitted country home couldn't rival the rich and stately houses in Cincinnati or San Francisco, but she wasn't going to give her brother the satisfaction of remarking on her lowered station.

She had written about the wealthy and educated society she kept and that San Francisco was a prosperous and vibrant city. Again, she left out the full story: that she had done a good deal of gardening herself and enjoyed it even though the stain of dirt clung to her hands and nails and no amount of salve could keep the dryness at bay. She didn't write about the occasional work she would do to help Martin and Jason or how she'd help Bell jar up produce or shop at the general store for fabric and sundries needed at the house. However, she wasn't old and pale or dowdy, as Chad had referred to her becoming. The life she had carved out was as good as she could make it. Her inheritance certainly helped to that end.

Lastly, she had inquired about their health and the state of the business. Having received a curt reply from her mother stating she was happy for them and that all was well in Cincinnati had left Jane suspicious, and the cold letter had hurt her more than she wanted to admit. The only upside was that her mother hadn't asked if they'd had children yet. It was a sore subject, and she would in no way find consolation from Elisha, only a stern warning for her to be more available to her husband.

When Martin came into the house from a long day, she showed him the telegram.

"I'm sorry, my dear," he said. Taking the telegram to read for himself, he remarked, "Couldn't Chad have sent a lengthier account?"

"What should I do? We can't both go, but I should see her before . . ." Tears welled in her eyes and dropped to her cheeks. Jane swiped them away, as they were uninvited.

He came to her, and they embraced. He kissed the top of her handkerchief-covered head. "You should go. Take Lacey with you. I think you would be sorry if you didn't say . . . goodbye."

Jane pulled away with a nod.

"I wish I could be by your side," Martin said. "Take whatever amount of money you may need. I'll ask the bank to provide that. We will afford first class for both you and Lacey."

"Thank you, Martin. That's good of you."

"Oh, Jane, don't let me off that easily. I know your thoughts. I'll be with you in heart and soul," he said. "It's no use for me to sit in your brother's parlor and lament over the present or the past. You know how it would be."

She did know, and he was right, yet it didn't help to alleviate the desire for his presence, for him to hold her at night and to wake in his arms the next morning with the reassurance of a united front as they faced her mother and brother together, as she faced the possibility of her mother's death.

With a nod, she turned her thoughts to what she would need to pack and the travel arrangements for the train trip.

Lacey would be thrilled to take such an adventure. The young woman had become more essential to Jane's life, as well as a trusted friend.

Her thoughts rushed to Harry. Would he have taken the time away from his farm to be with his wife on such an occasion, knowing what Martin knew about her family?

The disappointment in her marriage, which she had long kept at bay, crashed to shore. She fell into despair in the middle of her lovely parlor. The tears streamed down her face as her chest heaved with emotion.

"My dear, my dear," Martin said as he helped her to the couch.

Jane took her handkerchief from her embroidered shirt pocket and wiped her face, inhaling a deep breath. Looking down at her yellow calico farmer's dress didn't help her mood. It was a declaration of her life now. She closed her eyes. She would surely bring the proper clothing.

Chad's words bored into her like hundreds of termites eating away at her foundation. She hated how fragile she felt when it came to his and her mother's judgment.

Collecting herself, she stood. "I'll be fine, Martin. You're right, I should go to her, and I will ask Lacey to accompany me. Do not worry yourself over it." She looked at him and saw his concern. Perhaps there was hope he would make an exception and come with her.

"That's my brave wife," he said. "And buy yourself whatever you need for traveling clothes and city clothes." He scratched his head. "Whatever you need."

His words felt hollow. He was smoothing his guilt over by offering her what he thought would make her happy. It would add to the already tender wound his lack of attention and affection had formed.

"Yes, Martin, you are the farm, and it is you. I will never again ask you to leave it. Thank you for your generosity. I will go plan my trip."

"Jane, don't be angry. I just can't leave now. Maybe in a few years we can travel, go wherever we like, but not now."

She heard him pandering as she walked to her desk. After writing a reply to her brother and a message for Lacey, she summoned John to carry both to the newspaper. Martin approached her and placed his hand on her shoulder.

"Please, Jane, I'm doing this for us. We're becoming more successful. Folks are buying our produce and milk. We'll make a good profit this year, and there's still so much land to develop."

Turning to look into his eyes, Jane said, "Tell me, Martin, why is the profit such a concern to you? We do well because we have all the money we need. I wish you would focus on our marriage instead of every little penny spent. Or is there something you're not telling me? Is this about my brother? Has he threatened you?"

A long silenced followed.

"Martin? Please don't let that be the case. He's all talk sometimes. He can't touch us here."

Martin's blank expression caused her to step back.

"What is it?"

"I would, well . . ." Martin fumbled for the correct words. "He might tell you things about your inheritance. I would be careful of his vengeance toward us moving here and leaving him to run the business without us."

The acid rose from her gut. "What do you mean? Have you heard from him? Is the business in trouble? My inheritance?"

Martin looked flustered. "No, no, it's just that he wasn't happy about our move, and I know he can make trouble. That's all. I'm just looking out for you. I've got to get back to work." He kissed the top of her head.

A stab of warning hit her. She went back in time to the parlor in Cincinnati when they told Chad and her mother they were leaving to go West. She remembered the strange way Martin had responded to Chad's reaction—or overreaction, as it seemed to her. It was as if they shared a secret.

What lay ahead for her? Martin didn't want to talk about it. What could he be hiding?

The back door closed, and her husband was gone, back to his animals and his fields.

That night she couldn't glean anything more from him about the situation. She would have to find out for herself.

Before leaving for Cincinnati, Jane had to see Harry. Jason saddled up her horse, Minnie. The mild-mannered chestnut mare had been a godsend to Jane. Her rides through the countryside set her turbulent mind to rest.

She found Harry sitting on the porch of his humble home, a large log cabin built by his own hands. She had marveled at the tightly constructed logs and how graceful and simple it was inside. It was warm and inviting for a rustic home.

His legs were stretched out and rested on the porch's top rail, a pipe in his hand. Finding him in such a state of relaxation was unusual. Jane desired to join him and let the day pass them lazily by with all her worries carried away with the soft breeze.

Once he spied her, he sprang to his feet, placing his pipe down on the crude wooden table. She found his mounting block and waited for him to come over and help her down.

"What a pleasant surprise," he said.

Jane knew this was unprecedented. She had only visited his home with Martin.

Taking her by her slim waist, he brought her safely to the ground. She straightened her riding skirt and looped Minnie's reins to the post nearby. She wouldn't be long.

"I'm leaving for Cincinnati, and I wanted to say goodbye."

The smile left his face, and he rubbed his nose as if it had suddenly become runny. "Yes, Martin told me. I'm sorry to hear about your mother. I was going to come by the other day, but, well, I thought you'd be busy."

"Thank you for thinking of me."

"I think of you . . . too often."

Her legs became weak. She wanted his lips on hers, his hands in her hair as they lost control . . .

"How long will you be gone?"

His question brought her back to earth.

"I have no return ticket, so I really can't say."

"Oh."

"Not too long. I couldn't bear to be gone for too long."

The relief that came over his face accelerated her yearning for him. Gil came into view, and Harry stiffened.

"I hope it isn't too grievous," he said. "Will you be traveling with Lacey?" The question was rhetorical. He knew Martin was for Lacey accompanying her.

"My mother could be on her last breath or simply aching for

attention. I'll know exactly when I see her. And yes, Lace will come with me. Martin couldn't possibly leave the farm."

He nodded. "I'm sorry . . . I mean, I wish your husband could be with you. It's a long journey with plenty of time to think."

"It is. I have much to think about."

Harry agreed and stepped aside. "Well, safe travels. Thank you for stopping by. I appreciate it, Jane."

The awkwardness was palpable. Gil doffed his hat and shouted a hello, then walked off toward Harry's barn.

Jane waved at him, then brought her attention back to the handsome man standing in front of her.

"I will leave you to your porch and pipe, then."

"You caught me in a rare moment."

And then there was that beautiful smile of his. She was undone and had to do all she could not to shout, "I'm in love with you!"

"Harry, I think you and I have an . . . understanding?"

Harry chuckled. "We both understand what we might be getting into."

Their eyes met, and she could have sworn he was looking right into her soul.

"Have a good trip, Jane."

She knew it was time to end this meeting.

"Thank you, Harry."

She untied Minnie, and Harry came around and helped her mount.

Looking down at the man she loved, she could only say, "Good day, Harry. Watch over Martin for me."

"Good day, Jane. I will."

A moment passed, and neither of them moved. She extended her leather-gloved hand to him, and after a beat, he grasped it tight and held it for several seconds before releasing it back up to her.

"Until you return, then," he said.

"Until I return," she replied.

Taking the reins, she turned her chestnut toward home. With a light shake of the reins, Minnie went into a graceful trot. As soon as she cleared his road, she let the horse gallop through the open field between his farm and her home, the wind catching her hair and whisking the tears from her cheeks.

CHAPTER TWENTY-FIVE

THE CONDUCTOR'S VOICE RANG LOUD AND CLEAR. "CUM-BER-land Sta-tion!"

"That's us, Lace," Jane said, then folded the newspaper she was reading.

Lacey looked out the window and came back with excitement written on her face.

"Soon I'll be in the great city of Cincinnati! I never would have thought I'd ever see anything past the city of San Francisco or even Clermont City. And here I am, me, Lacey May Bennett, a world traveler!"

Jane didn't want to break it to Lacey that the world was bigger than San Francisco and their two-thousand-mile train travel. Then she remembered the first time she'd ridden the rail out West. She had to admit it was pretty exciting. She smiled at her and nodded with agreement.

The last bit of travel had Jane weary. It was a long journey. When she came from the train, she spotted her brother standing by himself. Had he not thought of hiring a coach for them?

Jane approached him with Lacey trailing behind, trying to help the porter with their luggage. They weaved in and out of the throng of passengers, some of whom stopped to greet their people while others milled about, looking anxious for more passengers to descend from the train. With her nerves on edge, the scene felt chaotic and most uncomfortable. A chill ran up her spine. The acrid smell of the steam coming off the train made her sick, and she longed for a smile from Charlotte and a hot cup of tea.

Chadwick extended his hand. "Hello, Sister. It's been too long."

Jane accepted his black-gloved greeting as he kissed her cheek. "Yes, it has. How is Mother?"

"She's been holding on for you to get here."

Lacey came up from behind.

"Chad, this is my secretary and friend, Lacey Bennett."

"A secretary? Why does one need a secretary on a farm? Hello, Miss Bennett."

Lacey returned the greeting, and as Jane had warned her of her brother's off-putting character, she seemed to ignore the barb.

A quick assessment of her brother showed Jane the once-handsome young man had dark circles under his wrinkled eyes and a bit of gray touching his temples. He had aged in such a short time. Her suspicions grew.

She'd had plenty of time to think on the train and mull over what he and Martin might be hiding. Her mind wandered too many times to Harry and their goodbye. She ached to be at his home again with his hand holding hers, his grip so reassuring.

The train's whistle startled her. She'd have to tread carefully in finding out what she needed to know. Chad didn't look that happy to see her.

They walked through the station, and Wallace welcomed them into the family carriage. At first glance, Jane didn't see anything askew, but on closer inspection, she noticed the shabby state it was in. Why had Chad let it go like this?

The old driver doffed his hat at Jane. "It's good to see the young lady of the manor again," he said.

"How have you been, Wallace?"

"Oh, same ol', same ol', Miss Wallingford. I mean, Mrs. Cabot."

Jane smiled at him, and Wallace slowly climbed up onto his seat and Chad helped the ladies into the cab. Jane settled into the velvet seat with Lacey beside her and Chad was across from them. She noticed several worn and frayed spots. How had the fabric come to be like this?

"My goodness, Chad," Jane said with a chuckle. "Are you renting out the carriage?"

He wasn't amused, and it alarmed her. Their satchels and purses had found their places. A thin blanket was brought up by Lacey, and she draped it across their laps. With the knock of Chad's knuckle on the small window, the carriage lurched forward, and they were off.

The coldness of the interior was odd to Jane. Her father always had Wallace keep a brass foot warmer filled with hot coals on the floor at this time of year.

"You can't afford a bit of coal for our feet?"

His empty stare added to the chill in the dim curtain-drawn carriage. The pungent odor of alcohol emanating from her brother gave Jane more cause for concern.

"There are better ways to spend my money. The heat from our bodies should be sufficient."

Jane gave a side glance to Lacey, who slid closer to her. The ride would take about an hour, and she placed her gloved hands under the blanket, deciding it wasn't worth her time to argue with him. Something was amiss, and she would find out sooner rather than later.

When they arrived at the house, a once-grand manor, Jane was shocked to see its unkempt state. The windows hadn't been washed, the front gardens were in need of cleaning and readying for the winter ahead, and the paint on the house was peeling in many areas. Mostly, she noticed the thin stream of smoke coming from only one chimney. She rushed inside and found her mother in the parlor lying on the settee, which had been placed closer to the fire, several blankets wrapped around her.

"Mother!" Jane rushed to the pale and shriveled figure. "It's Jane. I've come."

A thin veined hand came out from under the blankets. "Jane, is that you?"

Chad and Lacey had followed her in, and both stood aside while the mother and daughter reunited.

Lacey gave a sniffle. "Oh my!"

"Mind your place," Chad barked.

Coming away from her mother, Jane seethed in anger. "What is this? Why isn't she in her bedroom with a doctor by her side? Where is Charlotte?"

"Jane, please get Charlotte," her mother cried in a soft withered voice.

Chad went to his mother. "We have talked about this, Mother. She had to leave. Rest now. You can visit with Jane once she has settled into her room." Turning to Jane, he addressed her shock. "Don't give me that look, Sister. Where have you been for the past several years? I've been here trying to take care of the business and our mother. Do you think it's been easy for me?" He looked at Lacey. "I will show your secretary the kitchen, and she can tend to Mother while we talk. She's due for her broth."

"Miss Bennett is not your household help. Where is the cook?"

Chad left the room, and Jane and Lacey followed. He led them to the kitchen. The once-spotless, well-run hub of the household looked deserted, with only the warmth of the low flame of the stove. Jane slowly sat down on a stool at the worktable, taking in the room with a heavy heart.

"I can make us tea if you'll tell me where the leaves are," Lacey said.

Jane gave her a captious look but let her help. She got up and quickly showed her where the teas were kept, then joined her brother at the table.

"Tell me what is going on here, Chad."

Her brother squinted at Lacey. Jane knew that look of suspicion.

"Miss Bennett is my secretary and confidant. Now tell me, what is the reason for this state of affairs?"

He rubbed his beard and took a sharp breath. To Jane's dismay, she thought he was about to break down. Then he composed himself and looked at his hands as they smoothed the edge of the table.

"It's your fault. I didn't have your part of the monies to keep the business running as it should have been run. I made a few hasty investments, as I needed the cash to pay for the expenses, and . . . well, they turned out to be the downfall of me. Mother's illness didn't help. The doctor and hospital bills added up quickly. Martin agreed he'd help, but I had to take matters into my own hands."

Jane stared at him in disbelief. So, Martin and Chad had made a deal. "Martin didn't mention any of this to me. He agreed to help? How? And what about Mother's own inheritance from her family and what Father left to her?"

"Gone. Like I said, her sick bills had to be paid."

She remembered her brother's penchant for gambling and women. Had he spent his fortune so recklessly? And what investments? Her mother was her greater concern.

"Chadwick, how could you have done this to her?"

He pounded his fist on the hard wooden table, sending a jolt through Jane. Lacey squealed, and the china cups rattled in her hands.

"You!" he shouted at her. "It was your selfishness that brought us to this lowly state. You and Martin should have stayed to help run things and help our mother. The store downtown was Martin's to have. But no! Both of you are to blame, but I blame you the most for your high-minded stubbornness. Thank God I put in place what I had to, or we'd be sitting in the poorhouse!"

Jane's hands dropped into her lap. "Why didn't you wire me? I would have paid for Mother's bills. What do you mean by putting in place what you had to? What have you done? I demand to know!"

He stuck out his chin. "Father knew better, and so did Martin when he agreed."

"Chadwick, what did he agree to?"

"Never mind. It's over your head, and I have my pride."

He was talking like a madman. It roused more of her anger.

"How proud are you now to see your mother huddled by the parlor fire?" Jane stood, nearly shaking with anger. "And to blame this"—she opened her arms in appraisal of it all—"on me? How dare you, Brother!"

His hand came up to strike her, and if she hadn't been swift enough to back away, it would have caught her hard on the face.

Lacey let out a scream. Chad cupped his flushed mouth and drew back.

Jane stood frozen in place, her hand to her chest, the tears coming swiftly down her face. Lacey rushed to her side.

She patted Lacey's hand, which had come up to embrace her. "I'll be fine, Lace," she said, breathing heavily. "Get us that tea and let us settle down." She looked at her brother as she spoke and sat with caution.

The tea was soothing to Jane. She let the sweet aroma remind her of better days. Chad continued hesitantly but unapologetically.

"While you were traveling here, I had the attorney, Shipman, make arrangements to finalize the future estate plan. Martin and I came to an agreement. Your inheritance is mine. I can't wait any longer. We made a deal."

"What?" Jane felt the bile rise within her. The rush of clarity nearly knocked her over. Her husband had made a deal with her brother, and it had to do with her money. She rushed to their defense. "My inheritance is my and Martin's future. You can't have it. In spite of what you may have concluded, this was not my fault. I don't care what kind of deal you and Martin had. You said so yourself, you invested unwisely. You'll have to sell off some of the shares in the business. Take your profit to pay your debts and keep the stores running. The other stores aren't as big as the one downtown, but they might help restore some of the losses."

Again, Chad rubbed his beard, and Jane's heart sank.

"How many shares are left, Chadwick? How many stores?"

"A few. I have already taken your prescribed course of action. It hasn't helped."

"Oh, dear God." She placed her elbows on the table and clasped her hands to her mouth. "Father . . ."

If he knew what his dear son has done, what would he think of him? The empire our father was building, the future of expansion he had in mind. What would he think of me, running away from the business to some farm out West? Her perspective was altered, as she sat in the kitchen of the home she'd grown up in. What had she done?

"The lawyer has deferred your future endowments to the Wallingford estate. The money will go to pay off debts and start anew. I know I can bring it back. You will reap these benefits as a shareholder. I've already consulted with a new mine in South Africa. Their diamonds and other precious stones are less costly. We can recoup if we—"

Jane raised her hand to stop his tirade. "No, Chad. Father only bought diamonds and jewels that came from the most reputable mines in Brazil and India. How do you know what you're dealing with in South Africa? You cannot do this."

Chad let out a sharp laugh. "You are so naïve, dear sister. Do you think our father didn't deal with every company he could and become rich from some of the less desirable mines? Silver and gold and diamonds for the taking, no matter where they come from. This is the reality of business."

A silence engulfed the room. Icy rain pelted the dirty panes of glass high above the kitchen walls. Her father had dealt in unscrupulous business? No, it wasn't possible.

"I will speak to Mr. Shipman tomorrow," she said. "I don't think my inheritance can easily be deferred. Martin assured me he looked into it before we left. It's beyond your control."

"It's done, Jane. Martin and I had Mr. Shipman alter Father's will. I told you he gave me full charge of the finances. It's in his will, or were you only paying attention to your own money? Martin owes me. I gave him a chance to prove himself, but now I want my money."

Jane was shocked and confused.

Chad continued. "But go cry to Shipman if you wish. It's time you grew up and faced the fact that no one is going to give you everything with a little pout of your pretty lips or a conniving tilt of your richly adorned head. It's time to take responsibility for what you've done."

The acidity in his voice alarmed her. What had Martin agreed to? What was left of her money? Her monthly inheritance covered the expenses that the farm didn't cover and much more. She needed to see the accounts for herself. What would life be like if they actually had to rely on the farm's revenue?

Overwhelmed and exhausted, she took her teacup to the sink, rinsed it, and laid it on the sideboard to dry. She knew it would still be there tomorrow when she came down to breakfast, where there would be no cooked eggs, muffins, or other delights waiting for her as in the days when the family fortune had been well taken care of.

How did Father not see to securing my future?

"I will go to my room now," she said. "Tomorrow I will find out what this is all about. For now, I must insist you send for food, firewood, and coal. I will pay for it."

"Whatever you say, dear sister." His tone was full of scorn.

"Lacey, you will stay in the room directly left off the landing."

Lacey took her leave. Before climbing the stairs to her bedroom, Jane went into the drafty parlor. She looked down at her sleeping mother and brought the blankets around her in a cocoon.

Her poor mother—Elisha Wallingford, wealthy socialite. What had happened to her? Where was the priest who had always helped her through her troubles? Where were the friends in high places who could rescue her?

Jane wanted to sob in grief but couldn't find the strength, and it worried her heart. She would send Wallace for the doctor first thing in the morning. Her mother's labored breathing told Jane it wouldn't be long before her body succumbed to the illness plaguing her. She thought about her garden and medicinal herbs. The mixture she used to calm her and Martin's colds and other minor ailments had worked. When Harry had burned his hand, she had used a poultice of soothing calendula, lavender oil, and stinging nettles to help the pain. None of these remedies would be useful to her mother now.

She kissed her mother's warm, moist forehead and left the room. Homesick for her own bed and lonely for Harry's quick wit and playful teasing, she climbed the cold staircase. In her room, she felt little comfort. This home was no longer hers, and she felt completely removed from it. Then she realized that it wasn't the house she had been hard-pressed to leave; it was the people in it. Charlotte and Wallace, the gardener, the cook, her father and mother, Chad as his younger self, the families who visited, her friends, her job at the store, her friends at the paper. All of these things had filled her life and the house with activity and a sense of purpose.

There was none of it left.

She felt unsettled in the ghostliness of this once-fine estate. It was the people back in Clermont City and San Francisco who had allowed her to find contentment there. The land and her gardens too, not to mention her growing love for Harry. She felt an acute stab of loneliness. She had a home, and this was not it.

Back to her sudden financial predicament, she chided herself for not having been more forceful with Martin in letting her look at the financial books. She wouldn't lose the lifestyle she had created. Her money had kept them from becoming desperately poor on Cabot Farm.

Then a thought struck her.

Her jewels!

CHAPTER TWENTY-SIX

$\mathcal{T}$HE FOLLOWING MORNING, JANE HAD WALLACE BRING THE carriage around. She settled in and wrapped the woolen blanket around the lower half of her body, then stuck her gloved hands under the cover. She reminded Wallace to get more coal for the kitchen and wood for the fireplaces. "And for God's sake, get a foot warmer in this carriage!" She handed him a sum of cash for her comfort and additional money for food, then added an amount in for his back wages. She would have to get Martin to wire her more money.

She had left the doctor and Lacey with her mother. Chad had been gone when she came downstairs to breakfast—what of it there was. A few eggs and a loaf of bread was all Lacey could find. Jane had searched the cabinets. Other than several cans of beans and pork, she saw no stores for the winter months. Apparently, the grocer's man hadn't been around for quite some time. What had her mother been living on? She'd have to make sure the pantry was well stocked before she left.

After she'd paid the doctor the balance owed, he'd administered what Elisha needed. He told Jane in private her mother was not long for this world, adding he could have been more helpful to his patient had he been allowed to take care of her earlier on before the cancer had progressed to this state.

"She should be in the hospital under the care of doctors and nurses, Mrs. Cabot."

"Yes, I know. I will do what I can while I'm here."

Jane was enraged. Her brother hadn't taken care of their mother as he'd promised, and now she lay dying. She calmed her emotions and continued with the doctor.

"I am grateful, madam, to be able to help her now," he said as he pocketed the envelope of cash. "I'm afraid your brother has not kept me abreast of her situation. I have come to call several times, but I've not been allowed in to treat her. Then when he didn't pay his bills, I had no choice. I am not a charity."

Jane had to bite her lip from admonishing him for his lack of compassion. Had he forgotten how many hours she and her mother had volunteered at the charities he was the chairman of? How much money had the Wallingford family generously given to help the medical institute he was deeply involved in?

"I understand," was all she could say.

Alone in the carriage, she finally let the tears of grief escape her body. She shuddered with emotion. The ride to Wallingford Jewelers had her deep in thought about the consequences of her brother's actions. There had to be something she could do.

Focusing her attention, she exited the carriage and looked around. The square was bustling with activity. She inhaled the smell of the city in its late autumn clothes. The trees were alight with color, and a slight dusting of snow had gathered in places the sun hadn't reached yet—a sign of the winter to come. The familiarity nearly brought her to tears again, and memories flooded back.

Her father showing her the new store when she was young, his pride and joy bubbling over as his broad smile found hers and she took his hand. He clenched it in his large one, and she felt she was a part of him and their future. The warmth of a sunny day when she and Martin had lunch on the back stoop and gave each other longing stares. Catching up with friends as they all made their way to the shops and soda fountain. A sense of ownership of their city.

When a cold wind blew directly at her, she was taken out of her thoughts. As she turned to enter the jewelry store, she heard a woman call her name. The voice was quite familiar.

Sadie rushed to her side, a ripple of blue woolen skirt below a fine fitted overcoat fluttering around her with a fur muff hanging from her wrist. Her expression was full of curiosity.

"Hello, Sadie."

They gave each other a quick embrace.

"My lord, Jane! It's good to see you. How long have you been in town?"

"Not long. My mother is ill, and I came to see what I could do."

Sadie took her hand, and Jane felt the expensive materials of their gloves meeting in an awkward clutch.

"I'm so sorry. Is it really as bad as I've heard?"

Jane nodded. "I'm afraid so." Then she impulsively asked, "What else have you heard, Sadie?" Jane was almost embarrassed by her lack of communication with her Cincinnati friend. Sadie had written a few times, and she had responded, but that was the extent of their correspondence. Both women, Jane figured, had busy lives.

Sadie brought the back of her hand to her chin. "I . . . Well, Jane, there have been rumors, but I don't want to burden you with them, and besides, here we are together! We really must have tea while you're here. Leonard is out of town on business, but you must meet my two little boys and see our house on Rutherford Avenue. It really is the *jewel* of the city." Sadie laughed at her quip. Jane caught the reference and smiled.

"Oh, Jane, it really is good to see you."

"It's good to see you too, Sadie." Jane had to admit, her friend looked well and had a glow about her. She wondered what she herself reflected. Her own apparel was suited for the city, but had the farm taken a toll on her looks?

To her relief, Sadie commented, "You're still as beautiful as ever." Then she asked, "How long will you be in town for?"

"I'm not sure. Not long, I think. It's so busy back home with the farm and all." She cringed at her misstep. She wanted to add that she was part of the social scene in San Francisco and that her house was the talk of her little town, but Sadie gave her no chance to speak.

"Oh! So, you still live on a farm? I thought perhaps you would be able to talk Martin out of it. A sheep farm, as I recall? My dear, I'm glad I wasn't as adventurous as you. When will his appetite for the farm end? I thought you two would be back by now."

"It's quite nice actually. We enjoy the fine weather, and the society is good. I've made the house a grand country estate. I daresay the whole experience has grown on me, and I contribute a great deal to it." Jane suddenly realized that for once she had been truthful about her life on the farm. She quietly let the revelation take up residence in her. *Yes, it has grown on me, and I do contribute a great deal.*

"How interesting," Sadie replied.

It was obvious Sadie was being polite and had no point of reference to her life out West.

"I really must be going, Sadie. I have business to attend to."

Sadie shook her head, her curled blond fringe bouncing on her forehead under the fur-edged bonnet. "I'm sorry to hear about your brother's downfall."

It was tempting to agree with Sadie and find solace in a friend she had once had no secrets with, but Jane was upset with her brother's obvious misfortune. "It is his business now, not mine."

"And he's done a terrible job of it, I must say. Leonard tried to help him, but the drinking and gambling and . . . the rest have made him impossible to help. I want you to know we tried, Jane."

Taken with the sincerity of Sadie's comments, Jane warmed. "Thank you, Sadie."

Sadie bowed her chin, acknowledging what was due to her. "Besides," she continued in a lowered voice, "we invested in his new business. He named it Wallingford Diamond Enterprise, and we just about sank from it. Leonard refused to tell me the details, but I gathered the diamond mine in Africa was illegal and fraught with all kinds of trouble and even quite dangerous." Sadie leaned in and in a low voice added, "And children were being exploited. Now, rumor has it, Chad's looking at another in South Africa." She stood back and let out a puff of air, relaxing her shoulders. Then, in a regular tone, she added, "We recouped our losses though, thank God. My father was furious. We have our reputation to uphold, not to mention our standard of living. I hear many did not fare so well, and some are even going to jail. Serves them right. We pray your brother is not one of them. It's a good thing you live where you do after all, Jane. How would you endure the shame and humiliation?"

Gooseflesh ran up Jane's arms, and she was sickened by Sadie's revelations.

"I'm sorry, Jane. Truly I am."

"Thank you for the information, Sadie. I'm glad you were able to restore your lifestyle. If you'll excuse me, I really must run. It was good to see you."

"Jane, we really tried."

Jane placed her hand on Sadie's arm. "I know you did. Goodbye, Sadie."

Opening the door to Wallingford Jewelers, Jane was hit with a rush of stale air, and it gave her a flash of heat that rose from her stockinged legs to her head. She fanned herself, taking in a shaky breath.

Sadie's information was a lot to take in. It felt like teatime gossip, but it was her own family. She thanked herself for not arranging to get together with her friend—a friend now relegated to the past. What the two of them had once had in common seemed a lifetime away. Had she herself been so self-involved? Was she still? Jane was missing her farm even more. It was not just a feeling of wanting to be in her home, but a genuine longing and loneliness.

Looking around the store, she got a sense of scarcity. The shelves were not as full, the décor not updated to the latest style of presenting a simpler and more elegant display. There was so much old fabric and lace, and only three clerk girls behind three glass cases with the remaining store unattended. Half a dozen patrons roamed around, and Jane saw a lack of excitement on their faces. The air itself felt unwelcoming and a bit chilly, which was unheard of at this time of year, when her father had made sure their clients were as comfortable as possible. It was worse than she'd thought.

"Mrs. Cabot? Is that you?"

Mr. McMann stood above her. He looked thinner than the last time she'd seen him.

"Hello, Mr. McMann. I'm in town to see my mother. As you must know, she is ailing."

Mr. McMann's expression was pensive. "Yes, bad luck that is," he said.

"How is business, Mr. McMann? And please tell me honestly. The store looks rather . . . unwell."

He looked around, then took her aside, away from the patrons and workers. "Honestly?" He raised his furry brows.

"Please."

"Your brother is about to lose the store. That is as honest as I can make it, madam. I'm leaving at the end of this month. I'm going to Cleveland to work at my brother's clothing mercantile. That is how bad it is for me. My wife and I lost our savings in your brother's diamond business, and I can't continue to work for him

214

and stay true to my convictions. He swears he has new resources to draw on, but my wife and I just can't take any more chances. I don't know why I invested in the first place, but as you know, your brother can be very charming and persuasive. I also know that this is the last store to go. He sold the other five."

His reddened face told her this was difficult for him. He took out his handkerchief and patted his brow.

Jane couldn't comprehend what she was hearing. All the stores but one had been sold? She stared at Mr. McMann.

"Yes, I can see you are in disbelief. I have the accounting records in the back if you'd like to go over them. He did make a profit on the other sales, but, my dear, I don't know where that money went. It surely isn't here." He looked around and shook his head.

"I'm so very sorry, Mr. McMann. How terrible for you. I don't know what to say, only that I had no idea my brother was involved in such a shady enterprise."

"No, I suppose you couldn't have known, living so far away. But, if I may be so bold, had he not told you anything? Were you not asked to contribute?"

She shook her head. Then a thought came to her.

Her inheritance. Was that the new source of money?

There was little time to waste; she had to get to Mr. Shipman's office. As she gave a quick glance around the store, she noticed the glass case where Martin had placed his hand on hers when they were still newly in love. It was nearly empty, and what was there seemed of a lesser quality than what her father had once sold.

"We sell a lot of what they call costume jewelry," Mr. McMann said. "It's not the real thing. Mr. Wallingford has no more credit with the jewelers we once purchased from."

"I see. Oh dear, it's worse than I thought. Please excuse me, Mr. McMann. I must get to the bottom of this. I wish you good luck."

"Good luck to you as well. It seems the Wallingford name has fallen into the gutter and shall never return to its former glory."

She left the store, and the sting of his words hit her hard as a sharp wind lashed her face. She hurried back to the carriage, where Wallace waited patiently. He helped her in.

"The offices of Shipman and Shipman, please," she instructed.

JANE'S FACE TINGLED AS IT thawed in Mr. Shipman's warm waiting room.

At least someone can afford the heating bill.

Her anxiety mounted. From the look of the room, the law firm had suffered none of her brother's misfortune. Wallingford was one of Shipman and Shipman's wealthier clients. The richly appointed area was a clue to their ongoing prosperity. Deep-brown leather chairs sat on either side of the matching couch. Polished walnut side tables held large hand-painted lamps crafted from blown glass. The handwoven wool rug, Jane knew, was from Turkey.

A moment later, Mr. Shipman's secretary escorted her into his office, then on leaving closed the door. His office was of a high standard featuring the same décor as the waiting room. He sat behind his broad wooden desk and shuffled a few papers, then set them aside.

"Good day, Janey. How good it is to see you back in the city. And back in the family fold, or just a visit?"

She stared at him as her anger rose. His syrupy, condescending tone was not to be tolerated today.

"You know very well why I'm here, Mr. Shipman. And I will be addressed as Mrs. Cabot. I am no longer the little girl you liked to pat on the head."

The red flush on his face ran up into his balding scalp.

"I have been informed of my inheritance being taken from me due to a deal my brother and husband made with you. Is this correct?"

"Why, *Mrs. Cabot*, I had the utmost respect for your father, but to leave you with the full responsibility of such a large sum of money when your brother had undertaken the burden of your father's business . . . What they did was prudent, to say the least." He breathed in as he looked her over. "Your tastes are well-known to your brother and husband, and I hear you live in great style, albeit on a farm."

"It's none of anyone's business how I live or what I spend. My beloved father granted me that money. Now, tell me about this deal."

Mr. Shipman cleared his throat and clasped his hands on his desk. "As the attorney representing the family's interests, I—"

"How much do I have left?"

"Any of the farm debts will be paid up to present. As of December 1, your full monthly funds will abate to the amount of twenty-five dollars. Your brother isn't, after all, so unfeeling as to leave you completely out in the cold. The remainder of your inheritance will be deposited into his account. Your husband owes him the amount he was loaned from your dowry, but we can negotiate the interest Chadwick asked for."

"Twenty-five dollars?" She was astounded he could tell her that with a straight face. It was a mere stipend. Then it hit her. "Martin made a deal to give my dowry back to Chadwick? With interest?"

"Yes, the money from your dowry was a sort of loan. Mr. Cabot agreed to pay it back with 5 percent interest."

Damn it, Martin! How could you be so naïve? And to go behind my back!

She twisted her gloves in her hands.

"Please, Mrs. Cabot, have a seat. I see this is all very upsetting to you. May I have my secretary get you a cup of tea?"

"No, thank you. Tell me more about this deal."

"Indeed. It was agreed by your husband and brother to let you receive the previous amount for three years, letting you establish your enterprise. Given the state of affairs with the estate, however, Chadwick is keen to complete this business. The time has come to fulfill that agreement and also to have the remaining balance of your inheritance revert to your brother. I believe that's a sum of over $35,000. My, you have spent a good amount of it. I hope you have invested it wisely, my dear. Apparently, Mr. Cabot had great confidence in his farm. Three years is quite generous. I must agree with your brother in his efforts to save the business that brought about such wealth in the first place. Now, whatever resources you have in your property, furniture, and personal belongings will legally remain yours as long as you remain *Mrs.* Cabot."

Jane paced the office, nearly speechless, and when she found her voice, she didn't hold back. She stopped in front of Mr. Shipman.

"You advised my husband and brother to do this? What is your cut in this deal? Why was I not a part of it? Why? How could he take away what my father clearly gave to me?"

Mr. Shipman drew in his chin. "I was employed to do a service. Your father named your brother as the final authority concerning the business and the inheritance. I thought you knew that, Mrs. Cabot. I was going to contact you with the final figures, but since you are here, let me get them for you. Excuse me."

He left his office. Her thoughts spun in so many directions she felt the room tilt. Martin's unwavering belief in the prosperity of the farm may be their undoing. Most of all, she felt a sharp jab of betrayal. Her husband had found it necessary to hide something so important from her. A bond had been broken, and with it her heart. How could she face him without scorn? How would she ever love and trust him again? He'd gambled all her money on a sheep farm. Was that any better than her brother gambling on a shady diamond mine?

"Mrs. Cabot?"

She looked up and realized Mr. Shipman had come back into the room with the folder.

"What happened to the money from the sales of the other stores?" she asked.

His lips formed a line, and he scratched his head. "Now, that is a good question. I wrote the banknotes to your brother, and he cashed them. I fear he might have invested badly. I know nothing about it."

She took the folder from him and noticed his hand on her elbow. He was ready to have this meeting come to an end.

"Let me know if you have any questions," he said as he escorted her out of his office. "Some of the legalities might be a bit confusing."

"Yes, I will look them over."

"Very well. Good day, Mrs. Cabot. Give your mother my heartfelt wishes for a speedy recovery."

Jane faced the lawyer. "There is one more thing."

"Yes, madam, anything."

"Do you hold the key to the safe box my family has at the bank? I remember hearing my father talk to you about keeping them at your office."

Mr. Shipman smiled. "You were always one to keep your ears and eyes open wide. Yes, I have them."

"Before I left, I stored a few precious items in there. Now that I have a home, I would like to retrieve them."

"Very well. Are your husband and brother privy to your actions?"

She looked at him with imploring eyes. "Please, Mr. Shipman. A few baubles and some sentimental trinkets are all I want. Something from my childhood home to make my new house seem, well, cozy and familiar."

Mr. Shipman rubbed the back of his neck. "Oh, very well. I can't deny you this after the shock I feel I've placed on you. I am sorry, Mrs. Cabot . . . Jane. I hope you don't blame me for doing my job as I saw fit. Please let this be our little secret. I don't want to face your brother's wrath."

"Yes, of course." Jane saw the sincerity on his face. Perhaps her anger was misguided. Chad was the true villain in all this. And what about Martin's role? Once she got hold of her jewels, she would keep them safely hidden.

THE BANK MANAGER TOOK OUT the large safe box and placed it in a private room.

"Thank you," Jane said, then turned to retrieve what was hers and hers alone. She knew the worth better than most. It would keep them solvent for many years to come.

She turned the key and lifted the heavy lid to find envelopes—lots of them. She looked them over. Sales receipts, transaction documents, overdue notices, foreclosure warnings—a trail of her brother's mishandling of the business. Lifting the pile and searching the corners of the box, she found nothing more.

Her breathing became shallow, and she sat down on the one chair in the windowless room. The air was thick, and her head swirled.

Oh, not this, Chad. These most private of possessions. The diamond-and-emerald brooch her father had given her for graduating from the all-girl school. That day, he'd beamed with pride. The heart-shaped ruby necklace her parents had given her on her coming-out. The pearls, the rings, the bracelets and hatpins, all worth a small fortune, all gone.

It was as if a thief had come into her bedroom and stolen from her without a sound. The depth of betrayal made her physically sick. She took in several breaths. Returning to the lobby, she handed the key back to the manager. "Please return this to Shipman and Shipman," she said and slowly walked back to the carriage.

What was she going to do? How could she face this sudden loss of income and Martin's betrayal?

Another thought pressed her heart. Her mother needed to go into the hospital. Would it be in the paupers' wing?

CHAPTER TWENTY-SEVEN

"IT'S ALL FOR THE BEST, SISTER," CHAD STATED AS JANE WAS about to depart for the train station. Lacey was already in the carriage, and Wallace had secured the last of their luggage onto the back of it. "You'll see, Wallingford Jewelers will once again achieve the high standards we are known for. You are a shareholder now. Does that not feel grand?"

His breath stank of gin and tobacco, and his hand waved about in exaggerated expression. His flushed cheeks and glassy eyes gave her a deep feeling of dread.

How would she be able to get out of this shareholder business? She could lose even the twenty-five dollars a month if another of his deals were to sour. Although it was a scant amount of what she had once received, if it were gone too, she would have nothing but hard labor. There would be no more jolly visits across the bay or experiments with plants and seeds. Now that her jewels were gone, she had nothing to fall back on.

Confronting him on his thievery of her jewels had been a waste of time.

"I did it for the company! It was the least you could contribute. Why do you need such things on a farm anyway?"

It only proved to her how far her brother would go to sustain his dirty lifestyle and feed his drinking. Only her dresses, furs, and adornments remained, but after close inspection, she realized they had been rifled through and not returned to their original packing. The dank attic smell, along with the moths and mold, had tainted their once-glorious appearance.

"Of course, the shares are in Martin's name," Chad continued with less bravado. "But they are as if you own them too. You are one with your husband."

Jane could only agree as she pulled the satin gloves up her arms and donned her coat. For days she had listened to how her inheritance would make them all rich.

Her concerns about her mother's hospital stay had been cut short when Elisha died in the night. Jane had listened to the priest give her mother the last rites with a grief she recognized from the loss of her father. It was deeply painful. The funeral and burial were held quickly and quietly with a few of her mother's friends standing at the gravesite on the cold November day. The plot would have only a small stone, but Elisha would be buried next to her husband as had been arranged many years ago. Chad, Jane thought, couldn't have sold that at least.

SITTING ON THE TRAIN FOR long hours, Jane watched the scenery pass by and contemplated what to do. Her brother had stripped her of her wealth. She may have to sell off some of the artwork and what jewelry she had acquired in the past few years. Her investments were all in the house and furnishings. She had spared no cost in them. How could she not have invested more wisely? She would have to run the farm accounts no matter what Martin said.

He had lost all credibility with her now.

Perhaps she would push her concoctions with more purpose. Jane had made some well-known remedies already, and Clarence and Gladys had welcomed them into the general store. More research would be needed in running a profitable business. The thought nudged her melancholy away.

Lacey took notes when Jane's ideas became too big to contain. Jane drew maps of Cabot Farm, marking where to place more gardens. The enlarged stillroom would take on more duties, as well as the conservatory.

What to do about Martin and his deal with her brother still confounded her. She was angered by his betrayal and deception and felt less guilty for her feelings toward Harry, which were still hidden deep in her heart. Frightened and feeling desperately alone, she continued with as much courage as she could muster in finding a way to make this work.

With her head swirling with new ideas and profound losses, she finally gave in to the steady sway of the train and allowed herself to be lulled into sleep.

THE CONDUCTOR'S VOICE ANNOUNCED THEIR arrival at the Oakland station. Being home brought Jane's tangled feelings to the surface. She took in a ragged breath and let it out. Lacey gathered their belongings and looked out the window.

"I'll be right happy to be back in Clermont City," Lacey said. "You sure don't know what you have 'til you get away from it."

Her friend's words rang true. "I've been remiss in telling you how grateful I am for your friendship and service, Lace. I only wish I could give you a raise, but unfortunately, I might have to reduce your pay. I found out—"

"Let's talk about all that later." Lacey looked thoughtful. "I'm not going anywhere for now."

Jane took Lacey's hand in hers. "Thank you."

Lacey winked as she handed Jane her satchel. "I can't wait to get my teeth into some of my mama's home cooking. I'll be off as soon as we reach town if that's all right with you."

"Of course it is."

The coach ride back to Clermont City had Lacey dozing. Jane's nervous energy wouldn't let her rest, for she had much to deal with.

Martin came rushing up to her, and she let him embrace her tired body. Her own thoughts and feelings were not as welcoming toward him. He seemed to notice.

"Tired?" he asked. "I'm sure it's been grueling. Let's go home, and we can talk over supper. Bell has outdone herself for you."

Jane let the excuse of tiredness suffice. In fact, she was exhausted, and facing Martin with the truth would take strength.

That night at dinner, she enjoyed lamb stewed in fresh tomatoes, along with potatoes from her garden. The creamy butter she smothered them with had come from their own cows. This food had never tasted so good.

Back in Cincinnati, Wallace had somewhat stocked the kitchen, mostly with canned goods, and the meat had been questionable. Winter was never a good time for fresh fruit and vegetables or high-grade meats in that part of the country for those who couldn't afford them. Jane knew her brother would certainly refresh his household once he had the rest of her inheritance. Would that remove the stain from him? She doubted it. The fact that her money was going to finance his careless lifestyle remained like a shard of glass between her toes.

She gave a huff of annoyance. Keeping her anger to herself while she was in Cincinnati had nearly brought her to sickness, but she hadn't the stomach for her brother's excuses, and she feared his temper.

"Are you all right, Jane?" Martin asked between bites. "I'm sure it must have been difficult. May your mother rest in peace."

"I'm sorry. Can we talk after dinner? This is too delicious to spoil with conversation."

Cutting another piece of lamb, Martin nodded and continued to eat.

They sat in the parlor having tea and cake. Jane looked around. Her once-stable existence was threatened. Her plans to meet with Berta in the city after she came home were tainted. She couldn't and wouldn't reveal to anyone what her financial state of affairs was. She decided she would toil over the farm accounts to keep it afloat, then relish the generosity of others in the city where she was established as a wealthy woman, and so she need not pay for anything.

No longer able to keep her anger at bay, Jane faced her husband.

"Martin, why did you make a deal with Chad to steal my inheritance?"

Martin leaned forward as he choked on his bite of cake and sip of tea. She watched unflinchingly.

After coughing into a napkin and taking more tea, he wiped his watering eyes and looked at her. His sheepish expression maddened her.

"I thought you would find out sooner or later," he confessed. "I had no intention of letting myself fail."

"So, you did make a deal? And did you know that he has made good on it? We owe him the money you borrowed on my dowry. The three years ends December 1st. I'm to receive a mere twenty-five dollars a month and have none of my inheritance left but for that piddly amount."

Her anger grew as she gripped her china cup with both hands. She laid it on the table for fear it would burst. "It's over. We have nothing but the property and livestock going into a new year! He's taken nearly it all! And my jewelry! How could you do this?" Her voice was at a fevered pitch.

As if he had been hit, Martin shot back, "The property is no small thing. And . . . And all this," he said, making a sweeping gesture of the room they sat in. "Truly, what more could we ask for? I certainly didn't need all this frippery to be happy. Damn that Chad for being so dishonest, but Jane, we have the opportunity to truly be independent! What do you need with all that pomp and pretention? This is our life."

Her anger couldn't deal with reason. He had no idea what she would be giving up.

"If I had known you thought of life in such simple terms . . . I would have reconsidered your proposal."

"Jane, please don't talk that way. You knew how I felt about society, but I saw something real in you. Look at who you are now. Independent. Starting your own business. You wanted a life filled with meaning, filled with horticulture. By God, you have it! Leaving Cincinnati was the best thing that could've happened to you, to me. The farm will support us now, not your brother or father."

His words rang true, and she felt she had accomplished much, yet she faced a life of poverty. It was fine to work hard knowing you didn't have to; it was another thing to have to toil day and night to feed and house yourself.

"You don't understand!" She leapt to her feet and stormed out of the room and up the stairs. Martin followed her.

"Jane, for God's sake! I did it for us. I couldn't buy the land without your dowry, and Chad wouldn't let me have it unless I agreed to pay it back. I didn't know he'd—"

Slamming the door to their bedroom, she threw herself onto the bed and gave in to a crying fit. Every bitter tear stung her face.

Never in her life had she felt so miserable and alone. Martin had betrayed her, and he thought it was for her own good. Her heart was broken. She expected such actions from her brother, but not her husband.

She pounded her fist on the pillow. Her trust in Martin was gone, and in only weeks, their financial situation would be drastically changed. Where would she go from here? She felt adrift in a turbulent sea.

Chapter Twenty-Eight

December 1883

The sight of Harry's flatbed coming into her courtyard turned Jane's legs to jelly, and a flash of heat accosted her
heart. It had been a week since her return from Cincinnati. Why
had he stayed away? She stepped onto her large white porch. Martin was conveniently in one of the fields with Jason. Harry's timing
was impeccable.

"Hello, Jane," he said with a broad smile.

"Hello, Harry. It's good to see you." She felt a rush of excitement. She led him to the parlor. "I'll have Margie tell Bell to fix us
a small cart."

Harry chuckled behind her. "Oh my, I see we've been in the city
too long. A cart? I'll just take a cup of coffee if it's made."

She cringed. He'd been in her company for two seconds and
was already teasing her. Today she was in no mood. "Oh, damn it,
Harry. I was just being polite."

He laughed hard and grabbed her arm. "I'm sorry," he said sincerely. "You get that cart, and we'll see what's on it. I had a poor man's breakfast this morning: leftover biscuits and gravy. I need a cook or a wife."

"Never mind," she said. The mention of him having a wife stirred up her jealousy.

His brown eyes had that sparkle of mischief in them, and she melted. He came in close and whispered, "I missed you."

Margie was in the room, and Jane gave her the instruction for coffee, adding to place a piece of Danish alongside it.

"Or is the Danish too city-like for you, Harry Cabot?" she asked. His smile at her quip was intoxicating.

"We don't have any more Danish, but Bell made some raisin scones this morning," said Margie.

"That will do just fine. Thank you," Harry said.

Margie clucked her tongue and retreated to the kitchen.

Jane waited for Margie to leave. "Sit, Harry. Martin tells me you're as busy as ever. How goes the farm?" She sat down opposite him and arranged her skirt, swiping at nothing in particular. The blue dress she wore flowed naturally around her.

Harry crossed his long legs, placing his arms casually on his lap. The sight of him was like a delicious dessert after eating sour vegetables.

"I'm fine, but how are you, Jane? I spoke to Martin—or rather he spoke to me—about your inheritance. I'm sorry. Martin never was one for having great foresight. I had confidence he could make a go at this, and he's done well in my opinion. Or at least he's giving it all he has. I know a lot of its prosperity came from your money. It will be interesting to see how it goes without it. A challenge. Are you up for that, Mrs. Cabot?"

Abashed that Martin had confided in him with such detail, Jane wanted to lash out at her husband. She had not expected to be left in the dark as her mother had been with her father's finances. Harry knew her state of affairs, and she felt deeply vulnerable, though she couldn't figure out why. Whatever it was had eroded her pride. Her next thought was, *This is a tragedy that neither men seem to recognize.*

"Are you trying to make me feel better or worse?" she asked. "Martin didn't think I was important enough to tell me what was going on."

Harry uncrossed his legs, and leaning forward, he placed his elbows on his knees and clasped his hands. "Jane, I know it's a bad deal. I wish Martin treated you better. He was probably embarrassed to tell you. I would never leave you in the dark like that. Trust is what marriage is all about."

A flicker of lightness engulfed her, but she trusted no one today. She managed a smile. Harry looked at her, not leaving her eyes.

"I wish I could make this better for you." He took in a breath. "I can't. I see how you wanted your life to be. I've been to Cincinnati and saw from afar where the rich lived, how it was for them. It would be hard to give that up, for some. Martin didn't know that life. This farm suits him just fine." He scratched his chin. "Why didn't you marry a rich man, my dear?"

Wiping her nose, Jane didn't know what to say. Was she to blame for her own predicament?

He continued. "It's true, Martin doesn't have an innate skill for this. Some things you just can't teach. But hard work can go a long way. The other day I saw him bringing in the sheep, and he nearly landed them in my pasture again. His herding dog was as confounded as I was, but he worked with her, and by God, they got them right. If not for Jason, well . . . It's good he has him. He may just make a success out of this farm. Don't give up on him."

"Yes, of course, but this has shaken my very foundation."

"I know it has. But, to be honest, your foundation was built on someone else's hard work. It looks as if your brother took advantage of that, and you had no way of preventing it. I think I'd rather trust in myself and what I make of a situation without relying on others' generosity."

Jane's heart skipped a beat. The truth of it hit her hard. She had been relying solely on her inheritance. She hadn't thought of it as anything more than her right to have it for the rest of her life. And now it had been taken away without her having any say in it. How naïve she and Martin had been.

Dabbing at her cheeks, she said, "Thank you, Harry, for enlightening me."

He chuckled. "You'll be fine. You have more resources than you realize."

"Thank you for helping Martin. And me," she managed to say.

Harry looked deep into her eyes. The long-hidden feelings she had for him escaped their bonds, and another tear ran down her face. He came over to her, took her by the hand, and gently brought her to stand in front of him. He wiped her cheek with his finger.

"What am I going to do about you, Jane?"

"Do?" she asked with a trembling chest.

"Jesus, I'm not made of stone." He took a step back. "You were gone too long. I thought it would be good for me at first. I'd get you out of my mind. It worked in the opposite way. I couldn't stop thinking of you, damn it!"

"Here's the coffee and scone," Margie said in her loud, gruff voice.

Jane swung around and took the cup and plate from her. She surveyed the housekeeper's expression. What had she heard?

"That will be all. Thank you, Margie."

She turned back to Harry and handed him the refreshment. He seated himself again.

"I missed you too," she whispered.

Harry sipped his coffee and took a bite of the scone. He seemed to relish it. He swallowed and wiped his mouth. She watched him swipe at his whiskered chin. "Let's not start whispering, Mrs. Cabot. There's nothing to hide. We did nothing," he said, then took another bite of the scone. "Hmm, this is better than those hard biscuits."

Jane sat back down, her torso straight and her pride bruised. Romance might not have been in the cards for her. Was every man so matter-of-fact about love? Food seemed to take precedence.

"Yes, Bell is a wonderful cook. You must hire a cook, or as you said, get a wife."

He raised his brow at her statement. "A wife is what you suggest, huh?"

Jane swallowed. "Yes. It's time, Harry."

"Then I will be on the lookout for a fine woman who will cook and clean for me and help with the farm."

He finished his scone, washing it down with another swallow of coffee, then placed the cup and plate on the side table.

"Yes, and love, of course," she added, playing this dangerous game with him.

"I already love a woman," he replied. "I can't do anything about it though, and it kills me."

His words made her catch her breath.

Straightening her head and throwing back her shoulders, she tried to hide her desperation to hear more. "I'm as helpless as you. I have to focus on making a success of this farm. Knowing you are close, well . . . It makes it easy on my heart."

"I know you will make it a success. And I'm not going anywhere, Jane."

She nodded, and her chin wobbled. "I will count on that."

A weighted silence engulfed the room. Harry stood and went to the parlor entrance and slowly closed the French doors. The click of the second one gave the room the privacy they had never shared.

All at once, his hands were in her hair, his lips on hers. Jane felt helpless to resist. She met his passion with her own. They took to the couch, caressing and kissing each other with the urgency of two young lovers. She wanted him completely, and the headiness of this moment in his arms with his warm breath on her neck was like nothing she had ever felt with Martin.

After a long moment of pleasure, they came away breathless. They stared at each other, and then he laughed as he ran his hands through his hair.

"I've been thinking of doing that for a long time now," he said.

She found herself in a girlish giggle. "Me too."

He kissed her again, and when they parted lips, their foreheads met. She closed her eyes, taking in his closeness and knowing this moment could not last. Finally, he stood and offered his hand to her. Taking it, she rose and stood with him.

"What now?" she asked.

He shook his head as he thoughtfully wiped his lips with the tips of his fingers.

"I don't know, Jane. I don't know."

She gave a curt nod. What they had just done had opened up a floodgate she knew she would not be able to contain. Manage, perhaps.

"I do know," she said. "You and me, the farm, Martin. Damn it, I will make it all work." She was still breathing heavily.

He grinned. "I love your take-charge attitude. Underneath all that lace and lady, there's a fighter. I admire that in you."

"And under all that dust and indifference, there's a passion and a softness I look forward to uncovering," she said.

Harry raised a brow and cleared his throat. "I will definitely look forward to that."

They laughed, and soon the moment was over and the doors swung open. They immediately stepped apart.

"Keeping these doors shut doesn't allow for much circulation, Mrs. Cabot. You've said as much yourself," Margie barked.

Jane thought fast. "Margie, Mr. Cabot and I were discussing some business. I would ask you to knock next time before barging into a closed-door room."

Margie lifted her chin. "Pardon me for looking out for the wellness of the house, Mrs. Cabot." She turned on her heel and left, keeping the doors open.

"I'll be off," Harry said. He bowed and took Jane's hand and kissed the back of it.

"Oh, stop teasing!" *But don't stop!*

Raising his head, he winked, and then he left the room. She watched his strong body stride away from her. His sun-kissed brown hair touched the back of his neck, the neck she had just had her mouth on, the body she had pressed herself into with abandonment. The feelings he aroused were true, and nothing had prepared her for this depth of love she felt for another human being. It elated her and frightened her at the same time.

How much longer could she keep this secret from Martin?

CHAPTER TWENTY-NINE

Christmas 1883

THE TOWN WAS FILLED WITH SIGNS OF THE HOLIDAY SEASON. Wreaths of sweet-smelling spruce and eucalyptus hung in many of the store windows, and jingle bells chimed on the doors. Even some of the carriage horses had bells on their bridles. Garland swagged along the sidewalk posts, and candles had been lit in the windows on this moody gray December day. Jane stepped into the general store, where Gladys greeted her and took her list. It was quiet for the moment, and she was the only customer. Jane was glad for that since Gladys could get talking to the other customers, and she needed to get back home and start the Christmas baking. With Bell's help it would be like old times when the two cooked and baked an array of sweets and savories to feast on and sell. Jane was thankful Bell offered to come over for one day. Margie had also been given her notice and Lacey too. The latter being the most grievous. She and Jane vowed to remain friends.

"We just got in the fixin's for Bell's mincemeat pies. The spices smell like Christmas! I hope you'll be selling us a few for the store. They were mighty popular last year," the portly woman chirped.

"You're first on our list," Jane replied.

"By the way, where is Bell? She's usually the one to inspect every item on the list."

"She's buying some gifts at the shops, but she gave me strict instructions to get the finer flour not the coarser one."

"Yes, ma'am!"

They shared a laugh as Gladys scurried around the store collecting the goods. When she returned, she told Jane her beauty and medicinal products had sold well this month and the credit would be taken off her total.

Jane was elated and encouraged. "Thank you, Gladys. I will be making more soon. Meanwhile, I have some with me today. Jane placed her woven basket on the counter and took out several jars. "I just made these."

"Wonderful," Gladys said. "Just in time for Christmas."

While Gladys went over the list of groceries, Jane looked out the store window. She saw Martin was engaged with a few men, likely in conversation about their properties and how to store grain or hay for the winter. There was always some new idea about the job of keeping it dry and rodent free. Harry joined them, and she felt her heart beating in her throat.

My goodness he's handsome! His strong, lean body showed through his heavy cotton coat. She let out a sigh.

"What's that, Jane?" Gladys asked, then followed Jane's gaze. The store owner laughed. "A clutch of men. And they say women are gossips. These men know more than they let on. And Harry Cabot, still a bachelor! What are we going to do about him, Jane? You and Martin must find him a good wife. Do you think he's lonely? He must be."

Suppressing a laugh, Jane thought to herself, *Gladys probably knows what kind of tobacco he likes and his favorite dessert!*

"He looked mighty fine at the Christmas ball last week," Gladys said, then hummed as she continued her task. Coming back with an armful, she placed the items near the register. "Oh, Jane, you should have been there! City Hall was looking its best, and everyone was in their finest."

"I wish I could have, but as you know, Martin and I had the worst colds. I feel I'm just coming around. Last week's dance must have been wonderful. I'm sorry I missed it."

Jane thought of the ball she hadn't attended and her later questions to Harry about whom he'd danced with. It was bad enough that she'd been sick in bed that night, but then to have the sickness of jealousy on top of it had added to her misery.

His answer had been quite diplomatic. "No one caught my eye, and I thought of you the whole time." She'd called him a liar, and he'd kissed her on the mouth. A stolen moment. Many to come if Jane had her way.

By the time Jane left the store, the men had dispersed, and Martin walked up to her. She was still in a dreamy state of emotional unbalance from seeing Harry.

"Did you get everything you needed?" Martin asked as he took the basket from her.

"Um . . . yes. Let me find Bell, and we can head back."

"Harry sends his greetings."

"Oh, how nice of him. Let's go now."

Martin grinned. "Yes, a complete gentleman," he said in jest.

Jane's ears perked up.

"I hear he had quite a bit of refreshments at the ball," Martin said. "And danced with many a young lady. One might have caught his fancy. He's been acting strange lately."

"Is that so? Well . . . I have much to do. Where is Bell?" She walked quickly and with purpose to find the cook and go home, where she could unravel her thoughts and feelings by herself.

THE CONSERVATORY WAS WARM, AND the winter light beamed in through the large panes of glass. Jane sat on the wooden bench by one of the potting tables, surveying the plants and trays waiting for spring. The bright orange and red flowers on the brickellbush were still blooming, and she would arrange them among the greenery she'd foraged from the land to decorate the house with. Their vanilla scent made her crave Bell's almond vanilla cookies.

Her thoughts turned to Harry. Was the hurt of loving him worth it? The pain Martin would feel made her sad. He didn't deserve such betrayal. Did it match her feeling of betrayal from his actions? She wasn't sure it did. A thought kept emerging: she needed to begin detaching herself from Harry. She would throw herself into her business. The list of products she wanted to sell was growing. It was madness to feel this way toward her husband's cousin. But he wasn't just Martin's cousin; he was a man, the man she had fallen completely in love with.

She'd told Harry she would manage it all, but could she?

Lifting herself from the bench, she walked back to the house, where Martin and supper waited. Another day, another evening, and the sleep to come would take her away from the misery of loving someone she couldn't have.

CHRISTMAS DAY PROMISED TO BE a festive affair. Harry had given them a leg of lamb, which was now roasting above the fire pit. The two farmhands, Gil and Jason, both bachelors, were taking turns rotating the meat. Jane was pleased to see them scrubbed and in their Sunday best.

A salmon on a plank of cedar waited to be added to the fire, along with the seasoned root vegetables Jane had prepped earlier. The pies sat in the stillroom, along with sausage stuffing, hard cider, and an array of cookies. Jane felt proud of her and Bell's efforts.

Inside the house, a jar of colorful hard candy—a gift from Gladys—sat on the mantel in the parlor among the spruce and pine boughs and the bright flowers. Martin had cut a fine fir tree, which they had decorated last night with paper ornaments, pine cones, and popcorn garland. It had been a lovely rare moment with her husband—one she would tuck away in her memory.

Candles lit the room, giving off a soft glow. Jane came into the parlor, and her eyes went to Harry, who sat near the fireplace, a cup of eggnog in his hand. His longish hair was neatly pulled back, and he looked handsome in his new cotton shirt and black woolen pants. He looked up at her and raised his glass. The firelight struck his handsome features, and her heart fluttered.

"Merry Christmas, Jane, Martin," he said.

"Merry Christmas, Harry," she and Martin said in unison.

Jane took a sip of her eggnog and swallowed. The spiked drink went down smooth and warmed her insides.

Jason entered the parlor. "Time for the root vegetables and salmon. That haunch of lamb is nearly done."

Martin popped up. "I'll get it."

Martin was always good at cooking the salmon, and with the price of it at market, Jane knew he wanted to be sure it was cooked just right. With the last of her large monthly sum of money, she'd decided to take a bit of it and splurge on food and drink. It would be their last hoorah before they became poor farmers.

Harry was usually by the fire pit with the men, but today he stayed seated. So did Jane. When they were alone, Harry sat forward, reaching into his pocket. He took out a small box wrapped in silver paper.

"I have this for you. I hope you like it."

She took it cautiously. "You know it's our tradition for everyone to exchange gifts later, with pie."

Harry smiled and nodded. "I know, but this Christmas feels different. We were just friends in the past."

With a nervous hand, she unwrapped the paper and folded it neatly. Opening the lid of the small square box, she immediately teared up. It was a pair of gold earrings in the shape of hearts.

"I had them made special." He leaned in closer. "See, you can put them in the holes in your ears."

She placed the box down and took each hook-backed earring and found the holes in her lobes. Then she put her hands down. She could feel the weight of the gold dangling from her ears.

"How do they look?"

"Beautiful. Just like you."

"I'll cherish them, Harry. Thank you."

They stood together now. His hand brushed her cheek, and then his lips touched her mouth. It was dangerous, yet she couldn't pull away. They came apart as voices drew close. The brief moment reignited her desire for him with greater passion. She decided she would begin to detach from him after Christmas, when she could hide from him in her own world of business and duty.

At the rustle of men coming back into the house, they returned to their seats. Martin didn't notice the earrings right away, and Jane felt she needed to announce Harry's gift sooner rather than later. Nothing secret, just a gift.

"Martin, look what Harry gave me!" She brought her hands behind her ears to showcase the gold hearts. "Aren't they sweet? Did you tell him I had pierced earlobes?"

Martin inspected the earrings with a jeweler's eye. "Hmm, they look like real gold. Must have set you back some, Harry. My gift will pale in comparison. Thanks, Cousin," Martin said jokingly. His remark was light, but Jane saw something in Martin's expression that caused concern. Was he suspicious of her and Harry?

Harry's laugh broke into her thoughts. "With your jewelry background, I didn't dare get imitation," he said.

Exhaling, Jane gave a wide smile and was relieved she wouldn't need to hide them like she would her feelings for Harry.

The rest of the day was cheery, and at the end, Jane felt tired but happy. The mulled wine had her feeling giddy and hopeful. Perhaps Martin would be more attentive and love her again as he once had. Perhaps her feelings for Harry would dissolve, sending her back into the arms of her marriage. When she and Martin bid Harry good night, she didn't kiss Harry's cheek as was their custom, but patted his arm.

"Good night, Cousin," she said with a bit of a slur and giggle.

"Sleep tight, Jane." Harry laughed and kissed her on each cheek. It felt wonderful. *Damn him!*

CHAPTER THIRTY

April 1884

*T*HE NEW YEAR HAD BROUGHT A RENEWED SENSE OF BELONG-
ing on the farm, and by spring Jane had relinquished her thoughts
of living in the style she'd once known. She hadn't a choice. Sweat
on her brow, dirt under her nails, and long hours on the land and in
the conservatory, stillroom, and kitchen defined her lifestyle now.
Bell came only once a week to teach Jane how to cook and help
with preserving foods. With Margie gone, the laundry began to
pile up, along with the dust and dirt. Jane found herself surprised
at how fast it all happened. She would have to set the same schedule of cleaning as Margie had. She wrote it down and hoped she
could keep to it. The workload seemed overwhelming. Mostly, she
had relinquished her visits to Berta's, and her friend was not too
happy about it. Jane had not written since before Christmas, and
only in the form of a holiday card. After this long silence came a
letter from Berta in this morning's post.

*My dearest Jane, where have you gone to? It's been months!
We miss your beautiful smile and charming wit. It's so
needed! The New Year's party was dull, and I fear I'm
not as intrigued by my usual company. The spring brings
many parties and social events. Do try to make a few. You
simply must visit me! Your room awaits you. Cook says she's
anxious to make your favorite dishes again. Ned has deserted
me for a client of his. My God, the man is older than Zeus!
Whatever could Ned be thinking? Oh, Jane, I have no one
intelligent to talk with! Please come soon.*

Lovingly yours,
Berta

Jane laughed out loud at Berta's dramatic plea. She knew well
enough her friend would not be alone, yet she missed the robust,
cherry-cheeked Berta and her dreamy estate. It was the most luxurious of escapes. The contrast of their lives was becoming more
apparent.

Jane felt as if she was leaving behind all the pleasures she'd once
taken for granted. Born into wealth, it had never occurred to her
she would one day struggle to make ends meet, that the physical
work would take over her days, and the nights wouldn't be long
enough. Her dreams led her to places where she lulled on a chaise
in the shade of a large eucalyptus while sipping a cool drink with
not a care in the world. Sometimes Harry would be alongside her,
smiling. Other nights she would dream of lying in the turned-up
ground of the garden as if she had been planted there.

Today, Berta's letter made her anxious. Could she confess to
her city friend what her life was like now? How it had turned
due to her brother's irresponsibility and greed along with Martin's
culpability? Today she had laundry and more housework to do,
for the rugs needed beating and the dust was a constant. She had
to take the lunches out to the men and come back to put a hearty
stew on for them after work. Jason had become another mouth to

feed, as Martin had moved him into the annex next to the barn. He and Jason had turned it into a decent living space but without a kitchen. Martin reasoned that it was cheaper to offer him board and room than to pay him more wages.

Letting out a sigh, she closed the letter and began her reply.

> *My dear Berta,*
> *Forgive my long absence. I think I've found a calling here on the farm—*

Jane ripped up the paper. Cringing at destroying a piece of her expensive stationary, she knew she must be more in tune with her friend to get her to understand and not labor over her absence.

> *My dear friend,*
> *It has been too long. Forgive me. I have been busy with the society here. Poor as it is compared to yours, I still have an obligation, as my wealth and standing command it. I am well and look forward to our time together soon. Martin is enjoying his farm, and my home has become a jewel in the town.*
> *Don't give up on me. My regards to the Johnsons, Beechmans, and, of course, our Ned.*
>
> > *Sincerely yours,*
> > *Jane*

Knowing Berta would never come to visit, the letter was a safe response. Jane felt it also kept that avenue open should she ever need it.

Rising from her desk, she decided she hadn't the time to dawdle. Noon would be here before long, and the men awaited a lunch of meat sandwiches, apple tarts, and cider. She also made them a midday snack of a softer and sweeter take on hardtack. She had learned to make it from Bell.

Donning her apron, she began her chores with a swell of longing for a different life—a life not possible, for it included too many wishes. Feeling loved, respected, sharing the joy of not only having children but the making of those new lives together. Something was sorely lacking in her relationship with Martin. They hadn't fully recovered from his betrayal, and her love for Harry made it difficult to continue being in love with Martin.

Had her and Martin's first blush of love been a fleeting experience? Was her money all Martin had really wanted from her? The thought scratched at the open wound that had yet to heal. Forgiveness, along with her guilt, was a battle she fought with each day.

Focusing on her experiences with the land would bring her happiness. This was to be her thought for today.

Stopping to take a rest after delivering the lunch and snack to Martin and Jason in the fields, she let herself recline on the new spring grass against a giant spruce, its limbs sweeping gracefully toward the ground. The shade felt good, and she was able to steal a moment away from her world. The scent of the new honeysuckle beginning its winding habit around the trunk made this place all the more relaxing until the sound of someone coming alerted her and she sat up. She watched him walk past her.

"Hello, Harry."

Harry spun around. "Jane! Hello there. What are you doing? Hiding away?"

She laughed. "Yes, yes I am."

Harry tilted his head. "You look restful. May I join you?"

"I suppose. Weren't you going somewhere?"

"It can wait."

The California air was still and warm, a pleasure Jane would always love at this time of year, when there may still be lingering frost back in Cincinnati. This pleasure was now increased with his presence. Not a sound surrounded them except for the birds chirping and the faint bleating of sheep, which told Jane that Martin and Jason were far afield. Her belly trembled.

Harry sat down alongside her. He whispered in her ear, "Hello, my love." The sweet kiss that followed led to another and another as their passions unfolded.

Harry reclined her onto the thick grass, and they ignited their lust. His mouth was smooth and warm on hers as she fell into a dreamy state. He slid her kerchief off her head and ran his hands through her loosened hair, then along her calf and under her dress, up her thigh, and between her legs. She could barely breathe. She felt his hardness bulging from his cotton pants as he pressed himself into her body. The high neckline of her dress made it impossible for him to kiss the sweet spot on her neck. His large hand cupped her breast, his thumb catching in the cotton lace of her day dress.

"Too much clothing," he groaned.

They giggled as he gently bit at her lip. The sound of a man whistling shattered their intimacy. She jumped up and stumbled before righting herself as Harry quickly stood. They swiped at their clothes, removing any debris. He took sprigs of grass from her hair and found her scarf. She shoved her hair under it as she hurried from the scene, her heart pounding in her throat. She caught the sound of Gil's voice.

Trembling inside, she ran down the field to her home. Getting closer, she slowed her pace and warned herself to stop this madness before they were caught. She knew she was a coward, not ready to face the consequences of loving him. It would be too grave a situation to face. How could she have been so careless? What if Gil had been Martin? This could never happen again.

CHAPTER THIRTY-ONE

August 1884

THE SWELTERING AUGUST HEAT HAD JANE WIPING THE DRIP-ping sweat from her forehead under her wide-brimmed hat.

Joining Jane in the garden this afternoon was Sally Loggin, who had come down the hill from her homestead to help Jane harvest and sort the fresh plants for making salves and creams once they had dried. She had been a great help, and Jane enjoyed her company.

They had met at the general store and over the years had become friends. There was something about Sally's easy nature and the humble gentleness of her husband, Ben, that gave Jane an instant feeling of comfort. Though the Loggins kept to themselves, Jane and Martin had shared a meal with them a few times. It was mostly Jane and Sally who visited with each other or stopped to chat in town whenever they met coincidently. Their friendship was a nice surprise.

Since Jane could no longer afford to have Mr. Hill in employ, Sally had offered to help when she could get away from her own farm duties in exchange for a certain lavender salve she loved. Mr. Hill had only been by once for winter cleanup and preparation of the land for planting. The luxury of having his help came at the cost of a few mutton legs and a jar of face cream for his wife. Jane and Martin had spent hours making the soil ready. They would sell most of the produce grown on it, and she would dry or jar up the rest. Along with the sale of mutton and their own store of meat, they would not go hungry. With no Mr. Hill and Bell working at Carley's Restaurant, having Sally's help was invaluable.

Unlike Jane, the Loggins had a well-established good reputation in Clermont City. Jane had become aware of the gossip her change in lifestyle had caused. Just the other day at the general store, she'd overheard a woman talking to Gladys as she was out of their sight behind a standing shelf filled with flour sacks.

"I hear she may have to sell some of her artsy paintings and fancy furnishings to support them. She had to let go of her house-keeper. Who has such a thing anyway? And a *conservatory*. Fancy name for a place to start seeds and store grain. I suppose she must have spent her family's fortune."

"Have you tried her salve, Nan?" Gladys asked. "It's heavenly. My hands are so much softer for it. I have a jar here. You must try it."

"I don't need any fancy cream for my hands. Some good ol' pig's lard suits me just fine."

"It smells better than pig's grease, Nan."

"Well, I can't say I feel all that bad for her," Nan continued. "There seems to be plenty of money there. Her clothes alone could buy me and Alfred and the boys a year's worth of food. Still, it's a shame. We need the farms to do well."

When Jane emerged from her accidental hiding place, Nan Trundle's face went scarlet.

"Oh, Mrs. Cabot!"

"No worries, Mrs. Trundle. Martin and I are doing just fine. The paintings are still on the walls, and the furnishings are still in place. My clothes hang happily in one of the three ornate armoires in my large bedroom. Though if you're truly concerned, I would think a prayer rather than gossip might better help us."

Jane hadn't stayed for Nan's response.

She was hurt and angered. *They can say what they damn well please!*

Although the town welcomed Martin, Jane still had the feeling most of the townsfolk found her too high and mighty for their tastes. She still wore her city clothes into town, and why not? Fact was, she wouldn't be getting new ones, and no one would notice that most everything she wore was several years out of date.

None of this had bothered her until recently. Harry came to mind. She would surely be an outcast if they found out about their attraction to each other. That piece of gossip would truly upset the balance of things in a small town—or even in a big city. She vowed she would not give the likes of Nan Trundle the satisfaction.

Today a warm breeze and Sally's company were all she needed to feel right with the world. Sally bent down and brought up another bunch of calendulas, the orange flowers making an instant bouquet. "I love this with chamomile," she said to Jane.

Jane agreed. "Let's dry half for tea and half for balm. Let's get it into the conservatory, then have a cool drink." Jane was glad she had given strict instructions that the conservatory be built under the canopy of trees. Full sun would certainly scorch her tender plants and seedlings.

"That sounds wonderful. Do you mind if I take some for my soaps? I've harvested most of mine."

"Not at all! They've been growing like weeds."

A few strands of blond hair had escaped from Sally's bonnet, and she quickly tucked them back into place. She was a gentile,

God-fearing, upstanding woman, and Jane had learned to curb her offhanded remarks about the church or Pastor Evans. It was a small concession. Most of all, they accepted each other for who they were, and that endeared Jane to her.

Forgetting herself, Jane was about to call for Bell to bring them refreshments. With the sun hitting their backs, she and Sally walked to the conservatory with their baskets of flowers and herbs. Between the shelves lining each side of the long structure was a worktable filled with seedlings ready for the land. Hanging above it were bundles of drying herbs and flowers, including lavender, nettles, eucalyptus, and mustard. It smelled heavenly, and Jane could've spent hours in here experimenting for her beauty products and remedies.

She was honing her skills. The small business she'd started last spring was growing. Selling her products to the general stores in the county and her tea mixtures to the restaurants had proved not only prosperous but very satisfying. It helped the farm, though it wasn't nearly enough to let Jane rest each night without worry.

A light breeze ran through the open ends of the conservatory, providing some relief, but Jane knew they couldn't stay in here for very long; the heat was too great.

"Meet me in the shade of the trees, Sally. I'll get us a cool drink." Jane was thankful the iceman had come this morning.

Jane had set up a small table with chairs for this very purpose: to sit and rest with a cool lemonade.

"I'll bring down a few jars of pickles for you, Jane. I forgot this time."

"Don't make a trip just for that, Sally. But come for another visit. Next time just for iced tea and cake. I hate seeing you do extra work for me."

"It's been my pleasure, and my hands thank you for the cream. We farm wives must stick together. And . . . to be honest, you're a breath of fresh air for me."

Jane took a sip from her glass. "And you for me."

"Soon you'll have little ones running around, and I think I will be happy to come down here and help with that too." There was a tinge of sadness in Sally's tone.

"I feel a bit old for starting a family," Jane said. When she turned thirty, Jane felt she might have to close the door to that dream.

Sally grinned. "Mrs. Henderson just had her ninth, and she's thirty-eight."

"Oh my! Nine children to feed!" Jane said. "And what about you and Ben? If I may be so bold."

Sally shook her head. "No, I'm afraid Ben and I cannot have children." She raised her hand. "Please, no words of condolences. We are quite adjusted to it." Her smile lightened her face.

Jane patted her hand. "Auntie Sally would be most welcome!" she stated with false hope.

It had been over four years since she and Martin had consummated their marriage. She'd thought it would happen right away with little effort, but each time they made love, she sent a prayer up to heaven.

The doctor had confirmed she was capable, and though it was thought that Martin might be overworked, the remedy was to just keep trying. That was the answer. If only Martin was willing. He seemed less interested in having children and making love to her as time went on. In her heart, Jane felt Martin may not be able to give her a child. Like Sally, she would have to be brave and accept the hand life had dealt her. Perhaps she wasn't meant to be a mother after all. A sudden sadness pricked her heart.

"Truly, we are fine," Sally said.

Jane came out of her thoughts. "Oh, of course."

"Men get so busy with the land. Sometimes I feel invisible to Ben, but mostly we've come to a place where we cherish each other for our strengths and help each other with our weaknesses."

"I'm glad for you, Sally. I love what you and Ben have built up there. Though that road! It seems to be getting worse."

Sally laughed. "I know. It's been graded slightly, but after each winter it seems a lost cause with everything else that needs to be done. I guess I'm used to it."

Relaxing in the company of her friend, Jane sat back and pretended she was once again a lady of leisure entertaining a lady friend on a lazy afternoon. As she brought her glass to her lips, the dirt under her nails rudely interrupted her dream. They shared good humor and conversation, and soon it was time for Sally to leave and Jane to finish her chores of taking in the laundry and starting the stew for Martin and Jason. She'd already scrubbed the kitchen floor and beat the foyer rug. How was it always in need of cleaning? The day was only halfway through, but Jane's back hurt and her arms and legs ached.

MARTIN AND JASON ATE LIKE two ravenous animals. Jane took her time, though she was just as hungry. She looked at her husband. His tanned face had defined lines around his eyes and forehead. The soft, carefree expression had worn off, and his brows showed constant worry.

Was this the life he loved and cherished? Her once-gleeful husband who relished in this new and adventurous hobby had grown weary now that it was no longer a hobby but a way to survive. Was the reality of his independence from her inheritance and family finally hitting him? He would never concede to it.

Though her instincts told her to leave the subject for later, her impatience had her speaking to Martin about their lack of children. He joined her in the parlor for tea that night after dinner.

A yawn escaped him as he sat down heavily in his favorite chair.

"My dear, I think you should step up production in your area," he said. "Take some of the seed for growing the chicken scratch and sow it in the field near your cut flower garden. Sow heavily. I got the seed for cheap, and not all of it is viable, as you know.

We can sell some of the wheat to farmers for their livestock. And speaking of the flower garden, I intend to till it over next week for more crops. Jason and I will extend it to the east of the main vegetable garden."

Jane took in what he was saying and agreed with a nod of her head. She knew her beautiful flower gardens were doomed. They had produced very little for her products and were a waste of resources. Selling flowers was the least profitable part of the farm, but oh, the joy it had brought her.

"Martin."

He looked up from stirring his tea. "I know, but it can't be helped," he said.

"No, I wanted to talk to you about having children."

"Damn it, Jane! How can we afford a family? Tell me that. Do you have some hidden treasure? We've sold what jewelry you bought in the city!"

She bowed her head. She had been warned by her own instincts not to bring up the subject. Lately her heart ached for a child. Her breast ached to suckle a babe. She was desperate for a life to grow in her, to hold a child of their own. The strength of her desire was like none she had known. It confused her and made her speak in anger.

"If you hadn't made such a damn foolish deal with Chad, we wouldn't be in this—"

Her hand flew up to her mouth.

Martin placed his tea on the side table, stood, and said, "Good night, dear."

She had had enough of his dismissal of her. These discussions about children were rare, and now her pent-up emotions were ready to overflow.

"Oh! Sometimes I think you'd love to go back to my brother and work in that dark back room! Did the money tempt you more than me? My inheritance? I was just the pretty thing that went with it, wasn't I? You never loved me! You loved my money!" Her breathing was heavy. A dangerous line had been crossed, and she was on the other side in the wilderness.

Taking a deep breath and letting it out, Martin turned to face her. She stood defiantly.

"I fell in love with you," he began. "I also saw your inheritance as a means for us to have a better life—a good, natural life out here. The deal I made with Chad was in ignorance, I admit. I was excited, vain, naïve—call it what you will. I'm sorry. It seems it is you who wishes to be free of me and this land. Or it is you and Harry?"

Taken aback, Jane wanted to defend her feelings for Harry. At the same time, she shook at the thought of Martin knowing about them. How long had he suspected? Again, she wanted to believe she could detach her love for him and fall back in love with her husband. Martin's eyes softened and glistened.

"Martin, I just asked you to have a family with me. Harry and I flirt. It's . . . It's silly and harmless."

"Jane, please don't take me for an idiot. It pains me a great deal to see how you two are with each other. I've spoken to Harry about it, and he says what you say: only an innocent flirtation. I supposed he thinks of me as you do—simpleminded. I want to ask you, and tell me the truth. Do you wish to continue with me? If not, I will arrange your passage back to Cincinnati, or perhaps your wealthy friends in San Francisco might take you in."

Going back to Cincinnati was unthinkable to her, and living off of her city friends was so distasteful she couldn't bear the thought. Mostly, she couldn't leave Harry.

"Stop it! I have invested in our marriage and this land, and I will continue on it as long as you will have me." She looked down at the floor and then up into his eyes. "Trust has been broken. Can we mend it?"

"You know my sins, but do I know yours?"

"I have not sinned," she said and believed it.

Martin gave a sharp laugh. "No? Do you even care if God sees your sins? And if not, why should you care if I do?"

"It's true I attend church to please you and the town. I have my own beliefs. Can we please mend our marriage?"

With a nod, Martin reached out and took her hand. "I'm willing to if you are willing to let go of your feelings for my cousin."

It was a promise she wasn't sure she could keep, but she agreed for the sake of Martin and her marriage.

"Children will come when we've made a profit. Until then, we must be careful," he said.

"That doesn't seem to be a problem." She only hoped her love for Harry wouldn't take her too far and produce a child.

"For God's sake, Jane. I'm tired at the end of the day, and . . . and you give me no sign you are ready for me in that way."

"I see, it's my fault. Very well. I will make a note to be more available to you."

"Christ! I'm going to bed."

"Martin." Jane felt the time had come to be honest with him.

He turned and waited with hooded eyes.

"I think we should face the truth. One of us is incapable of having children."

"And I suppose that would be me? I am the problem? Of course! Christ! I'm going to bed!"

She let him storm out of the room. She cursed the Lord and God and the list of saints her mother had taught her to turn to for various reasons, for each one was apparently assigned a certain task. Sitting down, she racked her brain to find the saint who helped with stilted marriages and wives who loved men other than their husbands. Surely, she couldn't be the only one. No saints came to mind, and she sat in the parlor a good while, bemoaning her circumstances until she felt Martin was asleep and snoring. Sliding in beside him, she turned onto her side and tried to find sleep.

CHAPTER THIRTY-TWO

October 1885

THE MORNING MAIL WAS FILLED WITH BILLS FOR IMMEDIATE receipt, typical for this time of the month. However, one letter stood out for its heavy cream-colored envelope and official type. Shipman and Shipman Law Firm. Running her bone-handled paper knife along its edge, Jane took a breath and let it out. She opened the official-looking letter. Below the firm's heading, she read:

> *Dear Mrs. Cabot,*
> *I regretfully inform you that your brother, Chadwick Wallingford, has died of complications due to pneumonia. It came about very quickly and took him within days. He was buried alongside his and your parents on the 10th of October 1885.*

She stopped reading. As she stared at the table, her memories of her brother when she had been innocent of his true nature came rushing back. He had never regarded her with much love, but once in a while he'd shown her affection in the way of a gentle pat to her shoulder when a school day had been difficult or a gift of sweets when he had returned from town. As a child, the slightest attention he afforded her had made her day, and she'd wanted him to love her more than anything in the world. It was a void that remained unfilled. Coming out of her memories, she read on.

> *In regard to his estate, we are negotiating his debts and will keep you abreast of the remainder. After our initial review, it will not be much. Mr. Cabot will receive the funds, and we will then proceed to close the estate. The house is in foreclosure as I write. We are hoping for a quick sale.*
>
> *His remaining personal effects will be forwarded to you or, if you wish, given to a local charity. A telegram to our office will suffice on that account. May I suggest a charity since the cost of shipping may be a burden to you?*
>
> *I, or my office secretary, will be in touch with you and Mr. Cabot. A document has been sent to your husband for his signature. I thought it wiser, however, to send you this letter to inform you personally of your brother's passing and the state of his worldly possessions.*
>
> *My sincerest sympathies to you and your family.*
>
> *L. Shipman, LLB*

The typed letter slipped from Jane's hands. Her brother was dead. She checked her emotions for grief. It was a shock, but she had no feelings of sadness. It was strange how she had removed him from her heart so completely that his passing did not affect her. Perhaps the shock would wear off and she would feel miserably sad. His estate in debt? The house, her childhood home, in foreclosure? What about his investments with her money? It was all too disturbing.

Martin came to her later in the day with a cut on his thumb. She brought him into the stillroom, where she took a jar of balm from one of the cupboards.

"Have you received a letter from Mr. Shipman?" she asked while she applied the greasy ointment onto the cut and wrapped it with a strip of cotton.

"Yes, today," he replied, watching her work on his thumb. "How did you know? I took it out from the rest of the mail. I was hoping after dinner in the quiet of the evening I could tell you what he informed me of."

His large brown eyes were misty, and she wondered at his emotion for her brother.

"I received my own letter from him. Apparently, I'm more than just a name on my father's will document."

"Jane."

"So, he's dead, and you are to receive the remainder of his money, *my* money?"

Their marriage had taken on a quiet contempt, mostly on her part. Martin's civility had become a spur in her side. He was always more logical than her about any situation.

He took his bandaged hand away. "I'm sorry for your loss." He looked down at her handiwork. "Thank you."

She let out a puff. "You're welcome. Now, will you answer my question?"

"Yes, we will gain what is left of the money. I signed the papers, and they are on their way back. It's not yet settled, but he left nothing of value behind. It's a tragedy. He had so much and died with so little. I think we may receive less than a thousand from all of it."

"It's his own fault. I have nothing to say about it. Whatever we get, we deserve. Even if it's one dollar."

Martin came closer. "I agree." He looked at her thoughtfully. "I'm glad you've found a calling on our land. It's what I've prayed for."

Jane was surprised at this sudden recognition. It hit a soft spot in her.

"Martin, do you ever wish for more? With us, I mean. We are more like business partners and friends than a married couple. Are you no longer interested in me as a wife, a lover? Since we may not be able to have children, we don't need to be careful."

He looked trapped. She had backed him into a corner with her statement. His response stuck in his throat, as it always did when she asked about the state of their relationship.

"I work hard for us. Is it not proof enough of my love? I know it's not what you expected, but we have everything we need. What more do you want, Jane? What more can I do for you?"

"Are you happy, Martin?"

He scratched his head. "Happy as any man can be, I suppose."

She bit her lip and nodded. "Then that's all we can hope for, isn't it?" Wanting him to ask her in turn if she was happy was a fruitless desire.

She looked at his hand. "If the bandage becomes too bloody, come back in, and I'll change it."

"I will." He kissed her cheek and left.

A swell of anger rose from the very depths of her being, demanding her to act. She wanted to pound on his chest and scream, "Tell me you're still madly in love with me! Let's sell this damn farm and go live like normal people!"

Shaken, she gripped the built-in bench that held the jars of jam and stores of butter and breads, along with a pie Bell had generously brought by that morning. The back shelves were filled with products ready for market. The abundance around her gave her pause. A slow recognition welled up inside.

This was her work from her part of the farm. She went to the window and gazed out onto the vegetable and flower gardens. She had turned up the land around the gazing pond for more crops, and its water was now a useful resource rather than for viewing. The orchard, the wildflower meadow—both were her doing. She had made a difference.

She hadn't expected to find fulfillment on this farm, but in fact, that was what had been happening to her. She had found satisfaction in a well-run home, the gardens started from tiny seeds, growing into beautiful and useful plants. It nurtured her as she nurtured it, and it felt deeply satisfying.

If Martin came back into the stillroom and asked if she was happy, the answer would be an affirmative yes.

A WEEK LATER, A HORSE-DRAWN carriage came around the front, and Jane leapt to welcome Lacey. The women embraced. Jane had missed her assistant dearly, and they only met once a month for tea, mostly to catch up on the town's gossip and reminisce about their time together.

"Your timing is good," Jane said. "I need a friend right now. I learned my brother died."

"Oh, Jane." Lacey put her hand on Jane's arm.

"You know there was no love lost between us," Jane said.

Lacey came away with a smirk. "I can't say he made much of a good impression on me, but still."

"I suppose I should send flowers or something. He's already been buried. I have no idea what his funeral was like. He swindled many people, and according to the lawyer, it got worse. The house is in foreclosure."

"I'm terribly sorry. At least he can't take anything more away from you."

Jane puffed out a breath of air. "Well, that remains to be seen. I doubt I'll get another penny from my inheritance."

Lacey tipped the brim of her flowered summer hat. "I'm taking you to lunch."

"I have so much to do."

"I don't care! You are my captive. Get out of that apron and find your best bonnet."

With a smile of gratitude, Jane obeyed.

As usual, Carley's food was hearty and delicious. Jane sat back in her seat and wiped her mouth with the red paisley napkin. Carley made the cotton napkins herself, and they came in a variety of patterns. Jane's thoughts went to the Palace Hotel. The food was grand, but today in this sweet place, she felt as if nothing tasted better than Carley's home cooking.

A young woman and older couple sat a few tables down. Jane had not seen the young woman before. She was petite and quite pretty. The older couple, she had recently noticed in town. They were new to Clermont City, and according to Gladys, Burt and June Stanford were from Hartford, Connecticut. He was a retired lawyer.

Jane leaned forward and asked in a soft tone, "Lacey, who is the woman with the Stanford couple?"

"Their niece, Jessica Messing. She lives with them. I will have Carley introduce us."

Carley obliged Lacey's request, and Jane found herself engaged in polite conversation with Mr. and Mrs. Stanford and their niece. It struck her instantly they were from the East Coast, and Jane told them she was from Cincinnati. Their accents gave them away as the upper class. By the clothing they wore, she gathered they had wealth. Jessica's ensemble was head-to-toe haute couture. A prick of jealousy had Jane wanting to turn back the clock. How she wanted to dress like that again.

"Jane, Miss Messing asked you a question," Lacey said.

Jane flushed. "Oh, I'm sorry. I was just admiring your outfit. It's quite beautiful."

"Thank you," Miss Messing replied.

The young woman looked well-appointed, but there was sadness in her eyes that revealed more than her sweet smile could hide.

"Oh, I was just asking if you miss Cincinnati," Miss Messing said. "I've wanted to visit there but never got the chance. I traveled here by train and only caught a glimpse of that beautiful state. I hear it's a fascinating city."

"It is, and yes, I do miss it sometimes."

"Jane and Martin own Cabot Farm," said Lacey.

The three smiled at Jane and nodded. She felt their conservative politeness.

"A farm? How charming," Mrs. Stanford said. "Though I can just imagine how much work that must require. I need help with my own garden."

"Auntie is a lover of all things that grow, and she's a marvelous cook," Miss Messing said, a beautiful smile crossing her face.

"I can always do with more recipes, Mrs. Stanford," Jane said.

"Indeed, I have many!" the plump redheaded woman shot back with glee.

"Speaking of work to be done, I really must get back. It was a pleasure to meet you all," Jane said.

"Pleased as well," Mrs. Stanford replied.

Miss Messing smiled, and their eyes met.

Jane felt a connection to this woman. It was silly, and she shrugged it off. She was sure this family would not be toiling on a farm, so their paths may not meet but for the occasional greeting in town.

On the way home, Jane felt ill at ease. How lovely she had once looked in the gowns and dresses made for her at one time. She sighed. A farmer's wife.

CHAPTER THIRTY-THREE

October 1886

*C*OMING FROM THE BARN, JANE LOOKED OUT ONTO THE paddock of sheep. The early light of dawn touched the dewy grass they nibbled. The familiar sounds of the animals waking up resounded over the land. It was cooler now, and she could take in the fresh clean air and know that the coming day wouldn't be as hot. The lambs were growing, and soon the butcher would come along and take them away. Martin had met with the accountant yesterday and had told Jane the good news that this year may yield a fair profit.

Having to rarely deal with the livestock, Jane had joined Martin and Jason this morning as they got one of the cows back into her stall for milking. It had been a comical exercise, but Martin was now milking the often-belligerent Annie. Missy, the other milking cow, was the opposite of Annie. She was docile and the first to get milked each morning.

Wiping her hands on her apron, Jane walked back to the house to wash for breakfast. She had gathered the eggs and took out a thick slab of bacon from the storeroom. A fresh loaf of bread sat on the counter. Soon the kitchen would be filled with the aroma of another morning on the farm.

JANE BROUGHT HER NAPKIN TO her lap. She usually didn't have to wait for Martin, but this morning he was late. Once the bell rang, he was the first to the breakfast table.

The citrus trees had been plentiful, and she poured herself a tall glass of orange juice. Soon she would harvest the rest of the apples, lemons, and oranges to bring to market.

Jason came into the dining room and helped himself to the food laid out on the side table.

She looked beyond Jason. "Where is Mr. Cabot?"

"Still in the barn milking, I reckon. Maybe Annie's still acting up. I'll go out and see what's keeping him." He set his plate down and went to the barn.

Jane settled into her breakfast, as she was too hungry to wait for her husband. As she brought the glass of juice to her lips, she heard Jason shouting for her. Jumping out of her seat, she spilled the glass as she hastily set it down. She ran out of the house and followed another shout coming from the barn. As she entered, she found a horrific sight. She muffled a scream.

Martin's blood ran down his face, mixing with the white milk. He was limp in Jason's arms. The pail of milk was turned over, and the post behind Martin was bloodied.

Rushing to her husband's side, she shouted, "Martin, Martin. Talk to me!" Taking him by the shoulders, she shook him to wake him up. The blood gushed from the back of his head, and she nearly fainted.

Jason tore off his work shirt and wrapped it tightly around Martin's head. Jane fell back on her knees as Jason took charge.

"Help me! Get his legs!" Jason said.

Jane sprang into action. She held tight to Martin's heavy legs. Annie sauntered by her and back into the pasture, revealing more bloodstained hay. Her husband's blood.

She wanted to hold up her husband's head as it bobbed with the quick movement of Jason running backward, his hands under Martin's armpits.

"Be careful with him!" she cried out.

They laid him on the couch in the parlor. Jane stood aside while Jason placed a pillow under Martin's head. The blood staining Jason's white undershirt.

She knelt and looked at Martin's ashen face. She came close to his nose, wanting to feel his soft breath. There was nothing. She felt for a pulse on his neck, but there wasn't the steady beat she had felt whenever she had snuggled up to him. Her mind was stuck in place, and her body couldn't move. All she wanted was for him to open his eyes and tell her he was going to be fine.

"God damn, bitch must've kicked him into the stall post," Jason said, never one to mince his words to suit anyone.

His comment crashed into Jane as her husband's blood seeped into the light-yellow fabric of the settee with the matching brocade pillows.

Kicked by a cow?

"Jason! Get the doctor! Get the ambulance!"

Jason stooped down beside her and felt for a pulse on Martin's neck. Jane moved to let him place an ear on Martin's chest, her body unwilling to stop shaking.

After a few more seconds, Jason rose. His hand cupped his mouth.

"Damn it! Get the doctor!" she cried.

"He's gone, Mrs. Cabot. I'll fetch Doc Grant though."

"Hurry! And get Harry!"

Jane laid her head on Martin's still chest and wept.

"No, Martin! No!"

Harry thanked Dr. Grant for coming to confirm Martin's death. They placed a sheet on the carpet in the parlor, where Martin's wrapped body would wait for the coroner to receive him.

"Jason, would you show the doctor out, please?" Harry said.

Jason walked Dr. Grant to the door, giving Harry time alone with Jane.

Jane felt Harry's hand on her shoulder as she knelt by her husband's body. It felt heavy and annoying. She shrugged it off.

"Jane, please have tea. I'll put a shot of whiskey in it. It will help you deal with this and perhaps let you sleep."

"I have never taken a nap in the morning," she said sharply. "There's too much to do. And I don't drink in the morning either."

"I know. Let me help you to your room. I'll get the tea."

She knew today was not like any other day when her normal routine would be welcomed, even joyful compared to this unspeakable tragedy.

He helped her up and walked her toward the stairs.

Stopping abruptly, she turned. "I shouldn't leave him," she said.

"Let me take care of him. Go upstairs to bed. I will be there shortly."

Jane climbed the stairs to her bedroom in a daze. She lay on her soft bed in a state of shock.

Martin was gone. How was that possible? There must've been a mistake. This must be a dream.

Harry knocked on the door and entered.

"I don't need a drink, Harry."

"I do," he replied.

The tears dropped from Harry's face. The tension grew in the room. They both knew what they were about and that Martin had suspected their attraction to each other.

Fearful she would succumb to her love and need for Harry, Jane insisted he leave.

"Find Lacey and tell her I need her."

His stare of dismay did nothing to change her mind.

"Go, Harry."

He nodded and left the room.

Taking a deep breath, Jane looked around at the beauty she had created. It gave her no comfort. She had no place to hide.

Martin knew her love for Harry now. She was sure he was looking down on her and knew what she was feeling and thinking. Why hadn't she been brave enough to tell him the truth? Was this her secret wish? Had she caused him to die?

The guilt refused to let her sleep, and she eventually took Harry's advice and drank the whiskey he'd left on her bedside table.

CHAPTER THIRTY-FOUR

THE FUNERAL WAS SIMPLE. MARTIN HAD KNOWN MOST OF THE folks in town better than Jane did, and she saw a few faces she didn't recognize.

"Our deepest condolences," said Sally as she embraced her friend. "He was a fine man."

"Thank you, Sally. Yes, he was a good man."

Sally's husband, Ben, was at Jane's side and patted her back. "If you need anything at all, don't hesitate to ask." He then stood aside as others came to offer their condolences.

Jane was touched beyond words. The despair and loneliness that had engulfed her since Martin's death gave her heart an openness to those around her. She needed them. She needed Harry.

After the service and burial, Jane held on to Harry as he walked her to the carriage outside of the cemetery grounds. Jason drove them home. Martin would rest peacefully for eternity in the small gravesite beside St. Luke's Methodist. Jane had attended this church each Sunday with him only because he had asked her to.

"Attending church in a new town is the best way to meet the townsfolk," he'd said. "And who knows, Jane, you may become devoted to God someday. I know you have done battle with Him in the past."

It had become a ritual Jane was accustomed to. It offered her a place to sit without hurry, and the words of the sermon were as if a type of music played while she meditated on her life, her relationship with Harry, her gardens, her potions. Today she was grateful to have a place where she could visit Martin's grave.

Her husband's words sounded in her head. His words about God had held little meaning then, but today they rang true. She was always in battle with the powers that be. She had resolved to believe life was what she made it and the mystery of it all would remain just that—a mystery. She shook away any thought that might help her figure out the why of what had happened. It wouldn't help. Her husband was gone, and nothing, not even the most devout worshiper, could bring him back.

WITH A HEAVY HEART, SHE entered her home. Lacey had arrived before her, and Jane was greeted with a table of small bites and tea. Lacey and Bell were overly attentive. Margie was also present, and she spoke with an unusual softness.

Jane teared up. "Thank you all. Harry and I will be in the parlor. We need to discuss . . ." She paused. "Would you send in the food and tea, Margie? I will pay you for your time when—"

Margie held up her hand. "I'm here as a friend, Jane."

It brought more moisture to Jane's eyes.

Harry quietly closed the parlor doors after Margie left. He poured a cup of tea for Jane. "You need to eat something too."

She dutifully brought the tea to her lips and took a sip. She had no appetite though. "What am I going to do?" she asked.

"You're going to give yourself time. We will give ourselves time. This is a shock, and I can't even think to give you an answer. I lost a cousin, a brother." Harry paced the room. "I was going to tell him about us. I couldn't stand to go on like this. After all these years of this . . . this tension between the three of us. Martin sensed it. How could he not? Why were we all not more forthright? Damn it! We played as if we were characters in a fuckin' romance novel!"

His statement perked her up.

"What? I hope you were going to let me know before you told him." The tears stained her face. "Oh, Harry, I feel more married to you than I did with Martin. I feel I've lost a friend instead of a husband. My heart is broken. Why didn't we let him know?"

Rubbing his freshly shaven chin, Harry shook his head. "We should have, and now it's too late. I feel he's looking down on us with sorrow." His watery eyes met hers. "I hate myself for deceiving him. What were we thinking?"

Looking away from his torment, she took the cotton napkin from the tray and patted her cheeks. Her chest felt as if a dark, cavernous hole had opened up with no light to fill it.

"We were selfish," she said with a ragged breath. "It just . . ."

"Happened?"

Jane collected herself, ignoring the anvil of guilt he'd dropped on her.

"I will grieve for my husband and have courage for the future," she said. "The farm will run as is with Jason in charge of the livestock." She looked into his eyes. "You and I will stay away from each other."

Harry looked down at the floor, then up at her. He nodded in agreement. "We will talk business in a few weeks. Until then, may I come by to check in on you?"

"No. Lacey will stay with me and let you know how I'm doing. Please stay away . . . for now."

"Jane, we are related by marriage. It will seem odd if I stay away in your time of need. Am I to be seen as callous? Besides, I can't lose you too."

Jane shook her head, and a dull pain came to the back of her neck. "I don't care what you may be seen as or your loss. I want to be left alone."

Harry nodded and left.

Jane dragged her body upstairs to her bedroom, where a warm bath awaited her. Margie had also laid out her favorite dressing gown, and several candles were lit. It was her sanctuary.

A deep sense of loneliness engulfed her. She was now a widow at age thirty-three. No children, no husband, and nearly penniless. Had she missed her prime in society in exchange for working on a farm, for following her passion for horticulture? Would everyone call her Widow Cabot now?

Oh God! Martin, how could you leave me so soon? We could have worked it out. Harry and I would've told you about our love for each other, and maybe, just maybe, you would've been happy for us. We could have all worked together.

A sudden gust of autumn air slammed the shutter into the window casing.

Jane was jerked out of her thoughts. With her heart pounding in her chest, she went to the window and opened it and brought the other shutter closed, then latched them tight. *Please forgive me, Martin.*

THREE WEEKS LATER, HARRY CAME to see her. The house was empty, and Jason was out in the upper field. Lacey had gone home after staying a week. Jane twisted her hands over and over each other. She had thought of Harry, but her grief was still too raw to feel anything toward him right now. She welcomed him in.

"Good day, Harry."

"Good day, Jane. How are you?"

"I'm as well as to be expected. And you?"

"The same."

"Would you like a cup of coffee? I just made a fresh pot."

"No. I want to talk with you."

"Come into the parlor, then."

She sat still. Her breath felt shallow, and she coughed into the back of her hand, then clasped both hands in her lap. Since Martin's death, she had struggled with a heaviness in her chest and a cough none of her remedies healed. She yearned for Harry's strong arms wrapped around her body and to feel his love and concern. She wanted to wash away her guilt and start as fresh as a new bud on a flowering tree that bursts into the season in all its glory, then produces the most delicious fruit. The time was not yet here, and she steadied herself to listen to him speak.

"I've given this some thought," he began as he stood in front of her.

Was he about to say something he hadn't been able to express before Martin's death? Was his guilt about to break her heart? He seemed reluctant, and she could barely contain herself when he finally spoke.

"I feel it would be in our best interest to merge our farms. My accountant has gone over the figures, and he agrees. I think Martin's plan was to extend onto the east slope and buy up some of the land just south of my farm. We could merge and buy up the southern land and let the east stay as it is. It's not a good piece anyway." Harry sat down and swiped his nose with an intake of breath. "Just food for thought. It would allow you to make a better profit, and we could share the workload, hire a few more men. Mr. Hill is still available, I hear."

Jane looked into his wide-eyed, expectant expression. That was his thought? The farm?

"Our farms?" She got up and let out a puff of air and gave a sharp laugh. "I will have to think about it, Harry. I'm sure your accountant is right. It would be prudent."

"I know it's a difficult time to bring this up, but I thought before the season begins and all . . ."

"Of course. As I said, I will think about it."

"Good. All right. Now, how are you really doing?"

She reined in her emotions. "I'm getting along. It's been difficult, but it will just take time, or so I'm told. Thank you for thinking about me—or should I say the business."

Harry slumped his shoulders and looked at her. "That's all I can focus on right now."

It was all she was going to get, and she still had a few more chores to do before the end of the day.

"Then I should let you go," she said. "As you can imagine, I have many things to sort out. Most of the finances are in order thanks to me and our—my—accountant. There are still a few vendors to tell. I daresay they will not be happy to be dealing with a woman."

"That's where I can help, Jane. We'll be one business. I can take a lot of that burden from you."

"I didn't say I couldn't do it. I just said they wouldn't be happy about it."

She walked past him, and he followed her as she led him to the door. He stood in its open frame for a moment longer than necessary. It was a chilly November afternoon, and the sun was hanging low. A smear of reddish orange swept across the sky. It glowed behind him. Her heart swelled.

"Good day, Jane."

"Good day, Harry."

She stepped onto the porch and watched him mount his horse and turn it away from her and down the road. A sharp gust of wind had her closing the door and retreating to the fireplace, where she sat and contemplated what had just taken place. Had she expected him to take her in his arms and declare his love and devotion? The answer was a wretched, guilt-ridden *yes!*

Instead, he'd talked of their businesses. She had to admit, she had been going over every detail of her finances, and combining farms made sense. She had asked herself many times if farming the land was what she truly wanted to do. Perhaps she could rent an apartment in the city and leave the worries and hard work behind. She knew the jewelry business, and a store might welcome her knowledge. Leave Harry? All of these thoughts made her sick. The products she produced were a part of her life now. This was her farm and her responsibility. She had made a decision. Her farm would make a profit even if she had to work her fingers to the bones!

Chapter Thirty-Five

September 1887

$\mathcal{E}$VERY NIGHT SINCE MARTIN'S DEATH, JANE HAD KEPT HIS loaded pistol on her nightstand. She still hadn't gotten used to being in the house alone. And there was the information Sally had told her today: a few homesteaders had spied a small group of renegade Indians in the upper hills. They were just passing by as in the past and hadn't been a threat, but without Martin in the house, Jane felt exceptionally vulnerable.

Jason had moved onto Harry's farm. It was unseemly for a widow to have a man eating at her table. He still worked for her and she still fed him by way of him coming by to pick up the food. Although she had declined Harry's offer to merge their farms and had more work than ever, she didn't regret her decision. She was determined to continue what she and Martin had started, dog-tired and weary as she was. There was never enough night to satisfy her need for sleep. Some mornings she wanted to strangle the roosters and make them into soup. She knew her plight might bring her close to doing just that.

She doubted she would get a wink tonight. Her thoughts would not rest. The numbers in the account book filled her head. In her dreams, pieces of paper with amounts due for taxes piled up high to the ceiling, ready to topple down and bury her. She tried to ease her mind with thoughts of Harry, but that made her even more restless. When the sun set and the moon shined into her bedroom, she wanted him more than ever. The past eleven months had been lonely.

After breakfast it was time to start her day. With Sally's news, Jane felt a bit cautious of her surroundings. It was unsettling.

She put on her cotton shirt and tucked it into her brown skirt, which was worn at the hem. She had been meaning to have a few more skirts made, but they were low on the list of priorities.

As with every day since lambing season, she would meet with Jason to check on the babes to make sure they were dry and warm. Last month's rain and cold had worried everyone, and they'd struggled to keep the new lambs alive. She had even slept for several nights in the barn making sure the mothers didn't reject their babes. She had needed those lambs to make her a profit and to fill her belly with meat.

The garden needed weeding and planting. A batch of lemon-infused oil for the general store waited to be delivered, then a check on the accounts, and finally the mail before baking a batch of biscuits for dinner to go with last night's leftover lamb stew. She'd make some vegetable pies for her and Jason's lunch. Harry had checked in now and then over the past months. Jane was cordial and took his advice concerning the lambing business, but no more than that went on between them. She had sold the two cows and the pigs, which had given her the income to pay off some of the debt Martin had accumulated. Her idea of making the land a place to grow fields of flowers and plants for her products kept her going if only mentally. Branching out into beauty products was an exciting venture. What woman didn't love a scented cream to smooth over her face before bed, with the promise of smooth and supple skin in the morning? It thrilled her to pursue that avenue. Someday, she would no longer be a sheep farmer.

JASON APPROACHED HER AS SHE walked up to the field. With his usual larger-than-life presence, she felt her apprehension fade. She was safe.

With a curt nod, he bid her good morning.

"Good morning, Jason. How are they faring this morning?"

A few of the seven-month-old lambs followed him over to her, and she ran a hand through the soft wool of one nuzzling her leg.

"Very good," he replied. "I'm confident we won't lose any this year. I think we've come through the worst. Those damn rainstorms. Is Mr. Leary coming by to pick them up?"

"I'm weighing a few bids. He'll probably be my choice again."

"I've mucked the stalls and fed the chickens. The eggs are in the stillroom." He turned to the herd of lambs crowding under the shade of a large oak. "I'll take them up a ways today. I think they want to test themselves. Exercise will tender the meat."

Jane agreed and left him to do his work. She walked to the garden and grabbed her straw hat off one of the fence posts and picked up a large basket to put the weeds in. She reached into her apron pocket and took out the calendula cream and rubbed it on her hands before placing leathery gloves on. It was a routine that had helped, and she could confirm that to her customers. She breathed in the soft air and let it out. Another day on the land.

The sun bore down on her as she finished weeding and harvesting the large plot. It was time for a glass of juice. As she drank the sweetened lemonade, Jane looked at the glass. A pretty flower pattern swirled around the handblown crystal. She laughed out loud. *Well, my dear, at least you can still drink out of crystal!* With the day still ahead, she had no time to contemplate the lifestyle she'd once had. The stillroom was full of jars ready to be filled with her latest creams in mixtures of lavender and peppermint, calendula and rosemary, and citrus oils.

Back in her conservatory, she poured the oil, rendered from boiled sheep fat, over a bunch of lavender. The infusion would take several days. The sound of an approaching horse caught her attention. Stepping out, she saw Mr. Leary dismounting near the barn. She wiped her hands on a towel and walked over to greet him.

"Good day, Mrs. Cabot."

"Good day, Mr. Leary. Have you come with your best offer? I have several waiting to be addressed."

"I have come with my best offer. I'm afraid you'll find the other buyers will take advantage of your situation. I would be careful there. The market is ready, and you might feel pressure to take any bid that's offered."

"I'm not that naïve. Thank you."

"Why, of course. Excuse me."

Jane knew her correspondence with the other merchants had her selling low, but with the promise of taking the flock sight unseen, and as soon as possible with cash up front. Her only real income came from the sale of the lambs. A quick transaction with ready money was tempting. She prayed Mr. Leary wouldn't follow the lead of the others. The wool merchants would be next. Money from selling produce and her products had added to her income, but not enough to run the farm. She regretted selling the cows.

Mr. Leary took his hat off. "I'll be as fair as I was with your husband, ma'am."

"Thank you."

"May I say, why don't you join up your farm with Harry's?"

"I want to run things myself. I don't need a man to run my business. I think I can make a profit just as any man can. You are dealing with me as you did with my husband. I've checked the books. I know what the fair value is." *As good as any man!*

"Yes, well, the market can be fickle. I can give you eight cents a pound. I think Jason says there's fifty-two heads. I'll have to weigh them in a few weeks to give you an accurate account."

Jane's mouth dropped. "Mr. Leary, that's hardly what I expected. Last year we got nearly twice as much."

"Eight cents is my best offer. The taste for mutton and lamb isn't as popular as it used to be. My buyers in the East are finding their own ways of growing the meat. Once the rich loved it on their fair tables; now, not so much. The price dropped enough to be of great concern to me. I think I may go into the cattle business, as I suggested to Harry to do. I think you oughta do the same. The wool, however, is still a good price. You may profit enough off of it to make up for my offer. I'm truly sorry, ma'am."

"Don't be. I'll take your offer. Shall we write up the paperwork?"

Jane sent Mr. Leary off with her thanks for his honesty. Inside she felt a sense of defeat.

Cattle? How in hell's name am I to start raising cattle?

She had to talk with Harry. Her pride would have to take a back seat, as her love for him had for all these months; business would be the only topic. She rarely saw him, and when she did, a stoic politeness came over her. Still, her actions did not remove her guilt, and to her amazement, it was fading of its own accord as she worked hard to prove she could make the farm profitable.

Coughing into her handkerchief, she rubbed the ache in her chest, which had become her companion. The day was fading, as was her will to continue in her efforts. Each day ended the same with the same question she asked herself: How long can you keep this up? The answer was always the same: What else did she have? Where else would she go? Marry Harry? Settle onto his farm? Become a farmer's wife again? Would he want children? She wasn't a young woman anymore.

The thought of being with him was like dipping into a lovely pool of warm water as it caressed her sore, tired body. The thought was also a surrender of everything she had become, giving a sharp cold splash of water to her face.

JANE MET WITH HARRY THE next day, and they compared their profits from the sale to Mr. Leary. Harry had more heads, so his profit was greater, but Jane was proud of her sale.

"I have plans to continue my farm's growth," Harry said. "Leary told me about turning to the cattle business. I have the land. By selling the sheep now, I can still make a profit. I figure I can start off with about fifty head of cattle. I'd have to hire a team to drive them up here from Colorado. Consider my offer of joining up our farms."

Jane didn't want any more livestock. Her mind was clearly on creating more land for produce and flowers.

"Jane, are you listening to me?"

"Yes, Harry, he told me the same thing. I don't want to be a cattle rancher. I'm just getting used to being a sheep farmer." She tried to avoid his eyes, his face, the way his hair brushed his collar, and his lips—the lips she dreamed of kissing again. "I'd like to explore how I can make better use of my land for produce for my remedies and beauty products. I don't want to be a livestock farmer."

"I see. Well, that's fine. We can certainly do it all," he replied.

"What would the townspeople say? You and I together after the tragic death of my husband, your cousin?"

Harry humphed. "I don't really care. It would be a business deal. But if your reputation is what matters, we'll wait a while longer to make things official, though next month will be a year since his death."

Jane stared off into the distance.

"A while longer," she said. "I can't believe it's been a whole year. It seems like only a few days ago, and yet I feel as if I've been running this farm by myself for . . . forever."

"No more. You'll have me. You can spend all your time on your concoctions and potions, my little witch."

"Harry! I could be burned at the stake for such talk!"

They shared a laugh, knowing that at one time it had been so.

Jane pursed her lips. Why was she putting him off? She wanted him, but did she want his way of life?

Harry came closer and brought a stray hair away from her face. He bent down and kissed her cheek. Her insides softened, and her desire was reignited. It had been too long since he'd touched her.

"Harry, I don't think I'm ready."

"All right. Let me know when you are."

He pulled away, and she felt a hollowness that needed filling. The moment was ripe. They were alone. The dusk of the day was announcing the end of work. The years with Martin had been lonely, and the grief she carried was for both men, but the man standing in front of her was the one she longed for.

She drew him back to her, signaling her willingness. Taking her hand, he led her to the bedroom. He closed the door, though the house was empty. They quietly laughed together.

He untied her blue-gray apron, faded from washing, and tossed it to the other side of the room. She felt his fingers work their way down her back as he unbuttoned her calico dress. It dropped to the floor, and she stepped out of the heap of worn-thin material. A chill ran through her.

He undressed himself with urgency, and for the first time, she saw him in all his glorious nakedness. His torso was lighter than his tanned arms. His muscles were strong and well-defined even at rest, though there was little restfulness about him now. He breathed hard and swung her up by the waist. She landed on the bed, and a high-pitched laugh escaped her as he brought her under the fluffy duvet.

"Take the rest of your clothes off," he whispered.

She removed her chemise. With his help, the heavy knit stockings came off in two sweeps and were flung away, followed by her cotton pantaloons.

His passion rose, and she met it with her own. Closing her eyes, she felt the heady sensation of his warm body on hers, his lips on her lips. It was dreamlike. Then his lips left hers to explore her smooth skin. She moaned when his mouth found her nipples. It nearly sent her into a swoon.

After all these years of waiting. Finally, satisfaction! And she had never been more satisfied than at this moment.

He was inside her as smoothly as oil slipping down her fingertips. Watery, then rough, then silky smooth. Their bodies fit together perfectly. She arched up as his rhythmic movements sent her mind tumbling into a restless sea of emotion.

This was truly happening. So complete was their union, she wanted to weep. Never had she felt so satisfied with Martin as she did at this moment with Harry. This was what she had missed all those years.

He came off her with a throaty laugh. She waited, her heart beating strong in her chest. He lay beside her, and she felt his own heart in a pounding rhythm. They lay in silence, and then he slowly began to kiss her neck, then her lips. His hand slid over her thigh and onto her buttocks, where he grabbed her and brought her closer. His kisses became lusty. He wasn't turning over to fall asleep!

She was giddy and playfully pushed at him.

"Give me a moment to catch my breath!" she said, half laughing.

He grinned his grin, the one he saved for her, though now it was full of want.

They played and laughed and teased and made love until the night slipped away and dawn began to light up the sky.

FROM THAT TIME FORWARD, THEIR relationship took on greater meaning. In the light of day, Jane let the thoughts of him and their love play in her heart and mind while she tried to concentrate on her chores. Many more nights of lovemaking and many more days of toil and struggle followed. The polarizing of her world felt strange.

Tonight, she lay alone in bed thinking of her future, dreaming of her future.

Making a marriage with Harry would be the right thing to do, though it would mean compromise. He was willing to see her and her desires, but what would she have to prove? What if she sold all her sheep and livestock and began to focus only on her products?

The beauty products were selling well to wealthy women in Oakland, while the housewives purchased her remedies. She was greatly encouraged and hoped to eventually sell in other cities. She thought of training Jason to help her in the gardens instead of him tending to animals. The work would still be hard but more to her liking. How glorious that would be.

She knew Harry would work hard all of his life. It was something she understood.

Scrubbing her nails clean at the end of the day from laboring for her own profit brought her satisfaction. Would she be able to give it up now to cook and clean and take care of a husband and possibly a child? A small yet nagging voice inside her said, *He needs a farm wife.* Was she cut out to be only a farmer's wife? Or a merchant of fine creams and oils? A beauty boutique owner perhaps?

She sat up in bed. *Oh, stop dreaming, Jane!* Pounding her pillows into submission and lying back down, she decided to listen to her instincts. She would put off the merging of their farms as long as possible, along with the merging of their souls in God's name.

CHAPTER THIRTY-SIX

November 1888

THE MESSENGER BOY BROUGHT HIS HORSE TO A STOP IN FRONT of Jane's home. She came out to receive what news he had, though she couldn't think for the life of her what it might be.

"Hello, John. What have you for me?"

He leaned down from his seat. "Telegram, ma'am."

"Thank you." Jane took the paper and reached into her apron and gave him a penny. "It's all I have at the moment."

"No worries, ma'am. Thank you." He turned his horse around and trotted away.

Jane read the telegram. Her curiosity was duly piqued.

The family lawyer, Mr. Shipman, and his wife would be in Clermont City within a few days. How odd of him to come out here. The telegram was brief. He wrote he had information for her.

More bad news about her brother's affairs? Hopefully it didn't involve her money. Mr. Shipman would find no resources to settle any accounts here.

Then she wondered if she would have to entertain the lawyer and his wife. Her mind went to her larder. There was a cured lamb shank she was hoping would get her through until next month. If she cut it thinly perhaps? The end of the summer crop was good, and she had plenty of onions, carrots, and beets. With a few potatoes, it might all come together to make a good stew. She could arrange a plate of new lettuce leaves and radishes. An orange cake with lemon sauce for dessert.

Her heart sank. The wealthy lawyer and his wife might expect so much more.

THE DAY WAS STILL AND warm. Fall was a favorite season for Jane. Here it meant a mild winter to come, not the dreaded snow and ice she'd been brought up to know.

Mr. and Mrs. Shipman would be arriving any minute. Jane laid out a tea service and a small lunch of biscuits and the thin slices of cold lamb with her own red pepper and mint chutney. The orange cake and sauce were included. She had decided she'd have to direct them to Carley's Restaurant for their main meal.

She glanced up at the walls where her expensive art had once hung. She looked around at her fine furnishings, which had once seen better days. Not only did the sheepdog think her parlor was his on colder nights, so did some of the chickens on occasion. She wasn't always keen on wiping her feet as she came and went from the garden to the house. She had a hard time keeping the house as spotless as Margie had. Her best dress was a bit faded, and her skin was darkened by the sun.

Nevertheless, her tireless efforts yesterday had put a bit of shine on the home. She wished she could have done the same with her appearance. She had to remind herself that she had nothing to be embarrassed about. The graveled courtyard had been raked, and the pots of flowers on either side of her porch stairs were welcoming.

"Mr. Shipman, I must admit I am surprised to see you here," Jane said as she shook the older man's hand. He'd become even more ancient than she remembered.

"My dear Mrs. Cabot, I'm sure you are," he replied. "Here is my wife, Mrs. Shipman."

The women greeted each other, and Jane led them into her house. She noticed their inspection of it and tried to squelch the feeling of embarrassment.

"Mrs. Shipman and I would like to offer you our deepest sympathies for the loss of your husband. I take it you did get our card? But you seem to be doing well enough, Jane. I'm glad to see it."

"Thank you. I did. That was kind of you. Please be seated," she implored. "I'm sure the journey was tiring."

"We got here last night," began Mrs. Shipman. "We're staying at the sweetest little hotel. I must say, Clermont City is a charmer! And your home is a quintessential farmhouse, though I haven't seen many." She laughed lightly.

"And the land," Mr. Shipman said. "My, there is so much land between Cincinnati and here. Open land! I say, I must let my real estate friends know about—"

"The train was an absolute delight," said Mrs. Shipman. "So relaxing. We're having a marvelous vacation!"

This spurred Jane to get right to the point.

"I'm pleased you're enjoying yourselves. As I recall, Mr. Shipman, you have some information for me."

Mrs. Shipman clapped her hands and rubbed them together. "This is the best part!"

Jane sat in confusion, and she was a bit agitated. She had a list of chores to do.

Mr. Shipman reached into the briefcase he'd brought in with him and took out a paper with gold embossment on it. He handed it to Jane, a wide smile on his face.

"You are the proud owner of a diamond mine," he said with great satisfaction.

She took the paper and inspected it. Tilting her head, she gave the lawyer an uninterested glare. "You came all this way to hand me a worthless piece of paper? I don't need any souvenirs of my brother's debauchery in the diamond business." She offered it back to him.

"No, Jane. This one is a legitimate business, and it's making millions of dollars."

Jane looked at Mrs. Shipman, who sat next to her husband, grinning from ear to ear.

"It was signed over to you and your husband when your brother redid his will," Mr. Shipman continued. "Mr. Cabot had signed it over to you in his will, and now that he is no longer with us, God rest his soul, it goes to you. I doubt either man had a clue as to its worth."

She reexamined the piece of parchment. "My husband didn't have a will. What are you saying?"

Mr. Shipman looked at his wife, then back to Jane.

"He did indeed. His will was directed to me. I took care of it for him. I will have you refer to his cousin, Mr. Harry Cabot, for information regarding it. I'm surprised he didn't tell you about your husband's last wishes. And Martin didn't give you a copy of his will?"

Jane was taken aback with the extent of privacy her husband had dealt in. Harry, she decided, was an accomplice to the desires of his cousin. A men's private club, in a way. She would certainly tell Harry what she thought of it.

"What do I have to do about this diamond mine, Mr. Shipman?"

Sitting back, Mr. Shipman opened his hands. "You don't have to do anything. They have the right people handling it. I have investigated the business and decided to invest in it myself. You can sell your share of it if you wish." He reached again into his briefcase and took out another document. "Here is the value of your share as it stands today."

Jane slowly accepted the paper and read through some of the legal jargon, which she didn't understand. Near the bottom, a figure was written out: *$356,000.*

She pointed to the amount as she turned the document to face Mr. Shipman.

"Yes, my dear Jane, you are exceedingly wealthy."

Jane felt her head spin in disbelief. She brought her hand to her forehead.

"Oh, Lowell, I think this is a great shock to her," said Mrs. Shipman.

Jane slowly shook her head. When she came to her senses, she asked, "How long has it been this successful?"

"Oh, I would say at least four years."

Falling back in her seat, Jane was without words. Her mind reeled.

Four years? All the hard work she and Martin had put into keeping the farm going, every day she'd toiled to make it work with little help, and all the while she sat on this wealth? It was unbelievable to her.

She wondered what Martin would have done had he known of the riches this mine had brought them. Disheartened at his secrecy, she added it to the many questions that still hung in the air concerning her late husband. She had forgiven his betrayal of trust, but his secrecy still haunted her.

Looking up from her thoughts, she found the Shipmans staring at her with anticipation.

"I'm sorry, but this is a shock," she said.

"A very good one!" Mrs. Shipman said.

"I wish we could have found out sooner," Mr. Shipman said. "These foreign investments can be hard to track, and I had to be sure. My office looked high and low for assets to help satisfy your brother's estate debts. We worked long after his passing. I felt an obligation to your father and brother. When we found this, well, we were overjoyed. Of course, the estate was paid off first. The bank still took the house. It was sold at auction for a measly amount. His gambling debts—"

"Yes. I understand. Thank you for your work," Jane replied.

"You will, no doubt, want to discuss this with an investment lawyer," said Mr. Shipman. "I think the dividends alone are going to set you up quite well." He took a biscuit and layered the lamb and spooned a bit of the chutney on top. After a bite, he came away with wide eyes. "Mm, very tasty. Nothing like farm food, is there?"

Mrs. Shipman followed his lead and helped herself. "We hope this will bring you the joy it has brought us," she said as she took her own bite and agreed with her husband on the taste. After swallowing, she said, "I wasn't sure Lowell was in his right mind when he invested, but it turned out to be the best decision he's ever made. We are on a countrywide tour." She slipped her arm through her husband's. "It's wonderful to have him finally retired."

Mr. Shipman chimed in, "I have my best attorney to replace me, for your guidance." He reached into his coat pocket. "Here is his card. He deals with financial business."

Jane took the card. She placed it on her lap with the documents. The weight of the papers hid their worth. How could she be this rich? Richer than her father?

"Well, my dear, you have a lot to think about, and we must be on our way," said Mr. Shipman.

Jane walked them out, still in disbelief.

Mrs. Shipman took her hand before she was helped onto the carriage seat. "God bless you, my dear. Don't let this change you now. Money can do that. You have a wonderful piece of heaven here. I enjoyed meeting you. Good day."

Jane had no words but to simply say, "Thank you. It was nice to meet you as well."

Mr. Shipman gave her similar advice, adding, "Keep your guard up, and let no one know how rich you are."

Before Mr. Shipman entered the carriage, Jane met his eyes.

"Thank you," she said with all sincerity. "I feel I owe you an apology for my behavior when we met last."

"Think nothing of it. You were in distress, and I was not as compassionate as I should have been. Water under the bridge?"

Jane nodded. "Yes."

After the Shipmans departed, Jane walked inside the house and took up the envelope, looking at the card. A Mr. Phillip Rigby would be her attorney? Cincinnati? She wasn't sure she wanted anything to do with the city ever again.

She sat down and began to feel a rush of freedom pulsing through her. No more chores? No more worries? She would have to forgive Harry for his part in this. What did it matter now? They could begin a life of ease—together! San Francisco was wide-open to her. The possibilities were endless.

Chad came to mind. The end of his life must have been filled with heartache. The foreclosure of the house, the fall from grace. She hadn't dared ask Mr. Shipman where he had been living in the end or in what state; she didn't want to know. He hadn't gotten to enjoy the high life he'd so strived to achieve. Then she remembered him for who he was, and a part of her felt deserving of this windfall. She took it as a clear sign it was time for a change. The luxuries of life would be hers again.

Clutching the large envelope, she sighed and fell back onto the couch while tears of joy ran down the sides of her face, as she laughed out loud.

CHAPTER THIRTY-SEVEN

*A*FTER A SLEEPLESS NIGHT OF PLANNING AND REPLANNING, rehearsing her speech to Harry and indulging in what may lay ahead, Jane rose tired but with ease. The weight of the world had been lifted off her shoulders.

She sipped her coffee, and once again the joy of her new circumstance filled her with energy.

This was the opportunity she and Harry could grab with both hands. They could finally be a couple. The city would welcome them. The travel could be as extensive as they'd like. Her home would be everything she wished for. A city dwelling, and perhaps a cottage in Clermont City to stay in when she visited her friends. Bell would be her cook, and she would pay her generously. Lacey could come back as her assistant. Maybe even the prickly Margie would be her maid and housekeeper again. But why stop with them? A French chef for dinner parties? A dresser and dressmaker? Yes, she would have it all!

Coming back down to earth, she finished her coffee and joined Jason in the field.

Jane stood alongside Jason and approved his plans for moving the sheep and lambs to better grazing as she petted one of the furry babes and a few more who came near her. It was time to let them go. This was always a difficult season for Jane. She grew fond of the little creatures. She loved the lambing season even if it cost her to hire more hands and she worked twice as hard as any other time of the year.

The vast field was dewy and tinged with green, and it sparkled from the sunlight dappling through the trees. The sweet aroma of the changing season filled her lungs and her heart. A sense of satisfaction and well-being came over her, followed by a stab of remorse and sudden nostalgia for what she was about to leave behind.

Her mind was made up, however. No more caring about the cost of anything. *Will that lamb make it or not? What will the weather bring? Will the wildlife eat more of her gardens? It was always a chore to keep them at bay.* She'd lost six chickens this week to coyotes—a hardship she would no longer have to lament over. Someone else would care about all that. The production and marketing of her creams and ointments would be a wonderful hobby rather than a necessity. No more backbreaking gardening. No more damn sheep!

She stamped her foot. Freedom had come at last.

Jason turned with concern on his face.

"Felt a cramp coming on," she said. She smiled and felt relief soften her shoulders and strengthen her back. "I will be on Mr. Cabot's farm today. There's stew on the cooker and meat pies on the bench in the stillroom. Don't wait for me if you get hungry."

"Thank you, ma'am." Jason gave a nod and turned to his work.

Jane petted the last babe before it ran off to join its mother with the lovely thought of never having to eat lamb stew again. The most important task of the day awaited her. She needed to talk to Harry.

THE SUNLIGHT FOLLOWED HER TO Harry's home. The improvements he'd made over the years had transformed it from a cabin into a modern two-story farmhouse. She stepped up to the porch, almost giddy with her news. He greeted her with a kiss to her cheek, and she warmed.

"This is a pleasant surprise."

"I need to talk with you about Martin's will."

Harry stood back and let her enter. He offered her tea, and she was about to burst with her news, along with a tirade of accusations. They stood close in the kitchen, and she could feel him even though they did not touch. How she wanted him.

"Jane?" he said with an inquisitive grin.

The words rushed out of her, and she forwent her planned speech.

"Why did Martin not tell me about his will? What were you two about? Have neither of you any respect for me at all? Tell me, Harry, what was Martin thinking by keeping me in the dark?"

Harry scrubbed his chin. With his intelligent brown eyes below a furrowed brow, he searched the floor. Jane waited, her nerves pulsing. Finally, he looked up at her.

"Martin didn't want you to know he had left the farm to me."

"What? The farm is mine," she replied.

"He left the farm to me, Jane. He wanted me to take care of it and you if anything happened to him."

"And why didn't he tell me this?" Her cheeks were as hot as her temper.

"You would have been angry. Martin hated confrontation. He did it for your sake, so you wouldn't have the burden."

"But you wanted to merge our farms, and I refused. I really had no say in this from the beginning, did I?"

"I would have let you have a say in it. But I'd never let you get in over your head. I thought merging our businesses would keep me from having to tell you."

Jane turned her back on him. It all became clear. She was a woman, and so she wasn't entitled to any of the business between men. Martin had indulged her because she had money. She'd thought her hard work was for the good of her farm. She didn't know Harry was standing by ready to rescue her if she failed. How enraging! She spun around, her breath laboring from her anger.

"You both lied to me! Did Martin tell you about the diamond mine? Were you going to tell me about it?" She looked into his eyes, where she would find the truth.

"Jane, we didn't lie. We just wanted to protect you. And what diamond mine?" Harry paused. "Oh, yes, he had said something about it. I thought it was a worthless thing. We both did. It was listed in his will, but there was nothing to indicate it was a good investment. He left it to you. I thought it wasn't necessary to tell you that your brother had invested in a worthless mine."

"I suppose it wasn't necessary for either of you to tell me a lot of things. I was his wife, damn it!"

Gripping the counter near his kitchen sink, she turned to look out the window.

"Jane?"

"Give me a minute, Harry."

"I'm sorry," he said in a low voice. "I guess we thought we were doing something good."

Facing him, she told him her worth from the mine.

Harry's eyes went wide, and he let out a whistle. "I can only think that Martin didn't know about that. I'm sure if he knew what it had become, he surely would have—"

"Left it to you? Well, he didn't! It's all mine! I'm a very rich woman. Free and independent!"

"So you are. I'm happy for you, Jane. Please sit down, calm yourself."

She stepped back from him. "Calm myself? Isn't that what all men say when a woman confronts them? I thought you were different, Harry. Women are supposed to be docile and complacent? Well, enough of that for me! If Martin were here, I'd tell you both to go to hell!"

Her bodice moved up and down with her heavy breathing. This was not how she had envisioned this conversation between them, but it felt exhilarating to release her thoughts without a care of his judgment. She stood defiantly, and she was ready to take on any and all of his replies.

The room went silent. Then Harry spoke.

"Please, Jane, forgive me," he said. "You are certainly worth more than all this. I regret going along with Martin's plans. I think my guilt for loving his wife had me doing what he wished. It was wrong. I respect what you've done on the farm, before and since Martin's passing. As much as you might think, I wasn't waiting for you to fail. I was very much wanting and waiting for you to succeed."

With her anger abating, she took in a deep breath and let it out. Of course, he wouldn't try to defend himself; that wasn't Harry. Besides Martin's will, he had always been up-front with her. He was truthful with himself first, and Jane admired him for that. Had his loyalty to Martin excluded his love for her? She wanted that loyalty from him, and more so, she craved his respect.

"I feel betrayed by you and Martin, my brother, and my father. How can I trust you? I wanted to have a life with you, Harry."

"I'm still the man you've come to know. I'm sorry about Martin and your family, but they aren't me. You can't demand resolution from them through me."

Jane shouldn't have been surprised by Harry's response. He always saw right through her. She hated it at times, and this was one of those times. "Why must you be so damn . . ."

He took her gently by the shoulders and brought her close. "So damn what? Reasonable?"

He kissed her lips, and she returned the pleasure of it with her softened mouth. She pulled away. She was here for something else.

"Harry, I have money, we have money. We can do whatever we want! To hell with why Martin chose to keep his wife as a farm-hand." She threw her hands up in the air. "He didn't care for me, only this damn farm. We can sell the thing and be rich city dwellers. We can build a cottage in Clermont and have it as our summer home. Or we can return my home and land to the splendor it can be again. Wouldn't you love to sleep in? Have someone wait on you instead of trudging around the stalls and fields worrying about the weather or the market prices? Think about it. We could be together in the city. No one knows—"

"Jane." He let out a puff of air. "Why do you assume any of that appeals to me? Are we so opposite in our desires? I love you. I want you in my life. I . . . I want you to be my wife."

Stunted, Jane slowly left the kitchen to take a seat in the openness of his main room. He had just proposed marriage without any fanfare. She felt let down. He followed and sat across from her on the cushioned bench by the heat of the burning fireplace. He placed his hands in his lap, and she hugged her arms around her chest. She would meet his practical side with her own.

"Harry, I would very much . . . I . . . Yes, I want that too."

"Your money is yours to do as you wish, but I want to stay on my farm. As I told you before, we can merge the businesses. Of course, it will make things easier for you, but it's not my money."

"If we marry it will become your money. I'm not willing to give it up that easily. I did that once before. Besides, I don't want this for the rest of my life. Not now."

"This life is all I know," he said.

"Because you know nothing else doesn't mean that's all there is for you, Harry. There's a whole world out there full of possibilities. Travel, for one."

"I know it's what you've wanted. Martin spoke of the life he took you from, the places you've traveled to, the hope that someday you and he would be able to do that. Your visits into San Francisco, the style of life you're used to. I see how you have your house and gardens. Even with the loss of income, you manage to keep them neat and stylish. The conservatory alone is a piece worthy of any grand estate." He got up and sat beside her. "But I thought the farm life might appeal to you as you immersed yourself into it. I'm proud of you and the way you've handled all of this. The business you started on your own. Doesn't that mean something to you? I thought we would make a good team. But . . . I was imagining it. I guess my mind imagined us as I would like it to be, not what is true for you." He looked at his hard-worked hands and then back to her. "I'm seeing what Martin may have seen, and like him, I dismissed it for my own dreams and desires. I'm sorry. I know you too well to think you'd still want this life if given the chance to leave it."

Jane felt a hard lump in her throat, and her heart physically ached. She brought her hand to her mouth. *I will not cry.*

Harry took her hand. "Look at me."

She turned to his handsome face, his strong body, and she saw a man who loved her, but only on his own terms.

"Jane, we will build a new home. There's plenty of land. It can be ours. If you want to share your wealth, let's do it that way. I see the pleasure in not worrying about profit."

She lightened. "Yes, yes, and we can have a house in the city as well. Hire people to run the farm."

"I suppose."

His expression was complacent. She didn't like what she saw. This was not what she wanted from the strong man she'd fallen in love with.

"Is that what you really want, Harry?"

"I want to continue as I am, to be honest. You don't understand, Jane."

"No, I don't. I've worked hard, and I find little pleasure in it. It's necessity that drove me. My business is still a passion of mine, and I will continue it in some way, but now I don't need to work hard, and I can take pleasure in watching my gardens grow under someone else's labor." She brought her hands together and felt their roughness even with her balms. She thought of Berta's soft manicured ones. She would have fine hands again.

Harry rose and leaned against the stone hearth. The room was warming to an uncomfortable temperature. She felt his temper growing as well.

"The work of keeping my farm running is good work, and I get great satisfaction from it. I don't want the life you want. I can't have someone wait on me. That's not me, and by God, I would think you'd know that by now." His fist came down on the wooden mantel.

With a jagged breath, Jane stood. "I guess I did, but I thought you'd think different once an opportunity like this came your way."

"Money is not my life. Hard work and the well-deserved restful moments looking out onto my land is my life. Hearing the chickens and cows and sheep talk and knowing when they are content and when they are not is my life. The wind carrying the breezes filled with the scents of my land hitting my senses and nearly knocking me to the ground with joy is something I can't live without. I won't. Do as you wish, but I will stay here."

The tears streamed down her face. As with Martin, she recognized in both men a love for something more powerful than their love for her. The hurt was replaced by a heat that rose like the flames of a fire igniting a rebellion in her.

"Fine! Stay on your damn farm! Take what is yours and all the hardships that come with it. I'm not getting any younger. I want more from life, and damn it, I will have it!" She left his house with a slam of the screen door. Using his mounting block, she got herself up onto her horse and trotted away. The fall morning, so bright and full of promise, had become miserably clouded.

Arriving home, she sat on her porch, her veranda. She would have a finer one in the city. The wind had been sucked out of her sails, and she felt very tired. There were chores to do and business to take care of, but she ignored her duties and made plans to visit Berta. If only she didn't love Harry so dearly. She wouldn't let his pragmatic nature dissolve her excitement. Why was loving him so difficult?

The reality of their differences struck her and filled her heart with grief. She needed to get away. Jason could run the farm for a week or so. After a short rest, she went to her desk and penned a quick note to Berta. She didn't have her funds yet, but the small amount of cash she had on hand would be enough to send a telegram to her friend and pay for the ferry. She knew Berta would take care of her after that. She had kept in touch with her but hadn't visited in several years. She hoped her city friend would be welcoming.

CHAPTER THIRTY-EIGHT

THE RESTFULNESS OF BERTA'S PARLOR OF SOFT BLUES AND overstuffed furniture in light floral prints brought Jane the comfort of spirit she needed. She was tired from her travels that morning, first by coach, then ferry, and finally Berta's carriage, which had taken her through the bumpy streets of the city up the hill to her friend's mansion.

Tired and heartsick over Harry's rejection of the gem of a life she'd presented him with, she sipped on the expensive tea from China and let herself nibble on the ham and creamy cheese-filled butter-flaked bun. She'd had Jason inform Harry of her plans to leave for the city on a week's visit. It wasn't their way to not say goodbye, and it had added to her grief. The journey from home today was where she'd let her mind go over every word of the conversation with Harry. How she'd left it with him tested her resolve. What if she stayed with him? The thought rattled her, and she came back to the fact that there was a life beyond the farm waiting for her. She would experience that life to its fullest. Overlooking Berta's manicured lawn and gardens, she dreamed of her next home of similar grandeur. In this new freedom, she felt comfortable talking to Berta about her affair with Harry and where it now stood.

"Oh! How very disagreeable of him! My poor dear, you must be devastated. After all these years of loving him and taking that risk of being found out? Well, I think it's very poor manners on his part not to accept the wealth and all it could mean to him. This certainly explains your absence. A lover can be very time-consuming," Berta concluded as she stuffed a bite of cucumber-and-watercress sandwich into her mouth. Jane got the feeling Berta reveled in this new side of her.

"It wasn't like that. We rarely—I mean, we were not lovers in a seedy way."

Berta laughed. "Of course you weren't, my dear. I'm sure you were very civilized."

"Don't tease me. It's been very upsetting."

"I'm sorry. I've become cynical in my old age."

Jane nodded. "I'm glad I told you. I had to confess to someone!"

Jane had never revealed her lost income, so Berta assumed Jane was as wealthy as ever. Her new clothes would give that added credence.

As she sat in quiet companionship with her friend, she let herself contemplate Martin keeping her in the dark about his will and the diamond mine and Harry's plea for forgiveness. In truth, Martin had been a simple, honest man. He'd never appeared to be anything else. She would have to accept the fact that he'd acted in their best interest. There was nothing more tiring to her than trying to relive the past and puzzle out her late husband. But Harry was not simple. In fact, his complicated nature added to her love of him. He saw things others might miss. He was simple on the outside to any stranger who didn't take the time to get to know him. She had gotten to know him, and it proved now to be a heartache she wasn't sure she would ever recover from.

"I don't think I can change Harry's mind, Berta." Jane huffed and sipped on her oolong tea.

"Well, there are plenty of eligible men out there. You seem to choose such stick-in-the-mud types. I'll never reason it. I thought you said you were well-bred? Tish! Women are such fickle creatures!"

"Excuse me, but I like men who are down-to-earth. My father was practical and not silly in any way. I suppose that appeals to me. Sincerity is important."

"Of course it is," Berta said in her dismissive way. "My husband, God rest his soul, was never very sincere or honest but, he left me with a bundle." She smiled with satisfaction. "My dear, what does it matter when you can do just as you like? With money, women are free. Look at me. Do I look as if I've missed anything because this one or that one didn't agree with my lifestyle choices?" Berta guffawed. "I daresay no! You simply move on."

Jane gave a short laugh. However, she would not follow Berta's example. Rather, the other ladies of society appealed to her as she looked forward.

There was Mrs. Beechman with her slim beauty still intact and her regal manners to add to it. Her husband seemed still taken with her. Theirs was a good marriage as far as Jane was concerned. Or Mrs. Johns and her lovely, gentle way of being wealthy; she was humble, unlike Berta, who loved to flaunt her status. Another example she would take on was that of her father and his distinguished nature and smooth way of taking charge of his riches. She had nearly lost all such knowledge and training as she'd toiled on the farm. She bit her lip and touched her tanned arm and ragged fingernails. Even her own remedies couldn't make them young and smooth again.

"My goodness, how you've let your hands go. Whatever have you been up to on that farm?" Berta said as if reading Jane's mind.

Days later as Jane roamed the grounds, the sun peeked out among the clouds, yet the wind coming off the water was chilly. She had anticipated that and had packed her heavier shawls. The city was always cooler than across the bay in Clermont City. She wrapped the heavily woven shawl around her as she walked the grounds on Berta's estate. It was nestled among the other grand houses, and the borrowed views were pretty, yet the lack of forest was more evident to Jane than it had been in the past. No matter, she'd made up her mind to find the ideal house, one close to her friend.

At dinner, Jane and Berta sat at one end of the long dining table with Berta at the head and Jane to her left. Sunbeams shot into the room from the high windows, and the fireplace had a roaring glow. The feeling of warmth and pleasure engulfed Jane. The meal came in four courses, as was Berta's way of dining. She pressed Jane on buying the estate they had looked at the other day.

"You must grab up the Chatsworth house. Now that you are widowed, there is no need for you to stay on that farm," Berta said as she wiped her mouth with a gold-threaded linen napkin. Placing it back on her wide lap, she continued. "It's a bit on the older side and needs work, but you certainly have the time and money to make it just what you want it to be." With her large girth inhibiting her movements, Berta leaned over and tapped Jane on the knee. "How very exciting!"

"Thank you for helping me find it. And yes, I think it will be the very thing I need to occupy my time." Jane smiled, but inside she was in turmoil. Harry wouldn't be sharing her life there. "I could put in a nice garden. I love the taste of fresh vegetables, and it may fit a small circular conservatory for my plants. Also, I will have to have a stillroom for making my products. How do you like the lavender cream I brought for you? Yes, gardening will refresh me, I'm sure."

Berta nearly choked on her next bite. Jane jumped up to her friend's rescue. Berta waved her to sit and took a sip of water.

"I'm fine," she said as she wiped the tears from her eyes. "Oh!" She sat back and took in a breath. "My God! You can't be serious. My dear, please leave the farm across the bay! Next thing you will tell me is you want a sheep for a pet!" With a great boisterous laugh, Berta grabbed a square of cake from a platter of pastries set in front of her. After swallowing, she added, "The lavender cream is lovely, best I've ever tried. I wish it were for sale here, but sell the recipe and let someone else do all that work."

Jane didn't take offense to her friend's comments. She knew Berta wouldn't understand. A thought came to mind. The women in Berta's social circle would love her hand creams and hair oils. Her thoughts danced in her head as Berta helped herself to another pastry.

ON THE SIXTH NIGHT, JANE lay in the sumptuous bed with its canopy of fine satiny fabric overhead. The glow of the gold damask felt like a light shining down on her. The days with Berta had run into one another in a most languorous way. She felt renewed and light as a feather, yet throughout her weeklong stay she'd struggled to break loose of the feeling of profound loss. She'd thought she heard a lamb bleating in the distance one night. It was her imagination. She woke up worrying about rainfall and the lower temperatures and how it would affect her more tender crops. They must be harvested before it got too cold. Tonight, however, she had decided to purchase the Chatsworth house and make it a grand estate where she would host memorable parties and balls. She'd go see Ned tomorrow, after she shopped at the dressmaker's for a new wardrobe. Her credit was good until she obtained her funds. The aprons and boots she had worn all these years would remain in the conservatory where they belonged, not in her foyer as they were in her present home.

Berta's maid came in and drew the curtains closed and turned up the gaslights. "Is there anything you would like, Mrs. Cabot?"

"No. Thank you, Rachel. I think I will read for a while."

"Very good, ma'am. Good night."

"Good night, Rachel."

The door closed quietly, and Jane slumped back onto the fluffy pillows. She reached for her book on the side table and continued to read about a medicinal garden. She knew most of it by rote, but she had put away her books for the real work. Tonight, she let herself pore over all the lovely flowers, herbs, roots, and wild flora and their purposes as she marveled at the botanical artist's renditions. As sleep took her, she thought about her own gardens, the labor she'd put into them and the results. For now, her deep desire to find the person she'd been before she was forced into toil and sweat would overrule her sentimentality.

CHAPTER THIRTY-NINE

December 1888

HAVING FINALLY RECEIVED THE FIRST INSTALLMENT OF funds from Mr. Rigby's office, it took only a few weeks to sign the papers and become the new owner of the Chatsworth house. Even with her riches, Jane drove a hard bargain. She renamed it Wallingford Estate. It would be a nod to her father and mother and even her brother, whose dangerous investing practices had actually paid off and in her favor.

She sat in the Cabot Farm house going over her accounts. Paying the mounting debts was a great relief. Each month she would receive a large sum of money from her dividends. It would be more than she had ever had in the bank. A bank in San Francisco would be her choice, along with one in New York and one in Cincinnati. Mr. Rigby had suggested all three to spread out her wealth. Investing in properties would come later. She would manage her wealth as carefully as she had managed her farm, but with help from Mr. Rigby. Now it was time to tell Harry she was leaving.

He had come to visit only once since her return from Berta's, and it had been to deliver a stray sheep back to the pen. She caught only a glimpse of him from the kitchen window. He gave her a wave, and she held up her hand in return. This morning she'd received a message from him through Jason. He wanted to meet to discuss business. She tried desperately to focus on her accounts, but her anticipation made her stomach queasy. The knock on the door had her rushing to the mirror for a quick review of her hair and face. She smoothed the stiff bodice of her new dress.

Opening the door, she steadied herself. "Hello, Harry. Come in."

"Hello, Jane."

He stepped inside and stood too close. She took one step back and regretted the message it sent, but he didn't seem to notice.

"I have refreshments in the parlor," she rushed to say.

He gave a nod and followed her in. She took a seat, her back straight from her new corset. He remained standing with his folded hat in both his hands. The feelings that rose from his rugged good looks disturbed her. A party at Berta's had revealed the dandies swarming for attention around the available women, with her being the rich widow. Like the boys back home, those men were all clean and mockingly virtuous. Harry was real and sincere, and her heart ached for him as much as her body did.

"Before we start talking about business," he said, "I have to tell you how sorry I am that we left things so badly. I respect you too much to not honor your wishes for a better life. I didn't mean to disparage it in any way. It's not the life for me, but I love you, and above all, I want you to be happy. Shall we still be friends? Close friends?"

Friends? After what we've done together? What we've meant to each other? She pulled her thoughts back to the business at hand.

"I would like to think about it, Harry. For now, we need to settle the farm business between us."

Harry sat down and looked deep into her eyes. She wanted to drown in that look, but she couldn't if she was going to be strong and pursue her dreams. She couldn't live on the farm the rest of her life, especially knowing that it hadn't ever been hers. Even being back, she felt choked by its demands.

Touching the side of her neck, she glanced at the fireplace. The morning coldness kept it lit, and she caught herself worrying about having enough wood for the winter. Suddenly, the uncleared ashes called to her to do her duty and forget this nonsense of wanting more than she already had. She shook off the feeling.

"He left me with nothing. Martin gave you the one resource that I needed to survive."

"You don't need it now."

She rose from her seat. "I don't. I never will again. You can have it."

"He wanted me to care for the farm and you if anything happened to him," Harry said, pleading his case again. "He wanted you to be free of the burden."

Taking a breath and letting it out, she stood by the mantel. "Was I free of the burden?" She gave a sharp laugh. "So many plans. So many hidden gems, quite literally, that I have been ignorant of. What else, Harry? What else did you and Martin have planned for me? Here I was, guilt ridden and ready to go to confession twice a week to rid my soul of our love, our sinful lust for each other, and he hands me over to you as his dying wish."

Harry gave a huff. His voice was husky with emotion. "You don't have to put it that way. You are your own person. From the first day I met you, I knew that you had a streak of independence and self-assuredness. Truth be told, your beauty and sensuality alone confused me as to why you were with my mousy cousin. I've come to know you as a good and strong woman, someone I admire. Together we can accomplish so much."

Jane held up her hand to stop him from continuing. "I don't want to accomplish anything with you or anyone else. Martin had big plans for us. Look where it got us, where it got me. I'm free now. I will do my own accomplishing by myself if you don't mind." The words poured out of her without edit. She didn't want to sound so harsh, and yet everything she'd said was true.

Standing, Harry placed his cap on his head. "All right, Mrs. Cabot."

His formal acceptance angered her, but she had only one response.

"Good day, Mr. Cabot. And it's *Jane* Cabot."

Harry smirked and left.

Jane turned to the mantel and brought her fist down on the hard wood. "Damn it!"

This would end their relationship as she had come to know and depend on. It would sever her ties with the farm Martin had loved. Jane felt the stinging of her tears as this bittersweet moment hit her. *This is it, then*, she thought. She swiped her face of the tears. He saw a strong woman, and she was determined to be just that.

HER BELONGINGS HAD BEEN PACKED up and sent over to Berta's. The house had been packed up as well, and the furnishings would wait in storage as her new estate took shape. Harry came by while the carriage driver loaded her bags and cases.

"Hello, Harry."

"I wanted to see you off. I hope we can still . . ."

Jane sniffed and brought her handkerchief to her nose. "I'm happy the farm will be well cared for."

"Come around anytime to make sure of it. You are welcome anytime. Anytime at all." Harry wiped his own nose.

"The rest of my furnishings will be out soon."

"I'm not renting it until you say so."

"Thank you, Harry."

He took her hand. "Thank you for being in my life, Jane. Be happy so I know I've made the right decision in letting you go."

The lump in her throat left her speechless, and with a wobbly chin, she nodded her answer. Suddenly, his arms were wrapped around her, and she fell into his embrace. Their hearts beat against each other's as if they were struggling to join but could not.

Coming apart, she inhaled his scent and tried to be brave. Begging him to come with her on her new adventure was a waste of words. Instead, she would savor this moment. Her love for him would always be in this moment. His misty eyes, soft and generous; his powerful arms; his stance at the ready to welcome her back in a flash if she even hinted at changing her mind.

"Let's leave it like this, Harry. And hope the future will somehow bring us back together one day."

His expression was one of exasperation.

"Dear God! How you wrangle me in!" he said in a raised voice. "Do not give me hope, lady. I can't have hope, or I will be a rotten mess, and our—my—farms will suffer to no end. I will say good bye and wish you a good life."

Turning on his heel, he gave her no time to respond. She watched him leave while standing still in the muck of her making. Why had she let her romantic love for him surface with such a damn stupid comment?

I need to find my own way. I need to find who I am off this goddamn farm!

Part Three

CHAPTER FORTY

San Francisco—September 1889

 THINK THE BROCADE IN THE BLUE AND GRAY HUES WILL do well for the front room chairs." Ned's voice echoed in the expansive entry of her new house. The house was cavernous without the drapes and furniture and all the adornments. The many carpenters' hammers and their comings and goings among their makeshift worktables and benches littered with debris and lunch pails added chaos to the scene. The late-summer heat ran sweat down her corseted bodice, and she couldn't wait for a cool bath back at Berta's.

Wallingford Estate was not yet the luxurious home she envisaged. She'd moved into Berta's home, and it was going on nearly ten months of renovations. Off the hall, the plasterers were in the dining room redoing the intricately carved chair rails and the high patterned ceiling around which would eventually hang an elaborate chandelier. Jane loved the soft hues of blue and mint green she and Ned had chosen for the downstairs parlor. She followed his finger pointing to a leaf of fabric from the heavy book laden with samples.

"Yes, I think that would be fine," Jane said as she rubbed a temple with her ungloved hand. "Nothing bold or overly frilly. You know I despise the heavy, dark interiors of old Victorian homes. A new day is dawning. We'll be entering a new decade soon, and I want Wallingford Estate to shine bright with the modern era."

Ned turned to her and patted her shoulder. "Ah, I like your way of thinking, my lovely. Just as I did those years ago when we turned that old wreck of a farmhouse into a . . . well, decent home." He paused and continued to look at her.

"What is it?" she asked.

"I have to say, I was worried you had truly turned farmer's wife on me."

"Farmer's widow, you mean."

"I'm sorry, Jane."

For a moment, Jane saw empathy in Ned's eyes. It would be the first time she had seen anything like it from her city friend. He and Berta were very happy for her to come off the farm, and in fact, she sensed they might even be happy she had been widowed. It was more respectable than being a divorced woman.

"Thank you, Ned. It's been a difficult time. I don't know what I would have done without you and Berta."

"I know how hard it must be. I'm not all parties and jolly times. Life has its ups and downs for all of us. I can tell you, my love life is a mess right now, but I carry on." He clapped his hands. "Let's go upstairs. I want to show you the array of pinks I've chosen for your boudoir."

"Oh, Ned, not pink!"

They laughed as he took her hand, and she pretended to be dragged up the long, sweeping staircase.

I<small>N HER BEDROOM AT</small> B<small>ERTA'S</small>, Jane could relax and be herself. She was worn out and wouldn't let herself acknowledge how draining this effort of restoring and renovating the old estate was. The excitement and energy she'd once had in redoing her farmhouse was gone. Even with her ability to throw as much money as needed to the craftsmen to get the job done as soon as possible, it was still taking too much time. She was becoming weighed down with decisions.

Berta's constant parties and Ned's dramatic flair had begun to wear on her. She and her new gardener, Miguel, had argued over where the gardens would go. Of course, she got her way, but it had not been pleasant. She missed having Mr. Hill by her side, making it a true partnership resulting in a labor of love. She hoped their relationship would develop over time, as was her desire with the other staff she would hire. The interviews for a cook, undercook, housekeeper, and lady's maid, along with a carriage driver, groom, and stable boy had taken over her life alongside the constant demands on her choices for everything from the color of a pillow to the redoing of latticework on the arbor by the back entrance. Every detail had to be approved by her. Why wasn't this as joyful as the Cabot house and gardens? Maybe she was just getting old.

Tonight, as she sat in the tufted chair by the window overlooking Berta's gardens, her head hurt less, but her heart felt heavy. The nighttime serenade of Cabot Farm snuck into her thoughts. She couldn't stop thinking about Harry. She had also purchased a smaller home north of the city and by the sea for short getaways. Her seaside cottage. It, too, was being remodeled. She imagined herself and Harry there. Sipping her sherry, she let her guard fall away, and tears ran down her face. The light silk dressing gown allowed her chest the freedom to heave as her sobs grew deeper. As she came back from her emotional release, she swore she would not love again. Money would be enough for her. It brought her freedom and power in a world where most women had neither.

As the summer turned to autumn and the cooler nights and short days turned her mood more somber, Jane thought a visit to the Loggins would help her escape the renovation, which seemed to be never-ending, not to mention the noise of the city that surrounded her. Guarding herself from Clermont City's downtown and the farms, she would stay on the hill in the tranquility of the Loggins' homestead.

CHAPTER FORTY-ONE

October 1889

$\mathcal{A}$FTER SECURING THE WORKERS' PLANS, JANE LET HER contractor and Ned take over the last of the Wallingford Estate project. Once on the ferry, she realized how much she needed to get away and how odd it was that Clermont City had become a place to escape to rather than one to escape from. Life, Jane had come to recognize, was filled with such oddities.

The stagecoach dropped her off at the Clermont City station. She didn't bother to search the street for Harry. Sally had said he'd traveled up north to visit someone, the "someone" being a woman. Jane knew that in such a small town, everyone was aware of everyone else's business. It caused her to wonder if her and Harry's affair had ever made the gossip mill. Her jealousy was ignited, and it made her weak and vulnerable.

She emerged from the coach in her best tailored traveling outfit. The milliner had charged her a pretty penny for the peacock-embellished hat she wore atop her finely coiffed updo. Her gloves, a fine kid leather, fit exactly to her hands. Ben strode up and helped her the rest of the way down. She smoothed her skirt and her bodice trimmed with delicate hand-embroidered lace. She reached in for her small case, but Ben was ahead of her.

"Welcome, Jane! Let me take your bag. Come and I'll get you in my carriage, then get the rest of your things."

"I'm afraid there's quite a bit."

"That's all right. Sally wants you to stay as long as you want."

Jane settled into Ben's carriage and noticed its broken-in appearance. She'd have to remedy that. She tucked her skirt in as to not get it soiled. He got out in front and took the reins, and then they were off. The carriage swayed violently up the hill. She wanted to shout for him to take more care. With one hand on her expensive hat and another gripping the side of the open cab, she tried to keep her discomfort to herself. Besides, Ben didn't seem to take any notice.

Sally ran out to greet Jane, and they embraced and laughed, the friendship easily coming back to them. Along with Lacey, Sally was one of Jane's constant friends in town.

She instantly felt at home at the Loggins'; it was just what she needed. The attic room, now turned into her bedroom, was quaint and well-done in ginghams and rose prints. It was what Jane had expected. The opulence of Wallingford Estate couldn't match the coziness of this room.

A yellow-painted dresser was tucked under the eaves, and a small table and mirror with an upholstered chair sat to one side of the walnut wardrobe. A narrow yet comfortable-looking bed finished the room. The wardrobe would be adequate, yet she knew she'd brought too many dresses, shoes, and hats.

Relaxing her shoulders, she felt relief from the nagging headaches. She knew it was a warning her new life was causing unwelcome strain. Ned would keep her abreast of the progress, and that was all she needed right now.

If my money can't buy me peace and quiet, then I must be a fool!
She happily unpacked and settled in.

AFTER SEVERAL DAYS AT THE Loggins' home, Jane felt rested. Helping her friends with their homestead was satisfying, yet she had to admit she didn't miss the day-to-day worries and struggles of such a lifestyle. Her thoughts went to Cabot Farm. It tempted her. Today she was ready to come down from the hills. Sally would drive them into town to shop, and they would later meet with Lacey at Carley's Restaurant for lunch. Jane missed Lacey and had nearly convinced her to move to the city and become her full-time secretary. With Wallingford Estate nearly completed, she might win her case.

The rough ride down the hill caused Jane to declare, "My goodness, Sally! When is this road going to improve? It's been years! I must do something about this while I'm here." Turning to her friend, she saw a look of embarrassment on her face.

"Ben and Mr. Cantrell, and the Howards on the other homestead are all working on raising the money for the town to improve the road. Ben and Caleb, that's Mr. Cantrell, have done a fair amount already," Sally said. "The surveyor is still working on other properties. I think the area is growing in leaps and bounds." She held the reins tighter as she maneuvered around another pothole. "Hold on!"

Jane held on with a mighty grip, feeling as if the old thing's sides would give way and spill them both onto the rocky ground.

"What good is my money if I can't help my dear friends?"

The discussion was put to the side as they both concentrated on keeping their balance.

Once they were safely on the main road, they could relax and proceeded into town. Shopping in Clermont City was different knowing she might purchase anything she fancied. The town had grown, and there were more stores along the now-paved road. The general store had taken up two storefronts, and Gladys welcomed Jane.

"Well, hello, Jane! How are you? We all miss you being here in town, not to mention your creams and such. Will you be making more very soon?"

Jane hadn't given much thought to her products with the renovation of her house in San Francisco taking up most of her time. Gladys's question did spark a longing for those days. She pushed the feeling to the back of her mind.

"Hello, Gladys. It's nice to be back for a visit. I'm not sure when you'll see my products again. Hopefully soon."

"Well, it's good to see you. What can I do for you ladies?"

Jane bought most of the goods for the Loggins' home and pantry, such as a new butter churn, a few new pots and pans, and luxuries like a butter dish in Sally's favorite color: red. The staples of sugar and flour were also purchased, which put very little strain on Jane's wallet, yet she knew it meant a great deal to Sally and Ben. It was hard for Sally to accept, but she told her it was a way of earning her keep.

After the general store, they stopped in at Carley's Restaurant. It, too, had expanded to serve the growing town with more tables and workers, but Bell was still employed there, and Jane was pleased to see her ex-cook.

"The offer still remains, Bell," Jane said.

"You know I couldn't live in the big city. Though if you ever need me to join you here again . . ."

Jane laughed. "I don't know about that."

Lacey was full of town news, none of which intrigued Jane. Not the Manfields' prize cow dying, or the Flynns' family reunion being rained out, or the graduation of Missy Turner from secretarial school brought a lick of interest to her. She wanted to hear about one thing and one thing only: What was Harry Cabot doing, and with whom was he keeping company? Too proud to ask outright, she casually alluded to the subject.

"How did the sheep farmers fare in the market last year?" she asked as she raised her cup of tea to her lips.

Lacey got right to the point. "Harry says he did well. I visit the farms occasionally. He hired me to assist in some secretarial work. Nothing steady. Thank goodness I still have the paper for employment."

Jane took a quick sip and returned the cup to its saucer. "How is—"

"He's fine. He's seeing a woman named Celia Roddick. She's from Oakland, and they met here in Clermont City at the summer ball. It doesn't seem too serious yet. Her father has Roddick's Farm in Lamont, and, well, she visits him quite often, I hear. Harry is there now."

Jane coughed to clear the emotion gathering in her throat. Sally nervously adjusted her seat. Bell had seated herself next to Lacey, an empty tray in her hand.

"My, that's a lot of information, Lacey," Sally said with a side glance to Jane.

"I'll say," said Bell.

The world seemed to stop for Jane, and she found it hard to breathe normally. Swallowing the last bit of tea in her cup while her heart tried to find its rhythm, she did her best to look unconcerned yet interested. She knew she fooled no one at the table. Had they all known about her and Harry?

Bell rose. "Well, I gotta get these tables cleared. It was good to see you. Are you doing much with a garden in your new home? Can't think why those city ladies wouldn't want your creams and ointments just as bad as we do here. We miss you and them for sure. Gladys keeps waiting for you to start up again so she can place a big fat order."

"I hope to be setting up a garden patch for the plants soon. I have a new gardener, and, well, we've had our disagreements. Besides, the renovation of my new home comes first, and . . ." Jane stopped talking; Bell had lost interest.

"Well, come back in before you leave," she said and returned to cleaning the tables.

Bringing her attention back to Sally and Lacey, Jane let her money soften the blow of Harry's new woman and Bell's lack of interest in her life as she paid for the lunch ticket and reminded herself of the freedom she had. "Lace, have you given any more thought to moving to the city? Again, my home has plenty of space. I've missed you."

Lacey smiled and tilted her head. "I would love to, but I've met someone, and we've been an item for quite some time. I didn't want to say anything until it was certain."

"Certain?"

"He asked me to marry him!"

The sudden flush of Lacey's cheeks gave Jane a warm feeling, and she felt almost proud of her young protégée.

Jane took her hand. "That's wonderful news. And bad news for me. But I wish you all the best."

The time sped by as Jane and her friends talked about Lacey's wedding plans. It was hard to say goodbye to her and Bell. Leaving Carley's Restaurant brought a surge of nostalgia to Jane. She thought of the meal she and Martin had eaten here after his first day on the farm. He'd been so tired he could barely keep his head up. How different her view of Clermont City had been back then. It looked lovely to her today. She promised to keep in touch.

After lunch on the way back to the Loggins', Jane decided she wanted to make one more stop.

"Sally, I want to visit the farm."

"Jane, are you sure?"

"Yes. I'd like to say hello to Jason."

"Jason?" Sally said with suspicion.

"You told me he still works there."

"Yes, but . . ."

"Sally, there's no crime in seeing an old friend."

Sally steered the horse toward the country road on the outskirts of town.

"Hello, Mrs. Cabot. What a nice surprise this is," Jason said as he slid his dusty hat off his dark curls. He helped Jane down from the carriage as Sally decided to wait, still holding the reins.

Jane looked up at the big man and smiled. "How are you, Jason? How goes the farm?" She stood uninvited within the courtyard, and the tension was palpable.

"Very well, ma'am," he said, then glanced at the front door of the farmhouse.

Jane caught the farmhand's eye.

"We won't be long. Just wanted to say hello," she assured him.

He nodded and turned his back on the house. "We sure do miss you."

"That's kind of you to say."

"I'm not trying to be kind, ma'am. It's just the truth. The place is different. Harry—I mean, Mr. Cabot—has rented the farmhouse, and, well, I'm still expecting to see you coming out with a big basket and your floppy hat on. Instead, Mrs. Cobbs is older and quite stern. She's a good farmer's wife though, and Mr. Cobbs treats me well. He and Harry have made good on keeping up with things. We're slowly building up the cattle inventory."

Jason raised his chin and looked down his nose. "You brought a bit of artistry to the place, if that makes sense. A certain regale. And look how fine you are now. I suppose that bit of good luck with the mine sure has put you in a different world altogether now, hasn't it?"

"Mine?"

"The diamond mine, Mrs. Cabot. Everyone knows you had a bit of luck with it."

"Yes, well, just enough to buy a house in the city. An old house, I might add."

Jason nodded.

Jane's heart beat wildly. This town knew too much. Looking around, she realized she had left an impression on this land and on the people here. A place and time which no longer belonged to her. Again, the nostalgia rose up in her heart. She turned to Sally, who waited patiently, looking out onto the gardens with a stiff back. Jane knew she was quite uncomfortable with this unannounced visit.

"We'll be going now. Take care, Jason. You're a valuable asset to Harry, as you were to me."

Jason nodded, then placed his hat firmly back on his head. "Shall I give your regards to him?"

A panic rose in her. She couldn't open that wound.

"No, and as a matter of fact, I'd be much obliged if you didn't mention our visit."

"Sure," he said and helped her into the seat of the carriage, then wished them good day before walking back to the barn.

Placing a hand on Sally's arm to stop her from getting the horse to move, Jane let her eyes wander over the garden and land and her once-immaculate home. The front of the house looked a little different. There were no planters overflowing with flowers, and the gravel courtyard was a mixture of dirt and debris, the white stone barely visible. This was not a grand estate—rather it was what it had always been: a working farm. She took in a breath, and the sharp smell of hay and horse dung made her sneeze, forming tears in her eyes. She took out her handkerchief and patted her cheeks and eyes. Then she looked in the direction of her conservatory.

Oh my.

Through the dusty windows she saw a few plants, but on further inspection, the inside looked as if it was a place to store farm implements, bales of hay, and did she see a saddle on one of the benches? She turned away.

"Let's go, Sally. I don't think there is anything here for me to see."

THE DAY WAS TIRING FOR Jane, and she went upstairs to her room as soon as they returned. After changing into her plainer house dress, she lay on the bed and fell into a heavy sleep. When she woke, the amber light of autumn glowed outside the window, and the room had cooled. She wrapped a shawl around herself and thought of Harry's arms wrapped around her. The moment passed. Like the farm, he was no longer hers. Shaking the melancholy off as best she could, she went downstairs to help Sally in the kitchen.

At supper, Jane ate little and conversed only when necessary. Sally finally broke the silence.

"Jane and I went to the farm today. Jason is doing a fine job. He likes the new tenants," she said to her husband.

Ben looked at Jane. "That must have been hard for you. Why did you go?"

Sally frowned at him. Jane laughed.

"Now, you two don't have to worry about me. I'm sorry I'm not much company tonight. It's been a tiring day catching up with old acquaintances and all, but I can take care of my own feelings. Yes, Ben, it was hard, and I should not have exposed myself like that. I've made my choice, however, and I don't regret it."

"Very well," said Ben. "Let us toast to that."

They raised their glasses of red wine, and the room shifted to a lighter mood. Jane's heart was not light, and she wondered what her real motives for being here were.

After the supper dishes were done, she excused herself and went upstairs. The room had warmed from the rising heat of the kitchen. In her heart of hearts, she had wished to run into Harry, looking decked out in her finest dress and hat. She wanted to rub her happiness in his face and at the same time look into his eyes for the love they'd once held for her.

"Tsk!" she said aloud.

I have nothing to regret indeed! If he can carry on with his life, then so shall I.

CHAPTER FORTY-TWO

SEVERAL DAYS LATER, JANE HAD REGAINED HER CONFIDENCE in her life choices, and today she felt full of anticipation for what life had to offer. Ned had wired her about the progress of her house: nearly done, but not quite ready for residency. He advised she stay away for several more days if not weeks. She got the feeling it would be more like weeks.

The day started with the usual chores and a midmorning break for tea and cake. Jane had paid for the daily delivery of bakery goods from Carley's. With the exotic teas she had brought, new dresses for Sally, and a few bottles of fine wine for Ben, Jane was happy to introduce her friends to some of the finer things in life. As they sat in mutual accord, Sally announced that their neighbor, Mr. Cantrell, was coming for supper that night.

"Oh, how nice," Jane said.

She recalled the visceral reaction she'd had when seeing the tall blonde in town. It was always from a distance. He was almost beautiful, and she'd spent many days after such encounters struggling to get his face and long, lean body out of her mind.

She felt a quickness in her belly. She knew he had married the Stanfords' niece, Jessica Messing, and Sally was glad to have her as a neighbor. Jane's own life had not allowed for much more contact with the Cantrells. She remembered how shocked she was to hear from Sally last spring of Jessica's kidnapping.

"It will be a rare visit," Sally continued. "He's kept to himself ever since Jessica's disappearance. Ben and I think it would be good for him to do some socializing. It's going on half a year."

Jane chewed her bite of scone, then swallowed and shook her head.

"Yes, it's a terrible thing," she said. "What a hardship for the couple. I remember her as a sweet young woman when we met that time at Carley's. I'm sure they made a handsome couple. I've never met him, but I've seen him in town. I think Martin talked with him once or twice about homesteading. When you wrote of your fears of being in danger as well, I was ready to have you both come to the city."

"We appreciate that, Jane, but you know better. We couldn't leave our home. The Indians who supposedly took her haven't been spotted. The longer it takes to find her, the more hope fades."

"Odd. And is Mr. Cantrell giving up on her rescue, or is he still waiting?"

"He went searching for her up north and east of Sacramento. Even up to southern Oregon. He's familiar with the Klamath tribe up there. Nothing came of it."

Jane listened intently. How awful for the man. She was also intrigued. He was involved with the Indians. The mere mention of them frightened her, and she remembered the nights gripping Martin's pistol when she was told they might be passing through the area around Cabot Farm.

"With no news of Jessica, it seems each day takes her further from all of us. I pray every night and morning for her safe return. She and I were becoming quite close."

"I'm sorry, Sally. I hope she's rescued soon."

It was time to resume the morning chores. Jane brought the laundry into the small room off the main house. Sally pumped water into the large tub. Rubbing a bar of her strong soap between her hands, she swished the water, then plunged Ben's hard-worked clothes in, which turned the water an immediate brown color. Scrubbing one of his shirts against the wood-and-aluminum washboard, she and Jane conversed about the dinner menu.

WHILE BEN TOOK CARE OF the refreshments, including his hard cider and Jane's gift of wine, she and Sally were in the kitchen preparing tonight's meal.

"Ben says he's not the same man, and I have to agree," Sally said as she cut the potatoes for the pot of water.

Jane leaned against the sideboard, her hand becoming still from mixing the flour and water for her dumplings. She'd been told in more detail about the kidnapping of Jessica and how Caleb had searched for weeks for his wife. His homestead, Rail River Acres, had become his refuge, and he spent many hours alone there. Jane knew loneliness.

"Let's have a nice meal and a jolly evening, then," she said. "I for one want to enjoy myself seated next to friends and across the table from a handsome man." She nudged Sally with her elbow.

"Now, Jane. This is not that kind of invitation."

"Isn't it?" Jane said with a raised brow.

Sally shrugged. "I suppose Ben thinks it's time Caleb met someone nice. I think it's too soon. He says a woman in his life would be good for him. But a woman of his own kind."

Jane felt the jab. "So, I'm not to be the catch, but merely the bait? A rehearsal for when the right one comes along?"

Taking the kitchen towel from her shoulder, Sally swiped Jane's arm. "It can't hurt to have him seated across from a beautiful charming woman such as yourself. He's a farm man, a businessman with his silversmithing, a man—as Jessica once said—steeped in the Native culture."

Jane smiled. "He sounds very interesting." Sally's deterrent hadn't worked. She was more intrigued than ever. "He makes jewelry or kitchenware? Trinkets? I'd love to see what he can make for me."

"All the above, and they sell quite nicely." Then Sally changed the subject. "I should have said something about Harry. Ben said the last time he saw him in town he seemed content, but they talked mostly business. I wasn't sure if I should tell you about Celia. I've been meaning to apologize for not saying something sooner. I didn't think Lacey would blurt it out like that."

"Oh, I suppose I shouldn't have said anything about the farm, let alone visit it. I'm happy he's content. I know Martin's death was hard on him." A stab of sadness pierced her chest.

Sally gave her a cockeyed look. "You're being elusive again."

Jane laughed. "Am I?"

"You've changed."

"Have I?"

"Jane!" Sally pursed her lips. "I think you've become less, well, less soft."

Jane tilted her head. "Perhaps life has hardened me. I'm a widow and love has passed me by. I love my life as it is. It's not so bad now that I have a bit of money. There's no harm in flirting with a handsome man. Who knows where it will lead?"

She let Sally believe what she wanted to. Jane felt just as soft and vulnerable as always, and it confused her. Money was supposed to smooth out the rough edges of her life. When had her determination to lead a splendid, carefree existence abandoned her? She didn't know, and it felt disturbing.

She looked at Sally, who gave her a reluctant nod and then gingerly placed the cubes of potatoes into the pot and stooped to check the fire in the stove. After coming up, she took to cutting up the carrots. "Thank you for offering to buy us a new carriage and payment for a new road. You know Ben will have none of it, of course. We're doing just fine. We're happy."

"Very well." Jane huffed. "But the new dresses I brought you are staying, and you're wearing them!"

"Yes, ma'am," Sally said.

Jane gave her friend a wide smile. "It must be wonderful to be happy."

BEN COULD BE HEARD WELCOMING Caleb. Jane came up behind Sally as the two entered the room. Jane held a basket of biscuits ready to set at the supper table.

She wore her best figure-flattering dress with the cream lace bodice accented with the golden-yellow panels down the sides of the skirt. She had primped and prepared herself for this evening. Her hair was braided and sat atop her head, giving her more height, and there were a few curls around her face. The lilac cream perfume made by her own hand added a hint of fragrance on her long lace-covered neck. She wore all the right jewelry without being ostentatious, the right shoes in case he glanced down at her feet, and most of all, the correct amount of cheek and lip stain.

At seeing Caleb, her nerves flared. His long blond hair was pulled back, exposing his fine features, his cotton shirt was neatly tucked into a pair of black woolen pants, and the bolo tie at his neck presented a tall striking figure. He stood at least two heads above Ben. She hadn't noticed from seeing him at a distance just how intensely blue his eyes were.

She felt like a schoolgirl and wanted to shrink back. Scolding herself, she straightened her spine. After all, she was an independent wealthy woman of society.

"Caleb, this is our friend, Jane Cabot. Jane, our neighbor and friend, Caleb Cantrell."

Jane tucked the basket under her arm and extended her hand to him palm down. He gave a slight bend of his tall frame, and she was sure he might kiss it. Her cheeks felt hot. To her relief, he shook her hand politely. She felt slightly embarrassed at presenting a gesture she used in the city with men at parties who would indeed kiss her hand for giggles. This was different. She reminded herself of the company she was in.

"Good evening, Mrs. Cabot," he said.

His voice was as clear and smooth as his lightly tanned skin. She felt the expansion of her heart.

"Oh, please call me Jane, Mr. Cantrell. We're all friends here."

"Then please call me Caleb," he said in all politeness.

Jane nodded her head with a slight tilt. This was going to be a most "delicious evening," as Ned would say whenever an especially good-looking man made the scene at one of Berta's parties.

She set the basket on the table with a relaxed smile. Nerves under control, Jane dived in with small talk, then on to a more personal note. "I was so sorry to hear about your wife, Caleb," she said. "It must have been an awful shock to you and her family."

"Thank you," Caleb replied.

His eyes softened, and she felt a surge of empathy for him.

Ben proudly uncorked the bottle of spirits he'd brewed from the windfall apples while Sally brought more plates of food to the table.

"I was sorry to hear of your husband's passing," Caleb said, continuing the conversation. "I heard he worked that farm as well as any man could, considering he had little experience coming into it."

"Yes, he was . . . determined."

"Come now, supper is ready," Sally announced.

The small group fell into easy conversation. Jane found Caleb to be as intelligent and fascinating as she had hoped, and his opinions were thoughtful if not a bit unusual. His take on the Indians especially intrigued her. She listened attentively as he described his journey from the back trails of America to the Klamath Indian Reservation in Oregon. He talked about learning the silversmithing trade and how the Loggins' help had gotten him through the past several months.

She added her own experience in Cincinnati and on the farm, leaving out any of the hardships to avoid spoiling the narrative, as she felt Caleb was doing also.

She smiled at her friends. "Sally and Ben were so kind to me after Martin's death. I love San Francisco, but I will need the country air and friendly faces of Clermont City every now and then."

"Jane is staying with us through her home's renovations," Sally interjected.

Jane turned to Caleb. "The whole thing is a big mess. I sometimes wish I had bought another home entirely. I also have a little cottage in renovations as well."

Sally gave a short laugh. "Jane has money to burn. A house here, a house there." She waved her hand back and forth.

Flustered by Sally's sudden frankness, Jane shot back, "Now stop that, Sally. You have what money can't buy: a home with a husband in it!"

They all laughed. Caleb looked at Jane, his eyes penetrating her.

"Though being solvent can have its advantages," he said soberly.

Jane carried on. "Sally says you've built yourself a fine home. I'd love to come by and see it while I'm here." Turning to Sally with a smile, she was greeted with a stern look.

"You and Sally are welcome to come over. I keep the door unlocked. I'm mostly at work or in my shop."

"Now, ladies," Ben piped up. "Let's not intrude on a man without a woman to keep things orderly." The room went silent, and Ben looked away, then to Caleb. "I'm sorry, I didn't . . . I didn't think before I spoke."

Caleb sat back in his chair. He twirled the liquid in his glass. "No need for apologies, Ben. It's true. My home has been without a woman's touch. Fair warning."

"How about we try the wine I brought with the dessert?" Jane said. "It comes from the grape fields of France."

Jane heard Harry's voice in her head, *"France, huh? Well, aren't we continental."* She shut him up and turned to Caleb, who met her eyes and smiled. It felt as if he might be as mocking to her as Harry would be. Feeling pretentious, she added, "That's what I was told, anyhow."

"I think I've had enough spirits," Ben said sheepishly.

The conversation turned to talk of the weather, and everyone sensed the evening was winding down.

"Good night, Ben, Sally," Caleb said as he made his exit. Then turning to face Jane, he said, "It's been a pleasure."

She felt a slight blush come into her face. "It has indeed." Their eyes met for a brief moment, and something was exchanged between them. Or was she imagining it?

"Thank you for a very delicious meal, Sally."

"Jane made the biscuits," Sally said.

He smiled and placed his hat on his head and left without another word. His sudden cool manner left Jane confused. She hadn't expected much, but that last look he gave her had aroused something in her. Reasoning it was just his way, she decided not to take it personally.

She floated into the kitchen with the last of the dirty dishes. "Oh, Sally, I think I may have fallen in love tonight."

"How can you even consider it?" Sally washed the dishes with gusto. "My lord, you had barely been introduced, and suddenly you're on a first-name basis. It isn't proper!"

Jane rested against the sideboard and watched Sally, who seemed determined to clean not only the dish but Jane's immortal soul.

"Sally, I know you're a God-fearing, church-going woman, but I won't have you making this out to be a sinful thing. I'm kidding with you, but oh, he is something, is he not? Those eyes!"

Sally was indignant. "It's not something to joke about. Ben told me that he won't sign Jessica's death certificate so they can give her a decent ceremony. He'll never love you as he loved her."

"Of course not. He'll love me for me." Jane grabbed a cotton towel to wipe the squeaky-clean plate. "This is just what I need to take my mind off of . . . things."

Stopping mid-scrub with the next dish, Sally turned to Jane. "You're nearly six years older than him. What will people say?"

Jane paused to consider this. "Well, I don't care. Why should it matter? Love is love. And is there some law against it?"

Sally turned back to the bucket of suds in the sink. There was an awkward silence until she said, "I just don't think Caleb is ready."

Jane placed the damp towel on the counter. "I am sorry. I was just thinking about myself. It was wrong of me to express my desires to you like that. We're friends, and I thought you might be happy for me, for him. I know you miss her. Please forgive me." Again, Jane felt herself saying the wrong thing tonight. First boasting about the wine, now boasting about her feelings. She wished she could be as kind and humble as Sally.

"Yes, of course," Sally said.

Relieved that her friend's sweetness had returned, Jane took up her chore again.

"But what makes you think he's interested in you in that way?" Sally asked.

Jane laughed into the back of her hand. "Oh, my dear, you've been happily married for years."

"What does that have to do with anything? You were married for a good while yourself."

Jane shrugged. "Let's just say I can tell."

Wiping her hands on a clean towel, Sally became thoughtful.

"What is it?" Jane asked.

Sally raised her shoulders and lowered them with a puff of air. "I'm not sure I like the woman you've become."

Feeling speared in the heart by her friend's bluntness, Jane struggled to find the words to defend herself with. "I don't know what you mean." It was shallow, she knew, but it was all she could say.

"I'm sure you do. The money may have fattened your bank account, but it has taken something valuable from you."

"I have my freedom. That means more to me than anything. Let me have my way, Sally. I deserve to be happy."

"I worry that your meaning of happiness may bring you more pain."

Jane shrugged and looked away. "I'm going to pursue Caleb Cantrell, and that's all there is to it. If just for the sake of a brief affair."

The last word had Sally bringing her sudsy hand to her mouth and regretting it. She spit into the tub.

"Oh, see what you made me do?"

Jane handed her a towel. "Sorry, my dear. So sorry. I meant it only in jest."

That night Jane contemplated Sally's view of her. It felt good to change from the farmer's wife she'd been, but she wasn't sure it had made her a better person. Why would she want to pursue a man so out of reach as Caleb Cantrell? A distraction perhaps? She had to admit, she was definitely drawn to him.

She let her fantasies of him and her in an intimate way take her into a delicious night of passionate dreams.

Chapter Forty-Three

*A*FTER THE MEAT-FILLED PASTRIES WERE BAKED AND THE apple pie had cooled, Jane placed the lunch for two in a basket along with cider and hopes of a meaningful visit to Caleb's home. Taking one last appraisal in the Loggins' hall mirror, she turned to Sally.

"How do I look?"

With pinched lips and hooded eyes, Sally looked at her friend. "You look beautiful, as always. I'm sure Caleb cares less about the right hat, but it does go well with your plaid suit. The skirt should be heavy enough without being too hot. Those boots are quite delicate for a walk through the path, but if you're trying to impress, they'll do the job." She came closer and sniffed. "Lavender?"

Jane knew Sally was against her going over to Caleb's alone. Jane had seen him coming down the road the other day as she helped Sally bring in a calf who'd escaped to the edge of their field.

He had looked fine atop his horse as he tipped his hat to them. Her desire for him was mounting.

She would make room for Caleb in her heart as she pushed her feelings for Harry aside.

The wide path that connected the two homesteads was indeed a bit muddy from the last rainfall, but nothing she couldn't weave around with one hand holding up her skirt while the other balanced the basket of food. The walk helped to settle her nerves. Ben had said he knew Caleb would be working on his farm today. Chances were good he'd be wanting a hearty lunch. Why shouldn't she be neighborly and bring him one?

Finally, she reached his house, and it was plain, to be sure. She supposed, if it came to it, she could remedy that well enough.

She stepped onto the porch and gave a slight knock on his door. A dog barked, and she remembered him saying something about his rambunctious pup. After a long pause, she went to knock again, but the door opened, and there he stood. His trousers were dirt stained, his face held a surprised expression, and his dog was needling his way through his master's legs to get to her.

"Settle down, Boones," Caleb said. He held the pup away. Boones sniffed at her, and she petted the lively Labrador.

"Go lie down," Caleb commanded. Then glancing beyond her, he said, "You're alone?"

She felt awkward. She had invaded his privacy. Swallowing hard, she found her courage. "I hope you don't mind me bringing you some lunch. Sally was busy, so I thought I'd just walk myself over here."

He backed away from the door. "Come in, Mrs. Cabot. Jane."

She was about to leave the basket and retreat back onto the path with her tail between her legs when his expression softened.

"Thank you. I was about to have something to eat. You must have—I mean, you and Sally had this timed just right. Please." He waved her in.

Relieved but still shaky, Jane entered the small vestibule. A row of pegs on the wall neatly held his coat, a leather bag, and his hat. The floor needed a bit of sweeping, and she grew more curious about the rest of the house.

She entered the parlor and became lonely for the first time in weeks. It was warm and cozy and told the story of a man and woman who loved to sit in their chairs in front of the fire after a long day's work, the flames as steady as their companionship. The kerosene lamps gave off a gentle glow, and a basket of yarn sat next to the red paisley chair. A pipe rested on a silver tray next to the masculine leather chair. To complete the picture, the pup had settled on a rag rug near the hearth. The scene nearly brought her to tears.

Remembering her purpose, she unveiled the basket of food. "I think there's enough for two, if you don't mind me being so forward. The walk over gave me quite an appetite."

"Um, I suppose so."

She glanced beyond him at the doorway beside the stove. "Is the kitchen through there?"

Caleb followed her gaze. "Yes, that's the kitchen."

Making herself at home with the ease of one who knew their way around a country kitchen, she found the plates and glasses, then laid out the meal on the table. In the corner of her eye, she saw Caleb brush his hand over his hair. She knew she was being bold, and it might've been disconcerting to him, but she was forging forward. There was no turning back now.

"Once a farmer's wife, always a farmer's wife." She gave a slight laugh, and he smiled.

They settled into the food, and the conversation flowed. They started up where they'd last left off. He talked more about his upbringing and losing his family in a tragic accident, and she talked about her father's death before her wedding and her brother's mishandling of the estate. In a way, they had much in common, and she began to envision herself with him. She didn't talk of her marriage with Martin, and he didn't bring up his wife. Jane took it as a good sign that perhaps he would be able to move forward with another woman.

They sat at the kitchen table, wineglasses in their hands. She felt relaxed in this man's company. Each time his blue eyes cast their gaze on her, she wanted to melt into submission even though he'd made no invitation toward her. He was genuine and a gentle soul, to be sure. His manners were respectful, and she could see he had been well schooled in the social graces at one time.

A bark from the pup and a knock on the door brought them out of their engaging conversation. Caleb reached into his shirt pocket and took out his watch. Jane noticed the light outside had dimmed and the amber glow of the lamps had intensified. They looked at each other and laughed.

Caleb went to the door, and Jane heard Ben say, "Have you got our guest?"

Caleb answered, "My God, Ben, we lost track of time."

On entering the parlor, she witnessed Caleb's discomfort with their aloneness. She thought it was sweet.

"Jane was telling me of her childhood in Ohio, and I was . . ." He stopped at Ben's quick nod and wink. "We were having a friendly lunch."

Jane suppressed a laugh. "Are you here to walk me home, Ben?"

"Why, yes. We were worried about you."

"Oh, I was in good hands," she said and turned to Caleb to give him a generous smile.

"Thank Sally for the food," Caleb said. "Let me just transfer the rest of the pie and give you back the plate."

"No need for that." Jane waved a dismissive hand. "I'll come by and pick it up tomorrow. Will you be at church in the morning?"

Caleb looked at Ben, then back to Jane. "I don't attend church."

"Good for you. I find it not to my liking either, but when in Rome." She laughed. "I'll be by after we've attended."

"All right, Caleb," Ben piped up. "We'll be on our way. Enjoy that pie." He gave another wink. "We'll leave you to it."

On their way back to the Loggins' home, Jane fell silent, and Ben offered little but to say, "Sally is upset."

Jane came out of her thoughts of Caleb and how it filled her with gladness to spend the afternoon talking with him. "I know she is. I hope this doesn't harm our friendship."

"Knowing my Sally, she will forgive you."

Coming out of step with Ben, Jane considered taking up her defense right there, for she felt there was nothing to be forgiven for. She thought better than to try to explain a woman's heart to a man. Instead, she went back in her mind to sitting with Caleb and drinking in his looks, his mannerism, and mostly their mutual attentiveness.

Nothing could take away the joy of it and the bubbling anticipation in her heart.

CHAPTER FORTY-FOUR

*S*UNDAY MORNING SHINED BRIGHT AND WARM. LATE-blooming flowers dotted the landscape, and Sally's window boxes were a happy mix of pansies and small ferns. The wildflower meadows were showing signs of fall going into winter, but to Jane's mind it felt like spring again. A tinge of regret shadowed her happy mood. The heady aroma of the season had Jane wondering if the Cabot Farm gardens were being cleared for winter crops.

Are the herbal plants being cared for? The lavender will get too leggy if they don't cut it back, but not too hard so that it dies altogether. Did the new tenants remember to prune the orange trees just right so they get a good harvest? She shook her head to loosen the memories of tending to her farm and the daily and seasonal chores. *You're free from all that tedious work!*

"Jane, you seem miles away," Sally said as they walked to the carriage.

"I'm right here."

Ben helped the ladies in, and they were off to church, something Jane would rather do without. How confident Caleb had seemed in saying he didn't attend. She wished she could have such convictions. Berta and Ned attended regularly, and she knew she would have to continue to join them if there was to be a seamless relationship between her and society. It was their duty to set a good example.

When Jane asked Ben about Caleb's beliefs, Sally spoke up before he could answer.

"Jessica told me that he goes to the middle of his field and stands there for a while, then sits cross-legged and chants!" She brought her hand to her chest. "I wasn't sure how much to believe, but then I saw him once, quite by accident. I was bringing him some of my soap—by his request, of course—and I happened to look out, and there he was. On the knoll. I didn't mean to stare, but then the chanting began. Loud and clear. I pray for his soul each Sunday."

Jane furrowed her brow and cupped her mouth to hide her amusement.

"He has his own ways," Ben said in his diplomatic way.

"I admire him for that," Jane said, knowing Sally would find yet another reason to pray for her soul too.

After the service and a light midmorning snack, Jane set out for Caleb's home. When she stepped onto his porch, she saw the pie plate on the bench. The golden pup barked at the window, then retreated after she talked to him through the glass. Looking at the pie plate, she decided to come back later.

With her second try, she found herself in his parlor, sipping tea seated in the red paisley chair. The weather had cooled, and she was enjoying the flames dancing in the fireplace.

As with yesterday, the small talk turned into more substantial conversation.

"I'd love to hear about your beliefs," she said.

Caleb stared at the chair she sat in and then at her, but it was as if he was looking at a picture and not the real thing.

Of course, this was Jessica's chair. Did he want her to move? She looked around for another place to sit, but then he spoke.

"I suppose you could say my beliefs come from my experiences, and some of those experiences include my relationship with the Indians. Their beliefs and rituals seem more real to me than others." He scratched his cheek and cleared his throat. "To each their own."

"I don't know much about Indians. My mother and friends were afraid for me coming out West because of them. I see now that they were the least of my worries."

"From what you've shared with me, I take it you didn't much care to be on a farm."

"Not that one, anyway. I love land and fresh air, but . . . Well, Martin was not the right man for me, after all. I'm sorry he's gone, and yet I think I would have divorced him sooner or later."

Jane let her words sink in as Caleb's brows rose in surprise.

"I confess my first love is horticulture, but my parents would have nothing of it. I told you I also enjoyed journalism, but again, my parents believed differently. My father wanted me to be a boy and even confessed I should have run the business instead of my brother."

"I'm sorry you've been so unfulfilled in life."

Jane took offense. "Hardly! Anyway, I have plenty of money now and intend on living quite well."

His blue eyes met hers. "Jane, money doesn't bring one fulfillment, though it can be a comfort; I certainly know that. When I was out on the trails with nothing to my name but a knife, a piece of flint, and a change of clothes, I wished every night for a hot bath and a soft bed. Yet I felt alive and free, and I sometimes dream of being out there again."

His statement struck a nerve in her, and she adjusted her seat to keep her emotions in check. What was she missing in life? Was all her wealth giving her the happiness she craved?

"You're braver than I."

"Courage is not what I'm talking about," he said. "We take paths in life. Some lead to great things, some not so great. Life is a tapestry of all kinds of experiences. In my life right now, I'm experiencing loss. I wait for that path to come to an end soon."

"Perhaps our paths met for a purpose?"

Caleb chuckled. "Perhaps."

The conversation had hit a lull, and Jane stood and placed her cup on the table. "I should be going."

Caleb rose with her. "Thanks for the visit."

"It was my pleasure." She walked to the vestibule to retrieve her coat, Caleb behind her.

"Oh, the pie plate," she said, turning around only to meet him head-on.

His hands were on her waist, preventing their collision. The feel of them on her body made her weak in the knees. Suddenly, she was against his chest, her eyes turned up to him. He bent down to meet her. His hands cupped her face, and their lips met. The warmth of his body, the tenderness of his mouth—she gave no resistance. His hand traveled to her bodice as their kiss became more passionate. She melted into him with a moan, and he jerked away, causing her to step back.

"Oh dear! I'm sorry, Caleb."

Caleb ran his hand over his head. "No, forgive me, Jane."

"No need to ask for forgiveness. It was rather . . . nice."

Caleb smiled, but his furrowed brow told her he truly was sorry for his actions.

"Your heart is still attached to her. Of course it is. Maybe someday you will be free to love again, or she will return and you will be free in a different way. Grief is a terrible companion, Caleb. Will you let me be there for you?"

He looked overwhelmed, and she regretted her words.

"I'll get the plate," he said.

She waited in distress. He came back into the room, and she took the pie plate from him. Her desires had been set ablaze, and now she had to throw ice water on them.

"Good day, Caleb."

"Good day, Jane."

CHAPTER FORTY-FIVE

OVER THE NEXT SEVERAL WEEKS, TO JANE'S HAPPINESS, SHE and Caleb were together in friendly companionship, with her heart becoming completely lost in love for this complicated man.

The late-November air was cool, and the ground they walked on was damp. She wrapped her arm around his as they made their way back to his house from the field. He looked down at her and smiled, then bent to the ground and picked up a rock. They both inspected the shiny oval rock with white veins running through its smooth black shape. He handed it to her, and she felt as if he had given her a token of his affection. She took it and looked at it with sudden fondness before placing it into her pocket. She felt a little silly, but she wasn't going to throw it back to the ground. He gave a chuckle, and they continued to walk arm in arm back to his house.

Teasing the embers to produce a flame, Caleb crouched by the stove in the parlor while Jane made tea for herself and coffee for him. The flower-rimmed glasses she had bought him as a gift sat alongside the cups to later be filled with a bit of sherry for her and a shot of whiskey for him. She brought in the tray and set it down as their usual routine after a walk or visit before he escorted her back to the Loggins. She settled into the red paisley chair as he took his own seat. Boones slapped his tail on the floor as he settled on his rag rug.

"I tried to avoid you at first," Caleb confessed. "But I must admit, your company has brought me great comfort. Thank you."

Jane gave a tight smile. "I haven't exactly been shy about my feelings for you." She waited for his response, hoping he would say the words she desperately wanted to hear.

"The season will bring much work for me in my silversmithing business. Christmas is just around the corner. I'll be very busy. We might not get a chance to visit as often."

"Of course. From what I saw, I think every woman in town will want your jewelry and vases. I truly believe my father would have given you several commissions." She gave a slight laugh, trying to remove the press of emotion in her throat.

His eyes were pools of blue. She gave a curt nod and sipped her tea. Changing the subject, they talked of plants and her yearning to have a kitchen garden at her new home and a conservatory like the one she'd had on Cabot Farm.

"But smaller. I haven't the room at this house." She explained more of her recipes for tinctures, creams, and remedies for colds, cuts, and bruises and how she was eager to expand her beauty products. Jane noticed the tilt of his head and the playful grin on his face.

"What?" she asked. "I'm telling you the truth. A bit of calendula cream on your hands each night will do wonders!"

He laughed out loud now. "My dear friend, I'm sure of it. What amuses me is the way your eyes light up and your whole body engages in your words. It's easy to see that this is something you love."

Self-conscious of her enthusiasm, Jane leaned back into the chair. She wanted to play the seductress and have him sweep her off her feet and into the bedroom, where he would finally release the furious tension that had been building in her ever since she had first laid eyes on him. Instead, she had gone on about herbal recipes, and now he had laughed at her. Yet he was right. She felt alive talking about horticultural and her products.

"I think it's wonderful," Caleb said. "I hope you have exactly what you want in your new home. My wife, Jess, she also . . . Well, anyway, I think it's a great skill, and I admire you for it."

Jane set her tea down. "Caleb, may I be honest?" With her pulse pounding in her ears, she was anxious to reveal her true feelings for him and let the chips fall where they may.

"Of course."

She had his full attention.

"I . . . I've fal . . ." She looked into his eyes and saw a man whose integrity would not be compromised. It was something about the way he looked back at her—a cool steely warning. "I think you're right. It is a great skill. I admit, I miss it." A wave of heat rushed into her bodice.

He stood, and the strength of his presence in the warmth of the parlor shook her to the core. She had almost made a complete fool of herself, for he clearly wasn't returning her sentiments.

Holding back her emotions, she rose to meet him. He looked down at her, and again her lust for him was tempted without satisfaction. She was angry now.

"My feelings are not to be toyed with," she said without humor.

He brushed the side of her cheek with his thumb. "If I were free, Jane. But I'm not. My heart is committed to a woman who as each day passes becomes more ghostlike. The trail has dried up, yet I want to go out and search for her even if it takes me the rest of my life."

She turned to leave, but he took her arm and brought her close to him.

"The temptation is strong," he said. "I have feelings for you that go beyond friendship. However, I can only give you friendship."

"You play with me, Caleb. You come to supper at Sally and Ben's, and you laugh and flirt with me. We walk arm in arm, you engage in that kiss, and yet you cower at going further."

His furrowed brow and thoughtful expression gave her pause. Clearly, he had never been called a coward.

"Forgive me. I don't want to cause either of us pain. I for one can't afford it. I will try to stay away."

Letting out a puff of air, she turned and stomped into the vestibule. She grabbed her coat and hat.

"You are infuriating!" She tried to plunge her arms into each sleeve and pushed her hat onto her head, though it refused to stay on.

He took her by the arm and stopped her from going farther.

"Let me go."

"Not until we make amends." He held her arm and looked down at his feet, then back up at her. "In my own way, I have feelings for you."

Jane dropped her rigid stance. Her anger abated. "What are we going to do, then?"

He shook his head. "Only time will tell. Please give me time. I may be seen as a fool, but I'm still hopeful she will return, and I don't want you to get hurt."

"I understand. I will give you time."

She told him what he wanted to hear, but her feelings were hurt, and she felt anxious about their future.

"Thank you," he said.

He slowly bent down and kissed her lips, and then he was helping her with her coat. She left his home in a daze of emotions. Was she an adult who understood the workings of love or a foolish youngin' who knew nothing but their own wants and needs? At her age it should've been the former, but he left her with the feelings of an impulsive young girl. She hated feeling so vulnerable.

Walking back to the Loggins', her feet barely touched the ground. He had feelings for her. She decided to strive to give him all the time he needed. From what she had gathered, most Indian kidnappings did not turn out well.

Very sad, she thought to herself, but there it was. Their future together would be a life of compromise. Deep down inside, she knew she would be doing most of the compromising. As with Harry, she had fallen for a man whose life clearly defined him. What defined her? She didn't know. Who was she now? Living in one world when her heart was in another puzzled her. She tried to envision a life with Caleb.

His house would need work, but that shouldn't be a problem. Her home in the city would be their second home. She would work in the gardens at both and produce remedies for him and his hardworking hands and body. It might work. Her mind went to oil of lavender, chamomile, eucalyptus, and ginger. She created a recipe just for him and was anxious to write it down. Her imagination took hold as she walked closer to the Loggins' house. She would place the oil in a fancy little glass bottle, and when he had lain fully on his bed, she would straddle him and drip the heated oil onto his back and—

Sally came out of the house to meet her. "How is Caleb? Did you tell him about supper next week?"

Jane was shaking inside. "Yes. He would be happy to oblige."

Sally walked up to her. "Being in this cool windy air has made you all flushed. Come on, I'll get you some clear broth."

She took Sally's arm, and they went inside, where the meaty smell of the broth stirred Jane's appetite. Before partaking of it, she went upstairs and wrote down her recipe. She marked it *C. C.*

On Jane's next visit to Caleb's, Sally insisted on coming along. Jane gave no mind. She knew she'd be alone with him later that day.

As she and Sally sat together, Jane on a chair brought in from the kitchen and Sally on the red paisley chair, Caleb offered the ladies his own brew of coffee. Sally cut into the blueberry cake she had brought with her.

"This coffee is quite strong, Caleb," Sally admitted. She seemed to enjoy it, but both Jane and Caleb knew she much preferred tea.

Jane loved the change of pace and took in the heady aroma of the brew. After a short while, a knock came to the door, and Caleb pointed to Boones before he even let out a bark. The dog retreated. Jane felt a thrill at the way Caleb handled the pup. His authority over his life added to his appeal.

Caleb let in his company. A large man entered the room. Jane recognized the gentleman as Jessica's uncle, Burt Stanford.

"Burt, you know Mrs. Loggin, and this is her friend, Mrs. Jane Cabot. They came over with cake. Would you like a slice and a cup of coffee?"

With a wave of his hand, Burt declined.

"Mr. Stanford, what a nice surprise," Sally offered.

"Ladies," Mr. Stanford said as he removed his hat.

Jane saw a man who was flustered and uncomfortable. "I remember our meeting at Carley's some time back, Mr. Stanford," she said.

"Yes, yes, of course. It's nice to see you again."

Turning to Caleb, Burt said in a lowered voice, "I've got some bad news. Can we talk . . . alone?"

Jane and Sally looked at each other and rose in unison. They said their goodbyes, and Sally gave Caleb a squeeze to his arm. "If you need Ben or me . . ."

"Thank you, Sally."

Jane sensed Caleb's immediate tension. She gave him a smile that she hoped relayed her caring feelings. He didn't look at her as he anxiously saw them out.

At supper, Sally had mentioned seeing Mr. Stanford to Ben.

Jane suspected by Ben's grave expression he might suspect Jessica had been found, and not alive. It struck a chord of grief in Jane for Caleb. She would be there for him.

That night, she stirred in bed and gazed at the dark sky. The moon was a sliver among the stars that shined like diamonds. She agonized over what Jessica's uncle had to say to Caleb. She had so many thoughts, some of which she was not proud of.

AT BREAKFAST THE NEXT MORNING, Ben was midbite when he said he had talked to Caleb earlier that morning. The women stopped eating to look up at him.

"He told me Burt brought the sad news that Jessica's father had died."

Jane let out a sigh. She wasn't sure what this meant; she only knew Jessica was still out there. Who was she that she wished to have Caleb free from his wife? Not since she and Harry had gone out on Martin had she felt ashamed of herself. She didn't feel like a good person.

Listening to Ben and Sally's conversation, Jane sat in silence, stewing in self-loathing. Then she thought of Caleb's words about an all-encompassing love he would often tap into. She felt it sometimes when she was with him as they sat in silence, and it was wonderful. She wished she could feel it now.

Sally brought her hand to her mouth. "Oh, that is sad news. Jessica had mentioned her father was ill, but at the time, he was recovering. Her mother came to visit shortly after. If it were really bad, I'm sure she wouldn't have come."

Sally turned to Jane, and she came out of her daydream. "Jessica's mother came to visit, and my goodness, she certainly didn't approve of Caleb, the house, or the land. She was quite rude about it, Jessica told me. It upset the couple's life, and I can't help but think it caused quite a rift between them."

Jane had no connection to this woman or her family woes, but she answered with what was expected. "That must have been difficult. How her mother must suffer the loss of her daughter and now her husband."

"And her son. It's a complicated situation," Sally said with a roll of her eyes.

"Aren't all families complicated?" Jane said with a short laugh.

As the day unfolded, Jane found herself with little spent energy even after she and Sally had made marmalade, cleaned the chicken coop and laundered their dirty work clothes afterward. They also made a hearty lunch for the threesome and baked a cake to celebrate the Loggins' anniversary.

Jane decided a good ride on Ben's quarter horse might help to tire her pent-up emotions and sexual tension. It was nearly supper when she returned after having put the horse into a gallop across the field and then a good trot along the Rail River. Jane turned around as Sally entered the kitchen.

"Aren't you going to reprimand me for riding in the dark?"

"I'm not your mother, but Ben was getting anxious to get the horse back into the stall."

Jane gave a soft laugh. "Yes, he was." She approached Sally and put her arms around her friend's slim waist. "Thank you."

Sally patted Jane's hand. "You're welcome. I know how hard this must be on you. I feel it's my fault for introducing him to you."

"I hardly think we could've ignored each other the whole time. Don't feel bad. It's my own doing."

Finally, Jane felt tired. She went upstairs after the supper cleanup. Sally brought up a fresh pitcher of warm water for the basin. Jane had a clean-up, then slipped into her cotton chemise. Knowing how quickly the dawn came, she tried to clear her mind and let sleep take her.

Her thoughts wouldn't rest. What had she gotten herself into with this man? How could she have been so careless as to let his beauty and character sweep her off her feet?

Harry came to mind, followed by Martin, her father, and her brother. The men she cared for the most had caused her the most pain.

She soothed her heart with the thought of gardening and preparing her potions. She listed the seeds she would need, the splendor of her new conservatory, and the peaceful pursuit of loving and nurturing her plants. It would all have to wait as she waited for Caleb to make up his mind about them.

CHAPTER FORTY-SIX

THE DAYS PASSED, AND DECEMBER BROUGHT THE RAIN AND cooler days. Jane had to smile to herself when Sally declared how cold and dreary the season had become. Cincinnati in December was brutal in comparison.

Each year, Jane was thrilled to have the rain in her gardens at Cabot Farm and the coolness in the air. It charged her as she looked forward to the early planting season.

Ned had telegrammed her that the estate was nearly finished, and he wanted her back in time for Christmas. She was glad for it, but today she felt as dull as the gray sky. She hadn't seen Caleb in over a week, and Ben had simply shrugged when she'd asked about him. Something was amiss. When she approached the breakfast table, she noticed the gladness in Ben's face and the glow in Sally's.

"Good morning," Jane said. "You two look happy today."

Their moods shifted to a more serious tone. Jane sat down and, taking the hot kettle, poured the water into her cup of tea leaves.

The aroma of peppermint hit her nose. She placed it back down on the felted pad and waited. The anxiousness she felt in her stomach gave her warning.

"Ben, why don't you tell her?" Sally said.

"I thought you might in private," Ben replied, a bit perturbed.

"Yes, that might be best." Sally rose and asked Jane to accompany her upstairs.

Jane looked at Ben with questioning eyes as she got up and followed Sally. In her bedroom, she sat down at her dressing table and turned to face the room. Sally remained standing.

"Tell me before I burst with curiosity!"

Sally wrung her hands. "Jessica is alive and coming home any day now."

Jane felt as if she had been punched in the gut. She looked at Sally, whose tears flooded her eyes. The room went silent. Jane couldn't move. Sally leaned forward, and as if to touch a wounded animal, she laid her hand on Jane's shoulder.

With all the courage she could muster, Jane gave a smile. "That's wonderful news. She's alive. How wonderful. It truly is a miracle."

"Jane."

She felt Sally's hand on her shoulder and wanted to slap it away. Taking a few deep breaths, she instead patted her friend's hand and gently removed it. "I'll be fine. I always knew this day might come. I didn't think it would though. When did you say she's due home?"

"I think it may be today. Ben was over there early this morning. He had promised Caleb to help with the winch in his barn. You know how those two men like to get up even before the roosters. Caleb told him the good news. He's been a bundle of nerves and hasn't left his house since he heard from Mr. Stanford that she was rescued and on her way home. It's why we haven't heard from him. If this day hadn't been set aside for the winch, I'm not sure we would have found out until we saw her for ourselves."

"How? How did they find her?"

Sally took a deep breath and let it out. "Well, the details are not clear. Ben couldn't get much from Caleb. Something to do with her brother and cousin."

Jane looked at the floor. Her world had been tipped upside down, and Caleb's had been righted. How strange it all felt.

"Would you leave me alone, Sally?"

"Can I bring you anything? Can I do anything? I don't mind staying. You shouldn't be alone."

"Thank you, my dear friend. Celebrate her return with Ben. I know you feel joyous by it. I need a bit of time to arrange things. I think my house in the city is ready for me now. I will telegram Berta and Ned to let them know I'll be coming home."

Sally nodded, her lips pressed together and her chin wobbling. "I'll be downstairs."

The door closed quietly. Jane turned to her dressing table. The black rock sat by the bottle of oil she had mixed for Caleb. Her beautiful man and her future with him had dissolved like a sugar cube in the ocean. She crossed her arms on the table and put her head in them as sobs poured out of her.

THE EMPTY TRUNKS WAITED TO be packed with her belongings. She had acquired a few things for her new home, and Sally had offered one of her old trunks to Jane. Looking over the room she had occupied for the last several months, she gave a sigh. Her dresses were laid out on the bed, ready to be folded in paper and placed carefully among petticoats and stockings. Her jewelry, hats, scarves, and other accessories were grouped on the dressing table and chairs. The dismantling of this room felt as if she were taking apart the short but poignant life she had lived here on the Loggins' homestead and Caleb's Rail River Acres.

Opening one of the smaller trunks, she froze at the sound of his voice downstairs. Her heart leapt in her chest. So many thoughts raced through her mind. Was Jessica back, or was Caleb walking off his nerves? Had she come with him? She pulled herself together, looked in the mirror to check her appearance, and cautiously made her way downstairs.

"We are so happy for you!" Sally said. "When can we see her?"

It was confirmed: Jessica was home. Jane had to present a mature and confident woman. She was determined not to fall apart. Her pride was restored.

As she joined them, she saw Ben pouring the glasses and knew a toast was imminent.

"I'm very happy for you, Caleb," Jane said. "It's always such a blessing when our prayers are answered." Try as she might, she knew her voice lacked gladness.

"Jane is leaving us tomorrow," Sally said. "We will miss her very much."

Taking the glass of wine Ben offered her, Jane took a gulp and said nothing. Caleb's face was filled with light, and it shined from inward and out of his blue eyes. She was jealous of the woman who could make this man so happy. Sally was right: he could never love her as he loved Jessica.

"Leaving?" Caleb asked as he took the last gulp of his wine.

"Yes, my house is ready."

"I see. That's good." Caleb handed his glass back to Ben. "I just wanted to come over and let you know she's back and safe at home. A little worse for wear, but between us and her family, I'm sure she's going to make a full recovery."

He's not looking at me. He's done with me.

"I must get back. Goodbye."

The trio bade him good day, with Sally bringing her handkerchief to her eyes. They stood for a moment longer, and then Ben retreated to the kitchen. Sally, still wiping her tears, stood by Jane.

With unbridled emotion, Jane handed her glass to Sally and ran upstairs and scribbled her address onto a piece of stationary, then hurried out the door, passing her friend in the hall.

"Jane?" she heard from behind her as she raced toward Caleb. She spied him turning the bend, and catching her breath, she walked briskly and was soon behind him.

He stopped short and turned. His strength of presence was different now. He was different. She realized he had entered a different life path, and she couldn't be on it with him.

"I couldn't leave tomorrow without saying a proper goodbye. In private."

Caleb nodded.

She moved closer and took his arm. "May we have one last walk together for just a minute? One last visit?"

He acquiesced. "I must get back to my wife, Jane. She's quite fragile."

He stopped after a few steps and removed her arm from his. His eyes met hers, and she felt her grief surface.

"Thank you for your friendship, Jane."

She tipped her head to the side and swallowed hard. "It could have been much more, but circumstances have changed. I will remember you with great fondness and wonder what could have been."

"What would you have done with this man you have so little in common with? I have a past, I don't attend church, I drink, and I have been known to gamble. Not quite the ideal gentleman for a lady such as yourself."

Jane felt abandonment rise up to remind her she must remain independent or get swallowed up in the ever-changing sea of relationships.

"And yet we are friends. My life is more than attending church and being a proper lady, more than the right clothing and manners. I'm afraid you'll never see the real me."

"I was honored to see a part of you. I think you are more than all those things, and I wish you a good life. Cross over to your true path, Jane. Follow your heart."

"You changed my life, Caleb. I think you made me see myself. Thank you."

His luminous blue eyes and generous smile touched her deeply.

"If you're ever in need of a shoulder to lean on or an ear to listen, please think of me. Here is my address. I'd hate for us to never . . ."

His shoulders slumped, and he let out a puff of air. "I'm sorry."

She held the piece of paper out to him. "Won't you take my address?"

He reluctantly took the expensive cream-colored paper from her and tucked it into his shirt pocket. "Don't expect anything."

"Just knowing you have it makes me feel as if we are still friends."

She reached up and kissed his cheek, letting his scent become etched into her memory. She briskly turned and walked away before she became completely undone. Hearing his hurried footfalls in the opposite direction had her stopping and holding her stomach.

Closing her eyes, she hugged her waist against the tide of emotion. What had she meant to him? An affair of the heart and nothing more, or a deep connection he would never forget? She knew she would not forget their precious time together. Caleb Cantrell was not the kind of man one forgot easily, as with another man who had taken her heart and still had it. Caleb's last words touched her. She knew where her heart lay. Her head down, she walked back through the path and rallied her feelings.

Perhaps Berta is right—a woman with wealth may survive without true love. Is that what she wanted?

The chill of December wrapped around her body, and she hastened her step as she brought her shawl around her shoulders.

CHAPTER FORTY-SEVEN

After paying for her ticket and the many trunks to be transported back to San Francisco, Jane left the lobby of the stage station and waited patiently for the coach to arrive. The rain had stopped, and the sun came in and out of the passing clouds. She drew her shawl around her shoulders and rubbed her satin-gloved hands together. Ben hadn't stayed to wait with her at her request, and Sally had been in tears as they'd said their goodbyes at the house. Jane didn't want a scene at the station and had left her friend with a promise to return, or to at least write to her regularly. Adrift in her life, she would return to the Wallingford Estate and try to make it a home.

Shifting her weight, she noticed a few others had joined her who would be taking the same coach. It wouldn't be long now.

The town was quiet this morning. She looked down the long, paved road. The sidewalks were no longer boards but concrete walkways. Carley's Restaurant looked full. Bell would be busy.

A feeling of nostalgia engulfed her. She recalled the long days of setting up the fruit and vegetables with Bell for the winter larder. They'd conversed and laughed, but at what, she couldn't remember.

The town looked so different to her than when she had first arrived many years ago. Instead of the small nothing of a place she'd thought it to be, it now looked like . . . home. Her mind went to meeting Harry face-to-face on the boardwalk the day after they saw the ramshackle house—her restored farmhouse. He had sparked something in her that still remained. Martin's hard work, the secrets they'd kept from each other, his tragic death. All of it seemed so far away. She tore herself from her memories as she looked upon the little town with fondness.

Across the road, a few patrons were going about their business: a woman and child with baskets walking into the general store, Gladys and Clarence ready to serve them. A few men headed into the bank, and among them was a person who made her heart skip a beat.

Harry.

Would he see her standing here in her travel attire, ready to leave town for good? Should she wave, hoping to catch his eye? The road between them could be crossed with ease, yet it felt as if it were a treacherous stretch of land.

"Madam, the coach will be pulling up there. You might want to back away from the edge."

Jane looked at where she stood and stepped back without taking her eyes off Harry. A man approached him in greeting, and he turned her way. Her breath hitched. She held up her hand, and it caught his attention. Their eyes met.

Stepping off the walk, she felt a force grab her arm and pull her back.

"I told you the coach was coming!" the stranger said. "Are you in your right mind, madam?"

The answer was no. She felt a strong pull toward Harry, and nothing around her existed.

The large stagecoach sauntered in front of her. Once it came to a complete stop, she rushed around its back end, hoping Harry was coming her way. He was nowhere in sight. She looked up and down the road. Had it been her imagination?

She walked back and addressed the coach driver. "When do you leave?"

"After unloading and loading, about twenty minutes, ma'am. My schedule is there on the wall." He shook his head and walked away.

Without hesitating, Jane hastened across the street. She entered the bank and looked around for Harry. Where was he? She was beginning to think he *had* been only her imagination.

Confused and agitated, she walked out of the bank.

"Hello, Jane."

Turning around so sharply her skirts barely had time to untwine, she adjusted her dress, and with a pounding heart, she greeted him. His good looks still made her tingle inside. He smiled his generous smile at her. His brown eyes were bright and his body strong. He had been taking good care of himself, or had a woman had a hand in it?

"Hello, Harry. How are you?"

He stepped forward, and she wanted to release her wounded heart and embrace him.

"I'm well, thank you," he said. "And you? I heard you were in town. I'm sorry I didn't call on you, but I was out of town, and then the farm took my—"

"Oh, of course. I understand." She shook inside. *Remember, he's gone on with his life.*

His eyes did not leave hers, and they stood as if frozen in the moment. He broke the spell.

"Is that your coach?" He gestured with his chin toward the station. "Looks as if you're traveling. It will be leaving soon. I better let you go."

"I hear you are doing well with the farms, and there may be a lady in your life?" She inhaled and let it out. It had been said, and she couldn't take it back.

He looked at his shoes, then up at her with a nod. "A friend. She's been good for me."

Ruffled by his words, her jealousy rose with a storm of defiance. "How nice. Yes, I must be going. My home and life in San Francisco wait for me."

He gave her the look he always did whenever he caught her fluffing herself up: a tented brow and lopsided grin. She wanted to melt into a puddle of love and humiliation. How could he still make her feel so many emotions at once?

Adjusting the purse that hung from her arm, she swiped at her forehead, the fringe swaying from the pearl-encrusted body of the reticule hitting her in the cheek. Harry laughed and took her hand. She felt the gentle weight of his hand embracing hers, and she didn't want him to let go.

"It's good to see you, Jane. I have missed you more than I can say."

"But you have *a friend* and the farms. What else could one man like yourself need or want?"

He came closer, so close she could smell his clean earthy scent.

The tears in her eyes blurred his face. He dabbed them away without letting go of her hand. A cool wind blew from behind her, sending his longish hair swirling around his shoulders. His lips parted, and she felt herself about to kiss him. A bell clanged, and the coachman shouted last call. Her coach was leaving.

He gave a peck to her cheek and backed away. She leaned in ever so slightly to receive him, and then she straightened and walked across the street to her chosen destiny.

Sitting in the coach, she wanted to scream. She wanted to cry out to Harry, "Wait!"

The other passengers settled, the horses tugged, and the wheels turned as they left the station with her heart in pieces.

Chapter Forty-Eight

San Francisco—January 1891

The Wallingford Estate had become everything Jane had dreamed of all her life. In Cincinnati she'd thought it would be the house on Capital Hill, the one Robert Hale had bought for them. On Cabot Farm it would be the modest farmhouse she could turn into a manor. This was neither. This was the jewel of her life.

It was a year into a new decade and the continuation of a new chapter. What would it bring for her? She didn't know, but her heart remained bruised among her riches. She had everything money could buy. The freedom from want was heady and delicious. It was supposed to bring her joy.

Tonight, however, the heavy lump of melancholy in her gut remained. It angered her that she should feel anything but exuberance in her new life. The only thing that would calm it was gardening and making products from her harvest. She made a promise to herself she would strive to follow that passion. She'd allowed herself a small garden, but it was only for looking at. She hadn't put the time into caring for it. Her new gardener took it over, adding more structure to it. It matched the grand estate perfectly, but it wasn't Jane's vision for it.

Now that the estate was finished and the rooms were furnished to her and Ned's high standards, it was time to use the octagon-shaped conservatory for its original purpose. It had been used instead for lush plants and white wicker furniture, a design Ned had highly recommended and she had reluctantly gone along with. Friends marveled at the idea of it, and many wanted one themselves.

"How lovely to sit here in warmth under gray skies in the middle of winter and among such lush plants!" one had said. Another friend had gifted her two house finches in a large ornate gilded cage for Christmas. Everyone was taken by the ambiance they added to the space—except for Jane. The birds tweeted to no end, and she spent little time in there except for entertaining.

Yesterday she'd looked over at the windowed white iron structure and wondered how she had let her dreams slip away.

It's not too late, she reminded herself. What would everyone say if she turned it into a greenhouse for seedlings and common plants?

As she sat at her vanity preparing for another party, she took out the simple gold heart earrings Harry had given her that one Christmas when their love was new and full of lust and greedy anticipation. She appraised them with new eyes. Were they a mere trinket now of a time gone by? She placed the earrings in her lobes and swallowed. She was sure she would get called out for wearing such crude jewelry.

She sighed. Did she have to attend the New Year's Eve party? Would she even be missed? After a certain hour at these gatherings, the guests were usually too inebriated to care about anything or anyone but themselves. The Christmas balls and parties had been enjoyable last year and at the beginning of this season.

People had marveled at her renovated estate and the small elegant conservatory—the fun curiosity. Now, however, the gatherings had become redundant and had lost their luster for Jane. Her day-to-day life held little meaning. She was defined by her wealth and what she possessed. She had lost her direction. Her closest friends, Ned and Berta, were not as important to her.

Ned was off with another *client* in the most southern part of the state, and Berta had come down with digestive problems after her annual Christmas Eve ball. The doctor had her on a strict diet, and she was quite upset about it. Her company had become more tedious than enjoyable.

March would herald more social events as the warmer weather brought musical acts, outdoor theater, and alfresco dining. For Jane, spring was a magical time, not one of social events but of seedlings and plants. The society she had become a part of considered her an oddball. They already referred to her as *the plant lady*. It didn't take much inquiring about her creams for Jane to talk nonstop about how she sowed the seeds and what she needed to bring them to maturity and the way plants might react to the weather here in the city as opposed to the climate across the bay, and how she rendered the oils out of the lavender and calendula. She had been reminded a few times by Berta that the subject did not invite ongoing conversation among this society. It shut Jane up, but the nickname stuck. At the Christmas Eve ball, a drunken guest had come to her and asked, "Hey, plant lady, wanna make me grow?" Before she could tell him what she thought of such a rude remark, he was quickly dragged out of the party by a few other drunken fellows. It had dampened her spirits for the rest of the night.

This evening, Jane looked at herself in the mirror. A maturing woman looked back at her, a few threads of silver marking her black hair. A woman who wasn't quite old and yet one who had gathered some wisdom. The light of innocence was gone, even while her good looks remained.

Her time in the city made her tired yet restless. The women in her circle bored her. She found no joy in lunching with them and conversing about nothing of great importance. The things she could acquire bored her as well. How many dishes did one need? How many dresses could she wear in one lifetime? Hats, gloves, purses, and all the accoutrements of wealth crowded her armoires—all seven of them.

She picked up the diamond necklace on her vanity and placed it back in its case from last night's gathering at the Beechmans' home. The cost of that one necklace could feed and house and clothe so many of the poor in the city. How far could that go to make Cabot Farm a glorious place? She caught herself. Why did she think she'd want to go back to living on a farm?

She gave a small laugh, then descended the many steps that swept down to the grand foyer. She hadn't realized how lonely she felt. Winding her way down the many stairs, she wondered why she needed to live in such a large estate. The marble on the floor shined with the light, showing off its value. Standing in the middle of the cavernous space, she looked around. She felt cold.

Walking to the one room she loved the most, she opened the door to the library. The smaller room was lit with the glow of the fireplace. The black-and-white rock Caleb had given her sat on a shelf in the library near books on Indians. The white vein caught the light, making it sparkle.

Her readings of late had been on philosophy, Indian beliefs, and spiritual matters. How the Native People farmed their land and what they did with their produce. It was a new way of thinking and she welcomed it. Caleb had enlightened her in a way she couldn't deny. There was no hiding from the truth. She felt their paths had merged for a reason. The memory of him warmed her heart. She had forgiven the circumstances of their fate and looked back with fondness at knowing him. She wanted to hold tight now to the grains of wisdom he had imparted on her. Would she be worthy of them? There was no one to discuss her thoughts and feelings with. Harry might understand, but she had burned that bridge.

She leaned back on the comfy chaise, where she often fell asleep for the night. A blanket was always draped on it for that reason. She felt her waist. Was she getting plump? The food her cook made would tempt anyone to overeat. Her thoughts went to Berta.

Oh dear! I can't end up like her! I won't!

The dress she wore suddenly felt heavy and uncomfortable. She tugged at its waist. Her softer corset was too tight. Her dresser had gone home. She sat up and stared into the low flames of the fire. The thoughts that brought her joy began to fill her head. A jar full of cream she'd made from calendula flowers. Stinging nettle oil for soothing pain and healing wounds. Lavender for calming. So many more remedies and products for women to enjoy and benefit from—not the overly perfumed, but the subtle purity of nature's plants. Face creams! Hair treatments! Beauty products! It excited her to no end. What was she waiting for?

Jane went back up to her room and with a bit of a struggle removed her gown and underclothes. She stood naked in front of her mirror with only the earrings Harry had given her still in her lobes. She shook her head at her reflection. How had she lost her way? The thought she had of opening a boutique had faded. She'd let time pass without going forward with her dream. The renovation of this mansion and the company she kept had taken her attention away from what truly mattered. The society she had longed to be part of had nearly swallowed her up in its mindlessness. The unhappy feeling in her gut told her she was on the wrong path.

Placing on her robe and slippers, she went back down to the library. She doubted anyone would be missing the plant lady tonight, and she didn't care if they did.

Chapter Forty-Nine

September 1891

The wind whipped Jane's hair before she could get it under her hat. She decided to leave it off, and instead she took in the salty air as she walked back to the little cottage nestled among the windswept pines. The cozy, charming cottage, which gave her time to collect herself and sort out her thoughts and feelings throughout the summer, was one of her best purchases. The past several days had been the official closing of it until next spring. Her housekeeper, Doris, would keep it fresh until it was time for another getaway. The three-bedroom, two-bath bungalow was just right. Its inviting porch gave a view of the ocean and the steady rhythm of crashing waves.

Jane turned at the sound of the motor in the drive. It was time to put into action her plan. The nerves danced in her belly.

"Doris, please tell the driver to come get my cases."

"Yes, ma'am."

Jane looked at the cottage fading into the distance as the auto weaved its way down the driveway and onto the road. A part of her wanted to hide away in this place forever, but she knew what she had to do.

CHAPTER FIFTY

*T*HE CLERMONT HOTEL LOOKED SPLENDID IN ITS NEWLY painted facade. Jane walked into the renovated lobby. The new carpets and drapes were in subtle shades of beige behind beautiful floral prints. The walnut reception desk added a touch of class where there had once stood a smaller desk and chair. A bellhop greeted her and took her luggage.

"We've been expecting you, Mrs. Cabot. I will take these up to your room."

"Thank you."

Jane went to the front desk and checked in. The young lady offered to bring tea or coffee up to her room. Jane had to smile to herself. The first night she and Martin had spent in this hotel had been one of trepidation and disbelief on her part. She'd wondered what she had gotten herself into. At the same time, an unnerving excitement and anticipation had tickled her senses. Little did she know what lay ahead as she'd asked him that morning to call for room service.

"We're not at that kind of hotel, dear," had been his reply. Indeed, it had not been that kind of hotel back then, but today it was, and she would indulge in that service tonight instead of eating out.

Waking up to the activity of the small town was different from the roar of the ocean at her cottage. She liked the feel of it, with everyone going about their business. She had business to get to also.

Sally had written to her several months back telling her the news of the town and of Harry. He had built an addition onto his house but lived there alone. He no longer had tenants in the farmhouse Jane had renovated. It was now a country inn run by a couple hired from Oakland.

She marveled at his ingenuity. She was impressed with the fact he had given up on the idea of raising cattle. Part of his land was a pig farm, and the other part was producing crops of fruits and vegetables.

He even has a sunflower field, Sally wrote. *He sells the seeds as well as the flowers.*

After reading the letter, Jane had felt a wave of emotion come over her. It was the beginning of spring, and she hadn't started any seeds in her conservatory. It was still the decorated room everyone loved to come visit. Champagne flowed, and afternoon tea had become a thing there. She felt as if she couldn't stop it. She had become immersed in a lifestyle that had no room for horticulture. What was her purpose in life now? Harry had changed with the times, and Jane felt she had been indulging in the past. She was lost, but she was determined to find her way.

This morning she dressed in a plain brownish plaid skirt and a beige blouse with a large silk bow at the top instead of lace. She wore her hair in an upswept bun with no adornments. Putting on her matching plaid waistcoat, she went down to the lobby, where her carriage waited. She settled into the cab, her nerves on edge. She touched her earlobes, where the heart-shaped earrings hung.

Her hand was shaking. She grasped her hands together. This was going to take all of her courage.

As THE CARRIAGE CAME AROUND to the entrance of the farm, Harry stepped off his porch. It was a proper white-railed porch. Hanging baskets spilling over with flowers hung along its roofline. Jane came from the carriage, her heart in her throat.

"Hello, Mrs. Cabot," Harry said.

His handsome face, a bit older looking but still so appealing to her, had that grin she'd once owned.

"Hello, Mr. Cabot," she said with a smile.

He took her gloved hand in his. "It's good to see you," he said. "I thought you'd reply to my letter with a positive no, but I was so pleased you didn't."

"How could I think of rejecting a visit from the woman I still love?"

Jane was thunderstruck at his proclamation. "Harry, let's go inside. I have much to say."

"Very well. I made us some tea."

She looked at him as if she was seeing a new version of him but with the same outward appearance. He did look well and peaceful. It gave her a sense of calm, and she felt ready to speak to him.

The tea was jasmine and orange, one he'd made himself.

"All right, tell me what you've done with the sheep farmer turned cattle rancher I once knew," she said.

He let out a generous laugh. "I had to take a realistic look at my farms. My accountant and a few businessmen helped me to look outside myself, as it were. Who was I? A sheep farmer? A cattle rancher? I felt trapped in my own thoughts of who I was and how I appeared to everyone. It wasn't easy to start something new, to change the way I'd always done things. Losing you helped me to see that to be happy and successful, I needed to think differently. Very differently. Damn, I got a crop of sunflowers out there!"

He laughed, and Jane joined him. Her laughter turned to tears, and she quickly swept them off her face.

"Now tell me, what is it you have to say to me?" he asked.

She took in a deep breath and let it out. "I'm not happy. I feel I've lost my way."

"And what has that to do with me, my dear Jane?"

"Are you going to let me finish?"

He grinned and took a sip of tea. "By all means."

"I miss you. I don't miss working my tailbone off on the farm, and I don't miss worrying about money, but I can't have the life I want in the city, with those people. They overwhelm me! I thought it was where I belonged, but I was wrong. I haven't planted one damn seed since I moved there!"

"I'm sorry you're not happy. But again, what does this have to do with me?"

"Are you going to sit there and give me a hard time? I love you! That's what it has to do with you!" This was not going at all how she'd thought it would. He was supposed to look into her eyes and ask her to come join him and live happily ever after.

"I love you too, Jane. That never went away. I heard you had turned your attentions elsewhere, and I had to go on with my life. Unfortunately, I haven't found the wife I thought I would by now."

Jane became irritated. "Well, maybe she's here now." She pursed her lips and raised one brow.

Harry laughed. "Maybe."

The room was filled with electricity. Jane stood, and Harry followed.

They faced each other, and he took her hands in his. "Am I supposed to provide a way out of the woods for you?" he asked.

"No, I have a plan. I want to buy land and grow my plants again. I want to open a boutique where I will sell my beauty and health products. I'll hire workers to plant and care for my fields. I will ship my products to stores all up and down the coast and perhaps across the country, and I want to do all that here in Clermont City near you, with you."

Harry looked off in the distance. He became pensive. She waited.

He came back and looked into her eyes. He took her hand. "Will you marry me?" he asked.

Her heart expanded, and she felt she was going to burst. He wanted her in his life, and she was ready to fully commit to him.

"Yes, I will marry you, Mr. Cabot, but I'm afraid I can't be the wife who cleans and cooks for you. There's too much to do for my business! I'll hire people to care for us though." She saw the twinkle of tears in his eyes, and she moved closer to him.

"I don't care about that, Jane. I feel complete now. You've made me a very happy man."

They kissed sweetly, then more lustfully. Jane felt lifted off the earth with joy. At last, she had found her true path.

EPILOGUE

June 1900

*H*ARRY WALKED INTO THE SUNNY YELLOW-PAINTED KITCHEN in the cottage. Jane's heart swelled. He had come up from the sea, his face tanned from the sun and his hair ruffled from wind. She and Doris had prepared the house for their summer getaways last week, and she was putting some final touches on the rooms before they headed back to the farm. This was the first of several visits they hoped to have in the season. He smiled his smile, and it melted her.

"All ready for our summer escapes, eh?" he asked.

"All ready."

They kissed and held each other.

"Are you sure you want to get back so soon?" he asked.

"I'd love to stay longer, but the gardens are waiting, and I'm impatient to get the new crops in. I wonder if Mr. Hill got that special soil he promised. I think he said it contained more iron for some of the plants that yellowed last year."

Harry laughed. "We've only been away less than a week, my love."

She laughed back. "I know."

"It's been wonderful though," he said, then kissed the top of her head.

She looked up into his eyes. The fresh salt air at the cottage always ignited their passions in a different and lusty way. The freedom to roam about the house and land without a care. No one but themselves for miles. The abandonment at night when they made love with the windows open wide, letting in the sound and smell of the ocean, which stirred their passions even more.

Cabot Farm had become a modern working farm for their new business of selling Jane's line of products. With plenty of help, they were able to sneak away like a young couple barely able to contain their desires.

The farmhouse she had restored to a luxurious home many years ago had been renovated once more as a comfortable, more modest home that suited them both. Harry was not much for lace and chintz, and Jane was tired of opulence for opulence's sake. It was far from the cavernous Wallingford Estate, which she had sold to a wealthy family of eight. She was happier now than she had ever been.

The livestock were gone, but the chickens remained, for they loved the fresh eggs along with the aromatic bread Bell served them for breakfast. A housekeeper gave Jane the time to devote to her business. Harry was a gentleman farmer helping source and grow what Jane needed to produce her products, which sold off the shelves in stores throughout the country. Lacey and her husband lived in town, and she had become Jane's promoter. It was a wonderful partnership formed long ago, and Jane was grateful to have it continue.

Jason still helped on the farm, but in sales now, and he, his wife, and their three children lived in the now-expanded home Harry had once built as a cabin for himself. Jane and Harry had become Auntie Jane and Uncle Harry, and they indulged the little ones whenever they could.

Jane looked up at her husband. "Aren't you glad I talked you into a different way of farming?" she teased him.

"You didn't talk me into anything. I didn't want to live without you, my dear."

"Oh, Harry! Just admit it. I put us both on the right path."

"Be careful, Jane. Your vanity is showing."

She looked at him sheepishly. He would always put her back on the right path too. "Yes, dear."

"We're lucky to have each other, and I'm grateful for this new life," he conceded.

She let their embrace linger a while longer, then looked up at her husband with the feeling of wholeness in her heart. "Let's go home."

The End

TRAVELED HEARTS
BOOK ONE IN THE TRILOGY

The Traveled Hearts saga begins in 1885 New England, where Jessica Messing, a spirited twenty-year-old yearns to break free from the confines of her rigid, upper-middle-class life in Hartford, Connecticut, to become a well-known and respected artist. However, her family and society have different plans.

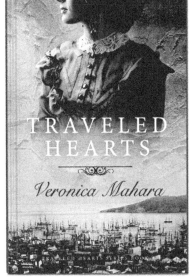

Falling in love with Jacob Stanford only complicates her life—a love affair she must keep secret.

Forced to bend to her father's wishes, she marries the charming yet deceitful English attorney, Frederick Moore, to help save the family's law firm. An arduous journey across America leads Jessica to her new life in San Francisco, California, where she finds herself trapped in life as a dutiful housewife. Compelled by curiosity, she secretly ventures into the heart of the city, where her artistic passion is fueled and her view of life is altered.

When her marriage is faced with jealousy and infidelity, Jessica is determined to carve out a truer life for herself, including her love for Jacob. Can she fulfill her dreams without destroying her reputation and her family's future?

SACRED TERRAIN
BOOK TWO IN THE TRILOGY

In book two of the Traveled
Hearts trilogy, Jessica Messing
finds contentment in her new
life, yet Jacob is still out of reach.
Promising to quit his roguish ways
before leaving her after their last
rendezvous, she remains hopeful
of him settling down near Clermont City. As the months pass
with no word of him, she is left in
doubt of his love.

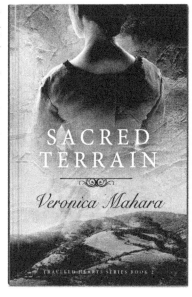

When the handsome and confident Caleb Cantrell steps into
her life, Jessica finds it difficult to
hold true to the man she has loved
for so long. Caleb's intellect and manners deny his rough exterior.
As Jessica's affection for Caleb grows, she must choose between
waiting for Jacob or living in the present, where a homestead on
breathtaking lands offers security and the love of a man who knows
what he wants.

Falling in love with two men was not her plan, yet her heart
cannot be reasoned with. Innocently, she becomes a pawn in Caleb's and Jacob's outlaw past. When she finally meets with Jacob
again, she has been through a harrowing experience that forever
changes her.

They come together, having been separated from society. The temptation is great, and the consequences are greater.

Secrets come to light while others remain to be seen. Above all, having been away from her home and art, she returns with a renewed purpose as she navigates the perils of love ... and loyalty.

UNENDING
TRAILS
BOOK THREE IN THE TRILOGY

Jessica Cantrell grapples with her feelings after the birth of her son, Henry.

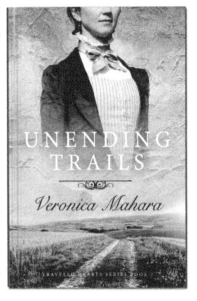

Her constant love for his father, Jacob, spills over to her infant and seals their bond. While her husband, Caleb, reluctantly agrees to take on the task of raising the child, the secret adoption puts a strain on their marriage as Jessica tries to make a home and family with Caleb.

Meanwhile, Jacob is settling down in San Francisco with her brother Will. However, the means by which they acquired the money for their new business comes under scrutiny and Jessica's ex-husband, Frederick is one of the most vocal. Jacob and Will must come up with a plan to keep the vengeful Frederick from destroying their new enterprise, but neither one expected what would happen next.

As Jessica's family grows and her art is recognized, the family is faced with the unnerving event of the 1906 earthquake. Jessica finds herself on a perilous journey to save her son, Henry. It reunites her with Jacob—a reunion that tugs at her heartstrings.

Unaware of Jacob as his birth father, Henry Cantrell grows up with both Caleb's and Jacob's differing views of life. Taking both to heart, he plans his future as a lawyer. With the 1918 pandemic comes the unthinkable and a shocking discovery sends Henry on a soul-searching journey—one that Jessica can only hope will not alter her son too severely, taking him away from her forever.

The Traveled Hearts trilogy is the saga of one woman's determination and courage to have a life that strikes a different tone in a time when women struggled to be autonomous and fulfilled. The family she loves will be tested alike, tearing her in many different directions and, in the end, forming a unique tapestry out of hardship, tragedy, and unrelenting love.

ACKNOWLEDGMENTS

Thank you to everyone at Enchanted Ink Publishing for helping me bring my fourth novel to fruition. Your professionalism and knowledge are invaluable. Not to mention the friendliness and patience you've shown me throughout the editing journey.

To all my readers, you add to my joy of writing. I think about you as I weave my way along the path of storytelling. Thank you so much for your support!

Thank you to all those headstrong women who came before me and left their mark on the world. My female characters are fictional but are based on what I've read about women in history. They've given me courage.

Last but not least, thank you and much love to my family and especially my husband Jeff. Your support and love mean so much to me.

Veronica Mahara

Veronica Mahara lives with her husband and two cats, Toby and Ginger, on their small orchard farm in the beauty of the Pacific Northwest. To find out more about the author and all of her publications, visit:

WWW.VERONICASUNMAHARA.COM

Made in United States
Orlando, FL
05 August 2024

49974494R00222